YOU LOOK BEAUTIFUL TONIGHT

YOU LOOK BEAUTIFUL TONIGHT

L. R. JONES

A THRILLER

THOMAS & MERCER

This is a work of fiction. Names, characters, organizations, places, events, and incidents are either products of the author's imagination or are used fictitiously. Otherwise, any resemblance to actual persons, living or dead, is purely coincidental.

Published by Thomas & Mercer, Seattle

www.apub.com

ISBN-13: 9781662508882 (paperback)
ISBN-13: 9781662508875 (digital)

Cover design by James Iacobelli
Cover image: © rolfo / Stocksy United

Printed in the United States of America

To everyone who ever felt invisible

Chapter One

> *Life asked Death, Why do people hate me and love you? Death responded with, Because you're a beautiful lie and I'm a painful truth.*
>
> —*Unknown*

Blood seeps through the cream-colored carpet, fading into the thick fibers, a river of life runneth over and under until death do us part. The same carpet that now absorbs one life and yet hugs my feet and cushions my body. Seconds tick by, eternal seconds, a clock ticking somewhere—loud, heavy, eternal. I try to draw in air, but I can't catch my breath. My throat is raw, my chest tight.

Run, I tell myself.

Run, before it's too late to run.

I rotate and immediately hit a hard surface—a piece of furniture, I think—banging my leg, pain radiating from my kneecap and down my shin. The room is spinning. The smell of death permeates the air, a scent no one can understand without experiencing it, *living* it while another person dies inside the horrific stench of it. Death has an energy, too, as contrary as that may sound, almost as if you can feel the grim reaper doing his work with a heavy pull that suffocates you in its existence.

I don't even know what is happening right now, how I got here, how this became a moment in my uneventful, unremarkable life. I blink the room—an office, a familiar office that once felt safe—into view and round the desk in my path. My heart is thundering in my ears, my breathing now raspy and loud as I make my way across the room and yank the door open. Freedom calls to me, and I stumble into the hallway before me, leaving the door open, sucking in fresh air. Looking left and then right toward the emergency door, I hear it promising safety and an escape from death and all the blood. So much blood.

I run in that direction, pain radiating in my head that I don't understand, but I push through it, my legs burning with the speed at which I travel, until I reach that blessed door, my hand closing on the long silver handle. The urge to look back behind me is strong, but I resist. *Run. Run now. Run hard and fast.* Shoving open the door, I burst into the corridor, and the hard steel slams shut behind me. I take one more step and halt with the realization that the smell of blood and death has followed me.

I look down and lift my hands to find the stains on my skin, gasping with the realization that I'm holding a long, silver letter opener stained with the same shades of red. Memories illuminate the darkness that is my shock. Oh my God. I can't run away from the killer.

I *am* the killer.

I drop the weapon—and it *is* a weapon—and a scream rips from my lungs, permeating the air as death had done—then I crumple to the ground and collapse.

Chapter Two

The past, two weeks ago . . .

When I was seven, my strict mathematician mother, who maintains a rigid schedule, picked me up from school an hour late. I'd stood there on a scorching Tennessee day, sticky and hot, gripping the straps to my My Little Pony book bag, and watching the other kids depart and head off to their blissful homelife. No one asked if I was okay. No one seemed to even notice me at all. I'd been certain my mother had been killed in a car accident or, at the very least, was lying on the side of the road, bloodied and dying. I'd been hunting for someone, anyone, to help me, when *finally* our gray Suburban pulled up to the curb. My mother hadn't even gotten out of the car. She'd popped the door open and yelled, "Hurry, Mia," as if I were the one running late. "We have to go to the store to grab ketchup for the meat loaf."

I'd done as she'd ordered, happy to be in the car, happy to still have a family, but as an adult, I have another take. I'd been traumatized, certain she was dead, and all she had said to me was we needed ketchup to make the meat loaf I didn't even like. Inside the store, I'd already forgotten the trauma of being alone and lost—kids are resilient like that—and I was considering how I might milk my mother's mistake quite literally.

I'd picked up a can of strawberry Nesquik to ask if we could buy it, and my mother was missing. Gone. Nowhere to be found. Panic had risen hard and fast, and frantically I'd hunted for her, walking past strangers, never making eye contact—my mother always warned me never to talk to strangers. At some point, I'd crawled under a bakery table with Memorial Day streamers sheltering me from danger. I'd been certain my mother would come by, screaming for me, at any minute. She hadn't. I'd waited there at least another hour before it was not my mother but my father who found me, and pulled me from under the table. Apparently, he'd emerged from the basement, where he'd been working on some new project, when he smelled the Wednesday meat loaf, and asked about me. My mother had freaked out, and my father had lost his mind with worry, and they'd fought. The result was that my father, and really the only hero in my life, had come to my rescue.

My mother had stayed home and finished the meat loaf.

That day I'd been invisible to everyone but my father, including my mother.

That about sums up my life and this very moment right now.

I'm sitting at the bar of the Tex-Mex restaurant, waiting on my friend Jess to return from the bathroom and trying to garner the bartender's attention to order two Diet Cokes and guacamole. Three times he's walked by me and ignored my various grabs for attention—the hand lift, the hand lift with a verbal "excuse me," and finally the shove of my dark-rimmed glasses higher up my nose to show seriousness *before* the hand lift with a verbal "excuse me." Three times. Three strikes. It's not even as if the bar is busy, but I remind myself he's preparing drinks for tables as well.

Jess joins me in a whiff of Chanel No. 5—the only perfume worthy of her to wear—sliding onto the stool next to me, her long blonde hair freshly sprayed and her lips newly glossed. "I thought you were ordering drinks and the appetizer?" She hangs her Louis Vuitton bag onto the back of her seat.

"I tried. The bartender ignored me."

"Oh good Lord, Mia, I hate that you still let yourself be overlooked." She waves at the bartender and immediately has his unbridled attention.

I grimace at his response and her comment. It's not like I let anything happen—it just did—but I bite my tongue. It's an argument I don't feel like having today.

The bartender steps in front of Jess. "What can I get you?"

"Two Diet Cokes and a guacamole, please," she says, glancing at her watch and crinkling her nose. "Can we dare to rush you? I have a meeting in forty-five minutes."

"I'll make sure to hurry things along for you," he assures her.

He's a tall, dark, good-looking, and baby-faced twentysomething, the kind of unestablished, inexperienced guy Jess wouldn't have even considered when we were still in our twenties, certainly not now that we're in our thirties. Nevertheless, his brown eyes glint with interest. He's enamored with her, but then everyone is enamored with Jess.

Jess and I are the definition of "opposites attract." She's blonde. I'm a brunette. She's beautiful. I'm objectively unexceptional, with pale skin and hair perpetually secured at my nape. On the career side of things, I'm a librarian who fantasizes about living the lives of the characters in books. She writes a wildly popular column called Living La Vida Local for one of Nashville's hottest magazines and lives a life that doesn't require she fantasize about anything at all.

We met when we were both freshmen in college, in the math lab, where I'd been tutoring, and she'd been failing. Yes, Jess has a weakness. She sucks at all things mathematical, especially algebra. I, of course, am the opposite, an algebra whiz, because *hello*, my mother is a mathematician and would have it no other way. I was tortured with extra math homework from the time I could even understand one plus one equals two. I mastered everything my mother put before me, just to be allowed time in the garage with my father, where he made the science of discovery fun.

Tutoring had been my mother's grand idea, not mine. Working at the lab meant dealing with people I didn't know, and that was less than ideal. But I was still living at home, and my parents were paying for my education, which meant I did what my mother said or she and my father would fight. The blisteringly clear fact was that fighting led to my father's misery.

Jess had sat down in front of me with perfectly glossed nails and shiny blonde hair, confidence oozing from her, while I was an insecure, basic girl with flat brown hair that had never seen a highlight. I didn't have on makeup because I made a mess of it when I tried, and I sure couldn't afford to get my nails done.

She'd reached in her designer bag, removed a book and paper before surprising me by saying, "Clearly, I'm an idiot." She'd slid a graded assignment marked with a failing grade in front of me and added, "Here's the proof. Can you fix me? And what do you want in return?"

What do you want in return?

That question had slipped inside me to that familiar part of my gut where I'd been keeping all the times my mother had made me pay for what I wanted, even beyond time with my father, by way of extra math homework. I'd felt bribed, held captive, and controlled. And, therefore, just that easily, I knew without ever being told that Jess might seem to have everything she wanted, but she paid for it, and not with money.

Jess had sucked at algebra, but she passed that class. And shortly after she and her father, who was a celebrity attorney on Nashville's "it" list, had a blow-up. He kicked her out and stripped away her generous allowance. She didn't know how to live without money and luxury, and I did. She needed me, and I'd been happy to escape my homelife right along with her. We'd gotten a cheap apartment together, jobs waiting on tables, and for just a few years, she and I were poor college kids, living la vida local, as she'd called it. And that became the title of her column at the magazine.

Then and now, we're an illogical pair, truly. She and I do not make sense in any way, but here we are, many years later, an apple and an orange, sitting next to each other. Her parents died in a car accident the year we graduated. Mine are still alive. Jess has a large social circle, but she doesn't let a lot of them past her walls. Just me, really. True to the opposites we are, I don't have a social circle at all, and by choice, but I choose to keep her present.

The bartender reluctantly tears himself away from the spot directly across from Jess, and almost instantly our Diet Cokes appear.

"I read your column today," I admit readily. I'm truly one of her most faithful readers. I love the way she covers everything to enjoy about Nashville, from the fashion and luxury homes to the scandals and dirty laundry. It's such an authentic mix of life in this big city. "Oh my God." I rotate to face her, shoving my glasses up as they slide down my nose. "Was that a true story?"

The story, part one published today, is of an aspiring singer here in Nashville who met a well-known country music star and became the protégé of a certain music producer who invited her to the "casting couch," so to speak.

"It is," she says. "I met her. I corroborated the story."

"Are you going to name names?"

"My editor won't let me," she replies. "Which I'm furious about, of course. Come on, the #MeToo movement should create a little more courage than cowardice. She just wants me to drag it out as a miniseries and end it with a warning about morality and protecting oneself. The magazine is afraid of being sued."

"That kind of stinks," I say, aware that any story of a woman being abused hits home for Jess. She was a victim of her father's depravity herself, years ago, before I knew her. She hides it all beneath the glamour, but this story really allows her an outlet. Not that she seems to need one. Ever. At all. "But I still think the message is an incredible one," I add. "With your readership, it will make an impact. I can't believe you didn't tell me about it."

The guacamole appears in front of us. "Would you like to order?" the bartender asks, speaking to Jess and Jess alone.

She glances at me. "What was it I got last time?"

"Enchiladas verde with beef that's well done," I say. "For both of us. Hold the sour cream."

He flicks me a look and then gives Jess a nod before lingering a bit too long, but Jess doesn't seem to notice. "I didn't tell you because I didn't think it was going to run for a month. They moved it up without telling me."

"Still, you didn't tell me when you were researching it."

"You always say you like to be surprised," she argues, "and speaking of surprises, I did something for you last night." She grabs her phone and punches a few buttons. "This, my dear, is the hottest new dating site. I put us both on it."

"Oh no." My hand goes up. "Never, ever, in this lifetime."

"It's for an article I'm writing. Two single girls, one dating app. I won't use your name."

"I'm not doing it."

"I went to that library conference from hell for you. You can't do this for me?"

"Are you really going to use that against me?"

"It was hell."

She's right, of course. There was literally a three-hour speech on library safety that included a slideshow about proper boxing techniques that made me, she who loveth all things books and libraries, fall asleep. On her shoulder. It would have been embarrassing if anyone had noticed.

"What do I have to do?"

"Like I said, I set-up your profile and—"

"Stop there. If you set-up my profile, I'm quite sure you turned me into Jess number two, which I am not."

"My only number two ever," she assures me. "And I did good. You'll see. Download the Duets app and take a look."

I crinkle my nose. "Could the name be any more cheesy? But I guess that's better than being called *Ménage*."

"Speak for yourself, honey," she teases. "*Ménage* sounds pretty inviting to me."

I snort. "Whatever. You are not that girl. You barely tolerate one man more than two dates, let alone two men at once."

"It might be less boring than my recent dates."

"I guess the real test for your article execution will come down to, Can I get to date number one and can you get past two?"

"I have no desire to get past number two, but I'll give a few guys a go just to write a good story." She grabs my phone from the bar counter. "I'll download the app for you." She punches in my code and takes a bite of the appetizer while she waits for the installation. Once my phone pings, she opens the app and slides my phone in front of me. "Your 'Invisible Girl' email and password."

Some people might think it's strange that she knows my passwords, but the email she references is one that she set-up for me and is not my primary email. Not to mention, we've literally known each other for over ten years, many of which we were roommates. She set-up half of my online shopping accounts in an effort to try to force me to be more present in today's world. All it did was make it easier to shop.

As for entertaining her with my dating entanglements, or lack thereof—been there, done that. Not interested in repeating those disasters. I grab a chip and guacamole. "I'd rather walk a plank over shark-infested waters than repeat my experiences on any dating app."

She rolls her eyes. "Such a drama queen. You get that from overreading."

I bristle. "You can't overread."

She ignores my rebuttal. "This is for my work, Mia," Jess scolds. "It's for *me*."

I press my lips together and pick up the phone, logging in to the app and immediately eyeing my photo. It's a shot of me she took one night when the lighting was perfect. It might as well have been one of those old glamour shots. It looks nothing like me. In fact, if I saw this photo, I wouldn't even think it was me, and I know myself pretty darn well. I'd think I was a gorgeous brunette with long silky dark hair, perfect skin, and brown eyes. The girl who wore glasses like a boss, not a geek.

Not the girl who woke up this morning with unruly hair, sensitive skin, and a round face that my limited makeup skills couldn't hide. I'd tied my hair at my nape, done my makeup the best I know how, which is not all that well, and finished the look off with the dark-rimmed glasses that allow me to see clearly. I'd forgotten the photo of the girl who might have been me.

Until now.

"This photo does not look like me," I argue, pointing at my face. "This is me."

"Oh, whatever, Mia." She gives me a little elbow nudge. "You already have three messages." She points at the little icon. "See? You are *not* invisible."

Good Lord, what has she put on my profile? I glance down and quickly scan the details:

Thirty-two
115 pounds
Only child
Addicted to books

Well, I'm 125, but I'll take it as a compliment that she put 115—unless she's trying to create one big fake Mia Anderson. Because the real Mia isn't good enough. That idea stabs like one of the forks in our place settings.

She waggles a finger at the screen. "Three messages and I just set-up the account."

"All of which are most likely new-account-setup messages."

"Only one is a new-account-setup message."

"You read my messages?" I challenge.

"Of course not, but I know what I got when I set mine up. One setup message. Just one. You have three messages, and two are the real deal."

I hate the funny little flutter of anticipation in my belly that will lead nowhere but a steep drop off a cliff named disappointment. "If they're like the ones I had with that other app, most of them resemble closet serial killers."

"That was years ago. The police have already caught all those people."

I smirk. "Not funny."

Thankfully the food arrives, another bartender setting our plates in front of us and briefly asking us about condiments and such. I think maybe I've escaped this conversation, but no such luck. Apparently I'm the one not ready to end it. "How many messages do you have?" Translated to: *How badly do I stack up?*

She unrolls her silverware. "None. I haven't gone live yet. I plan to after my meeting. Read your messages."

"No," I say. "Absolutely not." I shove my phone into my purse. "You have a meeting, remember?"

"Fine, yes," she concedes. "I do have a meeting, but are you going to help me with my article? And before you answer, I won't use your name."

"You already said that."

"I know you. You need to hear that promise more than once. Come on, Mia. It will be fun, just you and me."

Easy words spoken casually but with a big impact.

My entire adult life and hers, too, we've leaned on each other.

Jess's parents died in a car accident a month after she was hired at the magazine. She hadn't talked to either of them in over a year. They'd disowned her. Turns out, she still inherited everything. And yet, despite this, and her instant success at her new job, we were in the same understated apartment.

Flash forward three months later, despite her already proving to be a shining star at her new job, and me working part-time at a small library branch while working on my master's, we were *still* in that tiny apartment. We lived there until I graduated and *I insisted* she buy a place of her own. She resisted, but I knew it was time for me to go and for her to stop babysitting her college friend.

"Mia," Jess presses.

"I'll think about it," I say, because as much as I want to say no, this is Jess. I'm always there for her, and she's always there for me. As if I just said yes, she says, "I'll be over tonight, and we can read the messages together."

I set my fork down. "I do this alone or not at all."

"Then you agree?"

"I'll think about it."

And that's just what I do. I think about those messages through the rest of lunch, and even as I walk back to the library. I decide there's no harm in just reading a few messages. What could go wrong?

Chapter Three

My mother was the first person to take me to a library. I was two, and the influence of that trip on my life was captured in a Polaroid photograph of me and my mother. Me, looking cute as a button back then, in pigtails, holding a couple of books that were as large as me, with a grin on my face. The joy I'd felt inside a circle of books radiates through that image. Beside me, my mother's face had glowed. On that day, in that photo, we'd seemed the enchanted fairy-tale story of a mother and daughter destined to become best friends. As an adult I see that moment as one of my mother's early attempts to mold my views to her own.

She'd sought to create a mini-me daughter addicted to knowledge. Instead, she'd gifted me with my addiction to the written word. Some might argue knowledge and the written word are the same thing, but I would disagree quite dogmatically. When one hunts for knowledge, it's generally with a narrow agenda, such as my mother's infatuation with statistics. With the written word, the view is unlimited, our dreams often stirred, our lives influenced by perhaps only one turned page that opens our minds to new possibilities.

As for me and my mother, I'd wanted to read a book. She'd wanted to play a game that focused on problem-solving. I'd done as she wished to please her, but the joy I'd felt in that library wasn't present in those moments. That's really where our divide began, in those joyless moments, and so I'd faded into the background of her number-chalked school boards in academia. The day I told her I was going to focus on attaining a master's in library science, she cried. The day I got a job in a small corner library, she bit back scorn. The day I was promoted to the main library, I didn't bother to tell her, despite being a kid rewarded with the biggest piece of candy in the candy store.

As I walk into that library now, calmness washes over me and settles in my belly, roots there like a little bunny under the perfect bush. This place is home, my home, despite being a magnetic castle welcoming visitors. The central library is not just a library but more akin to a museum of the artistic mind, which might sound geeky, but it's true. We have three floors, an auditorium, high-tech presentations, a revolving art display, a play area for kids, a reading room, and even a café. When a new visitor walks into our location, you can observe their awe, the way their eyes look up, around, in front, and sometimes even behind their position to ensure they don't miss any of the tiny details, from displays to murals. It's a hustle-and-bustle location with never a dull moment, and in the busy downtown area, lunch hours are often filled with visitors who choose to enjoy the facility during their breaks. In the center of it all is the main library desk, where guests ask an information clerk for aid. On each floor and in each department, there's a checkout desk.

I work on the third level, the best of all the floors, in my opinion, by far. "Three" offers shelves filled with romance, adventure, and mystery. I step onto the floor-three escalator—two has its own—and as I always do, I turn to watch all that is below. The group of schoolkids being hushed by their teacher and parent helpers. The man at the checkout desk impatiently glancing at his watch. The woman at a table eating her sandwich while flipping a page of a book in earnest. I will never get rich or famous working in this place, but I am rich in knowledge and experiences, enchanted by some new discovery I find here every day of my life.

I'm now passing level two, noticing a little girl exuding excitement as she surveys a selection of children's books with glee. Her young mother—dressed in jeans and sneakers, as well as a long-sleeve T-shirt—is smiling, obviously pleased with her daughter's excitement. There's also a woman in the self-help section clearly fretting over her choice of books, her teeth worrying her bottom lip, her finger lingering on one title and moving to the next. If I were her librarian, I'd tell her to go home with both and find the voice that speaks to her. If I were her friend, I'd tell her to not just read the words but *use* them. And that little secret is easier said than done, or else I'd be a million exciting versions of myself I have never been.

My gaze shifts and lands on a man sitting at a table with a laptop in front of him, and I do a double take when I realize I'm not just looking at him—he's looking at me. As has already been established, *no one* looks at me. In all my years here at the library, studying people, often creating a story for them in my head, no one has ever studied me back. I blink, and I'm certain I'll discover he's really looking over my head or around me, but as I bring his dark, longish hair and strong, if not sharp, features back into focus, he's still looking at me. He's youngish, in his thirties, maybe, though I can't be sure. His fingernails are manicured, his watch expensive. I hold my breath, unable to process the moment with further articulate thought, and then he's gone. The escalator has delivered me to a higher level, beyond the wall, my signal to turn or be dumped on the floor of the landing.

I whirl around just in time to step off and then quickly turn back to the escalator as if I expect the dark-haired man to be racing toward me. Seconds tick by and nothing happens. In a huff of breath, I grimace at myself. What am I thinking? He was *not* looking at me. The end. I refuse to think about it, or him, for one more second. And even if he was looking at me, it was probably with peculiar interest as to why my simple black dress, basic boots, and dark-rimmed glasses were, well, simple.

I'm back to *the end*.

Time to go back to work.

Chapter Four

When I was eight and shunned by the other kids for being too awkward and shy, my father built me the most incredible playhouse in the garage, where he worked most days. It had a play kitchen, dolls, and a little comfy chair where I watched him fret over his projects. When I was there, I was in my safe place.

When I was twelve and dolls were suddenly shunned at school, therefore shunned by me, my father swooped in for the rescue again and converted my playhouse into a library, where I'd spend hours upon hours journeying anywhere my reading allowed me to travel.

Floor three is my adult playhouse. It's my safe place, my escape from the rest of the world, filled with books that deliver joy and adventure; therefore I've already left the man on floor two behind me. Some might say that I live between the pages more than I live a real life—okay, so *Jess* will say—but I'm happy here. And being happy matters.

Just as he was the day we met five years ago, my comanager of floor three, Jack Smith, is behind the half-moon-shaped service desk, assisting a single patron. Jack is my twin personality, a socially awkward book geek who lives for this place. But unlike me, Jack is not average. He's tall and fit—and he wears thick-rimmed glasses that, when paired with his favored sweater vests and ties, are kind of a hot schoolteacher look. His dark skin is perfectly clear and glowing even under the library's unforgiving overhead lighting, and I'm reminded that he's quite good looking.

At least I think so.

Unfortunately, considering our mutual geek status, and dismal dating lives, we just aren't that into each other, at least not like that. We tried. We went on a date, and two awkward people feeling awkward suffocated us both. It was just *too much* awkward. The best part of the night was when we burst into laughter and at the exact same moment said, "What were we thinking?"

I wave at him and motion to the back office we share just behind the service area, that holds two desks, facing opposite walls. It's a small space that ensures everything from a cough to crankiness becomes contagious. I've just sat down and put away my purse when Jack appears beside my desk. "Kara wants you to call her," he announces.

I inwardly cringe at our boss's message, which means I'll most likely be working with her on auditorium bookings today, rather than here on three, for fear I'll seem ungrateful for my new duties. Kara pushing me to expand my horizons resulted in a much-needed raise, considering my ever-increasing rent. Now I'm saving for a house, hopefully ending my mother's incessant pressure to stop wasting money on rent.

Jack, wearing a black vest, and checkered tie, motions to my desk, and my gaze lands on a napkin that seems to be covering a plate. "You missed Joan's birthday cake, and I know how you love to have your cake and to eat it, too." He waggles his eyebrows.

I laugh at his cheesy joke, because geeks together are geeks forever, and all that stuff. We'd known that from the day we met, when we competed for who knew the most quotes from books. He won round one. I won round two. And for the first time in my life, I experienced the phenomenon of instant friendship.

I rip away the napkin and eye the luscious vanilla icing. "Oh my God, this is from Julie's Bakery. I freaking love that place." I point a finger at him and chide, "You are never good for my diet," but even as

I do, I grab the fork he's dutifully included on the plate and add, "But thank you. I love you, too. I really needed cake right now."

"I love you, too," he says, sitting down in the chair next to my desk, his back to a wall, his gaze on my face as I shove a giant bite of cake into my mouth. I've learned to appreciate certain things about being invisible, such as shoving almost half a slice of cake in your mouth in one bite and no one noticing. Okay, well, Jack notices, but he doesn't care if I inhale cake. The thing is, he's invisible, too, but not with me, and I'm not to him, but I also feel free as a bird with him. Jack just gets me. He doesn't judge me. Jess is my people, too, but she's different. She's judgy; therefore I'm not free as a bird with Jess, but I'm okay with that. I'm also not invisible with Jess, or she wouldn't notice when I'm a slob.

"Do you know why I knew you'd need the cake?" he asks.

"Why?" I ask, licking icing from my finger.

"Because you had lunch with Jess. You always come back from lunch with Jess stressed."

Jess and Jack are what I call "my two Js," my people, the only people I confide in, count on, call family, no matter what their bloodline or mine. The problem is, they don't like each other. Not really. They'll tolerate one another when necessary.

"She doesn't stress me out. That's silly."

"You judge yourself by her," he states, his jaw setting hard. "Don't argue. It's true. You know it's true, and to your detriment."

The problem with people who know you well is they know you well. So, yes, he's correct. I judge myself by her, but that's my problem, not Jess's. Jess doesn't do that to me. I do that to myself. I am responsible for my own actions and reactions. I learned that in psychology class and in the books I obsessively read that semester.

That doesn't mean I put all I've read to good use, as right now I can't seem to deny or escape a defensive reply to Jack's analyzing me. "I wasn't aware you were now holding therapy sessions. Perhaps you need to stay away from floor two and the self-help books."

"Perhaps you need to visit floor two and the self-help books," he counters. "What did she do to upset you?"

"I don't know why you think I'm upset," I argue, setting my fork down quite precisely.

He eyes the plate and then me. "Oh, I don't know. The way you set your fork down with forced control. Or maybe because you inhaled that cake like you're a garbage disposal."

I quirk my lips to the side and think about what he said. Am I upset? No. *Upset* isn't the word I'd use. More like *uncomfortable*. Jess made me uncomfortable, and she did so with a hard shove out of my comfort zone. See, I was born in July, and that makes me a Cancer, the crab, and true to what the books will tell you, I like to live in a safe, comfy shell of my own making, and no one else's.

Jack folds his arms in front of him as if to say, "I'm not going anywhere until you spill the beans," and while I fight the confession, it wins the battle. "She's writing an article about dating sites. She wants me and her to basically register and document our experiences."

His eyes go wide and his jaw sets tight. "Is she using your name?"

"I didn't say I'd do it at all."

"Is she using your name?"

"I haven't even agreed to help her."

"Of course you're helping her. That's what you do when Jess wants something. Are you allowing her to use your name in the article?"

I could argue that he's wrong, that I don't always do as Jess wishes, but that feels like a bit of a moot point since he'll never believe me. Instead I say, "I'd never allow her to use my name."

"Is she compensating you?"

"If I do this," I state, "she'd pay me in love and friendship just like you would if I were doing you a favor."

He scowls his disapproval. "I wouldn't ask you to do something for my gain," he says. "I'm insulted that you think I would. And in case you've had a memory lapse, you had a hellish run last time we tried a dating site. Remember?"

All too well, I think, but I don't have the chance to assure him. The bell up front rings, an indicator Sally, our desk clerk, is calling for help. "I'll be back," Jack says. "Call Kara. Do not join the dating site." He gets up and leaves the room.

I don't tell him that Jess already joined for me. What's the point? Contrary to what he will believe, I am not Jess's puppet. I'm not going to put myself through dating-site hell again. As if on cue, my phone buzzes with an unfamiliar notification. I open my drawer and dig for my purse to find the dating app alerting me with three notices. *Notices,* I remind myself, not messages.

I tell myself to place the phone back in my purse and walk away from the dating app. Instead I click on the icon. I have one new notification and *four* new messages.

Chapter Five

Reality is created by the mind. We can change our reality by changing our mind . . .

—*Plato*

"Mia."

At the sound of my boss's voice, I drop my phone in my purse, shut the drawer, and twist my chair around to face her. "Oh," I say, taking in her pale skin, made paler by her dark hair, which is rather droopy around her face today. Considering she's usually as primped as Jess, I'm concerned. Even her light-blue jacket appears disheveled, not quite sitting on her petite body properly, a shoulder off-center or something. "You don't look so good." I stand up and turn my chair for her. "Sit down. Please."

She walks toward me but settles into my visitors' chair. "I'm fine here." She motions to my chair. "It's yours."

I hesitate but ease back into my seat and study her. Kara is forty-five and what I'd call a polished woman who comes together in an attractive way, but her singular features say she should not. Her nose is a bit plump. Her jaw is anything but sharp. I don't remember ever noticing her eye color. And yet she dresses stylishly, the rock on her hand compliments of her engineer husband, accessorizing with just about anything, and she claims every room she enters, despite a quiet disposition. She has what Jess has, in that her confidence clings to her presence even when she's as puny as she is today.

"What's wrong?" I ask.

She draws in a breath and pants it back out. "I don't know. I have a horrible pain in my side, and my heart is racing, which is probably from the discomfort. It started last night. I'm seeing the doctor in an hour."

"I'm so sorry you had to come and find me," I say. "I was about to come to you."

She waves off my concern. "You weren't tardy at all. I just need to give you some duties before I end up crashing and burning. I have that presentation with management tomorrow about the income projections for the auditorium. Can you please get them ready for me? I'll need it to look good, in full presentation format, but you worked with me on last quarter's update."

I blink at her. Wait, what? She wants *me* to put together the presentation that *she* will give and to which *she* will be judged? My rejection of this idea moves through me in what becomes a full-body experience. My muscles are tense. My throat is raw. My heart is racing.

"Go to my office if you need to in order to detach yourself from the activity on this floor," she adds. "I *really* need you on this."

Trapped like a rat chased by a cat that just plain outmaneuvered me, I swallow hard, quite clear on the fact that I cannot let her down. This is the woman who pulled me from my corner library, where the pay was low and, if I was honest with myself, which I wasn't until she showed up in my life, I was going nowhere. She saw me, just like "my two Js," and the compliment that was will forever stay with me. Kara delivered unto me *floor three* and with it a sense of joy and purpose.

"I'll handle it," I promise her. "You just go get well."

She is holding on to the arms of the chair. "Let's hope I do." She pushes to her feet and sways.

I'm already standing, catching her by her arm. "Do you have a ride to the doctor?"

"My husband's picking me up in a few minutes."

"Let me walk you back to your office."

"I'm fine now," she says, patting my hand. "It was just a little head rush. I know this project intimidates you, but you'll do fine. This is good for you. You tie your own hands with self-created insecurity."

With that, she walks out of the room, and I swear she's a little steadier than moments before.

Chapter Six

Kara's perfume, something sweet and oddly minty, still lingers in the air when my cellphone rings. I snag it from the deep, dark depths of the hell that is my messy purse, only to discover my mother's number on caller ID. I decline the call. It's not that I refuse to talk to her, or that I don't get along with my mother. It's simply that our conversations are always, for lack of a better word, *challenging*, and not well managed under deadline. Maybe if I went down to the self-help section on floor two, I'd find out I have pent-up anger issues toward her over her leaving me in that store years ago. I think I'll stick to my favorite romance novels for now.

I'm standing, gathering my things to find a quiet place to work, when Jack reenters the office. "Kara hunted you down," he observes, perching on the edge of his desk, arms crossed in front of his chest. "That's unusual. What was that all about?"

"Well, obviously, she doesn't feel well."

He frowns. "Obviously? She seemed fine to me. What's wrong with her?"

"Are you serious? She looked like death warmed over, not to mention she could barely walk."

"She did?"

"Good Lord, Jack. This is why you don't date. You don't notice things you should."

"Spoken as a woman with the wild and eventful dating life?" he challenges.

"If a guy doesn't notice the obvious," I shoot back, "a girl can't believe he'll notice anything about her."

"I'd give you all the reasons that logic is illogical if you were in the mood to hear it. She didn't seem sick to me." He eyes my oversize bag now on my shoulder, while my MacBook is in my hands. "Where are you going?"

"To the back room. Kara's going home sick. She's making me prepare data for her presentation. I need quiet. I can't let her down."

His eyes go wide. "You're preparing her presentation? Do you feel capable of doing that?"

I bristle with his obvious assumption that this is outside my comfort zone, which of course it is, but me thinking that and him thinking that are two different things. That's the contrary, irrational part of me I can't seem to deny or suppress. The part that doesn't want to be pushed but also doesn't want anyone to assume I can't handle being pushed, especially by someone who knows me well.

"I got this," I say firmly. "I'm not giving the presentation. I'm just preparing it."

The bell rings again, and he surprises me by smiling and saying, "You do. You got this, Mia." With that, he disappears into the other room again.

I realize then that he wasn't implying I wasn't capable of doing the job at hand at all. I'm simply a bit defensive after our conversation about Jess, and I projected my own self-doubts on him. Bottom line, Jack and Jess doubt each other, but I doubt neither. I'm not going to start now.

And with that, I add another "The End" to the topic.

Chapter Seven

The "back room," as we call it, is at the rear of our floor, where a singular wooden desk brushed with nicks of time and scratches sits among boxes of treasures, also known as the new books to be cataloged. There is also a conveniently located break room, which is home to a coffeepot and is walled off inside the same space. As work and caffeine go together almost as well as books and coffee, I start a pot brewing. By the time I'm sitting at the desk, with steam billowing from a ceramic mug, and I'm ready to work, my phone buzzes with a text message from my mother.

Call me. It's about your father.

My lips press together—and with good reason. It's *always* about my father.

For instance, some people might be curious as to why I would have such a visceral reaction to the idea of preparing Kara's presentation. The answer is simple: *my father*. Three years ago, he stepped out of his little creator's space, otherwise known as the garage, and onto the television screen. My father had done what thousands wish and pray to do by winning a spot on *Lion's Den*, the newest, hottest show competing against *Shark Tank*. He'd had merely two weeks to prepare his presentation, two weeks of nerves and practice pitches. He was ready. My mother and I had been backstage, rooting for him. We'd even held hands, which in and of itself was a miracle that passed that cold New York day. With excitement waving off us, we'd watched as he presented a new type of home window that conserves energy.

It was a disaster.

He'd frozen up, and then Big Davis, one of the most successful investors on planet Earth, mocked him. The longer Big Davis niggled at my father, the more painful it became, excruciating, to the point that I'd literally had to wipe tears from my eyes. Me and my mother's hands had fallen apart. My mother had stood there, saying nothing—what was there to say, really?—her fingers curled on her lips, looking as if she wanted to cry right along with me. Looking back, I believe that day my family was the closest and farthest away we'd ever been, depending on the time of day in question. From the morning, when we'd been united in a way I never remember us being, a team, flying high, jabbering about the future, to the afternoon, when we'd packed up and taken an early flight home, and we all welcomed the cramped plane that allowed no real conversation at all.

When I say it all comes back to my father, well, so do me and my mother. All the good and bad pieces of our relationship come back to him. She never agreed with my choices, even when my father supported me, which often pitted them against each other. On the other hand, she loves Dad as I love him, and for him, like that day in New York City, we unite.

When I was sixteen, I remember sitting across from the two of them in a restaurant as we celebrated him selling one of his patents, this one for a camping bottle with a flashlight in the bottom, to a private investor. He hadn't made a fortune, but he'd made more than my mother's annual salary at the time, a detail she proudly announced with a toast. That night, her love and admiration for her husband had shone in her eyes. It also wasn't an unfamiliar look she'd given him. It was just the first time I'd been old enough, and aware enough of the intimacy of relationships, be it a marriage bond or other, to understand what I was witnessing.

She loves him deeply.

He's my hero.

And, therefore, when he stood on that stage, embarrassed on national television, for a sliver of a moment, my mother and I were united in his pain, in our heartache for the man we both loved then and now.

In the aftermath, that moment when my hero was crushed for the world to witness left a mark on me and taught me a life lesson. Shelter in place, and like a good little July Cancer baby, I'm a quick learner. A crab likes her shell. Find my shell. Shelter in place. Maintain safety. Some might say I'm too quick a learner in this arena, but learn well I did.

Floor three has always been my playhouse, a.k.a. shell in the big backyard of the world, but after that day, it was more so than ever. Therefore, while I'm forced to take on duties that do not fit into my safe place—it's a small playhouse by design—I chose to stay on floor three and not go to Kara's office, which is on the first floor. The first floor is a place to be entered and exited. The first floor is a place to be watched from above. It's a zoo of unknown species entering from the outside world, and with it the kind of recipe for disaster I've generally avoided. Jess would say I play it too safe for my own good. There was a time when my father would have agreed. But he's not the same man anymore. Risks are no longer rewards, as he used to say often.

Worried about him now, I punch my mother's autodial number.

"Mia, oh good," she breathes out as she answers.

"What's wrong with Dad?"

"I'm headed out of town in the morning. I was hoping you might come by and bring your dad dinner. It would really make him happy."

My brows dip. "Since when do you travel for business?"

"Moving to the private sector in pharmaceuticals pays better than academia did, and it's also a new way of life," she says. "My boss wants me to deliver the statistical findings on several new drugs at a convention in Texas. I'm flying out tomorrow, delivering my little speech on Thursday, and then flying home that night. Your father will only be alone one night."

She's speaking of him as if he's a pet that needs a sitter, but then I've found mathematicians to be almost as clinical as scientists. Also, I frown with another thought. "Who is your new boss?"

"Dirk Michaels. He's the head of statistical findings for North America."

"And he wants you to deliver the findings? Why not himself?"

"I guess it's beneath him. You know how these stuffed shirts are." She cackles a familiar cackle, the same one she always lets out when the story of me being left in the store is told. She's uncomfortable and quickly shifts topics. "How are things with you?"

I open my mouth to tell her about my project but then press my lips together. She doesn't care how I am. She wants to escape, so I offer her an escape. "Actually, covering for my boss, so I'm super busy. Have a safe flight, and tell Dad I'll be by tomorrow night."

"You're a good daughter," she says, relief in her voice. "I'll tell him. Talk to you soon." She disconnects, escaping into the oblivion of a dead phone line.

I'm a good daughter? My brows dip. When has she ever, in all my life, said those words to me? What is going on? I sit there with each silent second ticking with heavy thuds as an uncomfortable thought lights up my mind and then crashes hard in my gut, where it screams to remain alive.

I quickly google "Dirk Michaels" and "Rochel Pharmaceuticals" before clicking on images. A photo of a man I guess to be in his mid-forties, with dark hair, a goatee, and chiseled facial features, appears on my screen. Oh Lord, my mom's new boss is good looking. Surely she's not—I mean—she would never have an affair. Would she?

Chapter Eight

By my estimate, I'm still more than an hour from finishing the proposal when the library closes. Jack pokes his head into my little workroom and says, "I hate leaving you, but tonight is Paige's dinner."

Paige would be his older, and only, sister. They aren't close, but since their parents are both passed now, they try to stay in touch. They lost their mother two years ago to cancer. Their father, before I ever knew Jack, to a work accident. He was a firefighter. They were divorced, a bitter divorce from what Jack has shared. Paige is a family law attorney, ironically married twice and divorced, and it seems she is always seeing a new man.

"Try to enjoy it," I urge, knowing all too well the way Paige pushes him to date more, calling him one step from being the guy's version of a cat lady, since he has three cats. She might be right, but Daisy, Doodle, and Donna are adorable.

"Don't say yes to a date with anyone I don't approve of," he counters.

"You don't approve of anyone."

"True," he says. "Because I may have to tell my sister we're dating. It would shut her up, and she already knows you."

"Dating I can fake, but I'm not marrying you to please Paige."

"Maybe we should make one of those pacts that if we're both not married at forty, we marry each other."

"That would be a great idea if I wasn't pretty sure we'll both be single at forty. And how does that affect us now? I'm too sober and busy to even think about screwing us up right now. Plus, your sister will never let us be fake engaged for that many years."

He grimaces. "My sister will be twice more divorced by then."

"Then maybe you should stop letting her pressure you to be her."

"If only you were as confident as your advice, Mia."

He's not wrong. If only.

He glances at his watch. "You leaving soon?"

"About an hour. You know I love this place when it's just me and the books."

"A little too much sometimes," he murmurs, but I don't even try to read between those blurry lines. I've been single too long to kid myself I would like his meaning.

Once he's gone, which is shortly thereafter, I dive back into my work, but Jack's words nag at me, insinuating themselves into the sentences on my computer screen. *If only you were as confident as your advice.* It reminds me of something I've heard, or perhaps read, somewhere, but I can't seem to figure out what or where. It bothers me. I don't forget things that feel important, and this oddly does.

I shake off the silly nagging thought that leads me nowhere but late to finish my work.

So much so that my stomach rumbles, and I'm forced to grab my leftovers from the break room fridge. I down what's left of my enchiladas with a diet soda. That doesn't mean I diet. I don't. I like my french fries and pizza. I simply dislike syrupy-sweet drinks. As for my eating habits, my mother didn't have high cholesterol until she was forty. I have some time to enjoy what I eat.

Once I've finally sent the presentation to Kara's inbox, I gather my things, and while I'd normally linger to enjoy the sounds the books whisper in my ears, I blink and I'm already on the escalator, thinking about the illusion of eating badly not affecting my health later in life, not because I'm worried about that illusion or my french fries. What I'm worried about is the larger illusion that might be in my life—one where my rock-solid parents are more brittle glass with a broken future.

I'm reminded of a book I read once. The main protagonist was a woman who was convinced she was blessed to be in the perfect marriage. Her life was a fairy tale until it wasn't, until every truth she knew unraveled and became nothing but lies. Perfect was an illusion. I believe everyone's story is riddled with illusion, and a big portion of that illusion is of our own making. Some might say that fiction allows you to hide from reality, to live inside a world of perfection rather than face your own illusions. Perhaps my father is also hiding from the illusion of a perfect marriage, too absorbed in self-hate to see anything but it, including my mother.

I blink and, without ever remembering the decision to do so, end up on floor two in the self-help section, specifically the relationship categories. Titles here range from *Who's Cheating on Who* and *The Wrong Bedroom* to *Broken Marriage*. I grab a book called *Open Your Eyes* that seems to be more about healing relationships than placing blame. I could easily blame my mother, but a lot of that is my own dirty history with her.

My father survived humiliation of a professional nature. To survive betrayal on the most personal level is another beast—and a brutal one at that. I'm not sure how he'll survive her cheating. I mean, what would it feel like to trust someone, to feel you know them, and know them well, and later discover they are leading a double life? I can't imagine trusting someone completely and finding out they are not the person you believed them to be at all.

I stop at the top of the escalator leading to floor one, where the hectic beats of a busy lobby have become absolute calm. I wait, watching below, expecting something to happen when I don't remember ever expecting anything but the joy of peace and quiet. I step on the escalator, that feeling expanding inside me for no good reason. Logically, I tell myself it's because I'm unsettled, but as my eyes fall on the seat where the dark-haired man had sat and watched me, my mind conjures a different take on that experience. Why wasn't I invisible to him? Maybe my mother's potential affair simply has my mind far removed from floor three and the romance section, but, rethinking the experience, it now feels a bit creepy.

Suddenly the silence inside the library is stifling, and I can't travel quickly enough to the exit.

Chapter Nine

Once I'm outside, in a coolish seventysomething Nashville September evening, that uneasy feeling fades. The high energy of a city that never sleeps replaces the quiet as a bus blasting loud music drives by, the party guests screaming to all who might hear. I barely do anymore. When you live and work downtown, it all becomes white noise. Even on Friday night, when we become a whole other level of party city. Beneath the rowdiness, though, are culture, good food, and, for me, everyone and everything about my life I love.

My walk is short, a whole two blocks, and I stop in front of a used bookstore, as my loft is above the retail area. Three years ago this past June, I was living in a high-rise apartment not far from here. I'd chosen a high floor, as it felt safer, but the elevator wait was forever, and it was not a fun way to deal with groceries. I'd been considering buying a small house, like Jack, only closer to downtown than his place, which is a fifteen-minute ride daily, and I considered it with such seriousness that Jess and Jack were tolerating each other to help me look for a place. I'd started the process feeling as if I'd earned this step in my life. After all, I was at the top of my pay scale without changing jobs. I was in a stable, happy place in my career in general. I dived into the hunt bubbling with excitement, only to discover that everything I found was small and expensive, and defeat clawed at me as imminent. Then one day at lunch, Jess and I had been out walking and the For Rent sign had caught my attention.

She must have seen my eyes light up, reacting instantly, pulling me around to her. "No. This will be loud, cheap, and not yours."

"I can't afford a house I want where I want it."

"I told you to spread your wings to other areas of the city."

"I like being a walkable distance to work."

"Move back in with me."

"We're grown-ass women, Jess."

"I know that, but you can save money and buy the same house outright. You know I don't touch my inheritance. I'll pay for half."

My heart had squeezed both with the generous offer and for the truth in those words. She *really* never touches that money, and yet she hasn't donated it, either. Jess owns a nice house, drives a nice car, and wears designer clothes, but she's earned it by being darn near famous at this point in her career. Sometimes I think she holds on to it to hold on to the connection it represents to her parents. Other times I think the connection it holds to her family disgusts her as much as they did.

One day we'll figure out what she needs to do with that money, or she will, and I'll just be there to support her, but it won't be spent on me. I'd squeezed her arm. "Jess, I love you. I do. Thank you, but no." I'd grabbed the For Rent sign, and the rest was history. Now, years later, the owners of the bookstore are thinking about selling it and the building, and I've saved enough to make all of this mine officially. But there is no way I'd leave the library to run the store, so soon I'll be house hunting again.

I unlock and open the building door, locking up behind me. I ignore the glass doors to the store and head right a few steps, then up a set of stairs. My door is the only one at the top of the climb, and I quickly enter my loft, walking straight up the black steel staircase to the bedroom, which overlooks the living area and kitchen. I plop down on the bed, set my bag beside me, and kick off my shoes.

My phone buzzes in my purse, and based on the distinct sound of that buzz I heard earlier, I'm fairly confident it's the dating app. The dating app I shouldn't even be registered for—*Thank you, Jess.* I shake my head and ignore it, pushing to my feet and heading to the bathroom.

Fifteen minutes later, I'm in pajamas and on the bed, with my MacBook open, when Jess appears in my instant messages.

Have you looked through your messages yet?

Of course she means from the dating app.

No, I reply. I haven't decided to even do this.

Please, she replies.

That word, *please*, is the start of a bigger push. She knows it. I know it. History knows it. My cellphone rings, and I answer with, "Tomorrow," though I'm already loading the app on my Mac. "I had to work late. I need to unwind and watch some HGTV or *Beat Bobby Flay*."

"You're such a geek, woman."

"You're more like me than you like to admit."

"I think it's you that's more like me than you like to admit. Tomorrow. I'm holding you to that."

"I know you are. Good night, Jess."

"I could come over and—"

"I'm in bed."

"It's seven o clock."

"Isn't it wonderful?" I counter.

She sighs. "Fine. Enjoy your HGTV. Lunch again tomorrow. Same place."

"Fine. Lunch again tomorrow."

We disconnect, and I don't know why, but I log on to the app. Alerts pop up. I now have fifteen messages, no doubt driven by that photo that looks nothing like me. *Thank you, Jess,* I think again. I search for my profile and quickly delete the photo. I upload one of my perfectly "geeky" images that actually looks like me, the real me. Now we'll see who really wants to message me.

Out of ridiculous curiosity, I click on my potential matches. I'm about four in when a surprising image appears. It's Kevin Rogers, a man I didn't think I'd ever see again. I'm not sure seeing him right now, even in a photo, is a good thing, either.

Chapter Ten

I dated Kevin Rogers. Me, the self-proclaimed Invisible Girl.

Sorta. I mean, I did.

It was all so strange.

I'd heard that Mary Beth Rogers, an elderly woman who'd been a regular at the library, had died. I'd noticed the address in the public announcement was walkable. Hoping to share my love for Mary Beth with others who loved her—she'd really become like a mother figure to me—I'd gone to the bakery, bought a selection of pastries, and dared to walk to the house.

I'd been awkwardly standing on the porch of a cute little home, second-guessing my decision to come here uninvited, when a tall, handsome, dark-haired man answered the door. Turned out Kevin was her grandson.

"Thanks," he'd said, accepting the baked goods from me. "You know where the funeral is, right?"

I hadn't planned to go to the funeral, but for some reason I just couldn't say no. Flash forward to the next day. He'd been there, of course, but quite alone. Turns out Kevin and Mary Beth were all the other had left on Earth. It had been me, Kevin, and some elderly friends of Mary Beth's. Kevin had cried and buried his face in my shoulder. When he'd asked if he could take me home, I thought he was just being polite. Turns out Kevin needed something I needed, too—a girl does have needs—and we'd ended up on my bed in what was a pretty fast and hard release.

I'd assumed he'd leave afterward. I was prepared for it. I didn't really feel less inconsequential with him because we'd had sex. I'm not sure he knew my name at that point. I also fully understood that he wasn't at my apartment for me. He didn't want to be alone. He was with me to be with someone, anyone. But Kevin didn't go home. He'd stayed the night. He'd eaten the breakfast I cooked. *Then* he'd left. I still knew nothing about him, aside from what he looked like naked and his relationship with Mary Beth.

It had been Monday morning when he'd surprised me by calling me and inviting me to lunch. During said lunch, he'd asked me to tell him about myself. He'd woken up from his grief and seen me. I'd radiated to the place of my heart and shared my love of books with him. In turn, he'd told me about his career as a programmer who developed games. Turns out he also liked to play them, which was fine at first. We'd been dating three months before I'd realized that we often sat next to each other on my couch while I read and he gamed, but we never actually talked. That's when I felt invisible again with Kevin. I comforted myself with the fact that when he met Jack, Jack had liked him. As for Jess, when Kevin met her, he didn't react to her beauty. She seemed invisible to him as well, almost as if he simply masked all of his true emotions to such an extent that I didn't really know him at all.

Curious now, my focus is back on the dating app, where I click on my messages, shocked to find one from Kevin. You look beautiful in that photo.

I lean back, straighten, blinking in surprise. I look *beautiful*? He never once in our short relationship told me I was beautiful, but then, I don't look like myself in that photo Jess used for my profile. I blink again when I realize his message just hit my inbox, and my photo, the one I replaced Jess's with, was already in place. I don't understand.

My mind goes to the day I knew he and I were over. In a rare meeting of the two Js, I'd been out to lunch with Jack when Jess had joined us. With both of "my people" present, it was difficult to hide my distress. I sink back into that moment, living it again.

Jack is the first to notice my state of mind. "What's wrong?"

"Nothing," I reply, not to lie to him, but rather to force my answer to be true. But it's not, which is exactly why I comfort myself by shoving one of the big, fat crispy french fries, which came with a much less interesting hamburger, into my mouth.

"Kevin again," Jess interjects as if I just confessed rather than suppressed my thoughts on the subject. "The mummified man that sits on your couch most evenings these days." Before I can answer, she adds, "You feel invisible again."

"Yes," I confirm painfully. "Kevin."

"I'm going to say it again, as I've said it ten thousand times," she states. "You are both"—she waves her fork between me and Jack—"what you choose to be. If you feel invisible, you are invisible. And you both feed this in each other. You use each other as security blankets. When was the last time you dated, Jack?"

"We aren't talking about Jack," I quickly chime in, trying to save him.

"In other words, a long time," she supplies. "You know, if you don't use it, it wilts."

I choke on nothing. "Oh my God, Jess."

"Just don't use it with her." Jess's fork is now pointed at me. "You two will wither away together if you go down that path, and you both know it, or you'd already have visited that option. Bottom line, believing you're generally unworthy has to stop." Then her fork points at Jack. "And truth be told, you don't like me because you know I see the truth and speak it." She lays her pointy fork down on the table rather primly, shoves her plate forward, and folds her hands in front of her. Her eyes meet mine. "Time for some of that truth right here and now. It's too late with Kevin. You've set a standard with him. You can't undo what has been done."

Jack sighs heavily. "As much as I hate to agree with her on anything, I do believe she's right about Kevin."

Hours later, I'd been back at the library when I'd texted Kevin and told him I thought we needed a break. He hadn't replied. Disappointedly, he also hadn't shown up at my loft that night. He was obviously okay with goodbye. That night, one year and three months ago, had been lonely, but I'd adjusted remarkably quickly. Right now, as I stare at his message, I remember Jess's words. *You can't undo what has been done.* I don't reply to the message. And I'm not sure why, but I do keep clicking on my matches.

I do a double take when another familiar face appears on my screen. It's Jack. Jack is on the dating app. I'm confused. He *just* reminded me about how bad it was for us both the last time we did this and encouraged me to pass on a repeat. And yet he's on repeat? I'm just not sure what to make of that.

There's an Oscar Wilde quote that says, "A man's face is his autobiography. A woman's face is her work of fiction."

I lie in bed that night, thinking about Kevin and Jack. Obviously, there is a story to each man's life that remains a mystery. This doesn't surprise me with Kevin, at all. He'd spent an excessive amount of our time together on his computer while I'd, in turn, had my head in a book. I'm not sure how either of us ever intended to know one another. On some level, I think we both simply needed to fill empty space. We were placeholders for one another. For a period of time, I now believe I chose to wear rose-colored glasses to view our relationship.

On the other hand, I've always believed Jack an open book where I'm concerned, as I am to him. I don't understand why he wouldn't just tell me he'd been trying online dating again. I decide perhaps he's embarrassed, though that still doesn't sit quite right. I'm his safe person, and he's mine, too, even more so than Jess in many ways. He never judges me. I never judge him.

When I finally fall asleep, it feels like the alarm buzzes almost instantly. I peel myself out of bed, my thoughts already jumping left and right, and both directions lead to Jack. Once I've showered, I apply the barest touch of makeup I dare apply with my limited skills, dress in a simple fitted black skirt and a black sweater, paired with boots, and head downstairs for a quick cup of coffee. With only a few minutes to spare, sitting at my kitchen island, with steam waving off my coffee cup, I can't help myself. I log back on to the dating site with the intent of finding Jack's profile. I'm able to search his name, but I come up with no match. Either I imagined his profile or he deleted it.

Chapter Eleven

In life, the people you call "my people" are those you feel safe and happy with when you're with them. And yet my short walk to work is shorter than usual as I debate asking Jack about the dating profile, which is insane. I never fret about anything with Jack. I walk into the side employee entrance of the library and cross the lower level before the chaos of a busy day erupts. Once I'm on the escalator, I turn automatically toward the view below that often engages me, for no good reason. I'm early. Visitors have not arrived as of yet, and my mind is still elsewhere. If Jack deleted his profile, the motivation might feel tangled, but it's also fairly easy to unravel. He did so with the hope that I would not see it before that happened. Jack and I have secrets from one another. I am sadly enlightened over the true state of our relationship, one not as open as I'd thought, and uncomfortable about seeing him for the first time ever.

Once I'm on floor three, walking toward the empty service desk, I hear, "Mia."

At the sound of Jack's voice, instinct kicks in, and I automatically turn to find him walking toward me, doing so with no hesitation.

"Coffee Cats had a short line," he says, offering me a cup as he joins me. "I got you the crème brûlée coffee you love."

He's looking exceptionally tall today for some reason. Perhaps it's simply that I feel smaller than usual, in the midst of my realization that he and I have secrets from one another.

"Thank you," I say, as we start walking toward the desk. "How was dinner with your sister?"

"About the same as your dinners with Jess," he says dryly. "She's been dating a new guy she's breaking up with because she's bored."

The reference to Jess has me wondering what secrets *she's* keeping, but then, I lived with her for years. I saw her good, bad, and ugly, and navigated her encounters with a father who abused her, right by her side.

At this point, I'm at my desk, and Jack's behind me, sitting at his, which faces the opposite wall. "Did you finish the presentation?" he asks, and I can tell he's rotated his chair to face me.

I rotate mine as well, sipping my coffee, which is sweet and warm, before I confirm, "Yes. I sent it to Kara before I left work."

Now he sips his coffee. "Did Jess convince you to dive into the hellish online-dating thing again?"

He asks the question without so much as a blink, and I start to doubt myself, wondering if I'd only seen someone who looked like Jack. "I was way too tired to deal with that last night, and I told her so. I'm meeting her for lunch."

"In other words, you're doing it."

He means the dating app, of course. "I'm still deciding."

"You're doing it. It's happening. Pencil me in, though. I need a plus-one the weekend after next for my uncle's wedding."

Jack and I have a pact. We're always each other's plus-one when needed. Since it's needed, I surmise his dating-site endeavors have not gone any better for him than I expect they will for me. "I didn't think you were close to your uncle."

"I barely know him, but my sister insists I go. She's bringing a date and told me to do the same, or everyone is going to start thinking I'm gay, which she said is fine, but she still wants to meet my partner."

I cringe for him. "She thinks you're in the closet?"

"Apparently," he states. "I told her I like women, and that if I didn't, I'd happily say so."

"Well, on a positive note, it's nice to know she'd accept you no matter your orientation."

"Right. Gay is fine. She just can't accept me as a loser who can't get a date at all, no matter my sexuality. Somehow that doesn't feel positive at all."

One of our morning staff members, Carrie, pokes her head in the door. "We need you, Jack."

Jack pushes to his feet and waves in her direction. "Coming."

Carrie disappears, and Jack lingers long enough to say, "The wedding is the Saturday after next. Mark your calendar."

"Marking it now," I assure him.

Once he's departed the room, I consider what I've just learned. I decide it's possible his sister pressured him about his love life to the point he felt he had to join another dating site. I mean, she knows he and I are platonic friends, so bringing me to the wedding won't end his sister prying into his love life. Needing a date is a logical reason to start a new dating profile. Hiding it from me is another story.

Chapter Twelve

Considering I finished my caffeine-laced latte a good hour too long ago, I'm running on low and am on the hunt for a pick-me-up. At present, I'm standing inside the minuscule break room, which Jack playfully calls "fun size" while filling a mammoth extra-large cup with freshly brewed basic coffee. My coffee love is not reserved for what one might call "upper shelf" beans with printed cups and juiced-up flavors. Hard, dark, and power punched with enough caffeine to pin my eyelids back for days is an afternoon favorite of mine.

I'm just stirring in some powdered creamer when I hear, "Mia Anderson," from behind me.

I abandon my cup and rotate to find my boss's boss, Neil Harper, standing in the doorway. Neil is what I call a librarian on stilts, his six-foot-five height made for basketball or high shelves. His ability to reach a book with nothing but a lift of his arm is impressive and enviable, to say the least.

"Mia," he greets again, a hint of a question mark accenting my name.

The uncertainty doesn't really surprise me, but I also suspect it's unrelated to my incredible ability to remain invisible to the masses. I'm not sure how Neil could possibly know my name or anyone else's. The man doesn't look down to the level where the rest of us human librarians dwell, let alone mingle with the staff.

"Yes, sir," I greet, confirming he has the right person.

He registers no relief or emotion whatsoever with scoring the right person he seeks. He hits his point hard and fast, leaving no room for empty space and chitchat. "Kara isn't coming in. We need you to make her presentation today. Be in the first-floor conference room at two thirty." He glances at his watch. "It's ten after ten now. That gives you plenty of time to prepare." He backs up and disappears out of sight.

I grab the counter behind me, the room spinning. He wants me to *what*? I attempt to draw in a wheezy breath and fail miserably. I'm hyperventilating and not for the first time in my life. I was twenty-two when I was one of a hundred people in a crash course on inventory control systems. We'd all been assigned a five-minute presentation, but on the day of the actual class, only twenty names were drawn to pull the trigger and grace the stage. I was one of them. I was prepared. I knew the subject. I was sure I'd impress everyone if I just conquered my nerves. None of that is what had happened at all.

I'd walked to the front of the room, knees weak, palms sweaty, stood at the podium, and started reading my notes. It had been uneventful. Someone in the front row had been asleep. Several others hadn't even been looking at me. It was the first time in my life that being a shadow in a room full of people had felt rather powerful. I could have done almost anything and no one would have noticed. A degree of calmness had splashed me with realization, cold water in the heat of a bad moment.

I'd actually become more confident after that day—until another day, that is. The day my father was humiliated.

I draw in another full breath. I am not my father. He was never invisible. Except maybe now, to my mother, but I can't go down that rabbit hole right now. I know the material today, just as I did that day so long ago. The material that documents the financial side of the auditorium will be the focus, not what some librarian filling in for Kara has to say, which works just fine for me. I'm going to back off the ledge and stop creating a crisis where there is none.

After pushing off the counter, I hurry out of the break room, exiting to the main library to find Jack and two of our staff members at the service desk, busy tending to a line of eager patrons. I walk behind the desk, pausing beside Jack to lean in near his ear and whisper, "I have to give Kara's presentation at two thirty. I'm going to the coffee shop next door to prepare."

I don't allow him time to ask questions or add to my nervous energy. I hurry to my desk with the hope of packing up and getting out of here without delay. By the time I've bagged my MacBook and it and my purse are on my shoulder, that hope is dashed. Jack is standing in front of me. "You're doing *what*?"

"Crazy, right?" I say, obviously aware of what he's talking about. Me doing a presentation isn't expected. "Kara must be really sick, because this is actually happening."

"You're giving the presentation?"

"I'm doing this," I confirm.

"Can I help?"

"Actually, yes. If I email you the presentation, can you have one of the staff make me forty copies? The attendees all have an email version to follow, but I want something physical for them to focus on that isn't me."

"Smart decision. By what time?"

"Two."

"Done. Do you want me to come over and drill you over lunch?"

He says that as if this is such a big deal that I need to practice, and I don't choose to be in that headspace right now. "No, thanks," I say. "I need to get in my own head."

He studies me a beat, his eyes sharp, before he asks, "You know you can do this, right?"

"We're going to find out," I say. "I just hope Kara is okay."

"I guess I was wrong about how sick she was."

I bite back a little quip about his dating skills that would be a natural wordplay between us but might give away my seeing his profile on the app last night. Unease is instant, as if I'm walking on a bed of dull nails just sharp and awkward enough to ensure each step torments me. It's similar to every conversation I have with my mother.

"I'll come over when I get a break," he offers, motioning toward the door and the desk. "*If* I manage a break."

Ouch, he's right. He really needs me here. "I can stay."

"No. No, I've got this."

"I don't want to desert you."

"You're not deserting anyone," he assures me. "You're supporting Kara, which is supporting our team."

He's right. I know he's right, but this isn't how I'd ever imagined myself doing so. "Call me if it gets too busy, and I'll come back," I offer.

"I won't call," he promises as the bell starts dinging, telling us both he's in demand. "You got this," he repeats and disappears out the door.

I exit the office and hurry beyond the busy desk and my guilt for leaving the staff behind, forcing myself to focus on what is before me, not what I'm presently leaving. With that idea in mind, I step on the escalator and text Jess to cancel lunch. Message sent, my gaze lifts and sweeps across floor two as it comes into view, homing in on one table. My heart hammers against my breastbone with what I find below. The dark-haired man is back, and I instinctively gobble up any details about this stranger and his intent—that word *intent* in my mind for no explainable reason. There's a book in front of him, a MacBook to his right, a coffee to his left. He seems to be here working, and yet, almost as if he does nothing but sit there and watch the escalators, his gaze is fixed on my location yet again. He's watching me, tracking my slow descent down to floor one. Isn't he?

And then he's gone. The escalator has carried me behind a wall.

Chapter Thirteen

In a rush of anxiousness, I exit the library and step onto the sidewalk. The air I didn't know was trapped in my lungs whooshes from my lips in what I can only call relief. When in my entire career have I *ever* been relieved to leave the library? Quite the contrary, in fact. I replay my two brushes with the man on floor two and decide he's a people watcher, as I am. That's all. It's nothing more, and people watchers see everyone.

Even those others ignore.

My phone buzzes with a text, and I start walking, telling myself to shake off the encounter as I read a message from Jess. Dinner tonight then?

Dinner with my father, I reply. My mother is out of town with her boss. Don't ask. Not now before my presentation.

My head was not where yours clearly is, she answers. I have questions. Coffee tomorrow morning. Coffee Cats. Non negotiable.

I blink and I'm already at the entrance to Caroline's Coffee and Bagels. The coffee isn't as good at Caroline's as it is at Coffee Cats, but the bagels are delicious, and the location is hard to beat. As for Jess, I don't answer her last message. She's made the decision. It's just another one of those "The End" kind of topics. What Jess wants, Jess gets. What I want is some time to myself, to calm myself down before my meeting this afternoon.

Entering Caroline's, I quickly find a corner booth, set my things down to claim my spot, and then head to the counter. There's a person in line in front of me, with Greg, the familiar college kid who is here most afternoons behind the register, helping him. Once the man finishes ordering and pays, he steps away from the counter, and I inch forward.

Greg looks right at me and then walks away.

Of course he does. Most likely he's just putting in the other customer's order.

And yet I wait. And wait. Greg walks toward me, and all seems well, but then he grabs something under the counter and leaves again. I grind my teeth and wait a little longer. He walks by me again and keeps on keeping on. Finally, impatience ticking in my jaw, I ring the bell. Greg appears behind the register. "Can I help you?"

"Did you not see me standing here?" I ask.

His brow furrows. "You were standing here?"

I grind my teeth a little harder. Of course he saw me standing here. I'm not literally *invisible*, but I'm feeling anxious to get back to work and let the confrontation tempting me slide on by.

"My usual," I say, trying to expedite this slow process.

His brows dip. "Usual?"

Is he *serious*? "I come in here several times a week and you wait on me. You don't know what my usual is?"

He just blinks at me. If I were Jess, he'd be falling all over himself to please me.

"Fine," I state. "A large honey cinnamon latte with nonfat milk and a cinnamon bagel with plain cream cheese." Yes, I drink nonfat milk in my coffee, and sugar and grease in everything else. I don't have to be logical to please my taste buds and belly.

Greg punches in my requests while I slide my card into the charge slot. Once the transaction is complete, he says, "Name?"

This man has asked me that question at least thirty times before today, and I fight the urge to tell him as much. Nevertheless, an uncharacteristically snarky reply slides from my lips and does so rather easily. "Invisible Girl," I say, and once it's out it feels good, as liberating as that presentation years ago had, in fact. I'm not allowing myself to be invisible. Take that, Jess.

In return, I expect Greg to grimace or make some smart remark. Instead, he grabs a cup, writes the name on the cup, and says, "We'll call you." He walks away.

I stand there a moment, just staring at the space where he'd been moments before, telling myself that the burn in my belly that resembles anger is the wrong emotion to feel. I should be pleased right now. Being dismissed supports the hypothesis that I won't be noticed enough in the meeting today to make a fool of myself. And yet this encounter with Greg doesn't feel good. Why can there be no happy medium?

I turn and walk to my seat, sitting down and pulling my MacBook from my bag before opening the lid and powering it up. My fingers drum on the table for far too long as I contemplate what a conflicted mess I am. I want to be noticed and yet, today, in that meeting, I do not want to be noticed. Apparently I want to pick and choose by who, when, and where I am seen.

Right then, the barista calls out, "Order for Girl!"

Girl. That's it. Just *Girl.*

I can't even get Greg—no, "the guy behind the counter," which is how I plan to think of him from now on—to write out "Invisible Girl" on my cup.

Why in the world am I worried about the presentation? Greg has made my point, driven it right on home to the parking lot in my brain. That point being that my father has never been dismissed. He is not me. I am not him.

"Girl!"

With that name filling the air again, I all but grind holes in my teeth. Pushing to my feet, I cross the room, bite my tongue, and pick up my order. Once I'm sitting down again, my gaze lands on the scribbled "Girl" written on my cup. I draw in a breath and sip from the coffee to discover it's not even a latte at all. It's just black coffee, and I've hit my limit with "the guy behind the counter." I stand up and march toward the counter.

The manager is behind the register, and I beeline to the empty counter in front of her. Loretta is tall, thin, and fortysomething by my first guess, and, people watcher that I am, I'm good with ages. And names. "Hi," I say.

"Hi," she greets. "Mia, right?"

I blink in surprise. "You know my name?"

"Of course," she assures me. "You're in all the time. What can I do for you?"

"I ordered a nonfat—"

"Honey cinnamon latte," she supplies. "Does it taste off?"

"It's just plain coffee." I slide the cup in front of her.

"Oh no," she says, her tone reading as genuinely concerned. "I'm so sorry." She lifts the cup to eye the order on the side and frowns. "Girl? He wrote *Girl* on your cup?"

The female barista, whose name I do not know, leans toward Loretta and says, "He can barely remember his own name."

Loretta scowls and murmurs, "Isn't that the truth," before adding, "I need a nonfat honey cinnamon latte, ASAP."

"You got it, boss," the barista replies, eyeing me to say, "Sorry about that."

"Thanks for making me a new one," I say, feeling my agitation floating away in a sea of kindness and apologies.

On that very note, Loretta casts me in a concerned stare, reaches under the counter, grabs a couple of cards, and hands them to me. "Coupons for a few free coffees. Sorry for all of this."

"Thank you," I say, and on a scale of one to ten, my frustration is now a zero. Loretta pretty much had me at hello. I went from feeling like an outsider to belonging right here in this little corner of downtown Nashville. "Really," I say, my mood uplifted as I add, "I do appreciate how you handled this. It was perfection."

She smiles as if she's found a new book she can't wait to break open and read. Feeling better than I have all day, actually, despite the impending presentation, I walk back to my booth.

I've just slid into my seat when I discover a white notecard on my keyboard that reads "Girl" on it.

My brows dip, and Loretta appears beside my table. "I told her to rush it and rush it she did. If that's not perfect, you let me know."

"I will. Thank you." But my reply is absent, my mind on the note card.

I don't know why, but I stare at it as if touching it will somehow change my life when it's just a note card. Which is ridiculous. It's probably from Jack, joking about me being called "Girl," and I glance around, looking for him without success. Still, I hesitate to open the note, and I don't know why. A note is not going to change my life. Chiding myself for my silliness, I pick it up and open it to read four simple words:

You look beautiful today.

Chapter Fourteen

I stare down at the note, blinking several times, confused, shocked, elated, flattered. It's as if a waterfall of reactions crashes down upon me, one on top of the other, drowning me in the sheer rush at which they assail me. Confusion wins, dominating the onslaught of my reaction.

What is this? Who did this?

It's not as if this is the kind of thing that happens to me.

No one *ever* tells me I look beautiful.

Correction, I think, no one who is not *my father* ever calls me beautiful, but then parental love—excluding my mother's, of course—is blind. Only, I realize, someone did, and just last night. Kevin sent me a DM on the dating app with almost these exact same words. I glance around Caroline's, looking for him, looking for someone else who might have left the note. I don't find Kevin, and the dining area is never busy at the lunch hour the way it is in the mornings, anyway. There are only a few people in line at present—two women chatting, an elderly man with a younger man, and then another woman who is texting at lightning speed.

Frowning, I return my attention to the note, deciding the script has a decidedly masculine texture to it, though I'm no handwriting expert, either. Ask me about the words between two covers, not the pen by which the story may, or may not, have been inked. I quickly log on to the dating app and find my alerts. I now have thirteen messages. I search for the message Kevin sent me last night, but there is none. I'm confused. I know I saw it. I know he sent it. Just as I know Jack was registered. Maybe it's a glitch in the dating app.

I search for his profile, and unlike my fruitless search for Jack's, I easily locate Kevin as an active member. The deleted message may simply be message remorse, and therefore he deleted the evidence. Still, Kevin knows I hang out at Caroline's, and the note on my keyboard sounds too much like the now-deleted message on the dating app for me to dismiss my ex as the culprit. I grab my phone and text Kevin: Did you send me a message on a dating app?

Seconds tick by, and he doesn't answer, but he's a slow texter, and we've not exactly been talking as of late, or anytime recently. He also never responded with urgency to my messages. Something about this entire situation is weird.

Unease is clawing at me when perhaps I should simply feel flattered by the random compliment left behind in the form of a note. This just isn't something that happens to me. I consider calling Jack and finding out if he did this, but if he didn't, he'll ask a lot of questions I don't want to answer. Same goes for Jess.

Turning my attention back to the dating app, I scan the messages, seeking anything that feels unusual. Could this really represent a random compliment? I glance at the front of the card that reads "Girl," which seems to indicate whoever did this heard that name called for my order. Of course, both Jess and Jack would also do such a thing to tease me, but not laugh at me. More a way to share a mutual joke. Of course that's what this is. One of them is being funny.

Time to end another chapter, this one rather silly.

I stuff the note in my bag and pull up the presentation.

Chapter Fifteen

With only fifteen minutes until my presentation, I stand inside the doorway of Caroline's, my bag on my shoulder, and watch the monstrous droplets of rain swell as they splatter the pavement.

The day my father was to appear on *Lion's Den* was a rainy day, one of his favorite kind of days. He called the days when a storm splattered about on the rooftop of the garage his most creative. Perhaps his love for the rain is how I came to love it as well. How I learned to appreciate snuggling in by a window, rain pitter-pattering against the glass, a book in my hand, a story enchanting my mind. I wish I could block that day out, but it's a snake in my mind, slithering about, at the most dangerous of moments, such as right now, right before I give an important presentation.

The television show had been filmed in New York City. We'd flown in the night before. I remember watching the rainfall over Manhattan from my parents' hotel room, my father stepping to my side and saying, *"Some people feel the rain. Others just get wet."*

It's a familiar quote he favors, and quotes often. He'd gone on to add, "I feel it and it feels lucky."

I'd felt his luck as well, almost as if it kissed the very air we breathed.

I also remember the moments after the disaster of his public humiliation on live TV, when we'd stepped outside the studio, a dank day remaining in the aftermath of the storm merely withdrawn to reinforce its massive downpour. My father had noticed the shift in the weather as well, holding his hands out in front of him, his eyes lifting skyward as he'd murmured, "The rain stopped." Almost as if my science-driven father was saying his luck ran out when the rain did.

While moments before I'd been willing away the rain to allow my return to my library home, suddenly I don't want to know when it stops. I'm about to make a run for it, allowing the rain to drench me in luck, when a man in a suit appears on the other side of the door, his umbrella high. I open the door for him, and he steps inside. He lowers his umbrella, pulling it inside and closing it, his dark hair neatly groomed, untouched by the weather.

I cannot help but notice his statuesque height. He turns to face me—no, he doesn't *just* turn to face me; he looks at me with striking blue eyes. Eyes etched with lines that age him into his late thirties, a worldly confidence to him I instantly envy.

"Thanks for the assist," he says. "Let me return the favor." He offers me the handle to his damp umbrella. "You look like you could use this."

Stunned by the offer, I am frozen in place, incapable of reacting. He not only *sees me*; he has not dismissed me but rather, gallantly, offered me a rescue. Thunder erupts above, rattling the walls a bit and jolting me into action. "Thank you," I say. "But I won't be able to return it."

"You don't need to return it," he states. "A stranger offered it to me. I'm passing on the same kindness. Maybe you can do the same for someone else."

"Yes," I say, pleased by this idea, even more so by being someone included in a circle of kindness. "I will. Thank you." I reach for the gift he's offered me, and once it's in my hand, he smiles a charming smile and opens the door for me.

A tad self-conscious as to how I'm going to manage to open the umbrella and step outside without somehow landing on my backside, I shove the umbrella out the door and pop it open. So far so good as I step out into the storm, protected by an umbrella that represents kindness.

The walk to the library is short, and as I reach the main entrance, the security guard opens the door for me. "Thanks, Doug," I greet the elderly man, stepping inside the foyer of the building and folding the umbrella shut.

"You're quite welcome," he replies.

At that moment, a young woman exits the main library doors behind us and approaches the exit. "Oh my," she says. "It's horrible out there." She glances at Doug. "Does the gift shop sell umbrellas?"

"Take mine," I offer, extending my arm to offer her the gift I'd received before her, her shelter from the storm. "And pass it along to someone else who needs it. That's how it came to me."

She blinks and says, "Really?"

"Yes, really."

"That's amazing," she murmurs, accepting the gift I've offered her. "I'll pass it along as well."

Doug opens the door for her, and she steps outside. As she disappears into the weather, Doug offers me a smile of approval. I'm smiling, too, until I reach for the door beyond Doug, the one leading to the floor-one zoo, and pause with a realization. Today I have been seen, not just once, but over and over again. By way of Kara's trust, by way of the man at the table on floor two. By way of Loretta's kindness. Then there was the note left on my table. And, finally, the man who offered me his umbrella.

I am not invisible, not this one day.

And it's the wrong day when I have a presentation to deliver.

It's with this thought that the young woman opens the door and exits into the rain, the umbrella sheltering her and no longer me. Something Jess said to me not too long ago flits through my mind. *"If you don't want to be invisible, stop choosing to be invisible. Don't dress like every day is a funeral. Wear makeup. Dare to make eye contact."*

"You know what I think, Mia," she'd said to me one day.

"I can guess," I'd said. "You don't have to say it."

"I think you're afraid to be seen."

"That's silly," I'd said, waving her off. "Why would I be afraid to be seen?"

"Hiding is always easier than facing judgment, but those who judge you are not worthy of you, anyway."

If only I were as confident as Jess, but something my mother of all people says often rings true as well: *"Fake it until you make it."* Of course, she didn't make that saying up. Who knows who originally did. Per my mother's friend who sold Mary Kay cosmetics, pink car and all, it was Mary Kay. Regardless of who said it, faking is all I've got right now.

With a deep, calming breath, I enter the main library, only to all but run into Jack. "I was about to come to get you," he announces. "You only have a few minutes before the meeting starts." He shifts the topic before I can reply. "I was able to set your presentation material on a table inside the meeting room." He dares to take a breath, his eyes narrowing on me. "How are you feeling?"

Antsy, I think, feeding off his hyped energy, and not in a good way. My heart is racing. My hands tremble slightly. But I also have a choice to make right now. I can choose to decide luck, like the rain, is on my side or choose to believe the universe has tricked me and set me up for a massive failure. I choose luck today; therefore I say, "I'm ready. Thank you for your help."

"I'm just sorry I didn't get over to Caroline's to give you a pep talk. It's been insane on our floor. I have to get back." He glances at his watch. "And you now have about three minutes to get in there." He squeezes my elbow. "Good luck." He walks backward, gives me a thumbs-up, and then turns and starts walking away.

I watch him step onto the escalator, the note burning a hole in my bag, the words playing in my head. *You look beautiful today.* Despite Jack never doing such a thing before, I think in the back of my mind I'd really believed him responsible and motivated by an effort to stir my confidence. He's distracted, though, his jittery mood a product of him juggling patrons and long checkout lines upstairs. I know him. I know that means he didn't have time to come next door and leave me that note.

I know him. I know Jack.

I repeat those words and think of his dating profile that was here one moment and gone the next. I'm reminded of my mother, who I've always believed loved and adored my father, but is now out of town with her incredibly good-looking boss. I think of me, waffling between wanting to be seen and not wanting to be seen. Do any of us really know anyone, even ourselves?

Chapter Sixteen

I hurry through the busy main floor of the library, my mind retraveling the past and why I must not let Kara down. Five years ago this month, she came into my little library branch. I was on top of a ladder, seeking a title I suspected had been misfiled. By the end of our first encounter, I'd found out my library was closing due to budget cuts, and Kara would be my new boss at the central library.

She saved my job. I can't let her down.

Nerves destroy me as I arrive at the meeting room and peek my head inside. There are rows of chairs filled with people, and at the front of it all I spy a projector and a podium.

Neil spots me and motions me toward the front of the room. "We're waiting on one more board member," he informs me. He gestures to a steel chair. "Have a seat."

Just that easily I'm dismissed, and it's sweet relief until I'm actually sitting down with a good forty sets of eyes. Forty times two is eighty. Eighty eyes on me.

A man walks into the room, and he must be the expected investor as Neil steps to the microphone. I barely hear him as he invites me to speak, but I'm aware of the rain that pelts the glass windows. "Luck of the rain," I silently murmur. I can do this. I *have* to do this. Kara is counting on me.

I stand, knees weak, chest tight, but I manage to step to the podium, carefully pressing my hands to the wooden top, hiding their tremble. I will myself to calm down and remember what a teacher told me once. Find one spot at the back of the room, focus there, and hang on to that one spot until you can breathe again.

The problem is the one spot is where the man, the newcomer, is standing. And that man is the one who was watching me from floor two.

Chapter Seventeen

It's hours later, and I haven't been able to reach Kara, while Jack has done his best to comfort me. I can't be comforted. I can't talk about the presentation at all. I just can't, and yet he persists. We're packing up our bags for the day when he says, "I don't know what happened in the presentation, but I know you. It wasn't as bad as you think."

"It was," I assure him. "At one point, I kept telling myself not to say certain things, and yet they came out of my mouth. And I think I used an English accent."

"You've been joking around and mimicking the dialogue in that book you've been reading. I'm sure you didn't actually—"

"I think I did," I say, the replay in my head about as brutal as one of my dating-app meet and greets. "Have you noticed the man sitting on floor two lately, mostly in the afternoons?"

"No," he says. "I tend to hyperfocus on our floor. Why?"

"He was in the meeting. Apparently the board has been watching us perform."

"You think they've had undercover patrons evaluating us?"

"I'm not sure," I say. "But if so, to what end? Maybe there are going to be budget cuts. That is how I got my job here. My branch was shut down."

"We're the central library. I think you're dragging yourself through a river of conspiracy theories that is going no place good."

"Right. Right. I'm sure you're right."

"Right three times in one sentence," he jokes. "Damn, I'm good."

I smile. "Right."

He laughs. "Why don't we go have a drink?"

"I have dinner with my dad. My mother is out of town with her new, hot boss."

He blanches. "Say what? She's having an affair?"

"They're at a convention, but something about it feels off. I don't know. I think she might be cheating on my dad, but I'm hoping to be proven wrong."

He rubs the back of his neck as if he's as tense about this as I am. "You want me to come by later tonight?"

"I do, but not tonight. I might stay with my dad."

His hands settle on his hips. "How are you getting to his place?"

"Uber."

He straightens, decided as he says, "I'll drive you."

"As much as I appreciate that, I need to clear my head before I see my dad."

Disapproval flattens his lips. "I'll walk you to the Uber."

"I'm good," I say. "I *really* need to think and clear my head before I see my dad."

"Don't wallow in that presentation going badly, Mia. It's done. It's over. It's behind you."

It's not, I think, but I don't push my point. He'll comfort me. I know he will.

Suddenly my fears over not really knowing Jack fly right out the window in my head. He's a good friend. He's always been a good friend. So what if he's on a dating site that he didn't tell me about? He was probably embarrassed in some way. Men tend to be more private about these things than women, I've noticed, especially with Jess around. In fact, as for deleting his profile, I doubt it was me he was hiding from. Most likely it was Jess, who isn't always kind to Jack.

I close the space between me and him and say, “Thanks for being a good friend, Jack. I really don’t know what I’d do without you.”

His eyes warm in that friendly way they always do with me. “If you need me tonight, I’ll be around. Call me. Okay?”

“You know I will.”

I step around him and head for the door, and it’s not long before I’m riding down the escalator, passing floor two. It’s as dead as a ghost town.

Chapter Eighteen

I step outside the library, a prickly sensation dancing on the nerve endings at my nape, for no explainable reason. The street is a hustle and bustle of nightlife, the decorative but practical outdoor library lighting casting me in a spotlight, a shield of light, a repellant to any promise of danger. Nevertheless, I welcome the ride that will offer the additional armor of a moving box on wheels, whisking me away from the war zone, where my presentation has left me bloody and bruised, if only in my own well-developed imagination.

I pull up my app and check the status of my ride. Joe, my driver, is no longer my driver, apparently. Jack, of all names, will now be picking me up in ten minutes. He's driving a black Kia. Joe. Jack. So many Js. *What is the universe trying to tell me?* I wonder.

Or maybe, just maybe, there is no hidden or subliminal message at all. I'm simply feeding fictional mayhem into everything that flutters a wing in my path, be it a bat or a beautiful butterfly.

I shiver against a chilly, damp night, rain still clinging to the air, an early fall evening, breaking from a hot summer. It's officially a busy, fun-filled season at the library. A haunted house will be a ticketed event, sweet treats will evolve into ghostly treats in the café, and spooky booklists will be handed out on all floors. During my childhood fall meant our house would soon become the "Halloween house" everyone wanted to visit, complete with a smoke machine.

My cellphone rings, and for the briefest moment, I assume it's Kara, nerves jangling a tune in my chest, but instead Jess's name flashes on my screen.

"Hey," I answer, wishing she really were Kara, wishing that dreaded call were behind me.

"I heard," she states.

"Oh good Lord, how did you hear? Has there been a public announcement, something like 'Invisible Girl escapes her invisible status to create a stir as the Stupid Girl instead'?"

"First of all, you are *not* stupid, and stop talking about yourself that way. And as for how I know, Jack called me."

"Now I know how pathetic I must seem. Jack never calls you."

"True, but Jack is also a protective little ninny, too. He allows you to wallow in pity, and therefore he turns your molehills into mountains."

She's not wrong. The pity party thing is, well, *a thing* between me and Jack. However, in this case, there are no molehills.

I flash back to the end of the meeting, when Neil had chased me across the main floor lobby and stopped my escape. "That was a disgrace," he said nastily. "I'm not sure why Kara thought you could pull that off, but she and I will be talking about your future, and hers, for that matter."

Jess is talking, and I realize I have no idea what she's saying, but it ends with, "I'll grab that pasta you love and meet you at your place."

"I'm going to my dad's, remember? Which you already know is a whole other thing we need to talk about. I think I told you already, but my mother may be having an affair or it's a molehill–mountain thing. I need to find out."

"Oh God, with the boss she is out of town with?"

"Yes, but I'm hanging up before you give me your opinion. I can't take hearing it right now." I eye the car that just pulled to the curb. *Jack* has arrived. "My Uber is here. I need to go."

"Call me later if you can. I have things to say."

"That's what I'm afraid of. Love you, Jess." On that note, I hang up before she can push back and rush to the car.

Once I'm inside, I pull my MacBook out of my bag and search for photos of the library's board of directors. I find them with unexpected ease, scavenging through each image, a pirate after my prize, but there is no chest of gold to be found. I do not see anyone who resembles the man from floor two, and the back of the presentation room, in any of the photos. With a wave of unease and more than a hint of motion sickness, I shut the lid of my computer.

He was invited to the meeting; therefore he's known in the library system. Logic tells me that means the only danger he represents is to my job. So why does it feel like more?

Chapter Nineteen

Jack, the Uber driver, is a twentysomething redhead, with curls and freckles, who doesn't talk, nor does he sing well, but sing he does. Not the country music you might expect to hear in Nashville, or "Nashvegas" as some of us call our great city. A nickname earned with bright lights and rowdy nightlife, but, truly, we're not all country vibes. Around these parts, we're a melting pot filled with variety. Driving home this point, as he literally drives me to my family home, Jack's performing Dua Lipa and Elton John's "Cold Heart," with two voices I assume to indicate each singer, defined in high and low octaves.

I quickly open the app to my father's and my favorite pizza joint and key in our regular order. After which I sink back into my seat and enjoy Jack's ballooning energy, which thankfully leaves zero room for the dreary, fretful self that I am tonight. As long as Jack sings, my mind sticks to the lyrics right along with him, and the escape is one I'd liken to the good ol' days, defined as most of those before this one. For example, days when I was not expected to stand in front of judgmental eyes and pretend I knew how to do so, without flopping. Days when I do nothing more than step onto floor three and my troubles fade into literary luxury while the world purrs like a kitten with my love of books. Days when I ride to my family home and worry that my mother will press me on my dating life rather than potentially exploring her own.

The ride is a short zip across the highway, exactly three replays of Dua and Elton leading Jack to Uber microphone stardom. Jack is belting out lyrics to "Cold Heart" when he pulls the Kia to a halt in front of my parents' house. "Thanks, Jack," I call out, and I open my door and step to the white picket fence in front of and around my family home.

My parents live in one of those old neighborhoods filled with character and charm—and trees with trunks the size of three or four, or even five, of me. An old neighborhood where the history whispers in the wind and sings with the drip-drop of rain on the rooftops.

I reach the front door and punch in the key code, which is my mother's birthday: 4-26-1964. She is, after all, the head of the house, at least these last few years. I turn the heavy steel knob, enter the foyer, snag my phone from my purse, and leave the latter on the entryway table. I wonder if she remembers he is only one hot patent, one big sale, from being famously wealthy. I wonder if my father remembers as well.

I find my father in the garage, in the center at a spread of elaborate tables, working on his newest inventions. He glances up and rips off his hat, his thick salt-and-pepper hair in expected finger-plucked disarray. His face lights with a welcoming smile, and I notice the crinkles at the corners of his eyes—deeper, it seems, each time I visit him. He calls them "wisdom lines," but I call them a wicked promise that one day he will be gone, and I will be lost. He's seven years younger than my mother, but as of late I do believe the opposite reads as true. I remember thinking my mother's recent obsession with Botox and microneedling was her desire to retain my father's interest.

Now I fear it wasn't my father's interest she had in mind at all.

"There's my beautiful girl," he murmurs, the tender greeting a reminder that I am the apple of his eye. But I do not miss the fact that twice now I've claimed that no one calls me beautiful, and twice now I've been proven wrong, though I dismiss the realization as irrelevant. My father wasn't responsible for that note left for me at Caroline's. Nowadays he barely leaves the house.

I round the table, noting his work uniform of khakis and T-shirt fondly. Already he's folding me into one of his famous bear hugs. My father is tall, a "hunk" as my mother used to call him, well over six feet, and while he was once quite fit, he's thinner now—*too thin,* I think. He pulls a stool up for me, and we huddle into the small space to chat. "Tell me what's going on in your life?" he orders.

He's surveying me with such eagerness, as if hearing about my happy life is the essence of his own happiness. I selfishly crave his comfort over today's events, but how can I dash his joy by sharing his daughter's ridiculous failure?

Thankfully the doorbell rings, ending my dilemma, at least for now. "That's the pizza," I announce. "I'll grab it. I'm starving."

"I am, too," he says. "I haven't had a good pizza since the last time we had one of our father-daughter nights. I'll grab the Cokes." He is already on his way to the fridge, and I'm dashing for the door, wondering what happened to the Friday-night pizza tradition he and my mother once shared. Traditions matter, even in friendships. Jack and I have once-a-month movie dates. We pick up coffee for each other a couple of times a week. Jess and I have lunch once a week and dinner out at least once a month. These things matter. They're to be planned, eagerly awaited, remembered with fondness.

It's a quick trip to the front door, where I snag the pizzas and accept the necessary and often underappreciated handful of pepper packets. Also underappreciated is the little box on top of the pizza filled with banana peppers ready to be squeezed on top of my cheesy slice. The driver tips his chin at me at the conclusion of our encounter. I linger to watch him walk down the dark sidewalk, not a star in the sky, a rumble of thunder and a gust of wind promising another storm.

Once I'm certain the delivery man has latched the wooden gate, easily damaged in the wind, I sway, intending to ease inside when my brows dip, and I hesitate. There, at the edge of the lawn, inside the sway of a weeping willow, is a shift in the shadows, an unnatural movement.

My fingers flex on the box, warm heat almost hot on the tender flesh of my forearms, but I'm frozen as if ice in a bitter cold winter storm.

Unexplainably, the hair prickles on the back of my neck, and blood whooshes in my ears. My eyes dive into the darkness, seeking the source of my unexplainable, irrational unease, when another gust of wind sends the long dress of the willow flying left and right, shadows dancing a tango across the yard. I laugh, a choked sound, and chide myself for my ridiculous behavior, which my father would call my masterful imagination, which often went to work on the old house's late-night croaks and creaks. I back into the house, shut the door, and punch the lock button on the keypad.

It's time to put my "masterful imagination," stimulated too often by edgy dark thrillers, to rest. No one is outside, lurking in my parents' weeping willow.

Chapter Twenty

My father and I convene in the sitting area of his little man cave, and we huddle around the coffee table, where we've created a pizza buffet. For a bit, just a wonderful, sweet, blissful bit of time, we laugh and joke, floating down memory lane, sharing stories. The chaos of this day fades, and my father's strong, square jaw relaxes, those lines beside his eyes somehow softer now than when I'd first seen him leaning over his worktable. It's as if the sunshine has burst through the stormy night and splayed its gold and yellow joy right here in man cave central.

We dash between subjects, from decorating the house for the holidays to firefly hunting and the preparation of Rice Krispies treats with various creative add-ins. "Mom hated when we made those," I say. "We had melted marshmallows everywhere."

He points with a slice of pizza. "Yes, but she ate her fair share, now, didn't she?"

"Yes, she did." I laugh. "She could put down the Krispie treats for sure."

He stands up, mimicking Mom, pretending to wipe a counter with one hand and shoving pizza, a.k.a. a Krispie treat, into his mouth. "If you took your time, the mess would not exist."

I'm a schoolgirl giggling now, in that way that only my father stirs in me. "That was *so* her." I grab a slice of pizza. "She loved, or I should say, loves pizza night, too, even though she always bitches about the scale the next day."

"No more pizza night," he declares grumpily. "Apparently your mother's cholesterol is high."

Apparently.

He says that word in that sticky way that dominates a sentence and highlights his mood. As if he's not sure he believes her. "Well, that's no fun. I didn't think it was bad enough to end pizza night." I shift the direction of the conversation ever so slightly, but I'm still hunting for clues to their relationship health more so than my mother's. "Why didn't you go to her event with her?"

"You know I'm not big on getting out these days."

I am instantly drowning in the quicksand of guilt for feeling I've done too little to lift him up since the mess on *Lion's Den*. If the situation were reversed, he would have done more to support me than I have him. I sometimes resist admitting that while he's my father, that day in New York City proves that he's also human, and therefore vulnerable, insecure, and fallible as well. "But you do like to support those you love. She's giving a presentation. She might be nervous."

He cuts his stare and picks up his soda can. "I might make her nervous." He slugs back a drink.

My fingers thrum on my knee, my thoughts jumbled up into mush in my mind, none of it forming coherent sentences. It's at this point that I must face my fear of hurting him. He catches my fingers, where they continue to drum my knee. "What is it you want to say to me, honey?"

"You have to live life with Mom, Dad, and being in the same house is not living life with her. Ever since—"

He withdraws his hand. "I made a fool of myself?"

"Honestly, Dad, that asshole from *Lion's Den*, Big Davis, is the fool. He came at you and made himself look like a jerk. It was all over the internet. You fall off the bike, you have to get back on."

"Yes, well," he says slowly, "*about that.*"

I perk up, my fingers calming, palms flattening on my thighs. "What does that mean?"

"I filed a patent last month that seems to be creating quite a lot of interest."

I blink and blink again, stunned that his hermit status has equaled obvious productivity, though I don't know why. He's a brilliant man who's been living for his work. "That's incredible, Dad. I mean, really, really incredible. What is it?"

He reaches in his pocket and produces what looks like a fuse of some sort. "This little baby will charge up with solar energy and then provide power for a fifteen-hundred-square-foot house for twelve hours. The fuses fit into a charging box that I created, with a solar panel on the side. As one fuse turns off and begins to recharge, the next turns on. I make the entire box and fuses for two hundred dollars."

"How big is the box?"

"Twelve by twelve. A ten-thousand-square-foot house would need only seven, which eliminates the need for the large eyesores that are the current panels."

"That's incredible, Dad. I mean, wow. It seems as if it's life changing—world changing, even. How long have you been working on it?"

"Five years, but since my incident in New York, I've done less outside the house and focused more on my work. It's ready now. The problem is that there's a lot of people in power who do not want something this cost effective in the market. If I don't tread carefully, someone will buy my patent simply to bury my work."

"How do you prevent that from happening?"

"I need an attorney, a good one, that can't be bought off by the same powers that be that would bury my work. I don't know who that might be."

"Jess might," I suggest. "She's got money and people helping her manage it. I'm seeing her Friday, so I'll ask. What does Mom say?"

His jaw transforms from that soft, relaxed state to solid steel. "Mom doesn't know."

My brows dive. "What? Why?"

"I don't want to disappoint her again. Once I have a check in my hand, it's real. Until then, I could die a *Lion's Den* death again."

In that moment I'm immensely relieved that I didn't tell him about my failed presentation and foolish performance. The last thing I want to do is convince him such bad luck is an inherited family trait. I'm a grown adult now, and as a daughter, my role is to become a mature person who doesn't need to be coddled, who now is strong enough to offer my father a ladder when he needs one. But not a crutch. That's where I had my role twisted and broken.

"That's not going to happen," I state. "And we both agree things happen for a reason, anyway. Maybe you were supposed to focus on this project, this happy ending."

His lips hint at an attempted smile. "Always my happy-ending girl. And yes. Perhaps it is, but it's not the happy ending I expected."

"Sometimes those are the best kind," I say, but in the back of my mind, I can't help but wonder if he believes Mom is cheating. If he plans to leave her, or her him, and he knows. My gut tells me not to ask, not now, and I don't know why.

"This would certainly show *Lion's Den* how wrong they were to pass you by, Dad."

His response isn't immediate, but slowly his lips pull and flatten, and the flatness in his eyes burns with something I can't quite name. "Yes. Yes, it will."

In that moment I wonder if I've been wrong about my father, lost in my own world, unable to fully view his. I wonder if instead of being depressed, he's been angry, and anger has transformed him in a way I do not quite understand. Nevertheless, if it leads him to a place where he shines, putting on a production, he's using that anger smartly. The idea pleases me, but there is a scratching at my mind as well that is uncomfortably present the rest of the evening with my father.

Later, much later, when the storm has passed, the night is lighter, and I step outside to the front porch, leaving my father in his man cave, lost in work. I walk toward my Uber that awaits on the other side of the gate, noting that the willow tree is no longer dancing with shadows, but rather in leafy slumber.

Once I'm in the back of the car, my new driver, an older man who appears to prefer the radio in the off position, barely greets me, which is fine by me on all counts. The noise in my head is quite enough.

Not only is my father excluding my mother from his great news, but he's not traveling with her. I wonder if he believes she's cheating. My mother underestimates him. His brilliance is not just evident in a lab. He sees things. He understands things. He observes and learns.

He was also different tonight. I'm not sure if that's good or bad. For the first time in my life, I think my father has secrets.

Chapter Twenty-One

I arrive home to the blast of hip-hop from the bookstore, a familiar problem when Ben, the cleaning guy, spends half the night destroying my sleep. I've fought with him. I've complained with the owners of the building, but they argue he's affordable, just like my rent, which they claim to be well below the citywide average.

Pausing at the bottom of the stairs leading to my loft, I am torn between the two choices of arguing with Ben or just heading on upstairs. Of course, today has gone about as well as me in high heels walking down a street, complete with ankle twists and face flops. Ben is my age, decent looking, but not a decent guy at all. The last time I confronted Ben, he stood there, in his overalls, a dip in his mouth, cowboy hat on his head, and told me my ploy to date him by being a bitch wasn't working.

I decide heading on upstairs is the smart move.

But then again, today I am not invisible. Maybe he will hear me when I complain this time.

I march to the bookstore door, pull it open, and don't have to go far. I all but run into Ben, who is standing on the other side with a spray bottle in his hand. "Whoa there, little lady," he drawls, backing up a few steps to allow me room to breathe and tipping his cowboy hat back a bit. The idea that he's wearing it while in the store at night, alone, is a little weird anyway. "The store is closed," he adds.

"But the dance club is not, apparently," I murmur beneath the volume of the music that is, ironically, "Cold Heart" all over again. I used to like that song. Can someone please turn it off, though? *Please.*

I reach in my bag and produce my earbuds. "I have a gift for you." I step closer to him again and offer him the earbuds. "The music plays right in your ears and not in mine."

He glances at them and then at me. "I don't like things in my ears."

"I don't like your music in my loft while I'm trying to sleep."

"No way it comes through the ceiling," he says, as if we have not had this conversation before now.

"Have you tried earbuds?"

"Never."

"They're comfortable and expensive, and they're my gift to you."

He smirks, giving me a dubious look. "You aren't too good at flirting, are you?"

My cheeks heat red. "I'm not flirting."

"Okay," he says. "Can you step aside so I can finish cleaning the glass on the door while you're not flirting with me?"

Heat rushes to my cheeks. "I'm not flirting with you."

"Because everyone offers some guy downstairs a hundred-dollar pair of earbuds?"

"I'm desperate for quiet."

He smirks, and I can almost hear his thoughts. *Desperate all right.*

"Okay," he says.

And just like that, I'm done. I could say more. I could push back. I could defend my honor, so to speak, but to what end? Another one of his snarky remarks? The landlord has not listened to my concerns; therefore Ben feels untouchable. More so, he seems to enjoy taunting me, and if that's true, I've likely only fueled his tank with my visit.

There is no solution to this problem that doesn't include me moving.

Without another word, I rotate on my heels and exit the bookstore. When the door shuts between me and Ben, the air in my lungs is thinner.

Once I'm in my apartment, I deal with Ben as I usually deal with Ben. I turn on my own music, a mix of yesterday's and today's tunes. I shower, hoping to wash away the new me and find the old version, the one that used to feel lost and alone. Turns out, being seen kind of sucks. *So does being ignored,* I think, now dressed in my long johns and sitting on the bed. My father knows this. That's why his efforts to be ignored were all about being seen again, but on his terms.

Or that's what I think is going on.

With him on my mind, I text Jess and confirm what time I'm supposed to meet her at Coffee Cats early Friday morning, then curl onto my mattress and open my laptop, aware that I owe her support on her dating-app project. Jess will help my father. In fact, she'll go out of her way to help my father. She adores him. He is a father to her, when her father was more monster, with wandering hands and lips that seemed to find all the wrong parts of her body. Or so Jess has told me, in those specific words. I haven't asked a lot of questions. I just listen when the tidbits of her pained childhood find a way to rear their ugly head, even in tiny bits, after she is triggered. Of course, she pretends she is not triggered and does so with the ease of practice. Quite skilled at such avoidance, she elegantly swoops whatever topic has taken us to her bad place aside and away. I can almost envision her as a magnificent white dove lifting her wings and flying high above the trees that shelter the beast lurking below.

The app loads, and my message box lights up. I now have eleven messages to what is most likely a hundred for Jess, but this isn't about comparing. Okay, maybe it is with her article in play, and I'm not sure how I feel about that. Uncomfortable, I decide, but I do believe that's about my own insecurity and sense of inferiority. An unimpressive, inappropriate reason to avoid helping Jess with her project.

I open the list of messages and find nothing from the ex, Kevin. But what I do find surprises me. I begin pulling up profiles, focusing on the ones that left messages after I changed my profile photos. One stands out. The photo is of a cartoon emoji man named Adam, and the message reads: You looked beautiful and natural in the first photo. In the new photo you just put up, you look guarded and awkward. As if you're afraid to be the woman in the first photo.

While it's possible there is truth to that observation, my defenses bristle and bristle loud and proud. I quickly write back and say: This from a person who's afraid to even post his real photo?

With that, I shut my computer screen, already done with this dating app, at least until Jess convinces me otherwise.

Chapter Twenty-Two

I wake with a jolt Friday morning, eye the clock, and panic with the realization I've overslept. I all but bolt to the closet, only to realize my dry cleaning is still at the cleaners.

Unfortunately my "basic" wardrobe of "basic" black is off the table. Well, not completely. I have one black skirt. My blouse options include white, green, and red—apparently my closet is the interesting combination of goth plus Christmas. Of course, I didn't buy the random rainbow-colored items. Jess and my mother did.

Surveying my options, I decide that red is for attention and expected from someone like Jess, who always shines in the spotlight, but for me it looks desperate. What I do not want to do is come off thirsty two days after I nose-dived while standing at a podium in front of the board of directors for the library and a stranger in the back of the room, whoever he may be. However, white collects stains, and green is a Christmas tree.

I grimace and pull on the red, luxuriously silky sweater, which can only mean Jess paid way too much money for it. I suppose it's a good thing I'm wearing it today, when I'll be seeing her. I doubt anyone else will even notice.

It's time to find out if I'm back to the uncomfortable comfort of being unseen and unheard again.

—

Despite my rushed exit from my loft, I manage to arrive at the bustling Coffee Cats a few minutes before Jess, claiming a spot in the ten-deep line. The woman ahead of me orders a vanilla white mocha, which strikes me as contrary as my need to remain invisible and also be seen—it seems meant to become my new drink. I order one with whip and nonfat milk, also rather contrary but highly appropriate. I also order Jess's usual nonfat hazelnut white mocha with an extra shot of espresso, no whip, and no foam. She doesn't try new drinks. People who know who they are and what they like don't have to experiment.

Once I've claimed a table, I head to the pickup area, waiting for my order. In a rush of sweet-smelling perfume, Jess joins me in line, and as if she's grabbing a page from my book, and me one from hers, I'm in color, and she's wearing all black in the form of a sweater dress and boots.

"Sorry I'm late," she breathes out, sounding flustered. "I've been trying to get an interview with a big music exec for weeks, and his secretary finally called me back. And no, I did not get the interview. She was a bitch. I'm not done trying, though. Do we have a table?"

"Back corner," I say, motioning to the spot I've chosen.

"Always back corner," she replies. "You are nothing if not predictable."

"Predictable sounds pretty good after my last forty-eight hours."

"Maybe we should be having Bloody Marys, not coffee."

"Me and vodka would make my feet forget how to walk."

She shifts her bag. "My bag is going to make me unable to move my arm at this point."

"Go sit," I say. "I'll wait for the drinks."

"You're the best," she declares, her eyes lighting. "You wore the red sweater. I love it on you." She smiles brightly and, with that, strides away.

"Seven!" the barista calls out an order, and I realize we have four before us.

With that in mind, and my workday creeping up on me, I hurry after Jess, sliding into the booth across from her. "Our drinks aren't even close to done based on the order they just called," I explain, "and I need to talk to you about something before we both have to go to work."

"Oh no," she says. "What happened?"

"It's not really an 'oh no' kind of thing. It's a good thing, actually. My father has a really hot patent right now. It's primed to change the energy industry to the point that some might try to buy it, just to kill it. He needs legal protection. Can you help?"

"Heck yes, I can help. I have a guy that looks after my parents' money and investments. I can call him."

I blink. Investments? I didn't know she had investments. I mean, yes, her parents left her money, but I thought she never touched it. Of course, she does well at her job, and she makes killer money. I don't know why this is bugging me, but it is. It does. Sometimes I think I know more about Jess than I do about myself.

But I didn't know this.

What else don't I know?

"This is exciting," she continues. "And I know how badly he needs this to go well," she adds. "And you do, too. I know you've been worried about him." She grabs her phone from the table. "I assume this is urgent. I can make a call now."

"Yes, please," I say, and the sincerity in her voice and actions has me blowing off my ridiculous thoughts. I mean, of course she has investments. I'm weird and paranoid right now. That's clear. I was even accusing the weeping willow of being scary the other night.

I almost laugh at my ridiculousness.

I'm about to tell Jess as much when I hear the barista shout, "Eleven!" which would be me, and a number is much better than being called "Girl."

"That's us," I say, but I hesitate. "My mother doesn't know about this, Jess."

She sets her phone back down. "Why?"

"I told you. I think there's trouble between them." My lips press together. "Let me get the coffees. I really need caffeine. I didn't exactly sleep like a baby last night."

Her chin bobs. "I hear ya, honey. Get the coffee. I'll make the call."

"Thanks, Jess," I say, pushing to my feet and crossing to the coffee bar.

Once at the counter, I pick up the two cups in my order and eye the sides of the cups to figure out which is mine. I blanch at what I find. There's a note scribbled on the side of my cup that reads: *Red suits you.*

Chapter Twenty-Three

Red suits me?

I blink at the cup and glance around, expecting someone familiar—Kevin, perhaps, after the message he sent me, or maybe Jack, trying to boost my confidence. Not that either has ever done such a thing, but someone did. The barista, a woman in her sixties, sets another cup on the counter.

Assuming she's been enlisted in the delivery of the message, I hold up my cup with the script pointed in her direction. "Did you write this on my cup?"

Her brows dip, her eyes squinting. "Hmm. Don't know how that got there. I don't even have a pen." She gives me a once-over and adds, "But that is a pretty red sweater."

"I, ah—thanks," I say, confused as heck right now and a little creeped out. This is two notes in one week, in two different places. The rules of logic tell me this isn't a coincidence.

I step away from the bar and rejoin Jess, who is still on the phone, a prickly sensation on my neck that's becoming way too familiar. I set her cup in front of her and sip my contrary vanilla white mocha to find it delicious.

Jess takes one look at me and quickly ends her call. "I'll call you later. Right. Bye." She sets her phone down. "What's wrong for real this time?"

Nothing, I think. *Everything,* I amend, but my head is spinning, and I'm not ready to vocalize my fears, which is why I say, "Did you talk to the attorney?"

"Yes. He's calling your father in an hour, but I want to call him before the attorney does. What's wrong?" she repeats.

I'm thinking about my serial killer dating-app joke that wasn't all that much of a joke, which spurs me to ask, "Did you put my personal information on the dating site? Like my address or workplace or favorite coffee shops?"

"Of course not. I'm many things, but stupid isn't one of them. Again. What's *wrong*? What just happened? Because between the time I sat down and you joined me, something transpired."

"Wednesday, when I was at Caroline's, someone left me a note on my computer, telling me I looked beautiful. It felt random because it was addressed to the fake name I gave the barista."

"That's kind of romantic," she declares. "You have no idea who did it?"

"None."

"Okay, so this was Wednesday, and I'm not sure it's something to be freaked about, but you are freaked out. From the time I walked in until now you—"

"Right. This just happened."

I turn my cup around for her to read the writing and speak my previous thoughts out loud again. "Two notes. Two different places. Two different days. Did you do this to try to build my confidence?"

She snorts and still manages to sound delicate. "I believe in fake forever things that elicit compliments, such as fake boobs or nails. Those things I will buy for you, as I did myself. But fake compliments that elicit no further compliments are worthless. And when would I have had time to do such a thing?"

She's right. She does believe in "fake forever," and she's not one to play games with me or anyone, for that matter. That's just not Jess.

"Maybe it's a coincidence," she suggests.

"Two notes. Two locations. Two different days," I repeat. "I've read enough crime novels to know that isn't a coincidence."

"Could Jack be doing it?"

"I thought of that, but he's never done anything like this ever. We're friends. We don't cross lines. It's not even in the air between us. We have zero spark. You know this. He doesn't tell me I'm beautiful."

"He was worried enough about you after the presentation to call me."

"The first note arrived before the presentation."

Her brows dip. "Hmm. Curious. Any other idea who might be stalking you?"

"Oh God. Are you serious? You had to pull out the *stalking* word, didn't you?"

"I'm joking," she says. "It's two harmless notes. Think harder. Maybe you already know who's doing this."

"Kevin was on the dating app. He sent me a message and told me I looked beautiful in my photo."

"You do, which is why I used it, but even the message feels out of character for someone so inattentive."

"Yes, but sometimes we value what we've lost more than what we already possess."

"There is truth to that. Maybe. I wouldn't call this his redemption, though. People are who they are. You've already seen his true colors." She tilts her head and studies me. "Do you really think it's him? Because I'm not reading that in you right now."

"Not really. This feels weird, Jess."

"Maybe you have a secret admirer who frequents the same places you frequent."

"Isn't that kind of creepy, too?"

"Maybe. Be careful, but don't go expecting the worst. Maybe it's something magical happening. Try to be neutral." She glances at her watch. "Unfortunately, I have to go soon. Are you okay with me calling your father on my way to the office?"

"Yes, of course. Thanks for doing this."

She waves the appreciation off. "I love your dad. You know I do. He's the reason I know all dads aren't creeps. Oh, and before I forget, there's a huge party for the magazine two weeks from now," she says. "I want you to come."

Which is a problem, considering the wedding Jack asked me to attend the exact same weekend. "You always want me to come and I don't."

"Yes, well, this is a big night for me. I'm getting an award. You're my only family, so you have to come."

Curiosity piqued, I lean in closer. "An award?"

"Yes." She waves this off as well. "Something about the most-read column."

I imitate her, waving off her success. "Oh, just *that*? No big deal." I scowl at her. "I hate when you downplay your wins with me. I'm not competing with you or jealous. I'm thrilled for you."

"I know that, my little chickadee. You're my ride or die. I also know my father was an arrogant jerk, and I try to remain humble and appreciative of what comes my way. You'll come?"

I don't even hesitate. Jack will understand. "Yes. I'll come."

"Excellent. Now I must run. I wish I had more time. I want to know more about your mom and dad. But we're still on for pasta and wine, right?"

"We are."

"And Jack is coming?"

"I haven't invited him yet, but I'd like to."

"I'd say no, but I can tell you need me to say yes. So invite him. I'll see you at your place at seven?"

"That works," I say and stand to hug her.

She rushes away, leaving the air dotted with the scent of her floral perfume all over again. It's a delicate, understated scent, while she is bold and confident. Though, sometimes, like this morning, there are those rare glimpses of a far-more-fragile side of Jess that only I would understand. For instance, when the contrast between my father and hers pricks at her protective shell.

I sip my coffee and think about how much this drink, the vanilla white mocha, sums up the contrary sides that construct most human beings. Such as the side of me that reads my cup once again, *"Red suits you,"* with mixed feelings. It's nice to be seen and noticed, even complimented, but somehow invisible just felt safer.

Chapter Twenty-Four

Jack's already seated at his desk in our shared office when I arrive on floor three. "I owe you," I say, setting a cup of coffee on his desk as I head onward to my own.

"Thanks," he says, rotating to face me and watching as I settle in my own little spot. "Hey, we were so busy yesterday that I never asked: How was dinner with your dad the other night?"

I turn my chair to face him. "He's got a hot patent pending. The biggest thing he's ever done, I think. I met Jess this morning. She's connecting him with an attorney."

"Really? That sounds exciting. You must be relieved to see him finally rebounding."

"Except he's not telling my mother. Honestly, I have so much to tell you. Can you come to a pasta-and-wine dinner at my house tonight?" I hold up a hand. "And before you answer, you need to know that Jess will be there."

"I don't hate Jess, Mia. I simply don't always agree with the advice she gives you. And since I'm certain tonight will be filled with lots of it, I need to be there. Especially when it's Friday night and there's no clock on the time she has to lecture you. Where are we getting pasta, because I know you're not cooking."

"Usually Maggiano's. I can't believe I've never invited you to pasta-and-wine night."

"Me either, since I love Maggiano's. You need me to pick anything up?"

"You're tolerating Jess for me. Just bring you. Oh, and on that wedding. What is the date?"

"Saturday the twenty-fourth. Why?"

"Jess is getting an award that weekend. I'm not sure if it's Friday or Saturday night. There's a big party. Can you go with me to that, too? If the timing works out? Maybe we'll already be dressed up."

"She didn't invite me, so you can go. And if you can't make the wedding—"

"I can," I say. "We'll figure it out. And you're invited to the party. I'll make sure of it."

"I'm not going because you're forcing me on Jess."

"Nope. You're going for me. You know how socially awkward I am." I shift the topic. The phone on my desk buzzes, and I whip around in my chair and grab the line. "Mia Anderson."

"Mia, it's Kara. Can you come down to my office?"

My heart thunders in my chest, a volcanic eruption threatening to blister a path right to my belly. "You're at work?"

"I am. Hurry now. I have a meeting soon." She disconnects.

Jack appears in the chair beside me. "What happened?"

Those two words—*What happened?*—are haunting me today. "Kara needs to see me. Now."

"She's back? Hmm. I guess she wasn't as sick as you thought."

"Or Wednesday's presentation went so badly she's trying to save her job."

"That's not what's happening here."

"And if it is?"

"It's not." The bell begins to ding at the front. Obviously, the doors are open, and patrons need help. "It's not, Mia. The sooner you get down there, the sooner you can tell me I'm right." He knocks on the desk, I guess to knock some sense into me, and then he's gone.

I stand up, and that volcanic eruption finds my belly and burns fire in my gut.

I think I might get fired. And I don't know who I am if I'm not the librarian on floor three.

Chapter Twenty-Five

The ride down the escalator is uneventful.

The man on floor two seems to be gone, in my mind, a stranger who swooped in, passed judgment, and cracked my solid world right in half, if I'm correct about how this meeting with Kara will go. The zoo below is as it always is—busy and chaotic—and as the escalator shoves me into the masses, I have a sensation of quicksand beneath my feet.

I've managed all of two steps when Akia Lee, one of the librarians in the zoo, steps in front of me. Akia is ten years older than me, fit, athletic, and confident. The only things we share in common are a love for books and being single, which one might think is enough to stir friendliness between us. We've spoken about three times in five years. And I'm kind of okay with that. I don't like to be around people who make me judge myself as worthy or unworthy.

Akia stirs that feeling in me, that need to look in the mirror and brush hair from my face.

He's not my kind of people. I'm not his.

And yet, here he is, greeting me, intentionally placing himself in my path. "Hi," he says.

"Hi," I say tentatively, really not sure what to make of this encounter he's forced.

"Listen," he continues. "I just wanted to tell you, Neil's a dick. Don't let him get to you."

My cheeks heat with the realization that he must have witnessed Neil confronting me Wednesday in almost the same spot.

"I don't know him well," I say, encouraging him to explain the "Don't let him get to you" comment in more detail.

"I do," he assures me, "and for ten years. Nothing is as bad as Neil makes it out to be. I promise. Hang in there." He gives my shoulder a consoling pat. He might as well have given me a chuck on the chin.

"Thanks," I murmur, but he's already faded into the crowd, and now, like Jack, he is gone as well. Only Jack's attention wasn't about sympathy. It was about friendship. Wednesday I was not invisible, and the impact seems to be overflowing into the rest of the week, and not in a good way. The only time Akia ever noticed me was when I was humiliated. Akia's attention, I fear, was all about pity. Now I'm wishing the quicksand would swallow me, but since that's not happening, I rush forward, and my fate feels as if it's hanging by a thread.

With my gaze down, hoping to avoid any further looks that might resemble pity, I travel down the same hallway I took to reach the presentation room Wednesday. Kara's office is down the hallway to the right, and I find her door open. I knock on the doorjamb and peek inside. "Come in," she encourages and stands to round her desk.

I step inside the doorway, and she adds, "Shut the door."

My heart is now charging at such a pace that my hands tremble, but I manage to pull the door shut. Once I bring Kara back into view, she motions to the chairs in front of her desk. I'm surprised at how alert and good she looks. Her skin is a normal tone, not pale and washed out. Her hair is neatly styled. Her tan-colored dress well pressed. "You look so much better," I say, claiming the seat.

"I had food poisoning," she informs me, settling into the chair beside me, and I do like this part of Kara, the part that never places the desk between us. She's not like Neil, who is always above us all and not just in his towering height.

"Honestly, I can't believe how much better I feel," she adds. "The hospital said I'd probably have lingering effects for days, but I think I'd already had it a few days before I crashed. Aside from a little dizziness here and there, I'm pretty darn good." She waves off the topic of her health. "Enough about me. Thank you for doing the presentation Wednesday. I'm so proud of you for doing it."

"Thank you? Are you serious? It was a disaster, Kara."

"The board loved the bottom line," she assures me. "And I think the way you handed out the physical presentation was a smart move. They had that to focus on during and after the meeting. The word I'm hearing is they are pleased with the income we're delivering with the auditorium."

"Neil told me the entire thing was a disaster—paraphrasing here, but that's the general gist."

She tuts and waves off that idea, just as she had her health concerns. "Neil overreacts to everything. And, on that note, or rather another note altogether as far as I'm concerned, I actually got you a little celebratory gift for making it through your first presentation." She stands and walks behind her desk to the credenza, returning with a long Tiffany-blue box with a white bow. "I have a thing for vintage Tiffany items. I bought this a while back and thought I'd find the perfect reason to gift it." She extends the box to me. "I do believe you finishing your very first presentation makes this yours."

"I did a horrible job," I say, holding up my hands in rejection of the package. "I don't deserve this."

"They liked the numbers. It's always about numbers, Mia. That's business. Take the gift."

Reluctantly, I accept the box and pull off the lid. Inside is a long silver letter opener that glistens in the light. It's simple and elegant, with "T & Co." carved in the center. It's also expensive. It's Tiffany, after all. "This is too expensive, Kara. I can't take it."

"Nonsense. I want you to have it. I know you might not open a lot of letters with it, but I thought it would make a cool bookmark. And hey, you walk home, which often worries me. Stick it in a book but use it as a knife if you ever need it, Lord forbid. That's a joke and a bad one. I hope you like the gift."

"Of course I do," I say, and with a forced serious voice, only a hint of laughter to be found in my words, I add, "Who doesn't want a Tiffany letter opener for a bookmark and weapon?"

She smiles widely. "Exactly. Now I must go to my meeting. And you need to stop being so hard on yourself. I know floor three is your safe zone, but it can just as easily be the prison that holds you captive. And the worst kinds of prisons, Mia, are the ones we don't know we're in until we've escaped. Because we often don't escape at all. Think about it."

With her statement ringing with a little too much truth, I push to my feet as well and walk to the door, pausing with a thought. "Kara," I say, turning to face her. "There was a man hanging around the library for a couple of days. He attended the presentation. He seemed important. Neil held the meeting for him. I looked at the board members' photos, but he isn't included. Neil mentioned budget cuts. Do you think he was some sort of outside auditor?"

Her brow furrows. "I don't know who that would be, but I'll see if I can find out. But, Mia, we are paying for ourselves with the auditorium. Think positive. Maybe he was here to learn how to do what we do in other places."

I nod and exit her office with my silver Tiffany letter opener, in a long, pretty blue box.

Chapter Twenty-Six

Listen to the silence for it has much to say.

—Rumi

Present . . .

There is silence all around me, hollow, empty, suffocating, as if I am in a box, a prison I am desperate to escape.

With a gasp, I blink into consciousness, my back to the solid surface, my gaze blurry, refusing to focus. Slowly, too slowly, images form. Stairs. Concrete. Railings. I'm in the stairwell of a building. What building?

A damp, cold sensation washes over me, centered in my core. I swallow against the dryness in my throat, and my gaze lowers, drawn to the ground, where it lands on something long and silver, stained with red. The letter opener. The Tiffany letter opener. It was . . . it was in my . . . bag. It can't be here, but where is here?

There's a sharp pain in the area where icy fingers wrap my belly, and I lower my chin, panting, a dark stain across the pretty fuchsia dress I was wearing. I love . . . this dress. It's ruined now. There's a flash in my mind of a struggle, and a sob escapes my throat, dampness clinging to my cheeks, rapid pants following until I scream. I just scream and scream some more. "No! No! No!" And then there are no more screams, no more words. There is just this quivering, quaking sensation in my body, and an odd, almost humming sound sliding from my lips.

I think I should run, but I don't know from what, and it doesn't matter.

I can't run.

Chapter Twenty-Seven

The past . . .

Even salt looks like sugar.

My father often says, *"Don't trust everything you see."* I don't think he made up that saying, but he uses it as a litmus test in his work. Right now, I feel that saying reflected in my life. For instance, my parents' pizza night being shunned is not really about cholesterol but rather the state of their relationship. The gift for filling in for my boss and making a fool of myself and her is not really a congratulatory gift, but rather a sympathy gift. And the notes I've been receiving aren't really random. I just don't know the truth behind them yet.

I'm still pondering my list of things that might not be what they seem when I manage to place my butt back in my chair in front of my desk, only to have Jack sit down beside me. "Well? What's the word? Are you fired or promoted?"

"Promoted?" I snort. "Hardly. That was never an option, and you know it. However, *oddly*, considering all, I was given a celebratory gift for finishing my first presentation. *This.*" I slide the box over to him.

"A Tiffany box? *Fancy.*" He opens the lid and glances at the letter opener and then at me. "Is this from Kara?"

"Yes," I say, and I go on to vocalize the answer to "Why?" as it hits me. "I think it's a pity gift."

"If she's bathing in cash." He pulls his phone from his pocket and punches in a few keys before glancing up at me. "A four-hundred-dollar pity gift?" He rotates his phone and shows me the eBay auction with the same item. "I don't think so, Mia."

My brows knit together. "Four hundred dollars?" I reach for his phone and stare down at the eBay listing in disbelief. "Why would she give me a gift this expensive at all, ever? I don't even give wedding presents this expensive."

"Maybe she gets a bonus if she hits certain goals, and you helped her do that."

"It's a *four-hundred-dollar* letter opener, which, by the way, she suggested I use as a bookmark."

"Her husband makes a lot of money," he reminds me. "But she could be expensing this as well."

"Neil yelled at me about budget cuts Wednesday. No way is she expensing a Tiffany letter opener for me, of all people. None of this makes sense."

"Maybe you're thinking too hard. Obviously the presentation didn't go as badly as you thought." There's a cackle of laughter from outside the door. "I better get back out front. The foot traffic is heavy today."

"I'm coming, too," I say, sliding the Tiffany box into my top desk drawer, but I don't immediately follow Jack out of the office. I linger on his perspective now, only to purge it with a hard rejection.

He's wrong, I think. The presentation did not go well.

My gaze lands on my coffee cup that reads, *Red suits you.*

That's wrong, too. Red has never been my color.

What is happening in my life right now?

Everything is contrary to the truth.

"Don't trust everything you see," I whisper.

Chapter Twenty-Eight

On my way home, I stop by the liquor store with the intent of grabbing a couple of bottles of wine, admittedly a little nervous about carrying a four-hundred-dollar letter opener in my bag, at least while it's in a box. As Kara said, it really would make an excellent weapon, and with that strange tingling sensation on my neck, I decide that if anyone tries to take it from me, I'll fight. I'll use the letter opener as a weapon. I almost laugh at the idea that I could ever do any such thing, my mind going back to my ten-year-old self. I'd freaked when I'd accidentally tripped my friend Ana, and she'd cut her arm open. I'd struggled to help her and soon discovered red really is not my color. The blood had sent me into panic mode, and I'd screamed louder than Ana. I think we all knew at that point that med school was not in my future. I was not, and am not, the bravest of them all—or anyone, for that matter.

I'm certainly not tonight, as the weirdest forty-eight hours of my life has me jittery and on edge. I truly can't finish up in the store soon enough.

I've just paid for my purchases, and I'm headed for the door when Ben enters the store. I suck in a breath at the unexpected encounter, and as if I'm in a jungle with a bear charging toward me, my gaze cuts left and right, in a wild hunt for safety, only to find the crush of people too deep on either side. By the time I've ruled out avoidance, Ben is standing in front of me. "You stalking me or what?"

"Would it convince you to wear earbuds when you clean?"

His lips quirk. "You just won't quit about the earbuds, will you?"

"It's a reasonable request."

"It's a free country and all that shit," he rebuts. "I can wear 'em or not wear 'em." He steps closer. "You're just as free as me." He steps around me and walks away.

I'm just as free as him?

I'm clueless as to what that means. He's an odd bird, and I waste no time placing space between me and him.

I leave the liquor store for my loft, and the busy sidewalk is both comforting and intimidating. While there is safety in numbers, there is also shelter to hide, and not just for me. Though I'm not sure why I feel like anyone would be hiding from me, aside from, of course, my note writer. I will not call them a secret admirer, as Jess did this morning. Something about the term "secret admirer" is actually uncomfortable right about now.

Thankfully I arrive home without incident, and about an hour before my two Js plan to join me. Once I'm inside, I lock up and easily settle into my comfort zone, my shell. Home sweet home is always just that—sweet. And even better, I do all this without using my letter opener as a weapon.

Some things go my way.

First up, I unpack my bags and pull out an ice bucket, placing a bottle of champagne on ice, a bottle of wine in the fridge, another that requires no chill on the counter. Next up, I unpack my purse, my MacBook first. Next, I remove the Tiffany box and set it in the center of my counter next to the bucket of champagne on ice. I study it a moment, thrumming the counter, curious about Kara and her motivations where this gift is concerned. We aren't friends, not really, but we have known each other for years. She's always encouraged me in all ways.

Still, it feels extravagant and over the top.

But I'm out of time to contemplate what I cannot know. Shaking off the thought, I hurry upstairs and change into leggings and a sweater, all black, of course, my true comfort zone, before I head back downstairs. I exchange a couple of text messages with Jess as she arranges the food—she always arranges the food.

With a pour of Meiomi cabernet sauvignon in my glass, I key my laptop to life with one goal: having the ability to say I checked my messages on the dating site, so I won't have to do it with my two Js.

Once I'm logged in, my inbox flashes before me. I now have twenty-one messages. I reach for my glass and sip deeply for courage. I then click on the icon. My eyes scan for the missing message from Kevin, but I still find nothing. We're matched, though, which allows me to see that he's online now. I double-check my phone and realize he never replied to my text. Hoping to solve the mystery of my little notes, I quickly type him a reply: I texted you the other day. Thank you for the compliment.

While I wait for his reply, I search members and look once again for Jack, but come up dry. I mean, of course I do. He deleted his profile to avoid me and/or Jess. That's a nonissue. The very fact that I had to warn him that Jess would be here tonight says it all. I begin tabbing through my messages and delete half just by way of age. Jess obviously was thinking I need a sugar daddy or father figure—no thank you. I scan a few more messages, and there is nothing even remotely exciting about anyone here. There is Lance, who is a doctor who can't spell. Jason, who is into gaming, and not much else. Been there, done that. I swear I attract men who will ignore me. At this point, Kevin hasn't even replied. Maybe the message wasn't even for me. Perhaps he was distracted gaming and sent it to the wrong person. I click delete on every new message I scan until I land on Adam, the guy with the cartoon photo:

> I'm not afraid to show you my real photo. But isn't it nice to be judged on character not looks?

I read our prior exchange all over again:
From him:

> You looked beautiful and natural in the first photo. In the new photo you just put up, you look guarded and awkward. As if you're afraid to be the woman in the first photo.

From me:

> This from a person afraid to even post his real photo?

I press my lips together and reply with:

> For someone who doesn't want to be judged by looks, you certainly assumed many things about me based on my photos.

After which I sit there and stare at the screen, waiting for him to reply, for who knows why. He doesn't even have a photo, which feels a bit like my note writer, hiding in the shadows. I sip my wine, and there's a beep with his reply that reads: I simply showed you how many ways a photo can manipulate impressions. Which woman are you? The one in the first photo or the second?

Why can't I be both? I challenge.

He doesn't make me wait for a reply this time. You changed that photo for a reason. I think you're afraid of one and not the other.

The word *afraid* bites. I don't like it. It rings far too true. Like you're afraid to show your face? I challenge.

I stare at the box where his words will appear, waiting. And waiting some more. I cackle at the idiocy of me sitting here, apparently on pins and needles, for this person's reply—the guy with a cartoon photo who's already criticizing me, of all people, and I don't know why. Why indeed? Why am I going back and forth with an invisible man? I'm cackling all over again as I whisper, "Because I'm an invisible girl."

My cellphone rings, and I grab it to find my father's number on the caller ID. I quickly answer. "Hey, Dad. How'd it go today?"

"I talked with that attorney Jess referred me to, and he's already in action. Thanks, honey, for making that happen."

"Jess is the one we need to thank. She didn't even hesitate to help."

"Yes, we will have to thank her. When this is all over, maybe you can help me figure out how."

"Of course, Dad. Is Mom home?"

"Her flight was delayed. I think she'll be late."

My jaw clenches. *One last quickie before she left her boss behind?* I wonder. It's a horrible thought I wish I could scrub from my mind. "You okay?" I ask, guilt stabbing at me for making plans tonight now that he's alone again.

"I'm wonderful, honey. I'm actually going to have another chat with the attorney after he calls one of the interested bidders. Good things are happening. I'll keep you posted."

"Oh. Well, that's good. Really good. You sound good, too," I add, noting his tone as warm and lifted.

"I feel good. What about you? Do you have a fun Friday-night date?"

My eyes go to the computer screen, where the box remains empty. "Jess and Jack are coming over. We're doing a wine-and-pasta night."

"That sounds wonderful. Don't let me keep you. I'm going to eat some of that leftover pizza before your mother gets here and talks me out of it."

Because he has to hide everything from her now. Because she is hiding things from him now, too, I think, but I keep my tone positive. "If you get news tonight, will you call me?"

"I'll text, but I doubt there will be much to tell. The attorney, Nick, he's setting boundaries for the bidding war."

"Bidding war?" I say. "Okay, that sounds exciting."

"Yes. Yes it does. Now go *have fun.* Love ya, hon."

"Love you, too, Dad."

We disconnect, and I look down at the computer screen.

Adam logged off. He's just gone. Without answering me.

There is a stab of disappointment in me I do not understand. The man has a cartoon emoji for a photo.

The buzzer for the door downstairs goes off, telling me at least one of my two Js is here.

I shut the computer and declare Adam out of mind.

He's the invisible man. And he's invisible to me.

As it should be.

Chapter Twenty-Nine

The two Js manage to show up at the same time, and in a rush of conversation, they overtake my tiny little loft. Jess is in a velvet sweatshirt and Jack in jeans and a tee, a casual night of fun in the air. As for the food, it's on its way, and while waiting, our little threesome gathers around the kitchen island, and soon our glasses are filled.

"What's this?" Jess asks, sliding the Tiffany box in her direction.

"From Kara," Jack supplies. "It's to congratulate her on her first presentation."

Jess tilts her head in my direction. "The disastrous presentation?"

"Yes," I assure her. "It *was* disastrous. It's a pity gift."

Jess lifts the lid and looks inside. "Expensive pity gift."

"Exactly," Jack chimes in. "Exactly."

"It's like a regift thing," I say. "She told me to use it as a bookmark. In fact"—I grab my bag and reach inside, removing a book I've been working on reading—"there." I open the cover and slide the letter opener inside. "Now it's a bookmark. It's actually a pretty cool bookmark," I add, giving it an inspection. "I like it."

"She is a library boss," Jess says. "I'd guess she knows what makes a good bookmark."

"Or weapon," I add. "She said I could stab someone with it as well."

"When I hear you say that again now," Jack interjects, "that is a little bizarre."

"For once, Jack and I agree," Jess concurs. "She said you could use it as a bookmark or stab someone with it? What the hell kind of boss do you have?"

"She meant for protection," I assure them both. "Because I walk home. And you two agree more than you realize."

The door buzzer goes off, promising the food has arrived. More chaos unfolds, and soon we have plates of food in front of us, and we're discussing my parents. "Your mom cheating on your dad," Jess says, wrapping fettuccini around her fork. "What a bitch."

"Jesus, Jess," Jack murmurs. "That's her mother."

"And unless she's gentle on your ears, we both know how she feels about her mother."

"She loves her," he argues.

"And hates her," Jess counters.

"Another topic please," I suggest.

"All right then," Jess obliges. "How about guess your secret admirer?" She points her fork at Jack. "Is it you?"

Jack blinks, looking a bit like a deer in the headlights. "What? What are we talking about?" He looks at me. "The dating app?"

"No," Jess says, "but we'll get to that, too."

I reach in my bag and pull out the note, sliding it in front of Jack. "Someone left this on my computer at Caroline's Wednesday. Then they wrote a note on my coffee cup at Coffee Cats today as well. Two notes."

"Two different places," he supplies. "That feels creepy to me."

My thought exactly, I think.

He looks between us and levels his stare on me. "It's that damn dating app. I bet someone recognized you from your photo."

"I find that highly unlikely," Jess states. "The notes started too close to the time I signed her up for the app."

"Exactly why it fits," Jack argues. "It's the same timeline."

"Actually, I don't think that's true. The window between when I signed her up and when she got the first message is simply too slim." She glances at me. "Have you been through your messages? Is there anything in the messages that reads like the notes you received?"

"Yes, well, I deleted about half because the men were old enough to be my grandfather."

"Without reading them?" Jack asks.

"Without reading them," I confirm.

Jess's lips purse. "You know there is nothing wrong with a hot, rich older man, right?"

I raise a pasta-filled fork to my mouth. "I'm ignoring that statement."

"What about the other messages?" Jack asks. "Any hints that one might be your note writer?"

"Enough with that," Jess grumbles. "It's not someone from the dating app."

Jack ignores her and gives me a squinty-eyed, suspicious look. "Well?"

I swallow and reach for my glass. "Kevin sent me a message and said I looked beautiful in my photo."

"You think the note writer is *Kevin*?" he asks, but he doesn't give me time to answer. "No. That just doesn't fit. He was a self-obsessed, inattentive asshole."

"Agreed," Jess replies. "There is no way Kevin did anything as romantic as leaving those notes."

"I'm not sure I'd call those notes romantic," Jack argues. "Walk up to her if you want to talk to her. Don't hide behind a note."

"Says the man who never walks up to any woman and talks to her?" Jess challenges.

"I might not be a ladies' man," he counters, "but I'd never leave a random note unless it was spontaneous and I knew I'd never see the woman again. It would be more likely to make her smile for the day. Two notes is a stalker."

"Unless the person knows me," I say. "Kevin makes the most sense in this equation."

"He doesn't live in the neighborhood," Jack reminds me. "He'd have to act like a stalker to leave you notes. And why would he do that when he knows you?"

"Maybe he saw me on the dating site and came to talk to me and chickened out," I suggest.

"Illogical," he argues. "He knows you. He dated you. The man has been naked with you."

"Jack," I chide.

"He's right," Jess intervenes. "This direction of thought you're presently partaking in makes no sense."

"Okay," I say. "He's responding to me trying to contact him. It's probably buyer's remorse. He thought he wanted me again, and then he started talking to someone else. In which case, my notes are over, just like me and Kevin." I let that simmer a moment, expecting it to feel uncomfortable or bad, but turns out it does not. In other words, the breakup with Kevin was a good decision.

"It's not Kevin," Jack murmurs under his breath, reaching for the bottle of wine. "I need a refill."

I don't argue with him. I'm not sure this topic matters enough to bother. It's two little notes I've blown up into more, most likely because it's one of the more exciting things that's happened to me in years. Instead, I tap my glass for him to hit me up with a refill as well. Jess reaches for the champagne bottle, which as of now is all hers.

"Before I forget," I say, sipping my newly filled glass and waving a finger between them, feeling loose enough now to tackle this topic, but not too loose to handle a conflict. "We need to compare calendars. Jess, is your party on Friday or Saturday?"

"Saturday," she says. "Why?"

"I'm going to a wedding with Jack that day," I inform her, leaving no negotiation on the topic. "What time is the awards ceremony?"

"Seven," she replies.

I eye Jack. "And the wedding?"

"Two," he supplies.

"Perfect," I say. "Then we can go straight from the wedding to Jess's event, already dressed to kill."

Jack and Jess stare at each other a moment, seconds ticking by before Jess says, "Fine. I'll ensure Jack is allowed to attend."

Who needs a dating app when just like that I have a date with not one friend, but two? As long as I leave the letter opener at home, it will be all fun and games, and no one will end up with a letter opener in the heart.

Chapter Thirty

Jack is looking at Jess with such disdain over her "acceptance" of him attending the party that I snort, at both his reaction and her being her. "You sound like such a snob, Jess. Good thing I know you're not. Okay, sometimes you kind of are."

"I'm selective about who I associate with," she replies. "That's a necessity to lead a safe and happy life." She presses her elbow on the counter, her chin on her fingers, and studies Jack. "Why don't you help out with my dating-site article, Jack?" she suggests. "I mean, you're obviously so single you're hanging out with us tonight."

"Pot, kettle," Jack retorts. "Where is your hot date, Jess?"

"I just prefer my present company to that of the unknown. *Yes*, even *you*, Jack. In fact, I'm glad you're here. A male perspective can be an asset to my article, and in many cases, it's harder to come by than a woman's. Men tend to act as if they just got punched in the balls when you say words like *feelings* and *commitment*."

"How very categorical and yet incorrect of you," he states.

"You'd rather we pretend it isn't so?" she challenges.

"I wonder how you'd like it if I made broad statements about women?" he counters.

"What broad statements would those be, Jack?" she queries coyly.

"That's a trap, Jack," I warn. "Stop now while you're still alive and kicking." I glance at Jess and solidly turn the conversation onto her. "Have you gone through your messages? I'm sure you must have hundreds."

"Not yet, but," she says, lifting her glass, "another one of these, and I should be ready."

Jack, however, is never ready. When Jess and I prepare to huddle up to read her messages, he turns on ESPN without the volume and sips his wine. I guess girls' night isn't all it's cracked up to be when you're not one of the girls, but looks can be deceiving. While some might think him uninterested, I know better. Jack is here for me, not Jess and her work project. If I trip into what he sees as bad advice trouble from Jess, he's here to catch me. That's called friendship, and as it should be, it's familiar, warm, and comfortable, like a favorite sweater that never grows old but does become cozier.

As for Jess, she's wholly focused on her mission to clear as many messages as she can and find the golden gooses, as she calls them. "You sound like my mother," I tease her.

"Jeez," she murmurs. "That's uncalled for, Mia."

I laugh and eye her remaining messages, unable to stop myself from mentally plucking through them for familiar names. Names like "Adam." But Adam is not in Jess's messages at all. The insecure, self-destructive person that I am cannot help but decide that means Adam believes Jess wouldn't give him the time of day. The man has a cartoon head as a photo.

For the next half hour, Jess reads and deletes, answering no one. We're almost to the end of her list when a message window pops open on her screen from, of all people, Kevin. Hi Jess, it reads.

Jess glances at me. "He won't respond to you, but he's going around you to me?"

"Who?" Jack asks, moving to sit across from us, on the coffee table.

My lips are tight. My shoulders, too. "Kevin," I murmur, watching the box as I wait for whatever else he's typing. Words appear, and my vision hyperfocuses: I contacted Mia again, and I told her she looks beautiful, but I have to be frank. She is who she is because you make her that person. It's not Mia I want to get close to again. It's you, Jess.

Jess shuts her MacBook with a solid thud. "Okay, enough of this. The idea was to de-stress you tonight. Screw dating sites. They're my work project. That's all."

A fist forms in my belly. "Open your Mac, Jess."

"What just happened?" Jack demands, his voice calm but punched with insistence.

"Kevin just hit on Jess," I reply, reaching for Jess's computer.

Jack curses under his breath, when Jack generally does not curse. He is, after all, unlike Akia, a stereotypical, quiet librarian, the geeky type. I like that about him. I also like that he's upset now, upset for me, that he understands how intensely I'm losing my mind in my head right now.

She holds on to it. "He is out of your life for a reason."

"She's right, Mia," Jack chimes in. "Let it go."

"Let me just be clear with both of you. I'm not going to *let this go* until I read whatever else he has to say to you, Jess."

Jess casts Jack a desperate, pleading look, and he sighs, scrubbing his jaw. "You're not going to win," he states. "We both know it."

Jess draws a breath and presses her lips together, slowly easing her grip on her MacBook to open the lid. Once she's signed back into the dating app, Jack slides into the seat beside her. On another occasion, the three of us here like this would feel like an accomplishment. Now it just feels like my funeral. Kevin's message reappears on her screen, but there's nothing more added.

"How do you want me to reply?" Jess asks.

I chew on my bottom lip. What do I want her to say? I just, literally just, reminded myself how much I don't regret breaking up with Kevin. This only serves to validate that point. I suck in air through my nose, reach across her, and shut her MacBook. "Nothing. I don't want you to say anything, but thank you for humoring me and offering."

"I wasn't humoring you, sweet pea," she says softly, a nickname she's randomly called me for a decade. It all began with my love for Popeye cartoons and my wish that something as simple as spinach could make one feel strong. "You're my sister from another mother," she adds. "I can't believe he put this between us."

"Let's watch a movie," Jack suggests. "I'll even agree to a chick flick." He glances over Jess to me. "But please don't say J.Lo's *Marry Me*. I *cannot*."

I liked that movie, I think, but a chick flick is the last thing I want to watch right now. "What's on the top ten on Netflix?"

I reach for the remote with every intention of dictating what comes next, at least on the TV.

Apparently life is a whole other thing and not my story to tell.

It feels as if someone else is turning my pages, and I'm terrified to start a new chapter.

Chapter Thirty-One

I blink into my bedroom hued with white light and gray ink, reluctantly allowing the drowsy haze of slumber to fade. The pitter-patter of another rainy-season storm on my steel roof is a symphony of music to my ears, and with it, the sweet promises of a perfect day lost in a book.

For me, weekends are about rise and shine, the earlier the better. I jog, I do my laundry, I clean up, and, when all my chores are complete, I allow myself the indulgence of reading time. In the middle of all this, I often meet up with one of the Js, and about every other weekend, I visit my parents.

But none of that, not today.

I stretch and glance at the clock, finding it early, 8:00 a.m., which is too early, considering the two Js left at two—way too late, but I didn't dare rush them away. When do I ever have the two of them together, in one place and acting civil?

Only when they think they need to be here for me.

And that, I decide, is pretty special.

But so, too, is a day for me.

An hour later I've showered, dressed in comfy sweats and a tank, and am sitting at my island with a steaming cup of coffee before me, my book ready to open and the rain a steady thrum above me. It should be a perfect moment in time, but today there's a slice of emptiness inside me, inching its way wide, and wider. I'm alone. This is my life. This may always be my life.

I have one instant flash of time when I imagine me and Kevin back in the day on my couch, side by side, a day like this consuming us. Only there was no us. There were just two people in the same room. That's not my dream. That's not better than being alone. It's another version of being alone.

That's the truth, and sometimes taking control means facing the truth.

I grab my phone as if I might actually call Kevin and tell him how I feel. Instead, I glance at my messages, where he has yet to respond, debating what I might say to him if I did actually contact him again. The answer is nothing. He doesn't get to drive my conversations or emotions. He doesn't get to decide what I do next.

Neither does Jess.

This, I think, as I slide my laptop closer and open the lid, is for me.

Sipping from my cup, I type in the dating site and wait for it to load. Remarkably, I have another ten messages. It's not the millions Jess had last night, but it's something. I click on my inbox and do what I came here to do. I find Kevin's name, and I hit the "Block" button. There, done. I'm about to shut down again when my gaze lands on Adam's last messages. His icon is no longer a cartoon character. It's a photo of a man. I click on the image and suck in a breath. Adam is attractive, with sandy-brown hair, a chiseled jaw, and intelligent eyes. Per his profile, which he's now filled out in detail, he's thirty-eight, a civil engineer, and speaks three languages: Spanish, English, and French.

I'm just about to convince myself he's just this good-looking arrogant guy who enjoys critiquing people, lesser people like me, when a message box pops up. A message from Adam that reads: You're judging me right now, aren't you? Just like I said you would.

My fingers hover over my keyboard and linger, denial eager to be pounded out, but I hesitate on what would be a lie. Guilt screams inside me. He's right. I *am* judging him, and for what reason? How he looks? Yes. Exactly. Seconds expand into a full minute, and my hands fall from the keyboard.

As if Adam can no longer endure the silence, he types: It's human. We all judge people on looks.

I grimace, my defenses rising, and suddenly my fingers are on the keyboard again: Like you judged me? I demand.

I didn't have to judge you, he replies. It's clear you do that for everyone.

"Says the guy who looks like a model," I murmur irritably to myself for finding him attractive, for mentally thinking about what it would be like to be with a man like this one, which is exactly why I type: You don't have any idea what I think.

Don't I? he replies. Why do you think I'm talking to you, Mia?

Mia.

As if he knows me. He doesn't know me. To tell me how much better you are than me? I challenge.

> Quite the contrary. Two photos, two sides to one woman. You're captive to your insecurities, which tells me I know you. We are the same, Mia.

I glance at the photo of the good-looking man talking with me, and my reply comes easily: You don't know me at all.

Don't I? he challenges. You feel overlooked, invisible.

He's using that word again: *invisible.*

How could he know *that* word?

Unease blisters my next reply: You expect me to believe you feel invisible? I don't think so. And how do I even know your photo is your photo?

His response is rapid-fire and unexpected: Send me your phone number and we'll video chat.

I blink and blink again. He wants my phone number? I swallow hard, that uneasy sensation flooded with a sense of excitement I have no business feeling. I don't know what this is, who he is, or what is happening right now. My fingers find the keyboard again: Post a video of yourself in our chat. Then I'll know who I'm giving my phone number to.

There's no vid option, he replies. I looked for it. I just found you on Instagram. I'll send you a follow request and send the video there. Then you don't have to give me your phone number until you're ready.

I draw in a breath in surprise. He found me on *Instagram*? How is that even possible? I don't use my real name on Instagram.

Chapter Thirty-Two

I reach for my phone and quickly pull up the Instagram app, which I literally use as a reading journal. "Nashville Librarian" is my handle, which admittedly isn't fun and exciting, but it says what it needs to say. I have a decent following of thirty thousand readers, bloggers, and book people that just somehow happened. But the truth is they're following my wide, sometimes eccentric reading picks, not me. People don't really know me at all. My name is nowhere to be found. My photo has never been included anywhere on the page, so *how* does he know this is me?

Because he does.

Right there in my inbox is a request from Adam Roth.

This is impossible unless . . . a thought hits me.

I glance at the dating app and pull up my profile, which clearly states that I'm a librarian at Nashville's main library. And, good Lord, Jess linked my Instagram account. Could she not keep anything private? And how did I let myself obsess over my photo and not bother to look at my bio a little more closely? I breathe out a sigh of relief. I can stop suspecting Adam of wrongdoing, at least to this end.

Returning to Instagram, I accept his follow request, reading his new message: Hi Mia. I'm making a video now. I'll send it in just a few minutes.

Trying not to read too much into Adam's attention, and still a bit skeptical about his looks and his interest, I remain on the fence about this entire exchange.

For now I click on his profile and scan his photos, which seem to date back a couple of years. The lake and boats seem to be his social media theme. He also appears to enjoy trying new beers, often posing with a cold one and labeling the flavor, or whatever terminology is appropriate. I can't seem to dig deep enough to find any photos of a man anyone would label as inconsequential as I feel most days of my life. Trying not to overthink things, I click off his profile, pick up my cup, and sip in an effort to focus on anything but the wait for the video. Turns out my brew is cold and in need of replacement. I walk to the sink, pour out my coffee, and refill my cup. Once I've added cream and artificial sweetener, I walk back to the island, sit down, and then pull up Instagram on my computer. The idea is to watch the video, if Adam really produces one, on a larger screen.

To my surprise, there it is. A video is actually waiting for me.

I click on it and enlarge it. Adam fills my screen, and he does not disappoint. Adam only gets better, the live-action version of the man outshining the photo. His sandy-brown hair is finger tousled. His Tennessee Titans T-shirt stretches over a chest worthy of any book in floor three's romance section. His green eyes are intelligent and fixed on the camera as he speaks.

"Hi, Mia. Let's see, where should I start?" He scrubs Saturday-morning "I haven't shaved" stubble on his square jaw. *"I'm Adam Roth,"* he continues. *"Thirty-eight, and a civil engineer. All that boring stuff you saw on my profile."* He holds up a finger. *"Fun fact. Confession, maybe? My photo was Scooby-Doo, and I actually love Scooby-Doo. I love all cartoons. Kind of a guilty pleasure of mine."* He grins. *"What can I say? My mom says there's a kid inside me, but don't let that fool you. I'm serious about my work. I actually moved here from Texas three months ago to work on a*

new highway expansion through Nashville. I do like to read. I suspect that's important to you, being a librarian and all. I favor action and adventure. The Gray Man is a favorite series of mine. Jack Reacher is another. The books are better than the movie or TV show. But, honestly, none of this is what you want to know, is it? You want to know why I say I'm like you. Or I was and not that long ago. I, too, was overlooked. I was insecure. I wasn't the man I am today. What changed? you might ask. I think this is getting too long. I'll load another video."

The video ends.

I breathe out. Oh my God. He's real.

Another video appears in my messages, and I click on it.

Adam reappears on the screen.

"Here we go again," he says.

"What changed for me? How was I like you and now I'm not? Ironically, I was in a car accident on a highway that I helped design. The truth is that had I not made certain safety adjustments to the layout, I would have died that day. My changes, the ones I'd insisted on, but barely because, you know, I was still the old me at the time—still the guy no one heard when I spoke—those changes were critical safety changes. I realized in the aftermath of my accident that (a) life is short, (b) my life has a purpose, and (c) it was time to take control of my life. And so I did. I purged everything and anything in my life that held me back. That's making it sound simplistic and far easier than it was. I'm running out of time again."

The video ends.

He's typed a message for me while I was watching the second video: Send me your number, if you feel comfortable. And I already know you don't want to talk on the phone or video chat. We can text.

I don't want to talk or video chat, I think, but how does he know this? How is that possible?

As if I've typed out the question, he responds: I know because I remember what it felt like to be the old me. We can text. Just text. For now, at least.

I stare at the message with the understanding that it's time to make a decision. Do I want to know Adam Roth? Seconds tick by, and I watch both videos again, processing his story, and God, what a story it is. He was like me. He *is* like me. And now his transformation is from me to the male version of Jess. The idea that he didn't just see me, but he *sees me*, really sees me, all that I am, all that I could be, and wish to be, stuns me.

As unbelievable as it might seem, the words that stand out the most are the ones that are unrelated to his changing persona. *"I'm running out of time."*

I don't want it to take me almost dying, or losing someone I love, for me to dare to live life.

I type my phone number in the message box and hit send.

Chapter Thirty-Three

The moment after I met Kevin, I called Jess to tell her all about him, and like then, my first instinct after sending my number to Adam is to text Jess. Jess has been a right arm to my left since college. My second is to think of that message Kevin sent her last night. I don't send the text to Jess.

Instead, Jack's words punch through my thoughts:

"You judge yourself by her," he states, his jaw setting hard. "Don't argue. It's true. You know it's true, and to your detriment."

Followed by Adam's first message: You looked beautiful and natural in the first photo. In the new photo you just put up, you look guarded and awkward. As if you're afraid to be the woman in the first photo.

I'm clearly not self-analyzing effectively enough at the moment to tie those things together, but I'm aware that these thoughts are two pieces of a puzzle. That puzzle being the reason I didn't send that text. Maybe there is nothing really to analyze at all. Maybe there is a time in life when we all don't just become adults; we accept that we are adults, no longer resisting that reality, and once that happens, it becomes natural and even necessary to hold some things as sacred and private.

That being Adam for me.

Ten minutes later, I'm glad I didn't text Jess for a whole other reason. Adam has gone silent. Thirty minutes later, same story. Okay, I think, forcing myself to be logical. Obviously, it's only a mere thirty minutes, half an hour, and life is going on outside our conversation, I remind myself. It's almost an hour later, and I'm settled on my couch, thunder rattling my walls, a book I cannot focus on open in my lap when my phone pings with a message.

I draw a breath and count to thirty, then repeat. Another breath, another countdown. Only then do I sit up, set my book aside, and reach for my phone. A new number is now live in my messages: Hi, Mia. It's Adam. Sorry to be slow. My boss called. He had a morning meeting and I'm dealing with budget issues for the new project.

Relief washes over me and I scold myself. I don't even know this man. Why am I so worried about the timeline in which he contacts me? Which highway are you designing? I ask.

It's a massive forty-million-dollar road project, which will not be focused on just one road, but to start, we're going to address the clusterfuck that is I-24 and create an underpass.

That sounds complicated.

It's what I do, he replies. For me, it's just like driving a car.

I actually rarely drive, I reply. I live downtown and walk to everything.

I live in the Gulch, he says. My employer is paying for my place for the six months I'll be here.

He's leaving, I think. This is a temporary fix, if that, and my world tilts left and right, unsteady, uncertain.

As for the Gulch, it's a high-end section of downtown with clusters of restaurants, shopping, and bars.

I love the Gulch, I reply and then ask what I cannot help but ask. You'll be returning to Texas?

Unless I have a reason to stay, he confirms.

It's a good answer. The answer a girl would want, and for that reason, I can't allow myself to accept it at face value.

From there, we text for a good hour, about his work, and mine, until he finally says: No video chat, but can I call you?

My fingers curl on my knee. Why is this a big deal? Talking on the phone is no different from texting. I sigh and grab my earbuds before I text: Okay.

A minute later my phone rings. "Hello," I answer.

"Hello, Mia," he replies, his voice just as it was on the video—low, masculine, warm. "This is better."

"Is it?" I ask.

"It is," he assures me. "Now we can talk about things that matter."

"We weren't already talking about things that matter?"

"Not the really important things, like why I'm like you and you're like me."

I laugh nervously. "We are *not* the same, and I find it hard to believe you ever were."

My phone buzzes with a text, and he says, "Look at the photo I just sent you."

I glance down at my messages to find a picture of a man that is Adam, and yet he is not. His hair is much shorter, almost buzz cut. He's wearing glasses. His entire persona is uncomfortable rather than confident.

"That was you," I say, and it's not a question.

"Yes. Now you know why I saw you beneath your photo."

"Yes, but you're not that person anymore."

"Yes I am. I have always been that person. I've just learned how to control that part of me. Once I did, it changed my life in every possible way. Even my career. No one was paying for apartments in the Gulch for me before I changed myself. Believe in yourself, Mia."

"Easier said than done."

"Until it isn't. I'll teach you how. If you let me."

Chapter Thirty-Four

He'll teach me.

If I let him.

"I'm a hard damn learner," I reply, my laugh that follows a bit choked, a familiar awkwardness in it and me that I simply can never escape.

"And I wasn't?" he challenges. "I had to nearly die to come to my senses. But the good news is that now I can help you in your journey."

"And what way would that be?"

"Ultimately to believe in yourself, but we both know that's a process that takes time."

"Forever," I murmur.

"Not forever, but humans are not creatures of change. I read a book on this topic years ago. Did you know that a woman who grew up in an abusive home statistically marries an abusive man? We gravitate toward what we know, even if that something isn't pleasant."

Thunder rumbles above, the walls vibrating with the low, deep sounds, a pummeling of rain on the rooftop, as if Mother Nature is demanding I sit up straighter and listen to this man, or perhaps listen to what the history of me tells as my own story. And once again I'm thinking about my presentation in college when I'd stood at the podium and amounted to nothing more than the passing of time for the audience. This time when I think of being ignored that day, therefore free of embarrassment and failure, it's not with the fondness of my previous framing of this moment.

We gravitate toward what we know even if that something isn't pleasant, I repeat in my head.

Invisible is not pleasant.

Invisible is safe.

Once again, he's in my head as he adds, "Sometimes the familiar becomes the crutch that holds us back and even tears us down."

My phone buzzes with another call, an intrusion to this insightful conversation with Adam that I resist—that is until I eye the caller ID, and my lips press together. "I have to take this," I say, and for reasons I cannot explain, considering I barely know Adam, I add, "It's my mother, who I have reason to believe is probably cheating on my father. She just got home from a weekend away. I need to take it."

He's silent a beat and then adds, "Just remember, sometimes moving on is living life. Change is not always bad, Mia."

"I don't want my parents to break up."

"But you want them to stay together and be miserable?"

"No. No, of course not." The line stops ringing. "I want them to fix what is broken."

"Sometimes the only way to fix what is broken is to force a change."

"Like her sleeping with her new boss?"

"If problems in the relationship exist, removing one problem sometimes creates another."

"You're not telling me what I want to hear."

"Is that what you want? For me to tell you what you want to hear?"

My phone begins to beep again. "She'll keep calling until I take this."

"I'll call you in an hour," he says, removing the question of when we will speak again, and just like that, he disconnects.

I don't even have time to process the impact of my conversation with Adam before I've accepted my mother's call. "Mom," I greet.

"Honey," she murmurs. Always the "honey" endearment when she wants something, as if years of salt can be removed by sugar.

"How was the trip?" I ask.

"It was fine," she replies dismissively, "but your father is acting strange. He's quite withdrawn. How was he with you?"

Good, I think, but then I'm not the one betraying him, but what I say is, "We had a great pizza night. He seems to be enjoying his work again."

"Oh, did he tell you his news then?"

I stiffen, confused by the direction this conversation is now traveling. Did my father change his mind and enlighten my mother on the pending patent sale? Did she find out on her own?

"What news is that?" I ask, my voice sounding appropriate, or inappropriate, depending on how you look at it, strained.

"I guess not then." She sighs. "Okay, I'm going to be honest with you. I intentionally volunteered for the convention to get out of town and give him some time with you. I thought he'd tell you what's going on, and then you'd do what you do and work your magic on him."

I blink in consternation. "What does any of that mean, Mom?"

"He was invited back to *Lion's Den*. It's a second-chance season, with the biggest flops now being offered the chance to become the biggest winners. All investments promised during the show will be automatically doubled by a pool of money established by the studio."

Confusion ripples through me. What the heck is going on? Why didn't he tell me this? And what does it have to do with what he *did* tell me? "He'll never go back on that show, Mom."

"You could convince him."

"He didn't tell me because he doesn't want to be convinced."

"I just want him to get the credit he deserves," she argues. "He's worked so hard."

There is tenderness in her voice, and my head is officially spinning, the ground with it. Is she or isn't she cheating on my father? And if she isn't, why is he hiding the patent from her?

"I think it will all work out, Mom. As Dad always says, there are more ways to fry an egg."

"It would be nice if it got fried while he's still young enough to enjoy it." She doesn't give me time to reply. "Anyway. I need to go. And by the way, your father is not supposed to be eating pizza. His cholesterol is off the charts. I meant to warn you. And before you assume as much, I'm not chiding you. I just want you to help me convince him to care about his health and his work."

It's my father with the cholesterol issue? What is going on? "He cares about his work."

"As long as he's safely locked away in the garage. Everything in life is not safe, nor does every risk end in disaster."

When my mother and I finally hang up, I set the phone down, an eruption of hail on the roof sending me seeking refuge in my windowless kitchen for cover. The way secrets seek refuge from the lies they may soon become. It seems everyone in my life, except Jess, has a secret. Then again, maybe she does. Maybe we all do. Even me.

Adam is my secret.

Chapter Thirty-Five

Present . . .

I gasp awake, hunching forward with my hand pressed to the stickiness on my belly, the biting pain stealing my breath. Air rasps through my teeth, my chest heaving, my gaze lifting to the stairwell around me. Now I know where I am. Images, horrible images, scratch at my mind.

"I . . . need out of here."

I need a phone. Where is my phone?

My chin lowers, and I search only for the knife—no, no, the *letter opener*. It's a letter opener. I lift my hand to reach for it, but my fingers curl into my palm, resisting the blood-stained silver. More images stab at my mind, and I shove them aside. I cannot go there right now, not when I'm still in this hellish place, dying, for all I know. The hesitation of moments before evaporates. My hand closes around the knife's handle, and I shift in an attempt to stand, fighting through the ache of my body. Somehow I manage to roll to my knees, crawling toward the stairs, inching my way closer and closer. Every part of me hurts, little dots swirling in my vision, but I pull myself forward. At some point the pain fades, and my body is numb, but my energy is nonexistent. I rest my forehead on the steel bars, telling myself it's just for a moment.

At some point I realize I'm dozing, and I jerk out of the darkness. That's when the distinct heavy thud of footsteps, above me and headed down in my direction, registers in my mind. My heart races, adrenaline surging through me in that fight-or-flight way fear overtakes us mere humans.

I don't know if I should call out or run.

Chapter Thirty-Six

A single lie discovered is enough to create doubt in every truth.

—Unknown

The past . . .

The hail ends as abruptly as it began, the way truth ends in lies in a few spoken words.

With her contact with my father regarding his patent on my mind, I dial Jess in hopes she might clue me in on what the heck is going on.

"Hey, you," she answers. "My God, this rain. It won't let up."

"Did you know my father got invited back on *Lion's Den*?"

"Oh good Lord, tell me he said no."

"He didn't tell you when you talked to him about the attorney?"

"Why would he tell me? No. Our talk was fast. I connected him with Nick Morris, the attorney I told you about. Is he going back on *Lion's Den*?"

"My mother says he was invited but on the fence about it. He didn't tell me."

"That's kind of strange, but, you know, maybe it seemed unimportant since he doesn't need them. He's on his own path."

"That my mother doesn't know about?"

"Well, if she's cheating—"

"What if she's not? What if it's not my mother who's cheating, but my father?"

"Oh come on, Mia. Your dad—"

"Is human and flawed."

"Okay. There's truth in that statement. We're all human and flawed. Only assholes think differently. But worrying about this won't change anything. They're adults. They make their own decisions. And maybe, just maybe, your father is simply doing what he told you he was doing. Surprising your mother with his success."

Did I tell Jess he said that? I don't remember. I must have. I tell her everything. "Right," I say and change the subject. "What are you doing today?"

"I agreed to go meet some guy for coffee. He's the president of some bank."

"Some bank? Just some bank?"

"I don't believe anything anyone tells me. You know that. I'll remember what bank when he's worthy of me remembering what bank, which is likely never."

"Cynicism is sinful."

She snorts. "Did you make that up just now?"

"Yep. Just now. I'm bubbling with brilliance today, let me tell you."

"You're snarky today. No more wine for you. Do I dare ask? Anything on the dating site?"

"Nothing worth mentioning," I say, and my secret cuts, while my answer borders on one of those lies I despise and try never to tell.

We chitchat for a few more minutes before she has to dart off to her date. I consider calling Jack for another opinion on my mom and dad, but he'll talk about more than them. He'll talk about me. The normal me would talk about Adam.

I don't want to talk about Adam.

As Benjamin Franklin said, "Three may keep a secret, if two of them are dead."

As guilty as I feel about keeping secrets from my friends, Adam is all mine right now. Only mine.

Chapter Thirty-Seven

If you're going to be two-faced, at least make one of them pretty.

—Marilyn Monroe

Are there really two sides to every person, or are some of us simply one point of view and in our very simplicity, content?

Then again, variety is seen in all forms of living. Light and dark chocolate. Red and white wine. Two sides of a record album, both with songs to sing along to with my father, as he tells stories of the days past, but not forgotten. As my father says, there can be more than one answer to a question.

I stand in the mirror on Monday morning, studying my image, thinking of the two sides of me represented in the dating-site photos. The one who is free and confident. The one who is anything but those things. Right now I'm her, the girl who has pridefully lived up to the geeky librarian persona with my dark hair neatly pinned at my nape, my thick-rimmed glasses solidly on my face. But is that pride about who I want to be or the limits I've placed on myself?

Adam's words replay in my head for about the hundredth time:

"You looked beautiful and natural in the first photo. In the new photo you just put up, you look guarded and awkward. As if you're afraid to be the woman in the first photo."

I let out a choked laugh. "How can I be afraid to be me?"

And yet I changed that picture with whiplash speed in denial of something, didn't I? Fear, I decide, is a bit like *those* relatives at holiday gatherings you dread seeing—in my case my aunt Betsie, who tries to recruit me to hot yoga to cleanse my karma. There's only one way to avoid Aunt Betsie, and that's to stay home, in which case I miss everyone else.

And so I don't stay home, not on the holidays, but it seems I do the rest of my life.

I'm tired of staying home.

I open a drawer filled with a variety of colored lipsticks, all of which Jess has gifted me with the promise, *"They look gorgeous, darling."* I choose the least intimidating, a pale-pink shade, and slide it over my lips. It's subtle, but it does seem to brighten my features. I also think I have a sweater that, contrary to my Christmas-tree wardrobe, is this shade.

With a quick pace, I walk to my closet, dig way in the back, and there it is. A long, silky pale pink, almost nude, sweater, also compliments of Jess. I quickly change into it and return to the mirror. The color changes to my lips and sweater are nothing dramatic, and I doubt anyone will notice anyway.

My phone buzzes with a text message from Jess that reads: Coffee? Lunch?

It's not that I don't want to meet her, but this new me, trying to be some other me, needs to do so on my terms. I text back: Can't do coffee ☹ Will text you midmorning and see about lunch.

She sends back two emojis: a sad face and a happy face.

I head down the stairs, and, truly, I don't recognize the girl who spent all weekend talking to Adam and who turns down coffee with Jess. I'm not sure that's a bad thing, though. To Jack's point, on many occasions, I do compare myself to Jess. I don't plan to snub Jess, by any means, but I'm not sure I can find me if I don't give myself a little time with, well, me.

I'm set enough on this strategy that I stop at a coffee shop a few blocks from my normal walking path, the Caffeine Castle. A silly name with sillier drink names, but they taste good.

I'm just about to head inside when a familiar face exits the coffee shop. Mike Adams, of all names, considering the current Adam in my life, is an old college acquaintance who is both good looking and successful. Mike is an FBI agent who personifies the television imagery of an FBI agent, dressed in a fitted suit with his dark hair cut short to the scalp. My knowledge of his career choice is not a product of a friendship but rather of him visiting floor three to show us photos of a suspect he was hunting. I knew the man but hadn't seen him in months.

"Mia," he greets, his tone friendly in a genuine way. "How are you?"

"I'm good," I say, and I'm struck by how comfortable I am with Mike. Truly, we really don't know each other well outside of our study group, but he has a calming presence, and he has always called me by my name. "Or I will be when I get my coffee," I add. "Is the FBI office near here?"

"It is, but I also live nearby," he says. "I just moved downtown to be closer to the office. You still at the library?"

"Still a book geek," I assure him. "I hope you caught that guy you were looking for."

"Not yet," he says, "but we will." His watch buzzes with a text message, and he lifts his wrist and reads a text that flits across the screen. "Damn. Gotta go, but I'm sure we'll run into each other again now that I'm in the neighborhood." He opens the door for me. "I highly recommend the White Elephant," he says, indicating his cup.

"I'll try it," I say. "Stay safe."

I head inside, the exchange leaving me with the sense of the casual but rather meaningless banter one shares with passing neighbors. Already my mind is leaving it behind, scurrying through the lost minutes and my growing urgency to grab my coffee and head to work.

I walk to the counter, order a White Elephant, which is a white mocha with Snickers flavoring, and then head to the bathroom. Or I plan to head to the bathroom but freeze just outside the archway leading to the sitting area, in shock at what I discover. Jack is sitting at a table across from a man, and for just a moment, from the rear, which is the only view available of the stranger, he looks like Adam.

Still, I find myself skipping the run to the bathroom.

I walk back to the counter, and I make sure the barista does not call out my name, not that this was ever an issue. When I pick up my cup, it reads only, "White Elephant with whip." I don't linger on the generic writing. My White Elephant and I rush for the door.

Chapter Thirty-Eight

The fragility of friendship is on my mind as I start the hurried walk toward the library, thankful that I'm the opening manager this week and due to be in the library before Jack today. This allows me the much-needed time to think, to process why I somehow feel as if him sitting with a stranger is a betrayal. Why I ran from him rather than greeted him. These reactions are illogical, but there is no denying their existence. There's something in the core of our relationship rotting away, and I do not understand how or why.

This idea journeys my mind through history again, landing solidly on my first lesson in that fragility. Ana, the childhood friend who I'd accidentally tripped, is at the center of that lesson. While I cried and worried about her after her fall, she told everyone I'd hurt her on purpose.

I hadn't been ignored when I was mocked and tormented by her friends, who were once mine. But shortly after I'd become nothing but a ghost to those I'd played with, celebrated birthdays with, called friends. So easily life shifts, night from day, sunny to stormy.

I'm back to why I ran away from Jack today.

My answer is one dirty word.

Secrets.

They're in the air, burning through the sweet smell of friendship and leaving behind a bitterness I cannot quite name.

I only know that as an adult, we are faced with the reality that secrets exist. They come at us in shades of many colors, in both small and large, layered with history, if only that of how we were raised.

Who was Jack sitting with, and why does it feel like a secret?

Why is my skin prickling, nerves jumping around?

My pace quickens with my heart rate, my mind jumping here and there, landing far in the past this time, in my childhood, where my own secret originates. When I was five, my little mind conjured a group of imaginary friends, four pastel-colored cartoon character animals. Only, pastel colors and cartoonlike characters do not represent friends at all. They were mean, stalking me, scaring me. No, *terrifying* me. Yes, I really did manage to transform cartoon characters in shades of pink and neon blue into demons. I'm sure a psychologist would tell me this is representative of a fear of the world—or myself, maybe.

Or something else I choose not to linger on.

Whatever the case, the entire situation feels weird, and no one knows about this part of me but my parents.

And now Adam.

I don't know why, but I shared this, and so much more, with a man who is virtually a stranger. The funny thing is he didn't laugh or suggest I'm mentally unstable. Instead, he confessed about his own imaginary friend, a bear named Billy, who was not a cartoon. We spent at least an hour discussing why our minds conjured up such creatures. In the end, we decided that somehow our imaginary friends represented our inherent insecurity, and thus our curses to become so darn intangible to the world.

This brings me full circle to the bond Jack and I have always shared in a way that Jess, my sister in so many ways, can never understand. Jack's friendship assures me that I am never completely unknown and unseen, as mine does him as well. In my mind, he's family, and I hide nothing from him.

Except you do, I remind myself.

He doesn't know about Adam.

He doesn't even know about my imaginary "friends."

And yet, I think again, *I told Adam.*

I step inside the library, the cool air of the chilled building washing over me as I cross the lobby toward the escalator. I'm halfway there when the fingers of awareness on my neck jerk my gaze left to the service desk, where I find Akia. I blink with the realization that he's watching me, a tiny pull at the corners of his mouth. I'd label the look amusement, rather than a smile.

The man who'd comforted me last week is laughing at me. Why is he laughing at me?

Can he just go back to ignoring me again, please?

I step onto the escalator, and the idea of not knowing what is at my back has me whirling around, leaving only my safe floor three at my back. Only, as I pass floor two and my gaze lands on the table where the stranger was sitting, it's not empty. He's there, at this early hour—he's there. His MacBook is open, a cup of coffee beside him, but his eyes are on me.

Almost as if he knew to expect me.

Chapter Thirty-Nine

One plus one equals two, except when the one plus one is me and Jack today.

Our energy is weird from the moment he walks in the door, a vibe of discomfort between us I've never experienced. Or maybe it's my vibe. I'm uncomfortable with Jack when I am never uncomfortable with Jack.

"That college group visiting today just overtook the lobby," he announces, peeling off his jacket and hanging it on his chair. "They're coming our way. As in the entire escalator is full."

I hop to my feet, and not in a panic over the craziness about to overtake our work life, but rather in appreciation for the separation between me and Jack the chaos will create. "Why in the world are they coming here?"

"I guess the speaker booked for the auditorium missed his flight, or that's what I heard downstairs. They're killing time. How was the rest of your weekend? I called you." There is a hint of accusation in his tone.

"I didn't see your message," I say quickly, which is true. I really didn't know he called. "I did think it was weird you didn't check in with me after the dating-site stuff with Jess."

"With Kevin," he says. "And you didn't call me at all." *There's that hint again,* I think. The accusation.

"I've been weird over the Kevin stuff," I say, which isn't a lie. Shockingly, considering how inadequate Kevin made me feel this weekend, I actually told Adam all about him, from our meeting to our breakup, to him hitting on Jess.

Instead of pity, he'd offered me, *"What a dick move. I hope like hell you aren't actually feeling hurt over that shit. He's not worthy of your emotions, Mia."*

Guilt stabs at me. Jack was worried about me, and even now my mind is on Adam, not this conversation. It seems like maybe I'm the problem, not him. "I stayed home and read through the bad weather. You want to go to lunch?"

"If this crowd even lets us go at the same time," he replies, as the bell up front starts a constant pinging. "College kids," he grumbles and heads to the front.

I stare after him, as uncomfortable with his departure from the room as I was with his entrance.

Chapter Forty

Chaos.

It's defined as complete disorder and confusion. Otherwise known as the present state of floor three.

The speaker planned for the morning in the auditorium down in the zoo was delayed to the point that the engagement is postponed until the afternoon. In other words, and as my father would say, we're presently running around like chickens with our heads cut off. Whatever that means, since I'm fairly certain a chicken would not be running anywhere without its head. Though half the questions I've been asked today hint that there are some people operating in a near-comatose state here, and I say this objectively, as one of the most patient people anyone will ever know. I am, after all, the librarian who spent three hours with an elderly woman, reading her the first chapter of dozens of books, because she couldn't decide which to check out. And did so without an ounce of irritation or regret.

She was lonely.

She felt invisible.

She was my people, too.

"We have to eat," Jack announces when we're both finally able to retreat to our shared office. "And I don't know how we are going to leave, let alone have time to stuff food in our mouths."

"Delivery?" I suggest.

"Delivery won't work," he replies, his hands settling on his hips, his favorite gray and striped tie hanging loose, with the absence of a sweater vest or his normal tiepin in lieu of the sweater vest, it seems. Jack is anal, his clothes perfectly pressed and matched. If there are books on his desk, the spines are in perfect alignment. I've always suspected this is his way of controlling everything when he sometimes, like me, feels as if he controls nothing. Like the time when he was a kid and his pants caught in his bike chain and no one stopped to help him. He lay on the side of the road for an hour before his sister stumbled onto him.

I blink as I realize Jack is still talking while I'm lost in the puzzle of his missing tiepin. "Anyway," he says, clearly finishing a thought I've missed completely before adding, "I heard one of the kids talking. Apparently Kara let the lot of them order in food, as long as they eat in the auditorium. Now all the delivery services are backed up." He glances at his watch. "And I have a call with my doctor in fifteen minutes."

"Doctor?" I ask. "What don't I know that I should know?"

"It's that old knee injury I got back in school acting up," he says. "I went for a run last week, and it just won't stop throbbing."

And yet he didn't tell me until now.

Normally, well, I'd know. Then again, normally he'd know about Adam, too.

"Proof I should never have tried to fit in by playing high school sports," he continues. "I looked ridiculous. I *was* ridiculous. If only we knew as kids what we know now. No one you knew back then becomes someone you know now. None of that even mattered."

My mind goes to the day when my mother had shown up late to pick me up, and the way everyone just walked right past me. The day I'd stepped to that podium and barely been noticed, despite being the center of attention. I'm not sure I agree that none of those experiences mattered, even Jack and his hurt knee. They taught us to accept being stuck in the shadows while others frolic in the sunshine.

"I'll handle the food," I say. "I'll call an order in to Caroline's and then run and grab us some bagel sandwiches. You take care of your knee."

His eyes soften with gratitude. "Thanks, M," he says, using a nickname he's called me for years, but, I realize now, not recently. I wonder why I didn't notice. I wonder why he uses it now.

Chapter Forty-One

I call in a lunch order for the entire floor-three staff, which is five people today. Purse on my shoulder, I hurry through the library before I end up caught in the hurricane of questions and requests again.

When I exit the library, I'm considering the idea that Jack is, or perhaps was, dating someone, and this shift in nicknames and behavior between us reflects this in some way. Maybe he didn't want me to know about his new love interest, though I'm not sure why. We've always discussed our dating lives. Always. It was literally only a month after I started working with him that he had a date from hell and spilled the entire story.

That morning I'd watched him with a female patron, seen his interest in her, the light in his eyes, the body language that was all about her and only her. She'd forgotten his name twice, and I'd felt his frustration. We'd gone to lunch that day, something that had already become our habit, and often. His order had been wrong, and he'd struggled to gain the counter person's attention with the same success—no success—which I generally believed was the kind of experience reserved for me and me alone. When he'd finally given up, defeat was written in his expression—scribbled frown lines and frustration.

"Happens to me all the time," I told him.

We'd bonded that day on a new level, creating a friendship that swiftly became enduring, solid. A few days later we were at the same burger joint when he'd said, "My sister set me up with her friend."

"And?" I'd asked eagerly, thrilled we were now at this level in our relationship, the place where we share things we might not tell others.

"She forgot my name," he'd ground out through his teeth. "The woman could not remember 'Jack' if her life depended on it. I even told her 'Jack, like Jack in the Box,' because, of course, I'm an idiot. I mean, Jack in the Box, Mia? I really said that. And she *still* forgot my name."

"Bitch," I'd said, which was the first time I'd cursed around him.

He'd blinked at me, met my stare, and then barked out laughter. I'd grinned and joined him, giggles overtaking me. After that our friendship shifted, deepened. We were no longer just work friends who aren't really friends at all but rather people we are forced to know and get along with. We were *friends*, with a growing bond that only grew stronger over time.

My thoughts shift back to present day. At this point, considering the invitation to the wedding, as his date, I'd assume anyone he was dating to be past tense, unless he intends to use me to shelter the new woman from his sister? Or use that time to tell me about the new girlfriend? These ideas burn in my belly in an uncomfortable way. Am I jealous? Maybe not as a woman, but as a friend who is fearful of a divide between us that I already feel present.

My cellphone rings, and I snake it from my purse to find Jess's ID on my screen, probably calling about the message I sent earlier to decline lunch. Jess, who I've shared an enduring relationship with since college, a bond my conversation with Jack has reminded me is exceedingly rare. "Hey, you," I greet. "Sorry about lunch. It's just a madhouse at the library. We couldn't even get delivery. The kids have them backed up. I'm having to run to Caroline's to grab bagels."

"I have a big story I'm working on anyway that's heated up today." She shifts away from lunch altogether. "Real quick. I wanted to talk about the dating-app story." I'm about to defend my silence on this subject when she adds, "I've decided to put it on hold."

About to enter Caroline's, I halt just outside and step to the wall, allowing the busy foot traffic to hustle past me. "Don't do that because of Kevin," I argue. "This does not affect me and you, Jess. I'm not upset."

"You call me every weekend, Mia. Not once this weekend. And I left you three messages."

I cringe as it becomes crystal clear that I've allowed my new relationship, or whatever this is with Adam, to cause the neglect of my two Js, my ride or dies. "I didn't check my messages," I say. "I wasn't ignoring you. I was reading. The weather and a good book, you know? I'm sorry."

The lie is bitter on my tongue, an acidic guilt washing up in words and bad behavior.

"I'm not doing the article," she replies firmly. "And good Lord, these men on the app are not the caliber I want either of us dating, Mia."

Except Adam, I think. Adam is different from all the others, but I'm still holding his existence close to my chest, my secret, and I don't know why. I just *am.* "This is your *Sex and the City* story," I remind her, refocusing on my friend, who remains forever important to me. "It's a good story," I add. "And the disaster that the experience is for me and you, including the Kevin situation, will make for a good read. Just don't use my name or his. And do *not* let Kevin get in between me and you or you and your work."

"I'm not letting him or *this story* get between us, Mia. We can talk about it this weekend. I'm afraid I'm so busy it's going to be Friday night again before we can grab a minute of quality time."

"It sounds like you're onto a big story."

"We'll see," she ponders cautiously. "I'll tell you about it when we have more time. Friday? Just me and you this time."

"Yes," I say, but now with a pinch of yet more guilt, this time at shutting out Jack, but still I add, "Just me and you this time."

"Later, beautiful," she teases.

I roll my eyes at the reference to my secret admirer, or stalker, or whatever I have, or had, going on.

"Goodbye, Jess," I murmur, and disconnect.

Hurrying inside Caroline's, I am shocked to find a line ten deep just to claim my pickup order. Good Lord, I cannot escape the campus that has taken over our little library and surrounding neighborhood. Ridiculously, I'm forced to take a number, as if I haven't already ordered. With the place bustling, and number three in hand, I claim one of the only open seats and shoot Jack a text: I literally had to take a number to even get our order. The kids are down here, too.

Snickers, here I come, he replies.

I thought you were cutting back on sugar? I ask, reminding him of the theme that was all last month.

His reply: I have no idea what you're talking about.

My lips curve at the familiar banter of the exchange. Could I be imagining our divide? My phone buzzes with another text, this one from Adam: Headed into a meeting but wanted to tell you that despite a day imagining grand highways and concrete, which, by the way, is the love of my life, you are still on my mind.

I laugh at the cute text and reply back with: It's nice to know I wiggled my way in between the highways and concrete bridges.

"Three!"

I slide my phone back into my purse and hurry toward the counter. A tall, thin kid with glasses, who seems to be new, greets me, accepting my ticket. "Order for Mia," I say, reaching in my purse and removing my wallet.

He punches it into the cash register, and I pay by credit card. Jack and I take turns paying for each other and have for years. Technically it's his turn to grab the bill, but I plan to refuse his money. The truth is, there is guilt driving this purchase as well.

"Your order is ready at the end of the counter," I'm told once my receipt is printed.

Hurrying to the counter, I offer the woman attending customers my order number. She, in turn, hands me my bag, and I'm out of here. Okay, not quite yet. I walk to the counter by the wall and grab forks, napkins, and salt. That's when I open the bag and toss the items inside and frown at the red writing on the back of what appears to be an extra receipt. Nerves flutter in my belly as I reach for it, straighten it, and read: *I like color on you, Mia. New challenge . . . wear your hair down tomorrow.*

My heart thunders in my chest. Whoever this is knows my name.

Chapter Forty-Two

Games.

It's all I can do not to whirl around and search the dining room for whoever is leaving me notes, a mix of emotions punching at me—left, right, left, right. I can't breathe with the impact. I can't seem to flip through the pages of my mind and decide which emotion wins—the part where I'm flattered and intrigued or the part where I'm terrified of what is really going on here. Do I have a stalker?

Me?

The girl no one even notices?

Adrenaline surges through me. This isn't funny anymore. This isn't flattering, either. It's creepy. I don't turn around. I don't scan the tables for familiar faces. I rush to the door, push it open, and all but run outside. *What is this?* Who would do this? I'm halfway back to the library when I stop dead in my tracks. "Kevin," I whisper. He's just trying to be mean. The message on the dating app. The notes. Contacting Jess. Something about me being on that dating app triggered him.

Anger is now the emotion that wins the war inside me—anger is what drives me to reach for my phone and punch in Kevin's number. The call dives into the dark, dark abyss of the voicemail he never checks. Of course it does, but I'm not ready to just hang up without saying my piece. "Stop whatever game you're playing," I snap. "Stop now, or I swear to you, I will go to the police and tell them you are harassing me."

I disconnect, pleased with myself for taking enough control to confront him. That's growth for me. For that I have to thank Kevin, no matter how much I wish I'd never met the asshole.

With no other option, I rush forward, aware I've been away from the library far too long. I've just stepped on the library escalator, leaving behind the lobby zoo, which *really is* a zoo of people today, when my phone rings. My heart thunders in my chest. Could Kevin be calling me back? No way. He won't listen to that message for months, but I want him to listen to it. Don't I?

The racing of my heart and trembling of my hands says otherwise. I shift my purse around and retrieve my phone. God, it is Kevin. I swallow hard and answer, but he doesn't give me time to speak, launching into an attack. "I don't know what you're talking about. Contacting Jess is *not* stalking you. As for the message I sent you, I didn't want to be rude and tell you this, but I had your profile up, shocked you were even on the app. I accidentally sent the message to you when it was for her. The end. Isn't that what you like to say?" And that really is the end. He disconnects.

I rotate on the escalator, away from my floor, facing the zoo below, trying to catch my breath before I exit to my floor. Only now I really cannot breathe at all. The man from floor two is still here. He's sitting at the same table, watching me watching him.

Chapter Forty-Three

It's an hour later when our floor-three team finally finishes the bagel sandwiches I'd brought back for them. Then, and only then, do Jack and I dare to retreat into the back room to eat our lunch.

I sit across from him at the tiny break room table, eating my bagel sandwich and listening to him talk about a potential knee surgery. I'm present but somehow numb to the moment, in tune with all the chaos of my life right now. Despite this, I am not unengaged with Jack. I am genuinely worried about his health, but with every question I ask him, my mind is cluttered up, secretly racing, charging in one direction and then another.

Kevin showed his true colors, intentionally trying to hurt me.

Does that mean he cared about me more than I thought or less than I ever imagined?

If Kevin isn't my note writer, who is?

Do I have a stalker?

What would Adam think of me if he knew my ex talked to me like I'm dirt under his shoe?

I told Adam about Kevin contacting Jess, but at some point I just look pathetic.

All these thoughts and more torment me, and yet I don't tell Jack about the note. I don't tell him about the confrontation with Kevin. I don't tell him about the man on floor two. When lunch is over, I also don't call Jess.

In the past, I would have told them both everything. Now it seems I tell them almost nothing.

I'm not sure what that says about the state of my life. It feels as if instead of turning pages in the book that tells my story, I'm slamming it shut before anyone reads the words. Even me, in some ways.

It's later than usual when I begin my evening walk home, well after seven, the sun hanging low, kissing the horizon a final good night. Mondays are the more peaceful evenings in downtown Nashville, with nary a party bus to be found, though there is *always* a party somewhere in this area of the city. While I normally enjoy the evolution of the city from week's beginning to end, the calm to the high energy this eve, the quiet is eerie and uncomfortable. The idea that my book is in my oversize purse, with a letter opener that resembles a knife inside, is remotely comforting, I suppose. But carrying a weapon and using a weapon are two different things.

Once I'm at the bookstore, it's a relief to climb the stairs and enter my loft to flip on the light, but I still find myself uncomfortable, scanning my surroundings for intruders before I lock up. Never have I ever felt that need before now. Once fully inside my home, I lean on the door as I allow myself a moment to simply breathe until I realize an intruder could be waiting on me upstairs. For no explainable reason, my heart thunders in my chest. Maybe I *do* need the gun Jack has suggested I purchase over and over throughout the years. His words play in my head now:

"A single woman, or man for that matter, living downtown, should be skilled and in possession of a gun."

For a gentle man with quiet sensibilities, this advice from him has always confused me. Hearing he was skilled with a handgun himself, even more so. *"I'll teach you to use the gun. You can keep one of mine at your place if you don't want to invest in buying one. However, a gun that is the right size for your hand, and feels as if it is a part of you, is a smarter decision."*

I reach in my bag, grab the letter opener, and stare at it in my hand. What am I doing? I'm not going to stab anyone. And no one is upstairs, either, and yet, as I move toward the steps, I find myself squeezing the silver handle tighter and tighter. Slowly I ease upward until I step onto the second level. Slowly I inch downward, settling on my knees and lowering my head to inspect under the bed. I pant out a breath of relief when it's all clear, as if I really believed the boogeyman was hiding there. I'm being ridiculous, I know, but when I stand, I find myself tiptoeing toward the bathroom and peeking in the door, surveying the area.

All clear.

But nothing feels clear at all.

I walk to the bed and sit down, allowing the letter opener to rest on my lap. In my head, I'm the little kid whose father let her watch the movie *It*, the original version, imagining clown hands grabbing my ankles from underneath. My heart thunders in my chest, a wild gallop—as if I'm about to appear in my own personal horror movie. And that is enough. I'm done. With my fingers wrapped around the silver handle again, I'm on my feet in an instant, kicking off my shoes and slipping my feet into my pink UGG slippers. Grabbing my bag, with my MacBook and phone inside, I hurry downstairs.

No wonder my mother was so pissed about me watching that movie. Apparently I'm traumatized for life.

A few minutes later, I'm sitting at the island, perched at the inner side of my kitchen, facing the door. My MacBook is open. A bottle of water and a steaming Lean Cuisine "gourmet" lasagna await my consumption to my left. My cellphone is at my right, with the letter opener beside it and within my reach. My cellphone rings, and I glance down to find Adam on the caller ID. Is this man really interested in me? What alternate universe am I living in? He's the kind of guy Jess belongs with, not me.

Nerves jangle in my belly as I slide my earbuds into place and answer the call. "Hi," I greet simply.

"Hi," he replies, and he has this warm cocoa voice, the kind of voice that drives away the chill of a cold night or a bad, confusing day. "How are you?" he asks. "How was work?"

My belly flutters in delight both with his words and the deep, sexy timbre of his voice. He's calling me just to see how my day was? When has any man, Kevin included, ever done such a thing? And when did any man ever stir such a warm sensation in my body, with nothing more than his words? What could this man do to me if he actually *touched me*?

"Weird," I confess, though I don't know why. I didn't share today's happenings with either of my two Js. Why would I share this with him? And yet, still, I press on, adding, "Work was weird."

"Weird how?"

"Just weird," I say, not sure what to add, not sure I should say anything at all. I'm back to my worry that at some point, if I keep telling him about Kevin dissing me, I sound desperate.

He's silent a moment, then two, before he says, "I don't pretend to know you well, but we spent the weekend talking. I have at least a small sense of who you are. *What's wrong*, Mia?"

Mia.

I like the way he uses my name as if he sees me without being here to see me at all. As if he sees me when those who are sitting right in front of me do not. My gaze slides to where the letter opener sits on my counter, a shiny decoration that could be used as a weapon. It's here for that reason, a decision on my part that opens my shut book and tells a story.

I'm scared.

That's the bottom line. The note writer is scaring me.

I need someone to talk with about this, someone who won't force a gun in my hand, as would be Jack's inclination. Or blow this off as nothing but fun and interesting, as I know Jess will. I love those two—I do—but guns scare me, and this is not nothing. Not when I have a makeshift weapon on my counter.

For the first time in years, I need someone other than them. It seems that someone is *Adam*. "Someone has been leaving me notes," I confess. "At the coffee shop mostly. They write the note on my cup or stick the note on my computer. They find an opportunity when there should be none. I can't figure out how they do it. The notes are compliments," I add quickly. "I'm beautiful or a random compliment to that effect. And while I know that sounds like a nice thing for this person to do, it's starting to feel creepy."

"I see," he says. "And who do you think is doing this?"

I should stop here, but I don't. "Today I decided it was Kevin. I thought maybe he was triggered in some way by me being on the dating site, angry at me."

He punches back with, "You think he wants to rekindle your relationship?"

"No," I say, the mean nature of Kevin's interactions with me a bit hard to swallow, even if I did bring them on myself, with that message I left on his phone. "Maybe it insulted him that I broke up with him," I suggest. "Those things bother some people, even if they have no real feelings for the other person. It's like an ego thing." I don't wait for a reply. It was never really a question. "I don't know," I add. "The whole thing just feels stalkerish, which is why I called him and threatened to call the police if he doesn't stop."

I hold my breath, dreading Adam's reply, waiting for it on pins and needles, seconds ticking by into more seconds, the silence awkward and heavy, and almost as weird as my day. "He denied everything," I quickly offer, filling the empty space I can no longer endure. "Maybe I'm wrong. Maybe it's not him. Whatever the case, I'm actually really creeped out and walking around looking over my shoulder." I breathe out. "Sorry." I laugh nervously. "I guess I just gave you an earful."

Silence fills the line again, a long, drawn-out silence. I shift in my seat and start to worry—is he not even on the line anymore? "Adam?"

"I have a confession to make, Mia."

Unease zigs and zags through me. "Confession?"

"Yes. I left the notes."

Chapter Forty-Four

The room spins, and I am unsteady when I am not even on my feet. He left the notes? *Adam* left the notes? How is that even possible? *How is that even possible?* Nothing about this feels right, and my instinct is to hang up. I'm about to do just that when he says, "Don't hang up. I saw you around the neighborhood, and then you were on the dating app."

"So you just left me notes? Were you *following* me?" I demand.

"No," he says. "No, nothing like that. I told you, I saw the old me in you. I liked the idea of giving you some space, of showing you how desirable you are, from afar."

"Without even telling me you were doing it?"

"I'm telling you now, Mia. Bottom line, I saw you and started leaving the notes before you showed up on my dating app. I left the first note on a whim. I couldn't resist. Then I saw you again, and you were with the person I now know is Jess. I didn't want to approach you then, but I wanted you to be *seen*."

"And today? We'd already started talking. Why stay in the shadows? I was alone."

"I had about five minutes to get back to work," he states. "It wasn't the time to tell you that, hey, I'm *that guy.* With the help of the lady behind the counter, I grabbed your receipt, wrote the note, and left with the hope I'd make you smile."

His explanation is almost too perfect. I think of the man with Jack at the coffee shop. "Did you speak with Jack this morning? Did you approach him?"

"What? No. I don't even know what Jack looks like. You've never told me."

"Well, if you've been watching me, you have to know what Jack looks like."

"I haven't been watching you, Mia," he says. "Our paths just happened to cross."

"Three times?" I counter. "No. That's not possible." But as my mind traces backward, I wasn't actually with Jack when I received any communication from Adam. Just Jess that one time, and he has admitted that already.

"It does feel impossible," he concurs, "and yet it happened. Our paths, even on the dating app, continued to cross, over and over again. It seems the universe wants our paths to cross."

If I were Cinderella and this was a fairy tale, I might buy this idea he presents. But I'm not. "I'm uncomfortable," I state.

"Sometimes uncomfortable is good, Mia."

Suddenly his use of my name no longer feels right. "I don't like to be uncomfortable, *Adam*."

"Which is why you remain *invisible* to the general population. Everything you do is about never feeling uncomfortable. I told you, Mia. I can show you how to be seen."

I think of the man on floor two, of the group who'd watched my disaster of a presentation, and of the notes that freaked me out. "I'm not sure being seen is what I want."

"And yet you don't want to be ignored, now do you?"

The comment hits close to home, but not in a gentle we-are-the-same kind of way this time. In a I-know-better-than-you-and-you-are-lesser-than-me way. "I'm hanging up now."

And that's what I do.

I hang up.

Chapter Forty-Five

I set my phone down and stare at it like it's some sort of alien from another planet.

Why have I been talking to a stranger? Why have I shared intimate details of my life with that man?

I think of the hours on end we chatted this weekend and reminisced about days past. Stories of my mother, my father, that dreaded day in New York City, when *Lion's Den* devoured my family. I told him my hopes and dreams. I told him about my father's new project and the bidding war.

And he told me about him. If I can believe anything he told me at all.

His parents are dead, both killed in a fire when he was ten. I wonder if the similarities between him and Jess drew me to him. Or maybe it's the fact that, like me, he's an only child. We connected on all those things, but do I even know anything about Adam? I wonder if he really is a civil engineer. Concerned I've been played, trying not to think about why anyone would scam me like that, I key my computer screen to life, I google "Adam Roth, civil engineer, Tennessee." The search engine does its work, displaying a rapid response but not a good one. My stomach is a twisty, turning mess when I find nothing. Desperate to prove Google wrong, I try again. This time I search for "Adam Roth, civil engineer,

Texas," and to my utter relief, I find him on a large construction and design website.

My tight shoulders literally slump forward.

He's not lying to me about himself, at least.

I wait a moment, savoring the information I've discovered, weighing my emotions. I'm still uncomfortable.

Shivering, I hug myself, then grab the very phone I didn't want to touch a few moments ago, with the intent of calling Jess. My finger hovers and then falls away. I set my phone down again, the ball of emotions in my belly rolling down a proverbial hill and crashing with an explosion of realization. I'm not ready to talk to Jess or anyone right now. Not before I understand what I'm feeling.

I press my hand to my forehead. Lord help me, on some level, the idea that he really knows who I am and is still interested pleases me. On another, I wonder what is wrong with this man. He is good looking, successful, and good natured, and yet he skulks around and watches me from afar. Why would he do such a thing?

He told you why, I remind myself.

Because he's like me or he was once like me.

Why didn't that feel more wrong than it did before now?

I reach for the phone again, intending to call Jack, but hesitate once more. What am I supposed to ask him? Has my stalker, dating-app mystery man I haven't told you about been chatting it up with you? I set my phone down again.

I'm not ready to talk about Adam to anyone.

Not yet.

Not until—I don't know when.

Just not yet.

Chapter Forty-Six

Present . . .

The footsteps above me on the upper stairwell grow louder, clunking down the steps, closing in on me, and I do the only thing I can do.

I run.

Someone is coming. What if it's the *wrong* someone?

I'm alive. I plan to stay that way, even if I have to use this damn knife again.

Adrenaline surges through me, fight or flight in high gear now, the human will to survive controlling me, driving me. With one hand gripping the steel banister of the stairwell, the other the steel handle of the letter opener, I sway, but my feet stay under me just as I'm hunched over, but not falling over. One flight of steps, two, three.

Finally the exit is before me and I turn the knob, and just like the stories you hear of a mother trying to save her child from a burning car—therefore she has superhuman strength—I yank the door open with a herculean force that I do not normally possess.

I all but hurl my body outside into the gusty wind, the dark sky above, darker than night, the kind of dark, ominous sky that promises dangerous weather. These storms favor Tennessee this time of year, even if those of us who live here do not favor them. I scan the empty parking lot, free of cars, no help to be found. A straight path forward leaves my back to the door and exposed to attack.

I go left, into a line of trees framing the parking lot and leading to the road. I've barely found the sanctuary of their coverage when the stairwell door is thrust open. Blood rushes in my ears, and I duck down behind a row of bushes, a tearing sensation in my belly shocking me, a loud whimpering cry escaping my lips before I can pull it back. Exposing me yet again.

I rotate left toward the main road and start crawling.

Chapter Forty-Seven

The past . . .

Adam doesn't text or call me back.

Hours pass, and my disappointment grows with each silent moment.

I'm in bed, a glass of wine on the nightstand, my MacBook in my lap, and I'm wearing my basic PJs with butterflies on the flannel that Jess hates and has replaced with silk and satin a million times. But tonight is about feeling like me, being me, understanding *me*. A task I'm not certain I'm capable of achieving. The truth is, I felt as if Adam was helping me travel a path of discovery.

Was I too hard on him?

Did I freak out over something that should have been romantic, would have been, in fact, to anyone else? But to me, I made it creepy?

Should I call him?

Instead, I open the dating app with no real purpose, not even sure what it is that I am looking for right now. My message box flashes, telling me I have ten new messages. I click on the icon, and the first message is from Kevin. Guilt jabs at me, all prickly and sharp, reminding me that I was wrong about him. Then again, I remind myself, he hit on my best friend and was a jerk about it as well.

It's right then that another message hits my inbox. This one is from Adam.

> Mia,
> I understand that you feel betrayed, but what you see as a betrayal, I see as me being spontaneous and romantic. I truly feel that if you believed in yourself more than you do, if you saw yourself as I do, you would have as well. Instead, you saw a stalker being creepy. We both know that's because you didn't think anyone who wasn't a creep would do such a thing for you.
>
> Well, I'm not a creep despite the fact that you all but told me I am tonight.
>
> And you're not unworthy, despite the fact that you always feel that you are.
>
> If this is the last communication we have, remember this . . .
>
> You're a beautiful woman hiding in the shell of an existence too small for what you deserve, Mia. All I ever wanted was to lead you on a journey of self-discovery.
> —Adam

I blink at the words, read them again, and again, and swallow hard. A journey of self-discovery? Does he mean sexually? The idea both terrifies and excites me. A little. I don't know. I think it should excite me a lot. I'm a little deprived of male attention, but I'm just weird with Adam. Interested, afraid, confused. I read the message again.

The words are written in past tense, as if he's done with me.

What am I doing? He's gorgeous. He's successful. He wants me. What girl doesn't want a man like this one to want her?

What have I done? What have *I done*?

My hands hover over the keyboard with the intent of replying, not even sure what to say, until finally I just type what I really feel. I'm sorry. You're right. People like you don't happen to me, Adam. I was just confused. The truth is, I still am, but I don't think you're a creep. I think—my fingers freeze a moment before I dare to add—I think you're pretty wonderful.

Seconds tick by, then a full minute, then two. No reply. I set my MacBook aside, throw off the blankets and sit up, pressing my hands to my face. *What have I done?*

My cellphone rings, and I jump, standing and staring at it as if it will bite me. I grab it and check the caller ID. It's Adam. Drawing in a breath, with a trembling hand—good Lord, I'm so very nervous—I hit the answer button. "Hello."

"Hello, *Mia*," he says, and the deep, intimate baritone of his voice does funny things to my belly.

"Adam," I reply, deciding the way he says my name is a good thing, not a bad thing. I do want to be seen, at least by him.

"Now that you know I wrote the notes, wear your hair down for me tomorrow."

Butterflies do a fluttery schoolgirl dance routine in my chest, and I am more alive than I have ever been before this moment. "Does that mean I get to meet you in person?"

"You're not ready yet. Wear your hair down."

Chapter Forty-Eight

Not until you spread your wings; will you know just how far you can fly.

—Matthew James Elliott

Adam was right when he said there is safety in what is familiar, thus why we repeat even what might be bad for us.

The next day I do not wear red, or tan, or light blue, or any color but black. To be specific, a black dress that personifies the me who has lived in the shadows, the woman who stands in front of the room and might as well be in the back. This dress, and its color, is my safe place. With the level of comfort that my normal attire delivers, I dare to do something that does not feel like me at all. I wear my hair down, long and brown, around my shoulders.

Nervously I head to work, walking down the street, skipping my preferred coffee stop, and heading straight to the library. No one will notice, I tell myself. A change of hairstyle does not shift the world on its axis. Me being seen and heard, beyond the embarrassment that was the presentation, would be that and more.

The minute I step inside the entryway, Doug, who is more often stoic in his guard duties than not, lights up. "Well now, Ms. Mia," he greets. "Look at you. I don't believe I knew you had hair."

"Of course I have hair." I laugh. "I wear it every day."

He grins. "You wear it well today."

"Thank you," I say, warming with his compliment and hurrying on my way.

I've just stepped onto the escalator when a tingling sensation on my neck has my gaze lifting and landing on the zoo-level customer service desk. Akia is presently staring at me. It's weird and awkward, and I turn away from him, facing forward again, running a hand down my hair, and ignoring floor two as I pass it by. Do I look that different? I flash back to the moment I stood in front of the mirror and stared at my reflection, my long, dark hair draping my shoulders. After wearing my hair up for a decade-plus, I'd felt as if I were looking at a stranger, but not an unpleasant one.

What am I thinking, though, really? Akia's still pitying me from the encounter with Neil, I suspect. His attention has nothing to do with my hair. I doubt that man could tell anyone what my hair normally looks like even if paid.

The escalator pushes me onto floor three and I hear, "Mia," from behind.

It's Jack's voice, and obviously, somehow, even with my hair down, he knows this is me. I turn to find him joining me on our floor and handing me a cup of coffee. "Hair down," he says, "lips shining. Am I in an alternate universe?"

"I think we both are," I confirm, lifting the cup. "Thank you. I need this." I motion to his tie, which is a bright color, when he tends to remain as muted as I do. "I like the red. Did I inspire you?"

We're still standing at the top of the escalator, neither of us moving toward our office area.

"You did, actually," he states. "You know I can't let you climb out on a limb by yourself and hang there. You take a risk, I'll take a risk." He points at his tiepin. "Even remembered to buckle up."

This idea that we are in things together warms me inside and out, even if my actions of late prove it to be less true than we'd both prefer. "Buckle up?" I laugh.

"A man can't have his tie flapping in the wind and smacking him in the face. But seriously, Mia, you look good. What's going on with you?"

What's going on with me? I think.

Talk about a loaded question with a complicated answer, one I think he'd understand more than most. This is why I decide to go with the truth, even if it's not the entire truth. "You know how Jess put up that one photo of me, where I don't look like me? And then I changed it to a photo that looks like me?"

"They both look like you, Mia."

"Well, I don't think so, but regardless, this stranger commented when I changed the photos. He said his read on me was that I am afraid to be the girl in the first photo. For some reason, despite him having a cartoon character for his photo, it hit home. I guess random remarks from objective outsiders can have more impact than I realized."

His eyes narrow, and he studies me for several beats before he says, "While I'm glad this cartoon guy inspired you, Mia, just remember this. Anyone with a fake photo has something to hide." He motions with his head. "Ready?"

"Yes," I say. "Ready."

I follow him to our offices with his warning in my head.

Anyone with a fake photo has something to hide. But Adam is not fake. His photo is no longer a cartoon character. I down a swallow of coffee and run to the bathroom. While in there, I stare at myself in the mirror again, starting to get used to seeing myself with loose hair. Who says a librarian has to be conservative and restrained in extreme ways? *I like this new look,* I think. I really do.

When I was five, I played dress-up in fancy Cinderella gowns and high heels made for little girls with big-girl dreams. I don't remember when I stopped fawning over beautiful dresses and shoes. I don't remember being teased or taunted. I remember being overlooked. At some point, clothes stopped being a path to being noticed, but rather a way to hide. That's what Jack doesn't understand.

I'm the one with something to hide.

Not Adam.

Chapter Forty-Nine

I've barely sat down at my desk when my phone buzzes with a message from Adam: I like it, Mia. Thank you for doing that for me.

I blink in confusion. Wait, what? He likes it? Oh God. He means my hair. Of course he means my hair, but I didn't stop for coffee. Isn't that how we've crossed paths in the past? How does he know what I look like today? Unease slithers through me all over again, but I warn myself to calm down, to ask questions, and to not claim assumptions as reality. With a trembling hand, I type: How?

> You walked right by me. I told you. The universe wants us to be together.

My brows dip and I type a combative: And you didn't say anything?

Is a random introduction on the street how you really want us to meet in person? he challenges.

"Hey, Mia," Jack says, stepping into the office doorway. "Mrs. Mackey is here. She says you have a book for her?"

"Right," I say. "Yes. It's in the back. I'll grab it."

"I'll let her know."

He exits the office again, and my phone buzzes with another message. I glance down to read: Let's meet this weekend. I have a surprise for you.

He has a surprise for me?

When? I type.

Saturday night, he responds. I'll text you the details in advance.

My hesitation is unexpected considering how much we've talked, and yet expected in that I am me and forever insecure. What if he doesn't like me in person? What if I don't like *him*? What if the magic of our calls is as awkward as it always is with everyone else?

I wet my dry lips and type, Saturday then, in confirmation.

I slide my phone into my pocket. It's official. I'm going to meet him. I will see him with my own eyes, touch him, I am certain, and look into his eyes, which I know to be green from his dating profile. Once I do all these things, once I know him, *really* know him, this entire situation will stop feeling weird.

Chapter Fifty

I wake Saturday morning, only hours from meeting Adam, with the incredible realization that he's still my little secret.

Not an easy task with the two Js in my life, but as proves true at random moments in time, neither is in tune with me right now. Jess is busy with work and even had to cancel our drink date last night. Jack, on the other hand, is battling his knee injury to the point that he missed two days of work this week. I've tended to him, brought him dinner, binged *Squid Game* with him, and ensured he was well medicated. He's focused on himself now, rightfully so, and trying to heal.

In a frenzy of nerves over tonight's meetup, I find my way to my kitchen and the coffeepot—rather quickly, even for me. Once my brew is ready, I lean on the counter, sipping from my cup, steam puffing from the top, and I contemplate why I've held Adam so close to my chest.

My mind slips back to midday Monday, when I'd made yet another run to the coffee shop, this time for the team on floor three. Loretta, the manager who'd scolded her staff member for labeling my cup "Girl," had been there that day as well. She'd not only greeted me by name, but she'd complimented my hair. *"Don't you usually wear it tied at your nape?"* she'd asked.

I'd been stunned that anyone had ever noticed, or remembered how I wore my hair at all. When my order was called, it was with a shout of "Order for Mia!"

I'd always thought that no matter what I did, I was dismissed, but that isn't proving to be true, not at all. This leads to the question, Was I ever really invisible at all? Or did I simply choose not to be seen? I don't know if I would have asked myself that question if not for Adam.

This is exactly why I don't think keeping Adam a secret is really about Adam at all. I think it's about this journey of self-discovery I'm traveling that needs to be raw and real and all my own. That said, I can't keep this up for long. Next weekend is the wedding and awards ceremony. I do wish I could ask Jess for advice about what to wear tonight, but I dismiss this idea. It's all or nothing with Jess, and today can't be about her. Today is about me getting ready for Adam.

The buzzer downstairs rings, and I straighten and set my cup down, expecting this is something I've ordered from Amazon, as it seems I'm always ordering from Amazon. The addiction is real. For the most part, my packages arrive when the main downstairs entrance is open, and therefore they make it to my apartment level. I open my loft door, surprised to find Jess standing there in a pink sweatsuit, with her hair piled on top of her head.

"I brought muffins from Julie's Bakery." She indicates the goodies in her hands.

"Get inside already," I say, taking one of the two bakery bags from her. "God, I love you, woman."

She laughs and heads toward the kitchen, where she helps herself to coffee. "I can't stay long." She glances over her shoulder at me. "I have to go by the office and chat with my boss about a story I have due next week, but I haven't seen you. That just feels wrong." She sips her coffee and claims the barstool at the end of the island. "How are things?"

I refill my cup and join her at the island. "Jack has a knee injury. He's been out of work for two days. I might run a muffin by him and check on him later."

"Good Lord, really? How is that even possible? He's young, not overly athletic from what I can tell, and probably doesn't even have sex. How did he manage to hurt his knee?"

I snort my coffee and almost choke. "Because knees are always involved in sex?"

She grimaces at me. "What are you even saying right now? Of course, if done right, he should be using his knees." She waves this off. "Enough about Jack. How are *you*?"

"The same as always. You?"

"Boring. I can't even be my own test subject on the dating app. I have no time. You won't do it. I mean, the project is doomed, but more importantly"—she sips from her cup—"have there been any more notes from your secret admirer?"

Heat rushes to my cheeks with just the idea of lying to Jess. Actually, I can't lie to her. So I don't. "One," I say. "Just one."

Her brows shoot upward. "And?"

"And I wore my hair down."

"Wait. What? I don't understand the connection between your secret admirer sending you another note and the hair, but"—she holds up her hands—"I need to get this straight. You wore your hair down to work? *You.* Mia Anderson, the Queen Librarian who goes out of her way to look the role." She presses her hands to her face and drags her hair back farther, as if imitating my normal hairstyle.

I shake my head at her antics. "I never wear it that extreme. But yes, I wore it down. And yes, I know. I'm just wild, aren't I?"

"So wild," she teases. "What in the world got into you? And feel free to connect the dots here for me at any point."

"It all ties back to that one guy on the dating app. I think I told you about him. The one who messaged me and said the girl in the second photo I posted looked like she was afraid of being the girl in the first photo you posted."

"Right. Right. I remember. He was kind of right on that." She doesn't give me time to argue. "Did he write to you again? Wait." Her brows dip. "Is *he* your secret admirer?"

"Okay, he insulted me, so I'm not sure how in the world you could surmise he's a secret admirer. But his comments did stick with me. I felt like he was being a jerk, but you know, he also jump-started my engine a bit."

"And?"

"I tried something new, and it felt good to wear my hair down. I got compliments."

She waggles her eyebrows. "You mean you weren't invisible?"

"You just couldn't help yourself, could you? You had to say that."

"You know I had to do it." She motions to the muffin bag. "Eat one. I know you love them."

"I can't eat and talk, and I know you're in a rush."

"Right. Yes. Damn my work. Okay, don't damn my work. I love my job, but I hate I'm rushed." She downs the rest of her coffee. "Before I go, I talked with your dad yesterday. He called and thanked me again for the referral. It seems like the bidding war is heating up."

"Yes," I confirm. "I've been chatting with him most evenings. He said the attorney is negotiating with everyone involved and has actually pulled an extra bidder into the mix. It seems to be going well. Thank you, Jess."

"Everyone keeps thanking me. I made a phone call. That's not a big deal, like, at all. However, I want in on the champagne celebration when it happens. Does your mom know what's going on now?"

"Considering she's cornered me into coming over for lunch tomorrow to talk to him about the *Lion's Den* offer, I would guess the answer to that question is *no*."

"Okay, that's just uncomfortable. Have you asked your dad why he's shutting her out?"

"No. And don't ask me why I haven't, either. I have no answer. I should have. I'm just not sure I can bear to hear that either of them is having an affair. It's like, you know, we just don't want to know our parents have sex with each other, let alone other people."

"Hmm," she murmurs. "True. So true. I give you a pass on this one. No wonder you haven't asked him directly."

"I might this weekend. He and I always spend time in his man cave."

Her cellphone buzzes, and she sets her now-empty cup down and glances at it, reading the message with an ensuing sigh. "My boss. He wants to know when I'm coming by the office." She slides off the stool and says, "You know, I might take a muffin to Jack and nudge him to be my dating-app guinea pig."

I push to my feet with the intent of walking her to the door. "You're going to take a muffin to Jack? You? As in my friend Jess who never has a conversation with Jack unless forced?"

"I'm forced. And I have extra muffins in the car. He can have two, but he has to wait until after my meeting." She grins and hugs me. "Gotta run, beautiful." She grabs her purse, and I follow her to the door. "Call me after your family get-together."

"I will," I say. "Good luck with Jack."

She's already disappearing down the stairs, and I shut the door, leaning on the hard surface and assuring myself that I didn't lie to Jess. I simply left out a few details, including the part where Jack was already on the dating app. He doesn't even know I know. I'm not telling Jess. That's his business, not hers, unless he chooses to make it so. The buzzer rings again, and I glance toward the kitchen, wondering if Jess left something behind. When I find nothing, I open the door to find her nowhere in sight.

My gaze is pulled downward, to the ground.

There's a huge white box with a red ribbon on it sitting right in front of me. My lips purse. What did Jess do now? And why so fancy a presentation? She normally just hands me the gift I'll object to while she will later refuse to allow me to decline. I'm not sure what to make of this, but I scoop up the box and bring it inside, then set it on the kitchen counter.

The card reads "Mia" in an unfamiliar script that is definitely not Jess's handwriting. Butterflies flutter in my belly, one part excitement, the other more of that unease I've been experiencing since meeting Adam. I slide the little white card from the small envelope and read:

Mia—

Your address is public record. I couldn't resist looking it up and surprising you.

Just one of the gifts I have for you tonight.

That unease I'm feeling expands, lifts its wings as wide as an eagle's spread, but curiosity wins the battle. I work the ribbon off the box and then open the lid. Inside is a silky red dress. There's another card lying on top of the garment that reads: *I told you. I like you in red.*

My heart thunders in my chest, and I draw a breath, eyeing the box again. The dress is sexy, the promise of something far more than conversation in the air between me and this man. But the seemingly romantic, intimate gesture is dashed away by my concern. There's no address on the box. Did Adam deliver this himself? Was he just at my front door? And how does he know where I live anyway? Is my address really public record?

I grab my phone and google myself. Sure enough, there is a way to find my address. That's news to me—and not good news. How is that safe?

My next move is to dial Jess. "Hey," she greets. "Miss me already?"

"Did you see someone at my door?"

"What? No. Why?"

"Nothing. Nothing. I'm having trouble with my delivery service. I'll call you later."

We disconnect, and my gaze lands on the dress.

Why am I ridiculously bothered at the idea of him knowing where I live?

Chapter Fifty-One

Present . . .

I cannot believe this is happening.

I managed to escape the building stairwell and even found my way behind the bushes framing the parking lot to the building. Then I blew it all by falling and yelping with the pain in my belly. The whimper of pain, truly the smallest of sounds, placed me in what I fear is almost an ideal position for whoever followed me out of the building.

I suck in a breath and curl my lips around my teeth, my legs trembling as I balance on my heels, my fingers curled around the letter opener with a death grip, aware, oh so aware, that it is my life it may well protect. Seconds tick by, laden with my fear that what comes next is more blood. More death.

But there is no sound, no crunch of boots on gravel, no movement, nothing to tell me whether the person who followed me from the building is moving toward or away from me. Silence lingers and breaks apart with a low, angry rumble of thunder, a bear in a cave, warning of its mighty rage, ready to explode upon the world below. A random icy-cold droplet splatters on my nose, almost as if it's calling me to action, telling me it's my time to run before the deluge is upon me.

I want to listen to this warning—I do—but if I run again, I risk the noise giving away my location.

If I stay where I am, though, I also risk being found, being attacked.

Despite how recent events might argue differently, I am not exactly the girl who wants to shove a knife in someone's body, nor am I a fighter. My love of jogging does not translate to me being athletic. I do not lift weights. I do not know karate. I didn't even participate in gymnastics as a kid.

This means staying and fighting is a bad idea.

The sky opens up, rain showering down from the heavens above, and when it does, so do I.

I start crawling right, down the line of the trees, biting my lip, silencing my whimpers of pain with another curl of my lips around my teeth, the iron taste of blood on my tongue. *Get up,* I think in my head, *run*, but my body is anchored in pain. Still, I manage to keep moving. Forward I crawl, *forward, forward*, and then a blast of awareness so strong rushes over me that I don't even dare look back. I just act. I push upward, rising to my feet, and run, run as hard and fast as I can. Fear drives me, consumes me, is a part of me as if it were my skin, my blood, my muscle. My hair is wet, draped over my scalp and face, my clothes a soaking-wet mop of weight on my body. But the road is near—it has to be near; please let it be just ahead—but I can't see it. I can see nothing but darkness.

And then it happens, that thing we all laugh about when we watch horror movies.

The girl always has to fall, and then she can't get up.

My foot catches on the unknown, and I am that girl, falling, falling, and I go facedown with a hard thud, my bones rattling, the mush of weeds and mud splattering around me.

For long moments I'm just there on the ground, rain pounding down on me, and I can't even think of moving. That's when the sensation returns, that now-familiar feeling that I'm being stalked, watched. I roll over, and it's too late for me now. Someone is standing over me.

Chapter Fifty-Two

A friend is someone who understands your past, believes in your future, and accepts you just the way you are.

—Unknown

The past . . .

On any other day, in any other situation, I would call or text Adam and thank him for the dress.

I don't.

I leave it in the box on the counter, sipping coffee and stuffing my face with bites of various muffins ranging from cherry to chocolate, while I think about how Adam snatched my address from the public record. Easy enough to believe except—my brows dip. Unless he really did talk to Jack that day at the coffee shop and Jack gave it to him? Maybe as a way of playing a part in my gift-box surprise? I reject that idea as fast as I've created it in my wild imagination. Jack did not give Adam my address.

Jack would never do such a thing.

I'm nibbling at another cherry muffin when my cellphone buzzes with a text alert from, of course, *Adam*. He's probably expecting me to confirm the dress has arrived and that I love it. I open the message to read:

I hope you like the dress

Tonight

9 pm

He includes an address that seems to be nearby downtown. My teeth worry my bottom lip. Now it feels as if I should call him. But if I do that, I fear this weird, distrusting side of myself will creep into the conversation. I don't even know why it's present. He told me how he managed to come by my address in the note. Nevertheless, I am uneasy with Adam, and I'm pretty sure if I act suspicious of him one more time, we're done. I think of our connection and the way he sets my pulse racing. I am alive when I talk to him, aware of myself as a woman, I think he is, too, and that feels good. I don't want us to be done, but I also don't want to be stupid. But who am I fooling? I can't not find out what is real and what is not with Adam. Bottom line: I'm going to meet him tonight, this man who says he's like me, this man I've talked with for hours on end. Pretending otherwise is a waste of time.

I stuff the muffins back in the bag and grab the box, carrying it with me upstairs. It probably won't even fit. He might know my address, but my size is another story.

I type a simple reply:

Thank you. Gift received. It's beautiful. Can't wait to see you tonight.

Mia

The dress is a perfect fit.

Standing in front of my closet, I study the formfitting bejeweled bodice and flared skirt that falls just above the knee. It's stunning, luxuriously silky, simple, and elegant, and I decide it's a Cinderella dress if I've ever seen one. I don't even know how Adam managed to pick a dress this close to my ideal dream gown with a perfect fit. Of course, we've talked for endless hours, and he's watched me from afar; therefore, I reason, it's likely he could guess a size. Not to mention, per the tags, he bought the dress at Saks Fifth Avenue, and the staff there is certainly paid well to be good at guessing these things. I decide not to overthink the dress fitting like a glove or Adam knowing my address. I've done a lot of looking for problems where Adam is concerned, and now tonight the speculation of what is right or wrong with our relationship, if that's what you call this, ends. The time to ask Adam about Adam in person has come.

I give myself one last inspection, replaying Adam's words in my head: *"I told you I like you in red."* I wonder if he will think I look sexy in the dress. I laugh nervously. My cheeks are flushed, my skin warm. I do feel a little sexy in the dress, and it's kind of wonderful. Maybe red *is* my color.

It's time to go feel sexy with Adam. *I'm ready,* I think.

The mystery of the man ends tonight.

I arrive at the address Adam directed me to via his text at ten minutes until nine—a girl does like to be punctual. The building is a fancy all-glass high-rise that appears to be an office building, but there must be a restaurant inside. There is no security at the entry, and I walk to the elevator and choose floor eleven, as directed by Adam's earlier message. With nervous energy lighting me up, I step onto the empty car, jab at the button, and then watch the doors slide shut.

Blinking at the vision of myself now reflecting before me in the silver sheen of the elevator, I barely recognize the girl in the red fitted dress and strappy black heels, her long dark hair silky around her shoulders. This can't be me, and yet it is. Somehow it *really is* me.

With a fist balled at my chest, I will my heart to calm while my chin lifts and tracks the floors as they zip past with far too rapid a pace. I enjoy Adam's company on the phone, I tell myself. Certainly I will enjoy seeing him in person. Still, my mind goes to a novel I once read about a woman, Sue Ann Miller, who was chatting it up with a man named Joe online, only to discover it was all a huge joke created by someone she knew. This person who set her up later released all the chats and even a nude photo that she'd sent to "Joe" on a Reddit thread that went viral. Sue Ann was mocked and shamed to the point that she eventually killed herself.

The elevator opens on my destination floor, and I shake myself. I didn't send a nude photo to Adam, and I am not going to be mocked. That's a ridiculous notion, fiction I'm using to scare myself. Jess is right when she declares me truly my worst enemy at times.

I exit the car and walk down a small hallway to an open door. I step under the archway and suck in a breath at what I find. The floor is unfinished, a shell of offices waiting to be built, but in the center of it all, just in front of a row of windows, sits a dinner table with flowers and a bottle of wine on top. I don't know if I should be charmed or afraid, but I quickly squash my fear. As Adam has observed, fear is my weakness. He wants to be alone with me. And when has any man gone to this much trouble for me ever?

Tentatively—no, more nervously—I cross the concrete floor and halt at the table, where there is a card with my name written on the front. I pick it up, open it, and withdraw a stack of note cards inside. The first one reads: *Follow the instructions and don't jump ahead. Your big surprise will await at the end.*

My nerves settle a bit, a smile touching my lips with this playful game. I glance around, wondering if he's watching me in the shadows, or if there's a camera somewhere, but it seems to be only me here, at least for now. My hope is that the surprise referenced is him, and I am eager to work my way through what looks like only a few cards. I flip to the next one that reads: *Pour yourself a glass of wine. It's the Meiomi cabernet you love.*

The man really listens to what I say to him, I think. He really does listen and remember what I share about my likes and dislikes.

I set the cards down and fill my glass, still feeling the pleasure of him remembering my favorite wine. Once I've sipped from my glass, I pick up the cards again and flip to the next one: *Sometimes feeling uncomfortable is necessary. Just as fear tends to do to us, discomfort reminds us how much we want to live.*

Something about the tone of the card snakes through me with a warning. I am no longer smiling. A ball of urgency forms inside me, and I flip to the next card: *Remember when I told you I'd teach you to leave the Invisible Girl behind? The most important lesson is to remove everything negative from your life. Clear the path for a more confident, happy you.*

There's nothing more on the card, but for reasons I can't explain, my hand is trembling, and my urgency to see the final card is a hundredfold. I flip to it and read: *You once told me the one thing you loved about Kevin. His apartment in the sky, the one you think you will never deserve yourself. The one you confessed to me, that he told you, you'd never be ambitious enough to own without him by your side. Pick up your wine, set your cards down, and turn to the window.*

I set down my wine and suck in a breath, a feeling of dread inside me. I round the table and stand at the window, the apartment across the street glowing with the brightness of what feels like a million lights. A man steps to the window, and suddenly I realize I'm standing across from Kevin's apartment, acting like a voyeur that I am not but have currently been forced into. Kevin is moving about in the room, and every instinct I own screams of danger. The cards fall from my grip, fluttering about as I struggle to retrieve my phone stuffed in my tiny black purse. Finally, it's in my hand, and I punch in Kevin's number.

He answers on the first ring. "Are the police on their way, Mia? What did I do this time? Fuck someone that wasn't you? Like Jess?"

I blink. Wait. What? "Did you and Jess—did you—"

He walks to the window and stands there, looking out across the city, as he often does while on the phone, and I wonder if he can see me, as I can see him. "What do you want, Mia?"

"Look across the street, into the building."

"What are you talking about?"

"Just do it. Now," I command.

He does as I say before murmuring, "What the fuck? Is that you?"

"Yes. Listen. A man called me and he told me—" That's when I see the figure in all black behind Kevin, approaching him. "Kevin, turn around. Turn around *now*."

But it's too late. The person, whoever the person is, jabs something in his neck—a needle, I think. He crumples to the ground. I gasp and cover my mouth, not sure if Kevin is sedated or dead. That's when I see the knife in the stranger's hand.

Chapter Fifty-Three

The person in black, standing over Kevin, retrieves Kevin's phone and with a gloved hand presses it to his ear. "Hello, Mia. I really must start this conversation by saying you look beautiful tonight."

Adam.

It's Adam's voice.

"What is this?" I demand, my tone calm. *I'm numb,* I think, in shock. Or maybe I'm in denial. Or not. Suddenly I'm screaming at him. "What did you do to Kevin? *What are you doing?*"

"Keeping my promise. I always keep my promises."

"What promise is that, Adam? *What promise* is that?"

"I promised you that I would teach you how to change your life, the way I changed my life. This is me showing you how to take control of your world."

"This is *not* taking control." I'm still shouting. "This is committing a crime." I suck in a breath and force myself to calm, reason coming to me. "Unless it's a game. It's a game, right? Kevin's in on it? *Right?*" My heart is beating too fast, a wild drum in my chest, punching hard. "Or did you . . ." I can barely say the words, my hand gripping my throat as I whisper, "Did you . . . *kill him?*"

"This is a means to an end, Mia," he replies. "This is me creating a traumatic event that shatters life as we know it and forces us to value each moment with a little more appreciation."

"I do appreciate life," I argue, praying Kevin is alive, praying I can save him.

"Wrong answer. You fear every moment. So yes, Mia. Now we play a game. Here are the rules. You control what is happening in your life, or I will. Your move dictates my move. And because I know how you think, I'll warn you now: don't even consider going to the police. I'll know. And they'll know you have a motive to kill Kevin. You are, after all, the shunned ex-lover."

"You don't have to kill him. *Please.* Please don't kill him." I press my hand to the window, and my voice is small again. "Please, Adam. Please, I'll do anything." A thought comes to me, and I push off the glass, my voice stronger now. "The police will know that I've been talking to him anyway. You can't kill him without hurting me. You've taught me a lesson. I'm ready to learn more." I sound desperate, I think, but I am. I am desperate, but maybe he needs to know that. Maybe he needs to know his plan worked.

I will do anything to save Kevin, and so that's what I say: "I will do anything to save Kevin. Do you hear me? *Anything*, Adam. What do you want? Tell me, and I'll do it."

"Be a good girl and your communication with Kevin will disappear forever, all of it." He pauses for effect and then adds, "Unless, of course, you cross me."

"That's blackmail. You don't have to blackmail me. I told you. Let him go and—"

"I'm not blackmailing you. I want nothing more from you than your participation in the progress of making your life better. Break a rule. Be punished. That's a promise. I *never* break a promise," he repeats. "And, Mia, anyone you tell about this becomes a liability. You're about to find out what happens to those I see as a liability to your future and my own." He pockets Kevin's phone and squats next to him. I gasp in horror as he slices his throat.

Just slices his throat, as if he were performing a menial task such as turning off a light switch rather than extinguishing a life.

For a moment, maybe longer, panic, shock, and fear collide, throwing me into the eye of a hurricane, where I am trapped, where the ground I am standing on might collapse under me at any time. I can't move. I am standing in the quicksand of blood and death, slowly sinking to my own—that is, until Adam disappears, out of sight, and my heart jackknifes at the idea that he's coming for me. "Move," I whisper. "Run. *Run!*"

Sticking my phone in my purse, I think about anything that might prove that I was here. The cards. I kneel and gather the cards; then somehow I gather the brainpower to snag a napkin and wipe the ground where I've touched. Once the cards are in my purse, I snap up the wine bottle and the glass that I also touched. My bag is small, and I can't fit these items inside it, but I start to run with everything in hand, halting as I remember the twist top to the bottle. I turn back and scoop it up carefully, cautious not to touch the table. On second thought, I use the second napkin I find left behind and wipe down the table. When I'm done, I carry it with me. Now I'm off to a run again, and once I exit to the hallway, I scramble toward the stairwell. I need to avoid cameras, and while it's likely too late to avoid them anyway, I have to do what I can do right now to save myself. Because Adam's right. I can't call the police for too many reasons to process right now. I'm Adam's prisoner. I'm his captive in ways beyond anything I ever imagined possible. Once I'm at the exit door, I use the napkin to turn the knob. I have no idea if fingerprints transfer from cloth to steel. Logically they do not, but there is no logic in anything happening to me right now. I run down the steel steps, my heart jumping against my breastbone, trying to escape the confines of my body the way I am trying to escape the confines of a man named Adam.

Once I'm in the lobby, thank God almighty above, I discover a side door, and exit to an alleyway. I ignore the dumpster that tempts me to dispose of the items in my possession. This area is too close to the location of the murder to be a safe dump site. I'm not a killer, but I might be called one, assumed to be one. Truly, I don't even know what a safe dump site looks like at this point. Without any coherent thought that tells me to do so, I find myself walking toward the police station, well beyond my loft, and onto Broadway, where there are people en masse. I stand across the street from the station, where officers come and go, tears streaming down my cheeks. Adam's words play in my mind: *Break a rule. Be punished. That's a promise. I never break a promise.* Who will he hurt to punish me for breaking his rules? I dump the wine and glass in a trash can right there, across from the station, and then hurry away. The cards stay with me, as they are proof of the "game" Adam is playing with me.

I've walked half a block when a tall man with dark eyes catches my arm and stares down at me, mascara no doubt drizzling down my face like thick black icing on All Hallows' Eve. "You okay, miss?"

Now I'm noticed? Now some stranger worries for my health and well-being?

Isn't that what Adam wanted?

Now this stranger is here, this man who isn't Adam. And he is a random stranger. I sense this. I feel his genuine concern. Some part of me wants to throw myself in his arms and beg for help, but I will doom him to nothing but pain. And blood. And death.

"I'm fine. Thank you." I dislodge myself from his grip and hurry down the street, cautiously watching for Adam but never finding him.

Once I'm inside my loft, I lock the door and lean on the wooden surface, slowly sinking to the ground, my legs two snakes of different minds, landing in different positions on the ground. I was angry with Kevin. I was hurt by Kevin. But I was not destroyed by Kevin. No one can do that to me but me. But now Kevin is dead. He's *really dead* and it's my fault. I should have never talked about him to Adam, a virtual stranger. I should never have ignored all the uneasy feelings I had about Adam.

If only I could turn back time and revel in being invisible.

Chapter Fifty-Four

Thou shalt not kill.

—Exodus 20:13

My Christian upbringing is singing in my mind. I glance down at the dress I'm wearing, the dress Adam gifted me, and that I oh so obediently wore at his bidding. It's red, so obviously, bright red, like the apple, the forbidden fruit from the tree of knowledge of all that is good and evil, that God forbade Adam and Eve from tasting. As my Bible teachings tell me, a serpent tempted them, Eve first, to taste the apple. Eve then convinced Adam to join her, to take just one bite. But the only serpent here is Adam.

He is evil personified.

Anger burns in my belly and my legs find strength. I push to my feet, my legs no longer tangled, but hands and fingers are tangling in the dress—grabbing at it, struggling as I reach for the zipper, fighting with the silk until I've kicked away the offending garment, thrown it across the room. Did he choose it and the color to represent blood? My bra and panties are red, too—my own sickening choice—as if he guided me to the sinful place of blood and lust. As silly as it might seem to another, I can't bear any of it touching my skin, and I wrestle with my garments all over again, tossing them all to the floor. I stand there, naked in my sin by association, hugging myself, trying to disassociate myself from all things Adam, all things sinful and evil.

I'm shivering when my mind starts thinking about the cameras, so many cameras that might have captured my image on this sultry, sordid night. Everywhere, every place has a camera nowadays. They are literally as common as cellphones. Me in that dress equals bad news. I rush upstairs and pull on a sweatsuit and sneakers, with a baseball cap over my hair. I hurry downstairs and shove all the clothes in a grocery-store bag. I'm now on the floor, staring at the bag as if it carries the plague. It has to go. But go where?

An idea hits me, and it's not long before that bag is in my oversize purse, and I'm walking down the street. *Act normal,* I tell myself. He'll be following me, watching me, and so I go to a place I go often. In this case Jessie's Diner, a joint only a few blocks from my loft. I find my favorite table and force myself to smile at Diana, the fiftysomething waitress, who I swear lives at this place the way I do the library.

"No hot date tonight, hon?"

"I've had it with dating for a while. Me, books, and my favorite beef potpie will do me right."

"You read too many romance novels," she accuses. "You expect too much of men."

Or, I think, too little. Adam overperformed. But what I say is, "Guilty as charged, I'm sure. I'm craving one of those famous potpies."

"I'll get that pie coming. Diet Sprite?"

"You know me so well."

She walks away, and I exhale air I didn't even know I'd been holding, my fingers fiddling with a knife on the table, eyes watching the door, expecting Adam to enter, but he never shows up. I burn to call Jess. She will know what to do, but my eyes squeeze shut with the image of blood spurting from Kevin's throat.

"Surprise."

I blink my eyes open to find the pie sitting in front of me, the crust flaky, the gravy bubbling around the edges.

"Your eyes were shut, so I said *surprise*!" Diana teases. "I hope you were thinking of good things. Need anything else?"

Help, I think. "No, thank you," I say, noting the Diet Sprite is already on the table.

I lift my fork and jab at the crust, the warm brown gravy pouring, but all I see is the red of blood dripping from Kevin's throat. Suddenly I'm imagining Adam walking into the diner. Imagining him approaching me, smiling as if all is well. Then me standing up and waiting until he's right in front of me before I start stabbing him with the fork, over and over and over. No. No. I'd use the knife. I'd kill him with the knife. And I'd enjoy it. I'd enjoy every last second of him bleeding out. I swallow hard with the realization that both knife and fork are in my hands. My grip softens and releases, allowing each to plop to the tabletop, and I pull my hands to my lap. I wonder if this is part of the game Adam mentioned. Him finding a way to turn my fantasies into murders, murders I commit. But I will never, ever be that person.

I've been at the table for about thirty minutes when I eye the clock, aware closing cleanup is approaching. I grab my purse and head into the bathroom. My heart is pumping with fierceness, and once the door is locked, I give myself only a moment to breathe. I need to move fast. I pull the lid off the trash can, dig in the nastiness inside, and bury the dress in the bottom of it all, beneath all kinds of stinky mess. Once I wash up, I climb on the toilet, move a ceiling tile, and stick the cards and notes Adam left me there, hidden, for only my eyes. For reasons I can't explain, I have second thoughts. I retrieve the cards again and stick them back inside my purse.

I return the ceiling tile to its proper position, climb down from the toilet, and wipe the footmarks from the seat.

I scrub up again and head out of the ladies' room, sit down at my table, and, with a plan in mind, not only finish my potpie but order a slice of peach to go.

Once I'm outside walking, there's something missing. I don't feel that tingling sensation of being followed. My cellphone doesn't ring. But then I guess Adam has his hands full. He's dealing with Kevin's dead body.

Chapter Fifty-Five

Kind words can be short and easy to speak, but their echoes are truly endless.

—Mother Teresa

The cards and notes burn holes in my purse, the words on them, especially those with compliments that read as sweet, instead bear bloody marks with a lingering impact. My steps are sure, though, my decision about where to hide them, how to keep them close, to protect myself, to show Adam's intent should I need to do so, solid. Aware, though, of everyone who passes me, of every sensation of eyes on me, I push myself to hurry, hurry, and do what I must do. Hurry and just get back home.

Once I arrive at the loft, I unlock the doors and quickly enter the building, locking up behind me. I breathe out, reveling in the facade of my safe place. I only allow myself a few moments to drink in this feeling before I launch into action again. I turn to the bookstore, unlock the door, flip on the light, and enter. Thankfully the owners are old school and don't believe in cameras.

"Who wants to steal books?" Old Lady Linda, the wife of the owner, once told me when I asked, which sums up why I almost bought this place. The family doesn't appreciate the value of a good book. Not one bit.

Once I'm sealed inside, I rush to the back storage room and find a ladder. I hurry up the steps, and just as I had in the diner, I open a ceiling panel, where I place the cards. It's not the best location, but it's the safest for now. Adam won't find them. The police won't find them. I hope. And they are close, and I just feel like I need them to be close. I climb down, move the ladder to another section of the books, and dust off my hands. Glancing at my watch, it's now almost midnight. I don't even know how that happened, but it's way past time for me to go to my loft and figure out what to do next.

Without haste, I walk through the store, flip out the lights, and step into the main foyer, locking the store. I rotate and gasp as I realize I'm facing Ben, as in he's toe-to-toe with me, the scent of his musky cologne suffocating that of the leather and wear of bound books.

"What did you just do?" he demands.

"Considering I have a key and access to the store as I wish, the question is what are *you* doing here?" I manage to snap back, irritated at the tremble in my voice that no doubt complements the overabundance of adrenaline surging through my body at present.

"What I always do. Clean up."

My brow furrows. "You don't clean on Saturday night."

"And yet here I am," he says dryly. "And here you are."

Yes, I think, *yes, we are,* and that sits about as easy as an egg teetering on the edge of an uneven counter, and about as messy as when it falls hard and cracks with nasty results. "Not anymore," I say. "I'm leaving."

His lips quirk in amusement. "Running away?"

That little quip rings a little too close to the things Adam has said to me, and I don't like it, not one little bit. A drum beats in my chest, a warrior letting out a battle cry that drives me to disengage, to get the hell out of here. And I do. I step left, intending to round his big body, and rush toward the stairwell leading to my loft. His big, meaty hand comes down on the wall panel, caging me from departure. "You aren't leaving with a book," he comments. "Why are you here?"

His breath is warm on my neck, the scent of him, that of a hamburger and french fries as if he just ate, and the smell curls my stomach. "Let me go or I'll call the police."

"There are so many ways that could backfire on you, don't you think?" he challenges.

The words read like Adam's warning, and now that drumming in my chest is faster, louder. Fight or flight becomes fight, anger bubbling in my belly. "Move. *Now.*"

His lips twist, amusement in his dark eyes. His hand falls away, and against all logic, I challenge. "Where are your cleaning supplies?"

"I keep them in the store. Would you like to come back inside and I'll show you?"

"I know this is hard to believe, but I'd rather go upstairs and read a book."

"The one you didn't get in the store?"

I could pull the book in my bag out, the one with the letter opener, and feel good about that bookmark, a.k.a. weapon, but I leave well enough alone. I say nothing. I simply step around him and force myself to walk evenly toward the stairs. Once I'm around the corner, I hurry up the steps, unlock my door, and shut myself inside my apartment. I drop my purse, grab the bookmark, a.k.a. letter opener, a.k.a. weapon right about now, and search my apartment.

When I'm done, I'm aware that there is no music coming from downstairs.

I don't know why Ben is there, but it's not to clean.

I grab my MacBook and open the lid, pulling up my dating profile. I search for Adam.

His profile is missing, completely vanished.

Chapter Fifty-Six

"Be a good girl and your communication with Kevin will disappear forever, all of it." He pauses for effect and then adds, "Unless, of course, you cross me."

I spent most of the night replaying Adam's words to me, pacing and pacing some more, fingers dragging through my hair, over my hips, wrapped around my body. Randomly I pick up my phone to dial Jess or Jack and then throw the damn thing down. Anyone I tell is a liability. That's what Adam said, and I believe him. With my resources at zero, I walk up and down the stairs to recheck the locks. At several points I curse myself for not learning to shoot a gun as Jack suggested or at least installing a security system. That changes tomorrow. I'm going to ask him to borrow that extra gun he owns. And I'm going to take firearm lessons.

But then what?

I stare at my phone on the bed, which is the last spot it landed, and I wonder what happens if I call Adam. Will his line be disconnected? What if it's not? What if it is? What does any of this tell me? Could this be one big joke Kevin pulled on me? No. Of course not. Or—could it? No. No. No. I saw Kevin die. Adam killed him. And how can he make my communication with Kevin disappear? Or reappear? I'm confused. I'm devastated. I'm alone. Kevin is dead. I can't go to the police. I can't call family or friends. *What* can I do? Ultimately, I do all I *can* do, at least for now. I open a bottle of wine and start drinking. This is followed by more pacing and more drinking. Me in the shower, sitting in the corner, naked, crying, *alone*.

At some point I throw up. At another point I fall onto the bed, wrapped in a towel, hair wet, and I must black out. This assumption comes to me only when the sound of the buzzer on my front door rings intrusively, over and over and over. I jolt up, queasy and in a panic. The police are here. It's all over for me. And it should be, right? I didn't even go to the police when I saw Kevin murdered. I wrap myself in a robe and my cellphone rings. I grab it from the nightstand to find my mother calling. Not now. No. I cannot deal with her right now. I toss my phone on the bed and rush down the stairs to hit the panel buzzer. "Who is it?"

"Your mother. How long are you going to leave me standing out here?"

My forehead drops to the door panel. *No.* That's all my mind can manage. Just *no*. But there is no such answer with my mother. I hit the button again. "Come up." I unlock the door and roll to lean on the wall.

As expected, she lets herself into the loft and steps in front of me. She's in jeans and a soft red sweater, as if Adam himself dictated her wardrobe, just for a good laugh. And of course, her dark hair is silky, her makeup perfect, her lips glossy. Whoever this man is in her life who is not my father—he's doing right by her. Or maybe it's my father having the affair, and she's trying to win him back. It's all a cluttered mess in my mind right now.

"You look like shit," she announces, glancing at her watch. "Did you forget lunch?"

I blink the memory into my mind. Lunch. I promised to go home for lunch. I did promise. I really did do that. Why now, though? Why today?

"Obviously that's a yes," she says, finishing the statement with a weary sigh. "Your father's excited you're coming. He's making a feast."

In other words, there's no backing out of this. I won't let my father down. "Why are you here?" I ask instead. "I'll be there soon on my own."

"I thought I'd give you a ride. That way we can game-plan on what we plan to say to your father. I'll put on coffee. You go shower."

The buzzer on the door goes off again, and panic jackknifes through me. Who is here? *What* is here? A box with Kevin's severed head inside? Would Adam do that? I think he might. Or I'm having a psychotic break and none of this is real.

My mother's brow dips. "What's wrong with you?"

"Nothing," I say. "Nothing is wrong."

I rotate to face the wall and hit the buzzer. "Yes?"

"It's me," I hear. "Jack."

Not a severed head, at least, but oh my God, why is he here? It's not safe to be near me right now. Still, I breathe out, "Come up."

I rotate again to face my mother. "Send Jack upstairs when he gets here."

Her lips purse. "Is that appropriate?"

"Mom, I'm not going to get naked with Jack, at least not with you here in the loft."

"Seriously, Mia?"

"Mom," I chide. "We're just friends. Nothing more."

"Is he gay?"

"No," I snap. "But why would it matter if he was?"

"I'm not saying that like an insult. I'm saying that like a mother who, knowing so, would not worry that he wanted to see you naked."

I press my hand to my forehead. She didn't just say that, and yet she did. "Just send him up." I don't give her time to argue. I hurry toward the stairs, climbing to the top, to my room. Once I'm there, I hit the bathroom floor, hugging the toilet to heave again.

The next thing I know Jack is kneeling next to me. "Oh Jesus." He hands me a towel. "I take it that wine bottle by the bed didn't mix well with your mother visiting?"

"Something like that," I say, flushing the toilet and then leaning against the door.

He sits down, one leg up, the bad leg, I'm sure, which I haven't even asked him about yet. "Talk to me. You don't drink alone, not that much. That bottle is mostly gone. Why the wine?"

Words want to spill from my mouth, so many words, but I bite back the ones that really matter. "Bad date. And then that Ben guy downstairs scared me."

His brow furrows. "The one that cleans and blasts his music all the time?"

"Yes. I went to the bookstore to pick a book—the owners let me do that. It was midnight and he was there. He scared me. He's creepy."

"Why was he there?"

"He said to clean, but he didn't have his supplies. And he never played loud music, which he always does when cleaning. It was weird."

"That's it," he says firmly. "I'm bringing you my gun. I'll give you a quick rundown, but you need to take lessons."

An idea that sounded good last night. Now I feel like I might shoot somebody and end up in jail. Like I might shoot Adam. Or worse, accidentally shoot myself. "Lessons first. Gun later. Thank you. Why are you even here? What is up with your knee?"

"It feels better. You know that's how it does me. It attacks. It recedes."

"Did you get your MRI results?"

"Yep," he confirms. "The docs want me to have surgery, but I feel better, so screw that."

"You know—"

"Eventually I will have to give in," he says, holding up his hands. "All surgeons want to operate. And now that we've had this conversation, we can move on."

"Okay. I won't lecture." I study him. "Why else are you here?"

"Jess stopped by my place, bribing me with muffins to do that whole dating-site gig for her. What the hell was that? She never stops by to see me, at least not alone. She uses you as an intermediary."

"She told me she was going to go by your place, but I honestly didn't believe her."

"And you didn't warn me?"

"I didn't believe her," I repeat. "It's weird, but I guess her boss is pressuring her to finish the article, and after the Kevin thing, she didn't want me involved." Just saying Kevin's name curdles my stomach again.

"Hmm," he murmurs. "You know what I think?"

"Probably more than I'm capable of thinking right now."

"I think she wants to marry me off and turn this threesome of ours into a twosome. She likes it being just you and her."

"She and I are like sisters," I say, "but we both have lives outside each other. Especially Jess."

"Well then, test her. Tell her we're dating."

I snort. "Are you serious?"

"We've never actually tried, Mia." He shifts, uneasy, his gaze lowering and then lifting. "You know?"

"We did try. We went out. We even joke about how we had, and have, no chemistry. And how can you bring this up *right now*, of all times, when I just threw up and look like shit?"

"Maybe that's the best time."

I'm confused, a jumbled mess, but I can have only one thought: I have to keep him far away from me. He could get hurt. A plot quickly forms in my mind. "Okay. I'll make you a deal. Do the dating experiment for Jess. If you don't find a perfect woman, we'll try a date. And I promise not to throw up. I'll even shower."

He laughs. "That's the deal. I have to do Jess's experiment, and then you'll go out with me?"

I don't laugh. "I don't want to lose you as a friend."

"You won't. We're friends no matter what. Remember on *Seinfeld*? Elaine and Jerry had sex and became better friends. They just knew it didn't work for them."

"You're comparing us to a nineties sitcom? You're such a geek."

"So are you. Why is your mother here?"

"I forgot I'm going to have lunch with my parents to talk about *Lion's Den*."

"Oh. Ouch. She still doesn't know what he has going on then?"

"Nope."

"All right then. I'll leave you to your great afternoon. Need help up?"

"No," I say. "I just need to sit here a moment."

"Call me and tell me how it goes?"

I nod and wet my dry lips. "I will."

He pats my leg, a friendly gesture that still feels just that, friendly. I mean, the truth is I'm just not sure the whole dating thing isn't about that pressure his sister is putting on him over his love life. The odd thing, though, is he still didn't confess the fact that he was on the dating site and deleted his profile.

Why does that feel off to me?

I shake away the thought. I've been through this with Jack. And right now, the truth is that everything feels off to me.

His steps fade down the stairs, and a thought hits me. The news. Kevin. What is happening? I grab my phone from the floor and tab for local news, careful not to look for anything specific enough to scream: *Hey, I saw my ex get his throat sliced last night.* There is nothing worth reading. I'm not sure if I should be relieved or worried. I mean, Kevin is a loner. Sundays are gamer days. He could easily lie on his floor, stiff and dead in a pool of his own blood, all day. It won't be until he no-shows to work tomorrow that trouble brews.

Chapter Fifty-Seven

Not once in five years has my mother visited my library.

Her interest in me is limited to what she wants and what she needs that I can help her achieve.

Yet she's taken over my kitchen, where she fills a thermos with the warm, wonderful brew for me to consume on the ride to my parents' place. Once we're in her car, I sip the concoction, and I'm pleasantly surprised. She's mixed hazelnut coffee, one of my favorite home flavors, with just the right amount of cream and Splenda. She's a smart woman. She knows more about me than she lets on. She keeps tools in her arsenal and uses them only as she needs them.

For herself.

"About your father," she begins, a stoplight away from my loft and three sips into my heavenly beverage.

"He doesn't want to do the show, Mom."

"And I certainly understand why, but—"

"We have to allow the people in our lives to be the people they are and accept them as they are," I say, and not without the bitterness of a little girl whose mother tried to dictate her future.

"You also cannot allow someone you love to fall off the proverbial bicycle and live in fear of getting back on it. You dust yourself off and get back on the bike. We've let him live in fear."

My defenses flare on his behalf. "Maybe he has another approach to getting on the bike again."

"This show could change his life."

"You mean *your* life?" I challenge.

"We share a life," she snaps. "Something I hope one day you'll understand."

And yet they don't share a life, I think. At least not the one my mother assumes they share. My father is doing one thing and telling her another. I don't know if she deserves such behavior or if he's the one out of line. At some point, does a daughter have a role to mediate with her parents, or is she out of line? It's confusing, too confusing for someone who just witnessed a murder and has no idea when her stalker—and Adam *is* a stalker—will reappear. As if I've willed him into existence, my phone buzzes with a text message.

I dig it from my pocket, and my lips curl around my teeth, my stomach locking up as I read: Morning, Mia. Don't worry about anything. That spill washed right up, never to be seen again. I'll take care of it all. What are you doing today?

I just stare at the message. And stare some more.

"Honey?" my mother asks. "Is everything okay?"

I wet my dry lips. "Yes." I glance over at her. "Yes. Of course."

But I'm already reading Adam's message again. How can he act as if nothing happened? And what is he telling me? That Kevin is gone, never to be seen, or found, again?

Mia? he prods.

I have to reply, I tell myself. If I don't, who knows who he'll kill. I quickly type: Going to my parents' place for lunch.

His reply is as quick and sharp as the blade he used to kill Kevin: And how are you going to take control of the situation with your mother?

Panic punishes me, heat burning my cheeks. I told him she was cheating on my father. Is he threatening her for her perceived sins the way he did Kevin? Is he trying to get rid of any problem in my life, even the normal ones all of us live with, like family squabbles? I hate the way he forces me to engage with him as if we were still just as we were before, prospective dates, but I quickly reply with: I'm not sure everything is what it seems. She appears really worried about him. I think he might be trying to surprise her with his success.

Interesting, he replies. Call me tonight and tell me all about it.

It's not a casual text like that one from Jess or Jack, who just care and want to know more. This message is a threat. Call or else.

Chapter Fifty-Eight

My mother pulls us into the driveway of the family home, and that weeping willow tree drags and sways against the pull of a windy day, a reminder of that night when I'd felt someone was here, watching the house. Watching me. Chills run down my spine, and I hug myself with the certainty that, yes, someone was watching me, and that someone was Adam.

When will he want to meet in person? When will I be forced to face him, kiss him, even touch him, just to stay alive? None of these things are options, and yet I am more captive now to him than I ever was to my own fears and insecurities.

My mother pulls the sedan into the garage of the family home and kills the engine. "Please tell me you will at least try to talk sense into your father." She glances over at me. "If he comes out on top this time, all his hard work pays off. Finally he will see his worth. He will believe in himself."

There is something in her voice, raw and raspy with emotion. She really is worried about him. She loves him. I don't know why I doubted that. I really never did. I just thought—I don't know what I thought. I guess it was more about them breaking down and falling apart over his self-induced hermit condition, which, she's right, isn't healthy. It's like not getting back on the bike. Or did he? He does have a new path to success. I'm confused by what is going on with the two of them and emotionally twisted in ways that I'm not sure will allow me to discover answers.

For now, I do what I can. I glance over at her and say, "What if he's humiliated again? Does he even come back from that?"

"I believe in him more than that. Don't you?"

It hits me that maybe, just maybe, she believes in him more than I do, and that carves a hole in my heart. I should be his biggest cheerleader. I'm not sure I have been. Maybe she has, and she simply isn't enough for him anymore, after all he went through. That idea twists me into knots. "I'll talk to him," I promise.

She surprises me and squeezes my hand. "Thank you. He's really shut me out." She sucks in a breath. "I don't know how to deal with it." She pulls back and grips the steering wheel, and in a rare confession she admits, "It hurts."

Vulnerability.

Raw, real, and uncalculated.

I don't know if ever in my entire life my mother has shown me that emotion, let alone been as real with me as she is now.

A ping in my chest comes with a question. Was my father so low after *Lion's Den* that he was thrown into a midlife crisis, and he is the one who sought outside attention? Is that where the confidence to say no to *Lion's Den* came from?

I don't know the answers, but I know one thing: if I don't have them when I talk to Adam later tonight, there will be consequences. But the answers I seek are not from Adam. They are from my parents. To bring them together again. To ensure their happiness. To keep them safe.

Chapter Fifty-Nine

A dysfunctional family is any family with more than one person.

—Mary Karr

My mother and I find my father in the kitchen, holding his famous lasagna with two big puffy pot holders covering his hands and a grin on his face. "Cholesterol be damned," he says. "It's been too long since I had you both here together."

Whose cholesterol? I wonder. His or hers, but I set that aside and focus on the bigger picture.

For instance, my father is cheerful, smiling, his hair in that mad scientist mussed-up mess that makes my father my father, but there is more, too. There is something under the surface of his happiness, a forced presence that reads like a secret. An easy read from me, the master of secrets these days. Oddly, though, so very oddly for me, more complex is the fact that my simple father *is complex* enough for me to wonder if he has one secret or perhaps more than one?

In that moment, I regret not calling Jess and checking in on my father's bidding war, but as she said, Why would she know anything? She just hooked my father up with an attorney.

"Just in time," my father announces, setting the hot plate down and removing his pot-holder gloves.

I round the counter and hug him. "Hiya, Dad," I greet, tilting my chin up to inspect him.

His brow furrows. "Hi, baby. What's wrong?"

"I'm about to indulge in your lasagna. What could be wrong?"

He studies me a moment and purses his lips. "Okay," he says softly, running his hand up and down my arm. "We'll get to it over the strawberry shortcake."

The next hour is what I would describe as a holiday with the Griswolds, minus squirrels in trees and fires. We're all together, our little family, and there is chitchat, but it's as awkward as a holiday word game where some family member makes up words that don't really exist. Or like the entire conversation is a Wordle puzzle, and no one knows the answer, so they just say random stuff.

The first moment of relief comes when my mother happily allows me and my father to retreat to his man cave. "Take your strawberry shortcakes and enjoy your father-daughter time," she offers a bit too agreeably, considering she's, well, her. And she's never really that agreeable at all.

A few minutes later, my father and I are settled in the cozy sitting area of his mad, brilliant scientist lab, indulging in our desserts when he says, "What's wrong with my daughter?"

It's as if I'm in the midst of a hurricane, in the calm eye of the storm, in a safe place where I could tell him everything. But then what? Destruction? Devastation. I know him. He acts on my behalf, and in doing so, could he become a "liability" as per Adam? My father has always been my rock, the person I love most in this world, which is exactly why his life matters more than mine.

I settle the bowl of deliciousness on top of the table and angle toward him. "I'm worried about you," I reply, speaking the truth if not the whole truth. "What is going on with your bidding war? And why are you not telling Mom? And why didn't you tell me about the *Lion's Den* offer?"

His expression tightens, and he sets his dessert on the table as well. "Your mother." His fingers are laced together, his gaze fixed forward, not on me. "I thought she was having an affair."

My insides twist and turn. "And?" The question comes out in a barely there whisper.

"I hired a PI." He glances over at me. "She's not, and now I feel like shit for having her investigated."

She's not.

I let that sink in.

It feels good.

It also feels accurate.

"Why do you think you were suspicious?"

"I was made a fool of on *Lion's Den*. I was hardly a man. Of course she wants a man. All women want a real man, not a fool."

I'm officially gutted, just gutted, hurting for him. "Dad—"

He holds up a hand and looks at me. "It's a thing, baby girl, and you know it. A woman wants to know her man is a man."

I'd push back on that, remind him that friendship, and love, are what matters, but he's in a headspace that is his alone, and right now he's letting me in that space. I need to let him talk and guide him to share more. "Is the potential affair why you're hiding the bidding war from her? Because she knows something is off between you. So much so she even told me."

"No," he says in a surprising dismissal of this idea. "Nothing like that. I wanted to surprise her, show her that her man came through and in a big way."

"Mom and I have our issues, Dad, but we connect on one thing: you. She loves you. You have nothing to prove to her."

"But I want to," he says. "I need to do this for her. And for me."

"Okay. I understand. But you need to know that she's pressuring me to get you on *Lion's Den* again. She believes you will rock their world. That's how much she believes in you. And I really wish you would have warned me about that whole situation. I was sideswiped when she told me about it."

"I should have warned you." He squeezed my leg. "I'm sorry."

"What is going on with that, Dad? Why aren't you telling her?"

He runs a rough hand through his hair. "It's complicated. Big Davis, that asshole from *Lion's Den*, is now bidding on my patent."

I blink. "What? Are you kidding me?"

"I wish I was. He's bullying the other bidders, threatening to pull out of other deals he has in the works with several key players. The asshole seems to have his hand in everything."

My brow dips. "Why does he want it? What is really going on here?"

"You know why. He made a fool of me. I can't be a winner now."

"Surely it's not that simple. That's an expensive I told you so."

"You're right. It's not," he confirms. "He wants to kill my patent because it hurts another product line he's involved in. In other words, your mother and I will get paid and paid well, but the work I did gets buried. It's not the ending I was looking for."

"Is there nothing the attorney can do?"

"He's trying. And I can say this—Jess hooked me up with the right guy. If anyone can fix it, he can."

"Why are you being pushed to do *Lion's Den*?" I ask. "Is that some game he's playing with you?"

"The attorney thinks he just hopes I'll want to save face and go on the show to get the press. The attorney also thinks that would be a foolish decision on my part." He looks me in the eyes. "I'll talk to Mom," he states again. "I didn't mean to put that pressure on you."

"You're sure about the affair? I mean her new boss—"

"No affair. I even had her followed at the recent convention. Nothing happened. Not even close. But I don't want her to know I didn't trust her. Please don't tell her what I did."

"My lips are sealed." I zip my finger across my mouth.

"I know they are, baby girl." He motions to my dessert. "Eat. You love strawberry shortcake, and so do I."

We both pick up our desserts, but he's not focused on strawberries and whipped cream. He's focused on me. "What's new in your life?"

In my head, I say everything I want to say. My ex was murdered in front of me last night, throat sliced, and now I'm being held captive by a madman, but what I say is, "Good books. Always good books." I leave it at that, and he lets me, when I know he knows there's more. I just don't think he has the capacity to truly worry about me right now. He needs me to be okay. He needs to believe my life is still just books, and more books. Without haste, I finish my dessert, and then I say my goodbyes to both my parents. It's time for my mother and father to talk.

Without me.

On the Uber ride home, my anger is palpable. That jerk Big Davis from *Lion's Den* is pure evil.

He ranks right up there with Adam. He really does. He destroys lives. If anyone deserved to die, it was him, not Kevin. And I didn't even like Kevin in the end. I just didn't want him to die.

Chapter Sixty

Once I'm inside my Uber, headed home, I dial Jess, needing to vent over Big Davis, the ultimate jerk of *Lion's Den*, but I end up in her voicemail. Next up is Jack, and he, too, doesn't answer. I want to scream in frustration, but my Uber driver probably would not appreciate my voice, even with a trade-off of a large tip.

I arrive at my loft while the bookstore is still open—of course it's open. It's Sunday and one of their biggest sales days. With my lips pressed together, I hesitate in the foyer that leads to the store or the steps to my loft, contemplating Ben showing up here last night. The entire situation was strange, and I consider entering the store and mentioning this to the owners, but thus far they're pro Ben. He can do no wrong. For all I know, he's a family member of some sort. Honestly, I don't know why I've never asked that question. I don't know a lot of things right now. I'm also not exactly in the best of moods to deal with them and not sure I'd handle myself well. Not to mention, I don't really need to be talking about my late arrival home last night with anyone, when Kevin died last night. While I watched. *Oh God, Kevin.* How have I not even thought of his death—no, his *murder*—in hours?

I hurry up the stairs and stop dead in my tracks at the landing. There's another box sitting in front of my loft door. *Another box. Another red ribbon.* My hands go to the top of my head. "No. No. No." All I can think of is that this is another dress, meant to be worn to yet another murder event. Or maybe this time this really is Kevin's severed head. This is, really actually, an insane thought. Of course it's not Kevin's head. It's not.

That was in a movie. I can't even remember the movie. Brad Pitt was in it, I think. Or maybe it was a book. But, damn it, right now it doesn't feel like all things fiction are really fiction at all, not anymore. Not for me.

I pace back and forth, resisting the idea of touching the box, opening it, even looking at it, but what can I do? *What can I do?* If I don't open it, maybe that's what makes him kill again. Maybe that's what sends him over the edge, as if he's not already there. I step around the damn box, unlock the door, and draw in a hard-earned breath. Pressing fingers to my forehead, I accept what cannot be avoided. I rotate and pick up the box, which is larger than the last, heavier, too, and struggle to lug it inside. I dump my purse and the box on the kitchen island, with my phone next to both.

"Oh my God, I might have to become a drinker," I murmur, willing my heart to stop trying to jump out of my chest. I swear I'd go see a doctor and ask for some good drugs to calm me down—I really need help right now, truly, I do—but Adam might kill him or her as well. Too queasy to consider wine anyway, I just stand there, staring at the box. There is also a lot of running fingers through my hair and pressing my hands onto my face. Finally I just do it. I work the ribbon off the box, puff out a breath, and lift the lid.

There don't appear to be any obvious body parts inside.

This only delivers a small degree of relief.

There's a bottle of champagne and another box inside. Who knows what is in that box. Of course there is a card on top of it all that simply reads: "Mia."

Oh, how I wish this man would forget my name. The Invisible Girl was so much kinder to me than this man knowing my name. My hand trembles as I reach for the card, and somehow I manage to open it to read:

The champagne is to toast a new beginning, your new beginning. The dress is for you to wear tomorrow. It will look beautiful on you. Move forward, Mia. Show me you can do this for yourself, so I don't have to do it for you.

Call me.

—Adam

Okay, so the unopened box is also not a body part. There is that. I grab hold of the small reprieve from my worst fear and cling to it.

The champagne is Veuve Clicquot, my favorite, which he knows because I told him. I told him so much, *too much*, about myself. And what are we celebrating? My new beginning? What does that even mean at this point? What did killing off my ex-boyfriend do for this new beginning? I mean, sure, he was an asshole, but the world is filled with assholes. Life goes on.

Except for Kevin.

He's gone.

Forever.

I literally force myself to reach for the second box, which I set on the island next to the bigger box. I lift the lid to find an olive-and-black-and-white tweed dress with diamond shapes mixing up the colors. There's a matching thick black belt. There are boots to match. Expensive boots. I can tell just from looking at them. I check the labels. The dress. The boots. The belt. They all bear the Chanel brand. And they're beautiful—truly they are—but I would feel ugly wearing them, wearing anything this man gifted me. Not only that—Jess would know Chanel from a mile away.

How would I explain owning items I cannot afford?

My cellphone rings, and I all but jump out of my skin. The caller ID, of course, reads "Adam." Why do I even have his name still in my caller ID? But then, what do I call him? Killer? Crazy man? Stalker? I could delete him altogether, but obviously that will do me no good. He'll call. I could block him. Then he might just kill again, maybe even me.

With that thought, I grab my phone, hit the record button, and answer on speaker. "Hello."

"You got the gifts I left?" he asks.

My lips press together. I'm no fool. This is his way of telling me that he knows I'm home right now. "Stalker" might just be the right name for him after all. "I just opened the boxes," I confirm. "It's too much, Adam. I can't accept such expensive gifts."

"I told you, Mia, I'm going to help you change your life."

By killing people? I want to scream at him, but he's already talking again.

"The shock you just went through was necessary," he states. "Just like my car accident was for me. This was, *is*, supposed to push you forward, not push you backward. You take control. Then I won't have to take it for you. Understand?"

It's not a gentle question. It's not a question at all. It's a demand. "I'm taking control of my life, Adam," I assure him, mustering a strong voice I barely know as my own. "I don't need you to do this for me."

"Wear the outfit tomorrow. Wear your hair down. Show me you're in control. Show me you know you're worthy."

I want to ask—worthy of what?—but my gut says that is one of those pass/fail questions that ends in me being given a big fat fail. "My friend Jess will know Chanel from a mile away."

"Good. You deserve it. If she's a good friend, she'll think so as well."

"She knows I can't afford it."

"Tell her you have a new boyfriend."

"She'll want to meet you," I counter.

"Then set it up."

I blanch. He wants to meet Jess? He wants to be that much a part of my life. "I haven't met you."

"Haven't you?" he challenges.

He means last night. I think. I don't know, but if he wants to come out of the shadows, I will have Jess on my side. Then Jess and I will figure out how to get rid of him. God, I need Jess right now. "When?"

He avoids that question altogether, instead ordering me, "Pour some champagne. Settle on your couch, then tell me what happened with your parents."

On my couch? What does he know of my couch? Has he been here? Are there cameras in my loft? Terror rips through me, as he seems to read my mind and adds, "And, Mia, keep in mind that I know things. I can erase facts. I can find facts. I can see and hear what you think I can't see or hear. You understand?"

Those words again. *You understand?*

I don't like them. Not one little bit.

And really? He wants me to just talk to him like nothing has changed, like we're still in a new relationship. "I can't open the bottle myself. It has to wait until you actually come over."

"Are you inviting me?"

No, I think, but something feels off, something in the way he speaks as if he's willing to be outed, to show himself, but he avoids actually doing so. This idea sends a rush of bravery through me and drives me to press him. "Would you come if I wanted you to?"

He's silent a beat that becomes three and then says, "Not yet. Go sit. Let's talk."

He's watching me. I know he's watching me, and I don't know what to do about it. There is a camera somewhere. Maybe many cameras. For now I must simply comply with his command. Stiffly, slowly, I pick up my phone from the counter, walk to the couch, and sink into the cushion. I start to question my paranoia. Maybe I told him that this is my spot to chat. It *is* my spot to chat. It's where I spent hours just talking to him. Maybe. I hope. Actually I'm not hopeful at all.

Especially when he seems to know when I'm sitting. "Tell me about what happened at your parents' place."

"My mother isn't cheating. My father feels bad about mistrusting her."

"How does he know she's innocent?"

"He hired someone to follow her." As surely as I say the words, I wonder if Adam is the man he hired. Could that be how he came to know me? To obsess over me?

"Why did he suspect her if she's not guilty?" he asks.

"He doesn't feel manly. He feels he let her down." The words flow easily, words that protect my parents, that keep them off his radar if my father wasn't actually the one who put us all there anyway.

"After the *Lion's Den* issue," he assumes, aware of this topic from our many talks.

"Yes," I confirm, and my anger flares, but not at Adam. All that happened today flows back to me, with nowhere but here, with Adam, to vent. "My father has a patent going to auction. That asshole from *Lion's Den* is trying to stop anyone from buying it, so he can bury it. It's good for the world's energy use, but it's bad for his business. He even tried to get my father back on *Lion's Den* to humiliate him again, I know. To destroy the project that is a winner."

"Does your father have an attorney?"

"Yes. Jess got him connected with a really good one that she uses. Now he'll likely go to war with Big Davis, but Big Davis is a billionaire. Those people are hard to beat. My father thinks, in the end, he will earn a big payout, but if Big Davis is involved, or anyone with a personal motivation that doesn't include taking this product to market, his product will be closeted. It won't be world changing. He's worked all his life to make a difference in the world. And did I mention he wants to make my mom proud? He doesn't know she already is. She so is. I was so very wrong to doubt her. When I saw her tonight, when we talked, I saw her pride in my father, her support."

"But you don't think any of this is enough?" Adam presses.

"What if Big Davis finds a way to screw my father all over again? I don't know if either of my parents will survive that." I pant out a breath. "I, ah, I guess I had a lot to say."

But at least it was just words, I think, and safe words at that. Not even Adam can touch Big Davis.

"What are you going to do to help your father?" he asks. "What are you going to do to take control?"

"What can I do?"

"Ask your father to take you to one of the meetings with the attorney. Speak up. Take control, Mia."

It's not bad advice, I realize, despite who it's coming from—that is, until he adds, "So I don't have to. That's the lesson. Take control so I don't have to."

"I'll set the meeting," I promise, and when I might argue I can't make a difference, I know in my heart, as my parents' daughter, I can. By being there. By protecting them. By, as he said, speaking up.

"Good," he approves. "Call your father now and call me back."

"Are you serious?"

"I'm always serious, Mia. You should know that by now. Call me back." He disconnects.

I swallow hard. I'm being ordered around—no, I'm a puppet and Adam holds the strings. But that doesn't change the fact that I like the idea of going to see the attorney with my father. I punch in my father's number. He answers on the first ring. "Honey. Miss me already?"

"When do you see the attorney again?"

"Tomorrow afternoon. Why?"

"Can I go? And just offer support and give you my feelings on the situation?"

"If you can tolerate your mother. She's going as well."

"You told her."

"I told her. She's relieved to know what is going on. And as you said, she claims to be proud of me no matter what."

"I'm glad. I knew that. I wish you knew that, too. What time is the appointment?"

"Four. Can you make it?"

"Yes. I'll be there. Text me the address."

"You got it. Love you bunches."

"Love you, too." We disconnect.

Almost immediately my phone rings with Adam's number. He's monitoring my calls. He has to be. "Hello," I answer.

"Wear the dress tomorrow."

"I told you, if I see Jess, Jess will know the brand and—"

"Tell her about me and the gift, Mia. Contrary to what you may think, I'm not hiding. And neither are you anymore. Good night, Mia."

With that, he disconnects.

Chapter Sixty-One

If you cannot be positive, then at least be quiet.

—*Joel Osteen*

While I'd normally linger in my loft, enjoy my coffee and a little me time, this morning I can't escape my place, my once-happy little place, fast enough. I'm out of my door, down the stairs, and on the sidewalk in a blink, as if a public place allows me to somehow become invisible again. I'm not sure I'll ever be invisible again. I witnessed a murder. I didn't report it.

I'm not me anymore. Not a me I recognize.

Eagerly merging with the bustle of morning walkers, I check the news yet again. Still nothing to note, not that I expected there would be. Kevin hasn't even no-showed to work yet. I'm almost to the coffee shop when my phone buzzes with a text message, and dread fills me with the certainty that it's from Adam. And, of course, it is: You look beautiful, Mia. Get rid of the glasses next. And remember: don't turn Jess into a liability. Tell the truth. We met on the dating app. We can't get enough of each other. We are always on the phone. I'm a man who wants to spoil you.

I halt and stop dead in my tracks, swallowing against the bile in my throat. He's watching me right now. He's here, somewhere in the crowd. He is *always* here.

Feeling as if I might hyperventilate, I slowly breathe in and out, and then I place one foot in front of the other, almost as if I'm a robot.

I'm being trained to be his robot, his puppet, his submissive. All these terms and words play in my mind, taunt me, promise me my future is this, his. I'm his slave. I'm Adam's Eve. Lord, help me, and I mean that literally. I need help.

I arrive at the coffee bar earlier than expected, but Jess is already present. She waves me down from a booth, motioning to the coffees already on the table in front of her. And here we go. Me, looking like another version of me, that Jess will have plenty to say about. Nerves do this little tap dance in my belly as I approach her.

She greets me on her feet, and with several gaping once-overs. "Okay, wow. You're in Chanel, girl. Your hair is down. You look *stunning*. I've literally begged you to let me give you a makeover, and you shunned me. *How* did this happen?"

I motion to the table. "I need coffee."

"Okay," she says. "But I need answers."

"Coffee. Answers."

She nods and we slide into our seats. "Talk," she orders. "Did your dad get that big payout for his work already and treat you? No," she says, rejecting that idea as quickly as she's spoken it, her brows dipping, "No," she repeats. "No way that happened this quickly, and this is more than that anyway. There's a transformation to you beyond the clothes."

"There is something," I say, the lies I'm about to tell burning on my tongue and lips. "I met a guy. A civil engineer. He just—wants to spoil me."

"Wait. *What?* And I don't know about this? Who the hell is he?"

"It happened fast. He was the cartoon guy on the dating app."

"The one who upset you?"

"I think it was more like him being the male version of you. He basically told me I needed to break out of my shell."

"But not as nicely as that."

"No. You're right. He was far pricklier about it than that, and he did upset me, but it also hit a nerve. Let's just say, he drove home your years of preaching."

"Okay. Maybe. I don't know. I don't feel comfortable with this. He's the *cartoon guy*. He literally used a cartoon character as his photo, which shouldn't be allowed. You don't even know what he looks like."

"I do. We did the whole video thing. He's actually really good looking." *Which is true,* I add silently. He *is* good looking. He's also crazy, but I leave that part out. "So much so," I add, still talking about his appearance, "that it felt like a joke that he was interested in me. He was the one leaving me the notes, by the way. He recognized me from the dating app."

"Hmm," she says, sipping her coffee. "I'd really hoped this was more romantic than creepy. Now I'm not sure what I think."

Go, Jess, I think. Thank you for being right there with me, even if you don't know you're right there with me, right now.

"On the bright side," she says. "You can now be a part of my dating-app story." She waves that off. "Or not. I'm unsettled by all of this. I'm just—I can't believe you didn't tell me."

"It's—this thing with him—it's only a week old. You've been busy, and I worried it was a joke."

"And that means what? We are us. We figure things out together. You didn't even tell me he existed."

"Well, I am now. I'm talking to you now. I'm telling you about him now. He even wants to meet you."

"He who? You haven't even spoken his name."

"Adam. Adam wants to meet you."

"And that's a hell yeah to a meetup. I need to assess this man. I mean, he has good taste in clothes, but those are some expensive gifts he's throwing your way after only one week. That feels a little fast and off. Then again, men can be that way." She holds up a hand. "Don't let me be a Debbie Downer. I'm happy for you. When can I meet him?"

"I'll see what I can work out." Eager to just get past the lies, I change the topic. "Speaking of the dating-app story, you actually went to Jack's place?"

"I told you I was. I'm desperate to get this article done. And by the way, his knee seemed just fine. Was he lying and just taking sick time?"

"Why do you always think the worst of him?" I challenge. "His pain comes and goes. That's the way bad knees can be, and he had an MRI. His doc wants him to have surgery. And by the way, I don't know what you said to him, but you must have scared him. He actually suggested he and I go on a date."

Her eyes go wide. "*What?* I scared him into asking you out? That is the most illogical thing I've ever heard." I open my mouth to speak and she holds up a finger. "Let's tell it how it really is. This new guy showers you with gifts and pulls you out of your shell, and Jack wants to date you now? How many times have I said it? Jack doesn't sit right with me."

"First, Jack doesn't know about Adam. And he wasn't serious about the dating thing. He's just afraid you want to marry him off, and then it's just you and me again."

"This is on me now?" She rolls her eyes. "Good grief. I have a life. He does not. I date and I'm thrilled you're dating. There is something off about Jack."

"He's a good friend, Jess. Be a good friend to me by being one to him."

She purses her lips. "He agreed to do the dating-app story for me, so I'm obligated to you and him." She waves off the topic and adds, "Enough about Jack. Tell me about your father."

I fill her in on what I know so far and end with, "I don't understand why my father wouldn't just reject anything involving Big Davis?"

She grimaces. "I fear he's trouble, Mia. I'm shocked but happy you're going to the meeting with the attorney. I'd offer to go as well, but I'm quite sure your mother wouldn't appreciate it."

My brow furrows. "Why do you say that?"

"I'm not really family, and she barely tolerates her own daughter."

I flinch and she grabs my hand. "Sorry. Raw nerve. Forget I said that. Back to the meeting. Let's talk strategy."

"I'm all ears. Throw me some good words."

"*You* be the lion in the room. Make everyone in the meeting focus on how dangerous Big Davis truly can be to a positive outcome of this negotiation. I know you can do it."

"Because I'm such a good negotiator and do it all the time?"

"Because you, my dear, are smart, and that, with the love you have for your father, is magic. Meanwhile, I'll make some calls and see if I can find someone who has something on Big Davis we can use, but I make no promises I'll find anything."

"You know I don't like to play dirty."

"That man humiliated your father. We both know he'll do it again if he gets the chance. He plays in the devil's sandbox and has fun. Remember who you're dealing with. The Bible says an eye for an eye. God told you that, not me. And no, I'm not being literal. I'm not suggesting you go poke the guy's eye out, but my point here is that you also can't wave a library book at him and get him to back down."

"Then what do I do?"

"In a perfect world, this project makes him money, the attorney writes a tight contract, and everyone gets rich."

"That's not going to happen. This product my dad created actually hurts his other projects, or so I hear. Again, I'm back to not knowing why he doesn't understand this potential business relationship to be the problem that it is."

"That's where you have to create leverage of some type. The attorney I hooked your father up with is a killer. That's why he's my attorney. But I'll see what I can dig up as well. It's important to know your opponent and know them well."

Killer.

Does she really have to use that word right now?

Guilt stabs at me. I actually wished Big Davis dead over Kevin.

What is Adam doing to me? Who am I becoming?

Chapter Sixty-Two

Jess and I exit the coffee shop and hug goodbye, promising to chat later in the day about Big Davis. Her choice of the word *killer* is still in my head, a broken record playing over and over in which I am as guilty of killing Kevin as is Adam by simply watching and doing nothing. By remaining silent out of fear of what the consequences of telling the truth might bring upon me. But my worry isn't about me, I justify in my mind. It's about what Adam might do to others, to people I love and care about, to anyone at all, really. Anyone. Kevin was wiped off this earth, deemed no more important than lint on a sweater, unworthy of continuing.

It's still early when I walk into the library, riding the escalators toward floor three and clinging to habit, to anything that feels familiar, therefore right and normal. I turn to survey what is below me now. The man that I've often seen on floor two is not present, but this is no surprise at this early hour; however, some part of my mind wonders for a fleeting moment if he's Adam. I dismiss this ridiculous idea, as I've seen Adam. He looks nothing like the man who I swear frequents floor two and waits for me, watches for me. Also a silly concept. That man has not been here watching me. Certainly if he was he'd be on floor three where I work, anyway.

I've just entered the office I share with Jack when he walks in. As we do most mornings, we unburden ourselves of our personal items and then turn to face one another.

"Holy Batman," he declares, reminding me what I don't know how I ever forget. He's a comic geek. "You look like Gotham on fire," he adds.

"Is that good?" I ask, laughing despite all that is going on in my world right now. Because that's me with Jack, I remind myself. He has a way of always making me feel lighter, better, more like myself—and right now that's especially golden.

"Well, it's not good if it's actually burning down," he explains, "but if it's all lit up and burning bright for a hot city night, yes, it's good. And that's what you look like. A hot Gotham city night."

"Well thank you," I say. "I always wanted to look like a hot Gotham city night."

We share a laugh I'd have thought impossible for me a few minutes ago, before he asks, "What's with all the change?"

Lies.

That is the word now lodged in my brain like a sliver of glass, slowly peeling away all the good that is me and leaving nothing but the kind of bad I do not want to know as me at all.

Because that's what his question demands I answer with—more lies. Lies I do not want to tell. So I don't. I just don't. I continue to cling to all the truths I can find, holding on to them as if my fingers cling to the ledge of a window, and if I let go of those truths, I, too, am as dead as Kevin. "I told you about the guy who commented on me changing photos on the dating app, right?"

"Yeah, you did. He told you that you were afraid to be the girl in photo number one, right?"

"Yes. Exactly. I'm telling you, that got to me." *Oh boy how it got to me,* I silently add. "I didn't enjoy his comments, but from the eyes of a stranger, sometimes we see the truth. I need to be braver. I'm trying."

"Yes, well, speaking of being brave." He studies me a moment, that weird, awkward thing we've had some of lately back between us. "When I said we should—"

"Date?" I supply, not at all shy with Jack as I am with other men, but no matter how we might wish it to be so, we don't snap, crackle, and pop, as I once heard my mother describe what she felt when she met my father.

Jack knows this.

We both know this.

Dating will right no wrong but rather create wrong where all is right.

"Yes," he confirms. "That. I don't want to lose our friendship, Mia. I was just—"

"Feeling pushed out by Jess?" I ask, but I'm really repeating what he told me himself.

"Yeah. Exactly."

"Never," I say. "We're friends for life, Jack." I think of the way he felt it necessary to delete his dating profile, without telling me about it, and add, "I'd like to feel I can cheer you on when you date, rather than have you feel like it means I'm not part of your life anymore, and vice versa. I mean, it will change us some, I know, if either of us finds that someone special, but it doesn't have to end us. And you do know that Jess dates, right? Believe you me, if she found the right man, we'd be planning a wedding."

"I'm not sure Jess is capable of that kind of intimacy. There's something cold about her, detached. Nobody will ever be good enough for her but you."

"Okay, that sounds like some stalker roommate movie, and that is not me and Jess. That comment is coming from the weird combative thing you two live by." I move on to something far more important right now. *Him.* I haven't given him enough attention, and as a friend, a real, true-blue friend, he deserves that I do. I point to his tie. "No pin again. You're in pain. Are you trying to hide it so I won't push you into surgery?"

"Actually, no." He smirks down at his offending tie, lifting it. "I can't believe I did that again."

"What's going on with you?" I press. "Is it more than the knee?"

"Maybe it's the wedding," he says, dropping the tie. "My sister and the dating thing has really started to get under my skin."

I think of Adam, and I do so with the icy certainty of disapproval of my attending that wedding as Jack's date, but I still say, "You've got me. We'll get through it together."

My phone buzzes on my desk and I rotate to answer it. "Mia Anderson."

"Mia, it's Kara. I need you to come down to my office." She hesitates. "Now."

I blink at the tone in her voice, which is both urgent and rather ominous. "Okay. I'll be right there." I disconnect, twisting around to face Jack, a hand pressed to the knifing sensation in my belly.

"What was that?" he asks.

"Kara wants to see me, and there was something uncomfortable in her tone. I'm telling you, the fallout of my bad presentation is still coming at me."

"Oh come on, Mia. She told you everything was fine."

"She said 'now' in this voice filled with dread."

"Now?"

I replay the conversation with him. "I need to see you. She paused, a heavy pause, and then, *now.*"

"You do know you're working yourself into a frenzy over nothing, right? There's an auditorium booking issue. There always is. That's all this is. You'll need to fix it with that magic you always work."

I inhale and nod. "Right. You're right. There is always a glitch, and I always fix it."

"So go fix it and get back here to work. I'll go put on a pot of coffee," he offers. "It'll be waiting when you get back."

"Thanks, Jack."

He pats my arm. “I got your back. You got mine.”

With his comforting words and support, I hurry out of the office, eager to just find out what the heck is going on. Once I’m on the escalator, I’m lost in my own head, unaware of all the happenings in the library that once brought me joy. I certainly don’t even look for the man on floor two. I’m replaying the call with Kara, then the exchanges with Adam, even the gift boxes at my door. I’m in the zoo of floor one as the front doors open and a horde of people piles in through the entrances. I’m at Kara’s door before they even have time to consume the librarians and inundate them with questions.

Her door is open and I poke my head inside. Kara is on her phone but motions me forward. She ends her call rather abruptly and rounds the desk, meeting me in the middle of the room and giving me a once-over. “Look at you,” she approves. “You look ready to take on the world.”

There’s an uneasy vibe to her that, in turn, makes me uneasy. “Why do I feel that’s a necessary place to be right now?”

“There is nothing here we can’t handle.”

I’m queasy. “What does that mean?”

“It means that Neil wants to place Akia in the role of auditorium coordinator. I told him absolutely not. You’re my girl.”

I swear the floor sways. “Because of the presentation?”

“He overreacts to the smallest of things.”

“That’s a yes. And he’s the boss. And Akia—I mean he—and I—and—”

Her hands come down on my shoulders. “You fought me when I wanted you to take this job, but it’s yours, and you don’t want to let it go. I know that. You need the money. I know that, too, and you deserve the raise the job offered you. I’m having a meeting with Neil today. I’m going to put my foot down. If you’d like to attend, I invite you to do so.”

“He’s known Akia for years. And he likes Akia. Do you know Akia had the nerve to comfort me after seeing Neil talk down to me?”

"Akia is, well, Akia. He's not a guy I'd recommend you trust. Do you want to attend the meeting?"

"I can do that?"

"Of course you can. This is about you as much as it is me."

"What time is it?"

"Four."

My heart sinks. "My father has a major patent going out to auction. I was going to ask to go to the attorney's office with him today at, of course, four. Can we do the meeting sooner? Or tomorrow?"

"First, and most importantly, congrats to your father, Mia. I know that *Lion's Den* situation was a real mess. I cried for you, and your family, when I saw it happen on live TV. As for moving the meeting, I doubt it. But I will try. And I'm your biggest advocate. I'll handle this if I need to handle it on my own. I'll let you know in the next hour. No matter what, go support your father."

"I'm worried, Kara. I do need this money. And I've worked hard. The presentation was a mess, but the work behind it was solid."

"I know that."

"Then why is he doing this? Because I made him look bad?"

"Perception is not always reality."

"He thinks I made him look bad," I repeat, pressing for confirmation.

"It doesn't matter what he thinks. As you said, your work, and mine, is solid. We got this. Neil is a moron, and I may or may not deny saying that depending on how much he pisses me off. Heck, I may say it to his face. More soon."

I nod slowly and back away.

I'm shell-shocked when I exit her office. Akia stabbed me in the back. That's exactly what happened, and I'm surprised at how easily anger materializes and burns like hot coals in my belly. Take control, Adam has commanded me, and right now I hope I don't see Akia, because I might do just that, and I'm not sure how that might look. Or maybe I do hope I see Akia. Maybe confronting him is exactly what I must do. Marching down the hallway, feeling intent simmering in my limbs, I round the corner to the main zoo, and there's a line of patrons formed in front of the information desk. Akia is unattainable behind said desk, the main contact for all those who wait for assistance. The wind in my sails dies, the thunder stolen from my brave moment where I might just have confronted him.

Or so I tell myself.

I never confront anyone.

I step onto the escalator and rotate, watching Akia attend to his patrons. When I leave floor one and bring floor two into view, the strange man is still not present. In fact, there is a mom reading her daughter a story at the very table he favors. This interaction, this normal, wonderful interaction, steadies me and draws down my hyperactive anger and energy. This person, me—I am this person—who loves books, and enjoys the moments others enjoy books, *is* who I am. I am not angry. I am not confrontational. I never wished to be those things. Nor do I now.

I rotate and step off the escalator, and while caffeine may well be the wrong thing for me right now, I walk past the help desk and straight to the back room, to the break area. I've just poured a cup of coffee when I hear, "What happened?"

I pant out a breath and turn to face Jack. "After my disaster of a presentation, Akia made a play for my job coordinating the auditorium."

"You've got to be kidding me."

"I mean, I don't know for sure, but that's how it seems to me. He seems to be Neil's pet."

"Yeah, well, that's Akia. What did Kara say?"

"There's a meeting with Neil at four today to talk to decide whether or not me or Akia will be holding the job. And I have to be at the attorney's with my father at four. She's trying to move the meeting."

"And if she can't?"

"She swears she's got this under control. I don't think she does, but then again, I've proven I don't, either, so maybe her going alone is best."

"You doing nothing is not the answer." He studies me a moment. "Fight for yourself, Mia. What are you going to do to fix this?"

"I don't know," I admit.

"Wrong answer. You earned this job. What are you going to do to fix this?" he pushes.

"I'll go see Neil," I state bravely.

"Good answer. Take control, Mia."

"And if he still gives the job and my pay to Akia?"

"Go over his head."

My brows furrow. "To who?"

"I'll see if I can figure out who that would be."

"You will?"

"Yes," he says firmly. "I will. What are friends for?" he asks. "We help each other." He winks. "Drink coffee. It makes you a better person. Bring me a cup. The desk is busy."

I nod and he disappears into the hallway.

Indeed, I think, *what are friends for?*

The answer is, helping you, and not with a knife in your hand and at someone else's throat.

I have to solve this problem before Adam does it for me.

Before "The End" is another life, not another chapter in a book.

Chapter Sixty-Three

It's midmorning, actually nearly lunchtime, when Kara calls my desk phone. "No go on the meeting change," she announces.

This is not unexpected, and I'm ready for what comes next. Motivated to save my job, I follow up on the plan Jack and I discussed earlier. "Should I stop by Neil's office before the meeting?"

"He's off-site at meetings," she replies. "He won't be back until right before our meeting time, but I'll ask him for a formal interview for you tomorrow morning."

"An interview for a job I presently do and do well," I say flatly, but that flatness morphs into anxiety, and more so, unexpectedly, more of that anger I felt earlier this morning. "Really, Kara?"

"If it's even necessary," she consoles. "I got this," she promises. "I got you. Okay?"

"I need to tell my father I can't—"

"Do *not* even think about missing that meeting with your father for this one. *Do not.* This will work out. Understand?"

Adam's words come back to me in an icy blast: *You take control. Then I won't have to for you. Understand?*

I do understand, I think. What I understand is that I'm juggling two critical situations at one time.

"Can you call me the minute you get out of the meeting?" I ask.

"I'll text in case you're still in with the attorney. Fair enough?"

"Yes. Great. Thank you."

We disconnect, and while I've been agreeable with Kara about what should be my priority, I immediately dial my father, hoping to move the attorney to an earlier or later time. He doesn't answer, and after a huff of frustration, I decide his lack of response is most likely for the best. Delaying the meeting is not an option. Not when the *Lion's Den* jerk is ready to gobble my father up and spit him out, broke and demoralized once again.

I have to be there. I have to look into the attorney's eyes and know he can play in the devil's sandbox with Big Davis and win. My father is too gentle to do so. My mother is too one-dimensional.

I've made the decision—I'm set—when Jack walks into the office. "Any word?"

I turn in my chair to face him. "There's no moving the meeting. I'll find out my fate here at the library from a distance. Neil is out of the office until the meeting."

"Okay," he says. "I've been thinking on this in case this was how this all played out. I do believe I have an idea, and it just might be a good one."

"I'm all ears."

"Well, it takes courage, but you seem to be all about that kind of move right now." He sits down and rolls his chair closer to mine. "I collected every board member's email. Why don't you write a nice letter to them all, apologizing for your nerves but also reiterating the stellar numbers you and Kara have produced together. You're good with words when you're able to hide behind a screen, Mia. I think it can work."

I give myself a moment to absorb this idea and push past what would normally be my immediate rejection. Once I do this, once I refuse to just say no, my mind resets to a hard yes. "I'll have to approve it with Kara, but I do think it's a great idea. Thank you, Jack. And you say I'm all about courage. You wouldn't have come up with this idea before. Maybe courage is contagious."

He gives me a warm smile. "Maybe it is. Call Kara. Get it approved, and then get to the back room and start writing. It's my turn to grab lunch. I'll hit that soup spot we love and bring you back some brain food."

"Perfect," I say.

Just that quickly, he's exiting the office, and I'm turning to my desk, reaching for my phone, and punching in Kara's number, spilling the idea Jack and I have concocted, and doing so with rapid, nervous rambling. When I've splattered all the words I can muster, and it's really, truly too many words, I hold my breath to await her reply, but not for long. "I like it," she confirms. "It's a great idea. I'm proud of you, Mia. You're taking initiative, taking control. These are things I knew you could do. That's why I pushed you toward the auditorium job."

I hate how every compliment reminds me of Adam, who's been remarkably silent most of the day, and yet he manages to scream like a banshee in my head. "Thank you, Kara. Do you want to read it before I send it?"

"Nope. I trust you. I'll send you the list of emails you need to make this happen, so just include me on the email itself. The sooner the better, though. I want this in our arsenal when I go to that meeting this afternoon."

We disconnect, and feeling motivated, I snatch up my MacBook and exit the office. Jack is standing at the help desk, apparently caught by a patron before he could escape to grab that "brain food." He glances over his shoulder and motions toward the back room. I give him a nod and a smile. He returns the smile and includes a thumbs-up. Just that easily I'm off to the back room again, this time to write a letter rather than a presentation.

There is a lift to my step. I'm taking control of my life, and it feels good.

But there is also a little voice in my head that says, "What if I'm not doing enough to please Adam?"

I sit down at the desk, and I open my MacBook with an ugly realization. I haven't looked at the news once since I got to work. I haven't worried about Kevin once this morning. All I've done is think about myself.

Chapter Sixty-Four

Of course, once I realize I've forgotten all about Kevin, I google the news. There is nothing to find, not yet, but there will be. Tonight, maybe? Won't his company miss him today? I expect they'll send his landlord and/or the police to do a wellness check? Surely they will.

The idea of all things Kevin and Adam becomes a distraction that has me struggling over the content of the letter. In an effort to focus, I stand, I pace, and I press a hand to my forehead. *Be in the now, Mia.* The now. I didn't forget about Kevin because I don't care about Kevin, I tell myself. My mind did what minds do. It's placed a barrier between me and what I cannot handle and survive. I know this from psychology class and more than a few books.

This is why people who get fired often blame their bosses, even if they're in the wrong. They need to believe they were in the right to keep moving forward. This delivers me to a horrible question for myself. I'm not doing that with the auditorium, right? No. I reject that idea immediately. I did a crappy job in the presentation. That is my only sin here. This idea motivates me, drives me toward a direction to write my email.

I sit down and get to work.

By the time I've eaten a bowl of tomato soup Jack brought me from a soup place down the road, I have a draft of my email. I send it to him and watch his face as he reads the contents, knowing the words even as he digests them for the first time.

Dear distinguished board members and esteemed library colleagues:

I'm writing to follow up on my recent presentation on the surge in auditorium profits, which you attended here at the main library. As obvious as an amazing fiction novel that rides its way to the *New York Times* Best Sellers list, I am not a master presenter, at least not in a group setting. Thus, I worked so very diligently to present the amazing success story that has been the billing dollars and storytelling the auditorium and its many events have brought to life. It's been a joy to work to turn our dream of creating a successful auditorium that manages to weave a story of its own inside a place that is all about brilliant storytelling—the main library.

Now, you might wonder how I've done such a thing, when I stand before a large group of board members, and can barely speak my name. With practice comes perfection. I've been sharing my love of books with people since I was young enough to speak. I've only stood in front of a room of prestigious people who obviously are committed to the world of books I love one time. If any of you sat with me one on one, my ability to talk about the auditorium, revenues, and business matters would be, and is, solid. I'd also most likely convince you to read a book I adore, and believe you would as well.

I thank you so much for the years I've enjoyed in the library system and invite you to ask me questions or chat with me about the presentation material, concerns, or, as always, a book you simply can't wait to connect with a fellow book lover to discuss. After all, books are the life of this operation. Without them, we are nothing. In the famous words of George Herbert, "Good words are worth much, and cost little."

Yours truly,

Mia Anderson

Master Librarian and Auditorium Coordinator

Jack's gaze lifts to mine, and I quickly say, "It's rough. It's not proofed or tweaked. It's just from the heart and—"

"It's perfect. Send it, Mia. You got this. You are in control. Not that asshole Akia. Then go to your meeting with your parents and bring the same Midas touch you did to this email. Maybe you should wear Chanel more often." He stands up. "I better go check on the team. Proof it. Send it." With that, he turns and walks away.

My brows furrow. *Maybe I should wear Chanel more often?* How did he know I'm wearing Chanel? Jack is not Jess. He's not a brand kind of guy. I'm confused right now. So very confused.

Chapter Sixty-Five

The whole Chanel-Jack thing bothers me all afternoon, and I don't know why. Jack is not Adam. Adam is not Jack. It's not until I'm sliding into an Uber to head to the meeting with the attorney that the nagging feeling abruptly takes shape. That morning I'd sworn Jack was sitting with Adam at the coffee shop is instantly center stage. The same morning that I ran into Mike Adams, ex-schoolmate, who is now FBI.

Could Mike help me deal with Adam?

But, truly, if I told him everything, would I just be admitting guilt by association where Kevin is concerned? Certainly, surely, blackmail would be considered a reason for my silence?

My cellphone buzzes, and I pull it from my bag to find a message from Kara: Great work on the email. Sorry, I didn't read it, or respond, until now, but others have. I've already received several complimentary replies about your written words. More soon! Good luck with your dad.

Any relief I feel by her reply, considering I've been hoping to hear her thoughts on my email for hours, is doused in the gas of my memory of Jack with that man at the coffee shop. Was it Adam, and he fooled Jack in some way into thinking he was just a random stranger? I trust Jack, but he and I have shared the same kind of insecurity that I've come to believe tends to lead to a certain brand of naivete. Could he be unwittingly being used against me by Adam? Nothing about my thoughts conjures anything resembling common sense, and yet my entire involvement in any of this defies all that I know to be my world.

I scan the news yet again. How many times is this now? Twenty? More? And still I feel like I haven't thought of Kevin enough. And *still* there is nothing in the news about a slaughtered man found with his throat sliced. How is that even possible?

My cellphone rings in my hand with Jess on caller ID. "Hey," I say, not sure what to expect, with bullets flying at me from all directions. "Do you have any good news on the whole Big Davis situation?"

"I wish I did. Big Davis is protected like the devil's own child. I can't get to anyone or anything that helps you knock him down. But one thing I heard over and over is don't trust him. Ever. He's the kind of guy who could be inside you and thinking of another woman. And, by the way, usually is. He's a real player."

Another time I might chide her for the crassness or just cave and laugh at her for being all that I expect of her and more, but not now. "This isn't surprising."

"You need to go into this meeting and push everyone to remember who they're dealing with," she adds. "Understand?"

I cringe with the now-familiar question that seems to be punching at me from all directions. As if everyone thinks that if I don't confirm understanding I'll do something stupid. I've never been stupid. I've been quiet and submissive. There's a difference. Then again, maybe there isn't. Maybe quiet and submissive equates to stupid. I've lost a real gauge on such things, it seems.

"I understand," I assure her. The car pulls up to the building that is my destination. "I have to go," I add. "I'm arriving at the attorney's office now."

"I have a dinner-interview thing tonight for one of my columns. Text me when you're done. I'll call you back if I can. But tell me what happens in the text in case I can't."

"Will do," I promise.

We disconnect, and I exit the Uber, glancing up at the high-rise where I'll meet my parents and attend the meeting with Nick Morris, the attorney, who I can only pray knows how to do his job in a hardball kind of way. Because if we have to resort to me telling him how to get down and dirty with Big Davis, my confidence in the end result of this negotiation is not good. That said, he works for Jess, I remind myself. He's no pushover—of that I can be certain.

I hurry inside the building, shiny floors and dangling lights surrounded by glass and more glass. Kevin lived in a smaller version of a building like this one, where the windows were the world, where the windows allowed me to watch his last moments in this world. I'm trembling with the idea as I sign in at security and hurry toward the elevator. Once I'm inside, I'm alone, and alone means I'm living in my own head, a cold, dark place where I'm reminded that Kevin only lives a few blocks from here.

Lived, I remind myself. He lived only a few blocks from here.

The elevator dings and the doors open. I'm greeted by a wall with the firm's long list of partners etched in some kind of tile. This is a big firm. Big translates to powerful, I tell myself. But I also worry about conflicts of interest. Out of every attorney on that wall, is there not one fan, or investor, in some Big Davis project? I turn left to walk toward the glass doors of the lobby. It doesn't take long for me to discover that my parents are already in a conference room with Mr. Morris. Nor is it long before the receptionist leads me to the same room, another room of all glass, where I join them.

There are four people in attendance, not including me. My parents, a man I assume to be Mr. Morris, and a pretty blonde who reminds me of Jess. Everyone stands. My father hugs me, my mother gives me a nervous nod, and then the attention turns to the man, who shakes my hand. "Nick Morris," he greets, confirming his identity before motioning to the Jess look-alike. I wonder if Nick knows her as such. A Jess look-alike. Is he as obsessed with her as most men, and could that work in our favor? "This is my associate, Erin Stanford," he says, introducing the blonde.

Just like that, all the niceties are thankfully over.

I sit between my parents, directly across from Erin. Nick, Mr. Morris, is across from my father. "As I was telling your parents," Mr. Morris starts, "Big Davis is the highest bidder on your father's project by a substantial amount. He's going to make your family quite wealthy."

I'm prickly, a cactus type of personality I normally do not like but which I seem to resemble right now. "And then bury the patent, right?" I challenge, glancing at my father for confirmation as I repeat, "Right?"

Erin answers for the room. "Big Davis assures us that won't happen. We're working on the contractual terms."

I glance over at her. I do not like her. She might resemble Jess in appearance, but she lacks her vibrating, confident presence. "Big Davis is not that easily agreeable or generous. There's a catch. What is the catch?"

My mother leans forward and glances at me over my father. "Did you come just to be negative?"

Her opinion of my opinion is never high, and I really don't care right now. My eyes go to Mr. Morris. "What's the catch?" I repeat.

"Not really a catch," he replies, confirming there is indeed a catch. "Big Davis simply thinks making the offering on *Lion's Den* will make for good television ratings."

"No." My hand actually comes down on the conference table rather firmly, surprising everyone, including myself, but I am not done. "Absolutely not," I add. "If this is allowed, Big Davis will humiliate my father and find a way to turn his invention into trash."

"Mia!" my mother proclaims. "Are you serious right now?"

My attention rockets to my father. "You know I'm right," I say softly.

Erin clears her throat. "We'll have the offer in writing before the show takes place."

My eyes are laser beams in her direction at this point. "Pardon me, Erin, or Ms. Stanford, but he'll find a way to outsmart you." I glance at Mr. Morris. "What's the backup offer?"

"Nowhere near as high."

"Does it allow his project to live on and not be shoved in a closet?"

"Yes, but—"

I turn to my father. "Take it," I implore him. "Take it and run far away from *Lion's Den*."

My father surprises me by saying, "The money I'm being offered will set you up for life, honey."

"How have you forgotten what happened on that show? How have you forgotten what that man did to you? Don't even think about doing this for me. Please. I beg of you. Do not go on *Lion's Den*. Do not take Big Davis's offer."

"If it's in writing—" my father begins.

"Please don't do this. I am literally begging you."

Mr. Morris clears his throat. "Mr. Anderson, may I speak with you one on one?"

I push to my feet. "I'll leave and make this meeting easier for you, Mr. Morris, but I'm not done making my case with my parents." I eye my father. "Don't agree to anything yet. *Please*."

He nods, and I walk toward the door. I don't even remember the ride down the elevator. I don't remember how I end up on the street, walking toward my home. My cellphone rings, and it's Jess. I decline the call. I cannot talk to her right now. I push forward, walking faster, harder, heart pumping with exaggerated thunder in my chest. I've just reached the bookstore, and my loft, when my cellphone rings again, and this time it's Kara.

I halt, drawing in a breath and accepting the call. "Hi," I say, a bad feeling churning in my belly.

"How'd it go with your father?"

I ignore the question. "Do I still have my job?"

"Look, Mia—"

"He gave it to Akia," I bite out. "Right?"

"It's not that simple. I believe, thanks to your email, you've opened new doors for yourself. We'll have a lot to discuss this week."

"But Akia got the auditorium job and the raise that goes with it?"

"Yes. But I managed to keep your pay the same. That's what I'm telling you. We have more to discuss. I promise."

"He still took what was mine."

"Yes, but—"

At some point I've entered the bookstore in a blur and walked up the stairs toward my loft. When I spy not one but two big boxes with a red ribbon, I stop dead in my tracks, aware Kara is saying something, but I have no idea what. "I need to go right now, Kara. I'll talk to you tomorrow." I do what I would never, ever do another time. I hang up on her.

I'm angry, the kind of anger I don't know as my own.

I unlock my door, open it, and grab the boxes. When they're on the island again, I am out of control. I set my purse down and dare to dial Adam. The minute he answers, I say, "I'm done. You're done. No more packages. No more games. No more gifts. I'm done." I don't give him time to reply. I hang up on him.

Chapter Sixty-Six

Present . . .

Rain suffocates me, and a roar of thunder is followed by a flash of lightning, a flash that illuminates the features of the man standing above me. I can see him; I can see his face. He is no one I know, but it doesn't matter, not with what I've discovered, what I now know as the truth buried beneath the atrocity of lies. I know everything now. Everything. Adrenaline surges through me, and I scramble backward in the midst of mud and slush, then rotate and push to my feet. Somehow I manage to place one foot in front of the other, to actually run, but my back is to the stranger. I'm a target, and I expect that at any moment I will be dead. A bullet will pierce my skull or my back. Or the stranger's big body will topple mine, and hands will find my throat, choking the life out of me.

Any minute now I am certain I will be dead.

This is always where the story ends.

This was always going to be my ending.

Chapter Sixty-Seven

The past . . .

Adam calls me back immediately. I don't answer. I decline the call. He doesn't try again.

I'm not sure what that means, but I don't care right now.

Energy consumes me, and none of it is good energy, either. It cuts, it slices, it has me shifting, pacing, uncontrollably moving here and there, and all around. Some might call this pacing, but it's more than simply pacing. There is no straight line. There is no place I can zig or zag where I feel settled and stable. Kevin is dead. My father is walking right back into the quicksand of *Lion's Den*, and it's going to swallow him this time, suffocate him. It might even end him. My mother—well, my mother is my mother. Always stuck on the numbers on the page, not the people behind those numbers.

And then, of course, there is me, the biggest fool of us all.

I'm captive to a crazy stalker, and I allowed it to happen.

I was foolish enough to actually think this good-looking, successful man saw me, really saw me, and was interested. *No.* No, that is simply untrue. I'm still invisible. That's why I lost my auditorium job, not because I screwed up the presentation. Akia is charismatic. He can meet a person one time and they are enamored with him. I stood at that podium, and while I thought I was seen as a foolish girl, I was as I always am—the Invisible Girl. My work didn't matter. My words didn't matter. Even my parents aren't seeing me, hearing me. My father of all people has gone dark on me.

The boxes with the big red ribbons catch my attention, and anger burns in my belly. Is he trying to buy me? Seduce me with money and gifts? And if so, why? Why is he doing this? I walk to the counter, grabbing one box and then the next, ripping away the red ribbons. I find clothes and shoes—Gucci, Dior, and Yves Saint Laurent among the labels. Three total outfits, all outrageously expensive. No one spends this kind of money on someone if he plans to walk away. Adam is not going away.

My fingers tangle in my hair, and I scream in frustration, literally scream. Loud music begins to blast from the bookstore below, and I eye the window. It's dark outside. My God, I didn't come straight home from the meeting. I don't even remember *what* I did. Where I went. I force my mind to calm and retrace my steps.

I walked home. No, I amend. I walked and walked before I came home, trying to calm myself. I check my call log and realize now that Kara called me at nearly seven. The meeting was at four. Why didn't Adam call me until then? And Jess *kept* calling me. Jack called me, too, a total of five times. I check the current time. It's now eight at night. Hours have passed me in a wave of everything wrong—and nothing right.

A new text hits my phone from Jess: Call me now or I'm coming over. Even Jack called me worried about you.

Damn it, she *will* come over.

I don't want to see her right now.

I punch her call button and she answers with, "Mia? What the hell is going on? You had us all worried."

"I just needed a minute, Jess, okay? I need a minute."

"Honey," she says softly. "What happened?"

"Akia took my job, and that attorney you sent my father to has a hard-on for Big Davis."

"A hard-on? Okay, you are really, really not yourself. You never speak like that."

She's right. Of course she's right. Nothing about me right now is me at all. "I told you," I say, "I need *a minute*." But as surely as I say this to her, I ramble onward, adding, "I'm trying to take control of my life, Jess, and it's not working. I just want to be invisible. It's better that way. I mean, I worked hard to build the auditorium revenue, and I did. I blew away expectation. I sold people on why we were the venue for every event. Yes, the presentation sucked, but why did that matter? Why did that one hiccup allow Akia to take my job? My work should have been enough. I even wrote an email to the entire board of directors pitching myself, and for what? He still took my job. Why can't I just be in the background, do a great job, and that be enough?"

"Mia," Jess starts, but I'm not done yet, and I say as much.

"I'm not done. I worked hard in that meeting with the attorney today to convince my father to do the right thing. No one listened. They all want to jump in the devil's sandbox and build sandcastles with Big Davis. My father is going to get screwed over, and I can't stop it from happening. So you see?"

"See what, Mia?"

"When I try to speak up, when I step out of my comfort zone, it doesn't work. Some people are just meant to be in the spotlight. You are. I am not. Everyone is not like you. You know that, right?"

"Okay, deep breath," Jess orders gently. "Deep breath. You're upset—"

"Ya think?" I demand. "Really, Jess? That's your reply?"

"Mia—"

My phone buzzes with a call, and I find Jack on caller ID. "That's Jack. Can you just call him and tell him I need a little time? I mean, you know me well. Once in a blue moon, I melt down. It happens, and then

I pick myself back up and I'm better for it. That's now. Just tonight, right now, I need to be with me, just me. Don't come over. Don't let Jack come over. Just let me think. Can you both understand that? Please."

"Okay," she agrees. "Yes. I know you. I know how this works. I'll come by in the morning, though, and we will walk to coffee together. Is that okay?"

If it just lets me be alone right now, I think, *I'll agree to about anything.* "Yes," I say. "Fine. That's fine."

"Love you, Mia."

"I love you, too. I gotta go." I disconnect and check my call log. My parents have not called. That's because my father is going to do what I begged him not to do and go on *Lion's Den*. In other words, he's going to be destroyed again. And the music downstairs is louder now. I can't take it. I've had enough. I google the news anyway. Still nothing on Kevin. I don't understand. Am I losing my mind? Did I imagine his murder?

An urgent need to prove I'm not crazy overcomes me. I hurry upstairs and strip away the stupid Chanel clothes—I don't even care if Adam is watching me. In fact, I hope he sees me pull on my Walmart sweatsuit and sneakers. I shove my hair under a baseball hat, and then, grabbing a jacket, I hurry back down the stairs and exit my apartment. Once I'm in the main foyer, I note the lodged-open door to the bookstore, the music grinding on my nerves.

I push it open and walk inside. Ben is nowhere to be found. "Ben!" I call out.

He steps from between two rows of books. "Yes, my lady? What can I do for you?" His tone is pure mockery.

"I'm going out. If I come back and that music is blasting, I swear to God, I will stomp your iPhone to its death. And I will repeat that every single night if necessary." I turn and exit the store and the building. I am not a killer in the Adam sense of the word, but if Ben thinks I'm joking, he's wrong. I've had enough. I will kill his iPhone in two seconds flat.

Chapter Sixty-Eight

There's a high probability that I really am crazy.

Otherwise, why would I be here, of all places, right now?

I stand across the street from the building where I'd gone to meet Adam for our first date, or so I'd thought. The building with a view right into Kevin's apartment. Which is exactly why I'm here now. I have to know if Kevin is alive or dead. I have to see him, sprawled on his floor, with my own two eyes, just one more time. Of course I'm worried about street and building cameras that might spy me visiting this location, but with my hair back and my hood over my cap, I'm incognito. And the truth be told, I just have to do this. I can't go on without doing this.

This area of town is no party sector and manages to be quiet this time of night, as is the case this eve. I scan the area, looking for and finding no sign of law enforcement. I mean, if there was a murder, wouldn't there be some police presence? Or maybe there would be, and there is, and I simply don't know. Maybe "they" are just watching for fools like me who return to the scene of the crime. But fool that I am, I'm doing this. I am *doing this*.

After hurrying across the street, I enter the building and rush to a stairwell, using the sleeve of my jacket to open the door. I left fingerprints before, I know—I had to have—but so have many others after me, to cover them up, to dilute the quality of my touch versus theirs. At least, I hope there was. This time, though, this night, I will leave nothing of myself behind—well, nothing I haven't already left. For instance, a part of my soul that is now doomed to hell and beyond based on my silence over Kevin's murder.

I didn't even call for help.

What if he was still alive when I left?

The walk up the stairs is unconscious for me again. Time and places are muddled about in my mind. *It's that survival instinct we all possess,* I think. That part of my mind, of all our minds, that is programmed to protect us, to ensure our sanity. I reach the floor where everything bad in my life feels as if it originates, though I know it was earlier than that night. It started with the first note from Adam. Maybe before. Maybe he'd been watching me for a long time.

I step into the open, unfinished office space, and my eyes rocket to the area where the table sat in wait for me the last time I was here. It's gone now. There is no sign I was ever here, that anyone has been here since. With leaden feet, I close the space between me and the window with the view into Kevin's apartment. The lights from across the street, from his home, glow brightly, as they had when I was here last.

Is he alive?

Is he home and living his best life?

Was this all a horrid joke played by Kevin himself?

Sucking in a breath, I step to the window and gasp at what I find. There is no joke. Kevin's apartment is empty, completely empty. There is no body. There is no furniture. There is only a vacant apartment. My cellphone rings, and I already know who it is. I don't even look at the caller ID. I answer with, "What is this?"

"I told you," Adam says calmly, his deep voice a vibration down my spine that frightens me for the simple fact that it soothes me in uncomfortable ways. "I'm helping you take control of your life," he adds, "not destroy your life, Mia. Kevin resigned from his job and wrote a quite-convincing note to his employer and landlord about being at a place in his life where he needs to travel and expand his life. He even paid off his lease. No one is coming for you. No one will hurt you. I won't let that happen. I've got you, Mia. That's what you need to remember. I've got you."

"I told you I'm done."

"Not even close."

"Stop watching me. Stop doing what you're doing. Stop everything. Do you have cameras in my loft?"

"No. I do not have cameras in your loft."

"You always know where I am," I accuse.

"There are ways to do that without me watching you on a camera like a perverted teenager. If you want to be intimate with me, Mia, that will be your choice."

"Never."

"That's your choice. I won't take that from you. I give. I don't take."

"Except Kevin's life?"

"That was a gift I gave to you. One day soon you'll see it as such. I told you. I don't take. I give."

"Why should I believe anything you say? And how do I know you're not watching me in my loft? Watching me in intimate moments that should be my own."

"I've never lied to you, Mia. Nothing I've told you is a lie. Call and try to reach Kevin at work. They'll confirm my story. I don't lie to you. I left you some gifts to enjoy. Enjoy them. This is not about hurting you or even controlling you. This is about you controlling you."

"Liar."

"I'm teaching you, Mia. Learning is never a gentle or fast thing to do."

I hang up on him again.

He doesn't call back.

Chapter Sixty-Nine

When I arrive home, the bookstore is remarkably silent. I have no idea if this has anything to do with my outburst, or simply that Ben is long gone and done cleaning for the night. I begin the climb up the stairwell to the right of the store, and my body is heavy, weighed down with the extreme rush of high and low emotions that have spent hours tormenting me.

I walk into my loft and lock the door. I don't even bother to check for intruders. At this point, if Adam is here, if someone is here, just let them come at me. I don't have the energy to care. The stench of guilt and death covered up by lies clings to me, and I drag my tired body up the stairs, strip down, and shower. Hot water pours over me until it turns as icy as my emotions. I have nothing left in me, not tonight.

Once I'm in my PJ set and in my bed, I lie there, staring at the ceiling, a rumble in my belly. I didn't eat tonight, and there is a growing necessity for nutrition. I shove myself up a bit, prop against the headboard, and open my bedside table, grabbing the bag of M&M's I've resisted for darn near a month. I eat them now, mindlessly consuming them.

My cellphone rings and I glance at the clock. It's midnight. I know who is calling—of course I know. One glance at the caller ID, and it's him. It's Adam.

I swallow my last M&M and answer on speaker. "You aren't going to go away, are you?"

"Not when you still need me."

"I don't need you," I say, though the combative tone of earlier is long exhausted. "You command me to take control. I try. It backfires. I was happier when I felt ignored. I'm invisible. And for that matter, so are *you.* You hide in the shadows. Hiding is what I've done my whole life. You're just teaching me to keep on keeping on."

"This isn't about me. It's about you. The minute I step to your side, it's about us, and me."

"If it's about me, let me handle my problems."

"If you're taking control, I won't, but you're going to have to talk to me, Mia. You're going to have to tell me what you're doing and why you think it's failing."

"Okay, fine. I talk. You listen. You let me handle my own problems. Is that our deal? No one else dies."

"We aren't talking about death. We're talking about life. Tell me what you're doing to control yours."

It's not the answer I want, but it's the only answer he's going to give me. "Fine," I concede. "I went to the attorney meeting with my parents to talk about my father's patent negotiations. They really believe Big Davis is the biggest, best bidder that ever rocked their world."

I can almost see him frown as he asks, "The guy from *Lion's Den*?"

"Right. That asshole. They actually believe him being the highest bidder, which is what I'm told he is, to be a good situation. My parents and their attorneys can't see he's setting them up. Big Davis wants to make the offer on live TV."

"And we all know how Big Davis and your father went down on live TV last time."

"Exactly. He'll demolish my father. This product my father created competes with one of Big Davis's products. If he humiliates my father and devalues the product, he doesn't pay my father, and he kills my father's future." My lips press together. "And maybe him in the process. I was strong in the meeting, Adam. I didn't even recognize myself. But it made no difference."

"Let me ask you this: Before you and I started talking, would you have stood up and fought for your father or sat back and watched?"

"I'd have talked to my father," I argue. "I'd have tried to convince him to do the right thing."

"By attending the meeting? By arguing with his legal counsel about what is right or wrong for him? Or by passively standing in the background, speaking only when spoken to?"

"Passively," I concede. "But my point is that there is no difference in the outcome."

"You don't know that yet," he points out. "And on that note, you have to shift your viewpoint, Mia."

"Meaning what?"

"You changing you doesn't mean others change with you. The fact that you do everything you can to make a difference instead of just sitting back and watching *is you* being in control *of you*. No matter what happens with your father's business dealings, you will *not* regret your actions or question yourself about if you could have done more. You can never fully control others, not even your parents."

It's terrifying to me that Adam is starting to make sense.

"You take control, Mia," he repeats, "and I won't. Just talk to me. Work through things with me. We all need someone to talk to, and for you, you're going to figure out that person is me. I'm that person who offers you unconditional support. You can tell me anything and not be judged."

"Sometimes we all need and deserve to be judged."

"And sometimes we deserve the freedom to say what we think and feel, and not be judged. I know more happened today than you've told me. I know we have more to talk about, but you need to rest, and so do I. We both have work tomorrow. Wear the Gucci tomorrow. You'll look like a stunner in it. And go to the eye doctor. Get rid of the glasses, though I must say you pull off the librarian look with a certain je ne sais quoi." He pauses a moment. "Good night, Mia."

With the French remark that basically means I have some unexplainable quality, a beauty I would only call appropriate to describe Jess, he disconnects.

Chapter Seventy

I wake the next morning with a numb sensation.

The tears, anger, and terror of the evening before are shoved somewhere in a deep, dark place inside me, no doubt my mind using my slumber to transport me to a place where survival instinct rules yet again. And, surprisingly, I *did* sleep. It's as if I'd simply reached a point of complete, utter mental and physical shutdown. My body and mind united and said: no more.

Once I'm fully up, moving, and showered, coffee in hand, I'm still in the same place.

I'm still numb.

I do as Adam has commanded.

I dress in the Gucci outfit, and while style hasn't exactly been my "thing," I lived with Jess long enough to know a few things about the big brands. Gucci is a bit eclectic, often designing with bright flowers, colors, and unique styles I typically find over the top for me. Remarkably, the dress Adam bought me is more classic, black of all colors, considering my rather goth wardrobe he's trying to replace. It's a fitted cotton material, with long silky sleeves, and accented with olive-green piping around the wrists, neck, and edges of the black, thin, rather elegant belt. I choose to pair it with the Chanel boots I wore yesterday rather than the Gucci high heels Adam has provided, which feel a bit delicate (translated as uncomfortable) for my active library job, as well as my walk to and from work.

The dress also comes with a $2,400 price tag. The tag itself has the price detached, but I google it via the Saks website. Who buys a woman he has no real relationship with dresses and shoes that cost as much as the items presently on my body and in my possession?

No one normal.

Only when the buzzer goes off to the downstairs door do I remember that Jess is walking me to work. Fortunately, no panic or dread follows this memory and realization. I simply don't appear to be reactive today, but then again, this is also Jess. She knows about Adam, at least some things about Adam. And she's all about a man opening his wallet for a woman. Jack will be another story. I haven't fully explained my transformation to him. If I tell him about Adam buying me luxurious gifts, he'll be worried in a way Jess will not. Therefore, where Jack is concerned, I may be forced to ride a fictional line with him that I'd rather not call a lie.

Instead of buzzing Jess up, I grab my oversize purse, in which my newest book is still marked with the letter opener "bookmark" at the same spot as days ago. Want proof I'm not me? I'm not reading. That's not me. It's someone I do not recognize one little bit. I stuff my Mac inside my bag as well, check the weather to decide whether I need a jacket, finding it mild and the jacket unneeded. Ready, or as ready as I can be for any day with Adam in my life, I head down to the door and then downstairs.

I meet Jess at the door to the bookstore. As usual, she is beauty and style personified, in a black pantsuit, a silky pink blouse beneath offering a perfect splash of color. I have no idea what brand she wears. Again, that's not my thing, but she knows mine, and right away.

She gives me an up and down and says, "Gucci. It looks good on you. He couldn't splurge on shoes to match?"

I roll my eyes. "Really, Jess?"

She shrugs. "Do it right or don't do it at all."

"He bought shoes. They're too high to walk to work and around the library."

"Then he didn't do it right, but at least he has footwear awareness." We start walking toward the coffee shop. "He must be some civil engineer to buy you Chanel and Gucci," she comments.

She's right, of course. This all seems extravagant for a civil engineer. "They did bring him in from Texas to design some highway, but maybe he inherited money like you did, too. We haven't talked about it."

"Hmm," she replies. "Yes, well, I don't use mine." She glances at me. "I would—you know I would for you—but you would never let me throw my money at you. Interestingly, though, this man is another story. You're letting him buy you things."

"Not really," I say. "He's just rather dogmatic in his generosity."

My mind hangs on that word, *generosity*, when I want to replace it with another, such as *threats* or *demands*.

"He must be," she replies. "When can I meet him?"

Never, I think. I don't want him anywhere near the people I love. "He wants to meet you," I say. "We just have to work out the details."

We enter the coffee shop and place our order before claiming a seat at a table. "You could bring him to my award ceremony," Jess suggests, picking up where we left off in the conversation.

"You already know I'm bringing Jack after I attend his uncle's wedding with him."

"And how does this man of yours feel about Jack?"

"Order for Jess!"

She lifts a finger. "Hold that thought. I'll grab our coffees." She stands and disappears, out of sight and mind for just a moment.

I'm no longer numb. Fear and worry form a fist in my gut. How will Adam react to me attending the wedding and the party with Jack? Do I tell him? Of course I have to tell him. He knows. He always knows. Seeming to hide anything from that man feels dangerous. He knows about Jack. He knows he's just a friend. And I'm not even sure Adam is really into me as a woman. It's more like a protégé or submission. Maybe *victim* is a more fitting choice.

Jess rejoins me, setting my coffee in front of me. "Where were we?" she asks. "Oh yes. How will the new man—Adam, right?"

"Yes," I confirm. "Adam."

"How will Adam feel about you and Jack attending not one, but two, events together Saturday?"

"I'm not sure," I answer honestly. "But I'm not letting Jack down."

Unless Adam forces me to in order to ensure Jack's safety, I think.

"I'm not surprised," Jess replies. "As much as I don't approve of Jack as your plus-one, I know you, and you are stubbornly committed to him."

"And you," I remind her.

"Yes," she agrees. "Which is why I tolerate him." She moves on before I can punch back on that one. "You and this Adam dude are new, so my advice you didn't ask for: either don't tell him about Saturday, or tell him and make it clear he has to deal with it or be gone. Don't do what you did with Kevin and stand in the background. Set the rules up front. Demand your own identity. I mean, him dressing you is all fine and dandy—but I only somewhat approve."

"Why? You love a man to break out his plastic."

"I don't like the way he's creating your image for you," she says. "He's choosing what you wear. You should be choosing how *you do you*. You always have, and I respect that about you. So much so that every clothing item I have ever picked for you just hangs in your closet."

"I wore the red sweater. You're very sweet and generous."

"Well then, on that note, stay over Friday night and pick a dress from my closet for Saturday night."

"I have to go to the wedding early Saturday."

"Fine then, I'll come by Friday loaded down with dresses."

"You don't have to do that."

"But I'm going to. What time? We can order in dinner."

"I have no idea what is going to be going on with my father and Big Davis, so let's chat about it Thursday."

"Anything from him this morning?"

"Of course not. He's already made up his mind. We're going back on *Lion's Den*."

"We're," she repeats. "Because what happens to him happens to you. I do love that about you and your father. What's up with your mother?"

I fill her in on the story. She listens intently and replies with, "Somehow it's just so hard for me to perceive of your father having your mother investigated. There's a side to him I don't think we fully know. Or I don't. Maybe you do."

"I think the *Lion's Den* situation just crashed his self-esteem to such a low level that he acted based on that insecurity. That's why I can't believe he would agree to go back on the show."

"Honestly, I can't, either. Just take the lesser money and make more over time."

"I agree," I say, "but as we talk about this, I can't help but wonder if he is just so afraid of Davis that he thinks he'll find a way to ruin any other deal, even after it seems over and done with."

"Considering what I learned about him, I fear you might be right. I'm going to try to get an interview with him."

"With what outcome in mind?"

"The power of the press, my dear, the power of the press. Plus, he's supposed to be handsy. I sure won't lead him on, but if he does that shit with me, I damn sure will confirm it to be true. You know how I feel about those kinds of men."

Because of her father. More and more, I wonder if Jack is right. Maybe Jess will never trust a man enough to love him, but he's wrong about her trying to get rid of him for herself. She supports my dating life. She supports me spreading my wings. "I don't think we even have time to go down that path with Big Davis, Jess. And there really isn't time anyway."

"What date is your father in talks to be on *Lion's Den* again?"

"I'm not sure. It's some worst-failures edition."

"Oh jeez." She punches buttons on her phone and then glances at me. "Okay. It's supposed to air live, late next month. That gives us a little time."

"Not really. My father is going to feel the pressure and sign whatever agreement the attorney places in front of him."

"Right. Of course he will." She sips from her cup, a thoughtful look on her face. "Okay, I don't know why we're worrying. My attorney is his attorney. He's not going to let him get screwed."

"Do you know he has some you-look-alike newbie attorney named Erin helping him on this? I get the impression she's highly involved, and I don't know, Jess. Call me nuts, but she looks *so* like you, it's a little freaky. Like maybe he has a thing for you that he's using her to live out. Maybe shades of you in Erin has him blinded by the light."

"That is an unexpected observation. I don't get that vibe from him at all, but I admit, it sounds worrisome. I'll call him. I'm on this, Mia." She glances at her watch. "I need to run, but one thing before I do: it's cool and all that you won't let Jack down, that you stand by him, that you are always a good friend. I also think setting boundaries with this new Adam guy is good, and you can use Jack and Saturday to do so. But the elephant in the room we didn't talk about this morning was your meltdown last night."

"Oh yeah," I say. "That."

"Yes, that. Mia, you know I have always felt you being invisible is a choice. You chose to be seen and or not be seen. When you chose to be seen and it backfired yesterday, you came down hard on yourself. I still believe, and I have always believed, Jack is your security blanket. It's easier to feel invisible together than be seen. Don't let that comfortable feeling you two will have together on Saturday make being invisible feel safer than being seen. Don't let Jack get between you and Adam. Don't let Jack hold you back." She lifts her hand in surrender. "No need to make your case. I'm done. That's all. Just my opinion. Love ya, sister." She squeezes my hand and pushes to her feet, and in a whiff of lingering perfume, she leaves me sitting there.

Jack is worried that Jess wants to keep him and me apart.

Jess is worried Jack will keep me and Adam apart.

I'm worried Adam is going to take everyone I love and just plain kill them.

Chapter Seventy-One

I've changed.

Or maybe I'm sheltering inside that numb sensation I woke with this morning, re-creating it now, cowering in a proverbial corner while a storm brews, deep in my soul, rallying for another big showing. Whatever the case, I walk into the library a few minutes after my coffee date with Jess, and I am fully aware, too aware, of the fact that I simply no longer feel the joy I once did when I stepped inside these doors. I no longer hear the imaginary sound of pages being turned in gloriously addictive books, as I once did every single morning as I started my day.

The happy version of me, the girl who loves books and her job, who usually greets everyone inside the walls of the library, even when I expect to be greeted by few in return, barely even speaks to the security guard. I whiz past Doug as if he's a stranger, my mind preoccupied with nothing at all, as crazy as that might seem, considering the content of my meetup with Jess. But some part of me just seems to know that if I allow anything, even one little thing inside my head, the effect will be a fast-rolling snowball down a hill that ends nowhere good. Even the sweet compliment on my dress from Wanda, one of the floor-one zoo employees, barely registers. I don't even think about visiting Kara's office to fight for my job in the auditorium, when one might think it would be the first thing I'd do upon my arrival this morning.

What's done is done.

I have no fight left in me, at least on this topic, not even when Akia—dressed in one of his perfectly fitted button-down shirts, in the same shade of green as his eyes—literally places his body between me and the escalator. "We should talk," he states. "Can we go to lunch?"

Translation: Can I teach him how to do the job I did well, just as well? The embarrassing truth is that there was a time not so long ago when I'd have helped him no matter the detriment to myself. Now is not that time. "No," I say simply. "We cannot go to lunch." I try to step around him.

He blocks my path, arguing his position. "I didn't do this. It was—"

"The man with one red shoe?" It's a joke based on the title of an old eighties Tom Hanks movie he'll never know, but I do. I do because my father loves that damn movie. And I love my father. My energy will go toward protecting him, not helping Akia.

"Tom Hanks," he surprises me by saying. "I actually love that movie. I watched it with my dad."

The comment on his part might open the door to a connection between us if I respond with my similar history, but I do not. I zip my lips, seeing him for what he is, a cobra who hypnotizes you and then strikes. I've already been bitten. Now is the aftermath. "I didn't take your job by choice," he adds, the shift in his eyes suggesting a lie, but I can't be certain. "It was forced on me," he continues. "And I told you. I know Neil well. When Neil decides he's done with someone, he's done. That's what happened to you. Truth be told, the only reason I've survived him this many years is that he and my father grew up together. My father shelters me."

But not me, I think, and he certainly knew that and took advantage of my fall from the presenting podium, so to speak. "Then you could have supported me and survived it just fine."

"I tried."

This time I'm certain *he lies*. I really do see it in the shift of his eyes that I've read about in hundreds of crime novels. This conversation is going nowhere but to a pile of more of those lies. Therefore I say what my father said about the *Lion's Den* disaster, "Things happen for a reason, even if we don't understand them until much later. I need to get to floor three. Good luck with your new duties."

His look is incredulous. "You're really going to blow me off?"

"I really am."

He grimaces and accuses, "I thought you were more professional than this."

I almost laugh. "No you didn't. You didn't think of me at all. Not until I served my job up to you on a silver platter. My mistake. Lesson learned." This time when I step around him, he doesn't stop me.

I close the few steps between me and the escalator, claiming my spot on the steel step.

I don't turn around. I also don't survey the library for fun tidbits of joy from those enjoying a book or family time. Nor do I study floor two for the stranger who I've convinced myself was watching me but may not have noticed me at all. I focus on what is above. My tree house, my safe place, floor three. The only place where I might just find the joy of reading and sharing book recommendations again.

The only place where I might find the ghost of Mia past. If I could find her, I feel like she'd know which book to pick up and find the solution to all this inside.

Chapter Seventy-Two

I'm actually the first to arrive on floor three for the day.

I quickly settle at my desk with the intent of relishing some time alone. Maybe if I step into the circle of books beyond this door, inhale the smell of the books, and listen, I'll hear the imaginary flutter of pages turning. I'll remember the love of books that grounded me in life, love, and family.

That hope is dashed a moment later when Jack joins me and shuts the door firmly behind him, ensuring our privacy. My fingers curl into my palms as I steel myself for what is to come. Jack is no Jess. He will push me harder on my meltdown last night, at least where my job is related. That's where our worlds collide, where we connect. That's where he will focus his queries.

Before I can even turn around, he's ranting. "Jess told me about Akia taking your job," he says. "I'm furious for you. I swear I've never wanted to punch someone, but I want to go punch him for you right now. Why wouldn't you take my calls last night? I was worried about you. I *am* worried about you."

I stand up to face him and lean on my desk, and that worry and anger he spoke of radiates from him. His jaw is tense and jutted forward, but there is more in his stare, a hint of hurt that I understand a bit too well. He feels second best, in this case to Jess, a sentiment that has been a theme as of late, it seems.

"I didn't want to take Jess's call, either," I say. "She threatened to come over by text if I didn't talk to her, and I knew she would. I didn't want to see her. I just needed a minute to myself."

He gives a nod, the shadows in his eyes lightening but not fading. "What did Kara say? Did the email you sent do nothing at all to help? I thought it was brilliant."

"The letter was good. She said it helped. I appreciate you suggesting it."

"It helped? Please explain how. You lost your auditorium gig."

"Yes, but apparently not my pay. She says she got calls about my email, and there is more to come on that, whatever that means."

"I'll be interested to see what that means, too. It's good you kept your pay, right?"

"Yes. Of course it is, but I guess the money wasn't what really mattered. I mean, it did, and it does—I need it—but the job and my duties were personal to me. I felt like I did good work that just didn't matter in the end."

"You feel unimportant," he supplies and then motions to my dress. "You're dressing for success, looking good, doing good work, and it just didn't seem to matter."

God, this man understands me. I do love and adore him. "Yeah. It sucks."

"Well, for the record, you're important to me. And I have to believe that Kara is telling you that there is something unexpected brewing for you."

He has no idea, I think.

"Can you believe that Akia actually asked me to go to lunch with him to 'talk'? You know, he wants me to show him how to look good. I told him no."

He arches a brow. "And he said?"

"This is not his fault. Neil is an asshole who just decides to hate people, and Neil is a friend of his father's, which works in his favor."

"In other words, he gets special treatment. Does Kara know that? You should go talk to Kara."

"Who knows if anything Akia said to me is even true. Kara warned me not to trust him."

His brow inches upward. "Really? She's never said anything negative about anyone in all the years I've known her."

"Same here, and yet she spoke that warning to me."

"Go talk to her," he urges.

"I need to just take a breather. I need to be here, right here, on floor three, and lost in books. I know you get that in a way so many other people do not."

He gives a nod. "Yeah. Yeah, okay. I do. But before I let you be, I have to ask about your father and the meeting."

Mentally I resist even talking about this again, but this is Jack asking. I catch him up and finish with, "So now you see, I'm sure that I just need to be here, really right here, lost in books."

He scowls and scowls some more before he says nothing more than, "Yes. Yes, I do believe I do."

It's a bit of an unusual reply from a man who is opinionated on my life, which comes to me with mixed feelings. He's acting weird, but thank you, Lord, for it, because I can't talk about this anymore.

My phone on my desk rings and I grab the line. "Mia Anderson."

"Mia, it's Kara." She sounds weak, her voice softer than usual. "I'm sick again. I can't believe the timing. I'm having more tests. Just please stay positive and hang in there. Akia might take the auditorium job, but there are things happening for you that you don't see yet. I promise." Someone speaks to her, and she says, "I have to go. Just remember this: I never break a promise. And I just promised you that things are happening for you that you don't yet see." She disconnects.

I share the information with Jack, and he uses her promise as encouragement, but later, when we're both back at work on our own,

I'm back in my own head and not in a good way. The conversation with Kara is now playing like a taunt.

She never breaks a promise.

Adam's words.

I'm seeing Adam everywhere I look, and I can't seem to look away.

Chapter Seventy-Three

You cannot depend on your eyes when your imagination is out of focus . . .

—Mark Twain

It's midmorning, and I'm in the paranormal section of floor three, just having finished up with a patron. My finger runs over the Vampire Chronicles by Anne Rice, a series that is truly about killers pretending to be just normal people. Just as I feel right now—like a killer pretending to be a normal human.

Exactly why I've stayed on the floor with patrons, and far away from Jack, one of the only people who knows me well enough to look into my eyes and see the shift from human to killer. A plan that goes right out the door as he hunts me down, rather ironically, right here, next to that vampire novel I was just contemplating. "It's almost eleven," he says, appearing distracted by some impending deadline he goes on to explain. "I agreed to twice-a-week PT for a month, starting today. It's supposedly my answer to not getting surgery, per my doctor."

My relief at his departure and my escape from his all-too-seeing eyes is immense, a tidal wave washing over me, but I manage to keep cool. "Well, maybe it is," I encourage him. "You want me to bring you some lunch back when I run out?"

"That would be appreciated."

"You got it."

He heads out, and finally I have the green light to return to my office and tackle the paperwork waiting on me while he's away. I've just settled in, sitting at my desk to get busy, when my cellphone buzzes with a text message. My pang of unease is instant, filling me with a sense of dread that is now a programmed reaction to any communication, when only weeks ago I felt no such thing.

Back then, which wasn't really "back then" at all, my text feed was filled with messages from my two Js, as well as my father here and there, all pleasant exchanges I looked forward to and enjoyed. With a leaden hand, I reach for my phone, unsurprised to find Adam in my alert box. His message reads: I made you an eye doctor appointment for your lunch hour. The address, my own personal eye doctor's address, which is only a few blocks from here, is included in the text. I wet my dry lips and swallow hard with the real message in this message. He knows everything, even who I use for my eye care.

He is always close and usually closer than I assume.

He must be a hacker or pay someone who is a hacker to monitor me. It's the only way he could know such personal details about me.

With her typical bad timing, my mother chooses then to call. Certain, without a question mark to be found, that I cannot handle her right now, I hit the decline button. Right after, and I mean *right after* I do so, I receive a text from my father: I trust the attorney handling the negotiation. We'll get a solid contract, honey. I promise. Thanks for worrying. I love you.

Defeat is imminent, I think, both his and mine. I forward the message to Jess. She replies almost instantly with: I'm having lunch with our mutual attorney. Erin will not be attending. I'll call you after. As for your dad, ask him to have a second attorney from a different firm read the contract before signing. Tell him it's standard practice with a contract this large. It's bullshit but it buys you time. I'll get you another name.

It's great advice, and I text my father: Jess suggests you have a second attorney from another firm review the contract when this much is on the line. She's getting us a second recommendation.

That's very kind of her, he answers. Can we get that name today?

That question—"today?"—tells me all I need to know. I was right. He was silent last night because he's already made up his mind about the patent. He was about to sign the deal with Big Davis. *Good Lord, and thank you, Jess.* She bought me and my father time. I reply to his message with: I'll text her now.

I forward the exchange to Jess and add a note that states the obvious: I think he was about to sign with Big Davis.

Her reply: I'll text him the second attorney's name. I already talked to that person. There won't be a repeat of what happened with Nick. I feel like shit for recommending someone who seems to want to sleep with me and Big Davis.

I actually laugh, when that really shouldn't be possible right now, and shoot her back a quick response, after which I glance at the clock and conclude the paperwork has to wait. It seems I have an eye doctor appointment, and my master and stalker will not be pleased if I do not attend.

After I check the lunch coverage with the staff, I grab my bag and make my way to the escalators. I'm on the way down, about to call in a take-out order to be ready in about forty-five minutes, when floor two comes into view, and my heart thunders in my chest. The man, the stranger who was in the board meeting but is not a board member, is there, and oh yes, he's watching me. Our eyes lock, his boldly holding mine, and I can feel the connection this time, and not a connection between me and him. Between him and Adam. Every instinct I own screams a warning in my head and body.

The minute the wall disconnects our view of each other, I start walking down the steps I would normally ride. I'm motivated, ready for answers where there have been none. Adam, the man who made me a killer in my mind, *is* invisible. This man, *this man*, whoever he is, is not.

Once I'm on floor one, I cut left, ignoring Akia, who I walk right past, and heading for the escalators that lead to floor two. Once I'm at the escalator, I am all but running up them, panting as I round the corner to find the man and all his things gone. He knew. He knew I was coming for him.

Chapter Seventy-Four

"Finally going for it, are you?" Dr. Smith asks as he rolls his chair in front of the one I'm presently sitting in. "I've been trying to get you in contacts for years. You're going to love them when you jog."

"I'm sure I will," I concede, all too willing to admit that glasses while jogging are challenging at best, and at worst a tad bit dangerous, considering they fall off, or fog up, when I keep them on, and I'm virtually blind without them. "You know why I've resisted," I add. "It's the whole finger in the eye thing. It bothers me."

"It becomes second nature. I promise."

He says this, and I know he means well, but he's still forced to spend the next fifteen minutes trying to convince me just to put the lenses in my eyes. However, once they're finally in, my glasses packed neatly in a case in my purse, I'm feeling pretty darn amazed about how crisp and clear everything around me is looking right now.

Once I'm at the front desk checking out, his tech Mauve, who actually has a shade of mauve hair, asks, "How do you like them so far?"

"Better than I thought I would."

"And even better a week from now, I promise." She hands me a sheet of paper. "This is your prescription, but don't order until you're sure the prescription feels right. We can tweak it if needed."

A few minutes later I step outside and reach for my nose to shove my glasses up, an obvious habit, but my glasses are not on my face. "I do like this," I murmur to myself, but I also dread the next time my finger must go in my eye.

Glancing at my watch, I find it's now pretty darn late, and I never even ordered lunch after the floor-two guy distracted me. With no time to think about how weird the entire situation with him truly is, I quickly call in the order.

Once that's done, I turn to start my walk back to the restaurant, only to jolt as I find Akia standing in front of me. "Akia," I say. "What are you doing here?"

He points to the taco joint next to the eye doctor, which I dislike immensely, despite loving tacos. "Our separate worlds get smaller and smaller, it seems," he comments. "I just talked to Neil, by the way." He holds up the taco bag. "I'm taking him back some lunch. He wants us to work together tomorrow. The whole pass-the-baton kind of thing."

Little spikes of displeasure punish my insides. "Of course he does," I comment, as dryly as possible. "I'll just need to confirm my schedule with Kara."

"Word is Kara won't be back until next week. She's pretty sick."

"I'll call her," I say, worried about her now, far more so than I am about Akia and Neil taking over the auditorium.

He shrugs. "Either way, let's just meet at the auditorium at eight in the morning."

It's not a question. It's an expectation I do not accept, my resistance obvious in my reply: "I'll call you this afternoon and schedule it."

"Right," he says, a smirk on his face. "I better get Neil his food." He starts to turn and then pauses to add, "Contacts work for you. So does the new wardrobe. In time you'll win Neil over. A group of us are going to happy hour tonight at Wildhorse right down the road. It's kind of a celebration of my new job, but you know, Neil will be there. You showing up would go a long way with him." He winks, a taunt in his action, before he firmly offers me his back as he walks away.

I watch him depart, aware now that Akia is not in a class of his own. He's devious, in the same class as Adam, only I assume he hasn't escalated his actions to murder. But you don't have to kill people to hurt people.

I have no doubt right now that the only reason I didn't lose my pay level was that email Jack convinced me to write. It won some of the board members over, people more powerful than Neil. The way Adam is more powerful than Akia.

By the time I'm walking toward the restaurant, I'm dialing Kara, thrown directly into her voicemail. "Hey," I say, "it's Mia. I'm worried about you. I heard you might be out all week. I'm going to train Akia in the morning. I won't rock the boat. Let me know if I can bring you anything. Food, maybe? Okay. Well. Call me or text me and let me know you're okay."

I've just ended the message when another call comes in. I'm unsurprised to find Adam on my caller ID, but I literally have to force my finger to hit the answer button. "Hello," I manage.

"What happened with Akia?"

His demand riles me up, and while I suspect he expects my submission, I surprise myself with the momentary warrior in me. "Do you really need me to tell you?" I challenge, thinking of the man on floor two. "As you said, you know things."

"I do know things," he confirms. "But I don't know what only you can tell me. Let me make this simple for you. Go ahead and assume I know everything. What are you going to do about Akia?"

I *do* have to assume he knows everything—of this, I've already decided, even before this call. "I haven't decided yet," I reply, buying time to figure out a better answer, for him and me.

"Wrong answer, Mia," he replies, and just as I reach the restaurant door, pausing by the wall, he adds, "Get your food, Mia. And *Jack's.* We'll talk tonight."

I don't like the way he says Jack's name, as if he's scorned, and my warrior returns, fighting through the submissive me that he's been dominating. I have to fight back. It feels right. Therefore I say, "I told you, I don't want to talk anymore."

"And I told you, talking is the way to control you and me."

"Talking to other people, not you, *is* me taking control."

"We agreed to talk last night. We agreed you would explain what you are doing and why, and then, and *only* then, would I allow you to become your own solution."

"I don't remember that exact conversation."

He's silent for a heavy beat before he says, "I don't want to take things into my own hands, Mia. Just remember you left me no choice." He disconnects.

Panic rushes over me, and I redial his number, regretting my warrior side hard and fast, *hating* my warrior side. It goes straight to voicemail. Over and over, I try him back, and over and over, my attempts land in voicemail. My phone buzzes with a text, and for once I pray it's Adam, only to find Jack nudging me to return to work: Starving. You almost back?

Damn it, I have to grab the food and get back to work before Jack is suspicious—or worse, Akia uses my tardiness against me in some way. I text Adam: I'll talk. Tonight. And I'm surprised how much I like the contacts.

I pray I've said enough.

I rush inside, grab the food, and hurry back to work. Soon Jack and I are sitting at the break room table, eating our sandwiches while he freaks out about me giving up my glasses. But I can barely hear the words he's speaking to me because Adam hasn't replied to my text message. All I can hear in my head is his words: *Just remember you left me no choice.*

Chapter Seventy-Five

My afternoon is spent once again avoiding Jack while worrying about Akia. Is Adam going to hurt him? Even when Adam is silent, I cannot escape his presence, in what I liken to being captive on Alcatraz, with the devil as my master.

Thankfully Jack and I have only about ten minutes to shove down our food before we're back on the floor, handling patrons. Otherwise I don't know how I would possibly manage to keep him from figuring out there is mania going on inside my head.

I check my phone for updates from my father, Jess, and, most importantly right now, Adam. The later it gets, the closer to happy hour, the more I wonder if I should just go with Akia, stay by his side, act like a clumsy, stupid girl with a crush. Anything to keep him close.

I don't have to like him to want him to live.

I've decided that's exactly what I'll do when Jack finds me in the office, packing up for the evening. "Kara's not just sick. She's in the hospital."

"I heard she was out for perhaps the rest of the week. Are you sure? How do you know?"

"Akia," he replies with obvious reluctance. "I went downstairs to check on her. He told me. I'm going to call and see if I can get an update on her." He grabs his phone, and I claim the chair next to his desk.

A few minutes later he disconnects from the nurse's station. "They aren't going to talk to me. You want to go by the hospital and see if we can find out anything?"

How am I supposed to say, sorry, no, I have to go to happy hour with Akia?

Happy hour, I tell myself, *is safe*. And the more I think about it, the worse I think it is that I be near Akia. Adam wanted me to watch Kevin die. That could be his thing. If I am with Akia, and maybe he expects that's exactly where I'll be, trying to protect him, Akia may well be in worse danger.

"Yes," I say. "I'm in. Let's go check on her."

Jack scoops up his bag and we head out together.

Akia is on his own, but it's my gamble to keep him alive.

I tell myself he's safer without me.

Chapter Seventy-Six

Kara isn't at the hospital at all, nor is she answering her phone.

"Why would Akia lie about such a thing?" Jack asks me as we exit the hospital a few blocks from my loft, then quickly adds, "I'll walk you home."

Just that easily, all my time spent avoiding Jack is null and void. I can no longer run, and it's a feeling that is broader than just our stroll down the sidewalk. It's a windy night, chilly but not cold, the sound of music as a party bus loudly passes reminding me that Akia is at happy hour. Akia is a target. And Adam still has not contacted me.

"I agree," I reply. "Obviously, Akia lied. I don't pretend to be in that man's head, but . . . I did tell him I needed to check with her before I trained him. Let that lead your thoughts where it might."

"He used me to make you feel that wasn't possible," he assumes.

"Maybe," I say. "I really don't know. Like I said, I don't pretend to know what is going on in that man's head."

"Nothing that goes on inside ours," he assures me. "You want to get a pizza? I promised Jess I'd do the dating profile tonight. You can help me."

It's weird to me that he hasn't told me he has a dating profile he paused, but maybe that's his plan tonight. The problem is, What happens if Adam calls? Or sees Jack at my loft and has a problem with it?

And how do I hide the killer I've become from Jack in such an intimate environment?

By finding a dark place that isn't my loft to substitute, I decide. "How about Mexican instead? That little taco joint we love? We can order a drink for your dating-profile courage."

"Sure," he says, patting his briefcase. "I have my computer with me, and you know I love that place."

"That place." I laugh. "We never remember the name."

"No, we do not," he agrees, chuckling with me.

A few minutes later Jack and I are in a dark corner joint with cantina music playing, and we both have salted Mexican martinis in front of us. "I have a confession," Jack announces, salting the chips.

This, I decide, is when he tells me about his dating profile. "I hope it's scandalous."

"It's not," he replies. "I signed up for a couple dating apps a few months back. I know, I know, I'm pathetic. I chatted with a few people, went on two miserable dates, and decided I just didn't have the energy. I'm going to give Jess the rundown on those dates and chats, and call it done."

I'm surprised that he did this without inviting me to join him or at least dishing on the activity, but maybe he felt I was bad luck. And he still didn't tell me about being on the one Jess suggested and then deleting it the minute I joined as well, but I decide to just let it go. There're much bigger problems to worry about right now.

For instance, Why hasn't Adam called or texted? And what will I do if he does either when I'm with Jack?

For now, I stay in the present and dive further into the topic of dating options. "We could hit the party buses," I joke. "Or," I add, "Carly on floor two met her husband at a wedding. Maybe you shouldn't be taking me as your date, but rather a friend. Then you leave your options open."

"Well, we can tell my sister you're my date. If there's some gorgeous woman who hits on me at the wedding, I'll disappear, and you can tell her I'm an asshole for cheating on you. She'd love it."

"Oh gosh, maybe we should plan it and make it happen. If only we could get Jess to attend the wedding and play the game with us."

"I'd rather it really happen," he comments as the tacos are set in front of us.

"True," I say. "Maybe it will."

"Or maybe we're getting married in ten years, two best friends who are both losers with the opposite sex."

"Good Lord," I say, finishing off a bite of taco. "Now you've wiped away all flattery over your dating proposition."

"I could do worse," he comments, dabbing his mouth with his napkin.

"Okay, stop while we're still friends and have not killed our ten-year safety net."

His cellphone rings, and he snags it from his pocket, glances at it, and says, "I need to take this. I'll be right back." He slides off his stool and leaves me and his food behind.

I frown as I watch him appear outside the window just a couple of tables down. Jack has never taken a call and not told me who it was before, let alone left the building to speak in private.

What the heck is going on?

Chapter Seventy-Seven

When Jack returns after finishing up with his mysterious call outside, he doesn't explain himself at all, and I don't push him. Lord knows, I've checked my phone for anything from Adam numerous times, and I even considered a run to the bathroom to try to call him.

Thankfully we fall back into our easy banter, and Jack never questions me or my weird behavior. That could translate into me managing to act normal. Or maybe whatever is going on in his life that he's obviously not telling me about is distracting enough for me to earn a pass for the evening. I'm not sure I like either option.

When dinner is over, we begin the stroll back to my loft. "I'm just going to write up dating-site app notes for Jess and email them to her," Jack says decidedly, as if the topic has been under grand debate, when it has not. We haven't talked about it at all over dinner. "Then I'm just done with this," he adds. "You could do the same for the last time you were on the sites."

"True," I say. "And I might just do that."

"How formal is Jess's awards ceremony, and where is it?"

"You know, I didn't even ask," I say, "but I assume at her offices. They have an auditorium. I've been there a couple of times. It's actually a really nice building."

"They're owned by some major publication," he replies. "That really doesn't surprise me."

We near my loft, and I'm already debating ways to convince him he doesn't need to come up, but it turns out that's not a real challenge. Once we're in the building, Jack is ready to head home, glancing at his watch. "How is it almost nine already? We both better get some rest. You have to deal with Akia in the morning, and I have to deal with my sister on Saturday. Maybe I need to go get one of those vitamin drips at that place down the road at lunch tomorrow in hopes of combating the stress of her for an afternoon and Jess for an evening."

"Maybe we both do," I say, and neither of us is laughing.

The two of us understand stressing over little things that feel big to us and small to others.

I open the door to the building and pause. "I think I'll start with wine tonight. Per Akia I'm to meet him at eight in the morning to pass the baton. And Kara is radio silent. I do hope she's okay."

"Maybe she'll show up tomorrow, but drink the wine in case you're stuck with Akia."

We say our good nights, and I head inside the building, pausing as I notice the bookstore door cracked open, with no sound blasting from within.

Curious if Ben actually listened after I threatened to murder his iPhone, I ease into the doorway to find a short, middle-age woman in a frumpy dress cleaning the store—sweeping, to be exact—instead of Ben. "Hello," I greet.

"Oh, hello," she says, smiling at me, her hand settling on her robust belly, while the other holds the broom. "You must be Mia, the tenant upstairs. I'm Blanca."

"Where's Ben?"

"I have no idea. I've never met him. I work for an on-call cleaning service. Me and Yvette are here working. She's in the back somewhere. We go wherever we're sent. Can I help you with anything?"

"No," I say. "No, thank you. Happy cleaning."

She smiles brightly. "Thank you. Have a good evening."

"You too," I say, but I hesitate, confused by their presence, before I back out of the door and head upstairs.

I'm standing at my island, staring at my message thread with Adam, willing him to reply when an ugly thought hits me. This is what he wants, for me to fear his silence. He's teaching me to never defy him again.

Hours later, I lie in bed and do what I have not done in too long, what I always did each night with my father before bed. I pray and not for myself. I vow to never defy Adam again if only Akia survives the night.

Chapter Seventy-Eight

I barely remember falling asleep, but the next morning I wake with a jolt to a sitting position with the realization that the buzzer for my door is going off. Someone is holding down the button. I grab my phone and check the time, which reads forty-five minutes before my alarm is scheduled to strike its attack on my slumber.

This has to be Adam-driven in some way, and even as the buzzer assaults my ears, I check my messages, expecting something from him and finding nothing.

For a whimsical, wonderful moment, I dare to think maybe he's gone.

Could he be gone?

I reject the stupidity of my own thoughts.

No, he is not gone, and whoever is at my door is probably holding another delivery from him, which is a daunting prospect. Somehow I doubt it's clothing this time.

My cellphone begins to ring in my hand with Jess's number. I decline the call and throw away my blankets, walking into my closet to pull on sweats, a tank, and slippers. The buzzer is still going off, and my phone dings with a text.

I grab it to read a message from Jess: I'm downstairs, woman. Answer your door.

Relief washes over me. The buzzer has nothing to do with Adam, but good Lord, Jess is so melodramatic. She probably has muffins, warm from the oven, and doesn't want me to sleep through the delight. This wouldn't be the first time she woke me in crisis over baked goods.

I walk down the stairs and hit the button to allow her entry, then walk into the kitchen to start a pot of coffee. I've just filled the water carafe when the door opens, but Jess isn't alone. Jack is with her, both of them looking like they rolled out of bed and threw on whatever was nearby. Jess's bare face confirms as much. This was no planned, organized visit. My two Js are not only together; their faces are etched in shadows, the kind that speak of tragedy. My chest freezes, air locked into my lungs. I set the pot down and step to the island, bracing myself on the counter for something horrific, something I may not survive.

I can feel my body quaking, my heart beating at warp speed, a panic attack threatening to claim control over me. What has Adam done? "Please tell me it's not my parents," I whisper.

"No," Jess says, rounding the counter to stand in front of me, catching my shoulders, and turning me toward her. "Akia was stabbed to death last night in a bar fight."

I blink at her, not quite digesting the words she's just spoken.

Jack joins us, shrinking the size of my little kitchen with his large body. "You didn't wish this on him, Mia, but I know you're going to blame yourself."

I rotate out of Jess's grip to face Jack, still not fully processing what has happened. "Akia is dead?"

"Yes," he confirms, and I swear I hate myself for the avalanche of relief that crashes over me, for just how thankful I am that it's Akia who is dead, and not my parents, or even one or both of my two Js.

I turn away from them both, afraid they'll see the poison Adam has created in me, the ability to be happy that one man is dead versus another. I tell myself that I'm not cold. I'm not heartless. I'm just—trying to digest it all, trying to survive Adam's menace, his reign of terror.

I grab the counter by the kitchen sink, holding on to it as if I were holding on to the last of my own soul, and maybe I am. Adam is changing me. I feel it in my bones. "Apparently there was a big brawl in the bar," Jess explains from behind me. "It's not Akia's first fight. He's apparently an instigator, but when it broke up, something happened in the bathroom. Someone stabbed him. It's all over the news."

I rotate to face them both. "Do they know who did it?" I ask hopefully, truly hopefully. I need this to end. The right camera footage could deliver that gift.

"There was no camera footage," Jack replies, as if he's read my mind. "The police opened up a tip line." He moves toward me and the sink. "I'll make the coffee."

I nod, in shock, I think, because I don't seem to be capable of reacting with anything more. I'm not crying. I'm not screaming. I'm not speaking, not more than I have to, but I'm also not numb.

There is an icy tightness in my chest that feels as if it might squeeze the life out of me at any moment.

"I'll turn on the news," Jess offers, rounding the counter and walking to the living room, where the remote rests on the coffee table.

A few minutes later, I sit on the couch with my two Js on either side of me, in my hand coffee that I am not drinking, but the warmth of the mug somehow eases the iciness of that ball in my chest. Jack ignores his coffee cup as well, where it sits on the coffee table, flipping through channels as we look for various news stories on Akia's death.

"Which of you found out first?" I ask, the only thing I've spoken in fifteen minutes.

"Me," Jack replies. "Kara's husband called me. He said she's very sick, but she was worried about how you and the rest of the staff would handle this today. Which is why I need to run home and shower and get to the library."

"I'll be there," I promise. "I'm okay. I have to be okay."

"You didn't wish this on him," he repeats, and only when he reaches for my mug do I realize I'm trembling.

He sets it on a coaster next to his cup.

"But I benefit from it, right?" I challenge. "I get the auditorium back."

"Or you turn it down," he says. "Do what feels right, Mia. As for now, we'll just focus on helping the staff get through this. In fact, I'm going to let my family know we aren't attending the wedding." He eyes Jess. "And I won't be attending your event. I know that breaks your heart." He returns his attention to me. "I'm going to volunteer to cover Akia's spot."

"I'll work with you," I offer quickly, thankful that I won't be his plus-one at the wedding. This shift in events may well protect him from gaining Adam's attention. At least for a little while, I add, but not forever. I know this now. I know it in every part of my being. Jack will become a target if I don't do something to end my connection with Adam.

"I'm going to go now so I can get to the library as early as possible," Jack states, dragging me out of my head and back into the conversation.

I nod, and he hugs me before exchanging a look with Jess and then standing up. I'm staring at an image of Akia on the television when the door opens and shuts.

"I'll come stay the night," Jess offers. "I need to bring you dresses for tomorrow anyway. Or would you rather stay with me? Or I guess you could stay with Adam, right? I forgot you're seeing him now."

Just the mention of Adam's name out loud grinds through me, threatening to thrust me into a cesspool of bad thoughts, destined to lead me to an inappropriately timed meltdown. "The last thing I want is to be with a man I barely know tonight," I say, and the truth is I would rather stay with her, sheltered in her home, not mine, but I don't dare. I'm terrified that if I run to her house, hide with her from Adam,

I somehow turn her into Adam's enemy and a target. "I'm probably going to need to be alone tonight. How about just pizza and dresses?"

"Sounds good. You okay if I go home and get ready for work?"

"I'm okay," I assure her, standing to reinforce the statement.

We hug, and I lock up after her, leaning on the door.

Adam killed Akia. I know this.

I run up the stairs and check my phone. When there's still nothing from him, I try to call him. The call goes to voicemail.

Chapter Seventy-Nine

The tears, guilt, and helplessness hit me in the shower.

My body quakes, tears mixing with the hot water of the stream from above, a storm erupting with a fierceness that I cannot control. My knees wobble, unable to hold my weight and the burden of the crash happening inside my body. I end up sitting in a corner, whimpering like a baby, losing track of time, space, and even the water that is icy when I finally come back to reality, my new reality.

I am a prisoner to a monster.

There is no escape.

It's not until I finally calm myself down—or perhaps blow through enough emotion to find that calmness—that I'm able to haul my now-chilled body out of the shower, wrapping myself in a warm towel. I sit on the edge of the bed, and it's then that I begin to use my brain, not my emotions. It's then when an idea, an escape passage of sorts, opens in my mind. Mike, my old friend from school, the FBI agent. He's the answer to every question in my life right now. I have to go to him. But how? How do I go to him without Adam knowing?

There lies the problem, and it's not a small one, at all. If I reach out to Mike, there will be a price, and that price will be written in blood. I pace and pace some more, trying to formulate a plan that finally comes to me. I text Jack: I am going to be late, but I'll be there.

No problem, he replies. You okay?

I'm okay, I answer, and I am, I think. Because I know how to get to Mike, and Mike will know how to get to Adam.

An hour later, I've inserted the contacts with no problem, refusing to let a finger in the eye be important right now. There are lives on the line. They matter. That is my focus. I've also dressed in one of the outfits Adam gave me, ensuring he knows I'm still following his orders, even if I'm not. This one is a cream, fitted knit Valentino dress, complemented with simple black piping across the bust. I once again wear my boots, as I am certain I'll need to be fast-footed today.

Once I'm ready to walk out the door, I go nowhere. Instead, I get to work on my plan.

I sit at my kitchen island and meticulously put together a file of text messages, links to a Dropbox folder with recordings of calls and everything and anything I can think of that might help Mike catch Adam. Details of Kevin's murder are the hardest to document, but I don't hold back. I end with a note: The most important thing I can leave you with, Mike, is this: he seems to know everything I do. He has a digital footprint as well. Be careful. We can't meet. We can't talk. He'll find out. And he might kill us all.

Once I'm ready to leave, I grab my bag, the envelope stuffed inside, check my phone for messages, and, when I find none, hurry out my door. Once I'm downstairs, I stand in front of the bookstore that doesn't open for an hour, unlock it, and then shut myself inside. I drop my purse by the door and rush through the building, halting under the tiles where I hid the cards Adam gave me the night he killed Kevin. I knew I saved them for a reason, and the reason is now. I've written about them in the notes to Mike, and I climb a ladder to retrieve them.

When I push aside the ceiling tile and reach for them, panic overtakes me. They're not there. They're gone.

Chapter Eighty

Adam knows and sees everything.

The missing cards drive home that point with brutal force. He must have followed me that night. He must have seen me place the cards in the ceiling. Or maybe there are cameras in the bookstore I don't know about, and he tapped into those. Either way, the cards are gone, and I have a decision to make. Abort my mission to communicate with Mike or continue onward with it.

I can't abort, no matter what the risk.

Two people are dead.

One was too many.

More might follow.

I do briefly consider randomly mailing in everything I've collected to the police station, or to the FBI offices where Mike works, but how long will that take to get to anyone who reads it? How many piles of tips and mail do they process daily? No. Time matters, and I cannot back down.

I have to act now, not later.

I hurry down the street to the quirky little coffee shop that Mike frequents and do so earlier than I've noticed him arriving in the past, in hopes of arriving before him, not after. Nerves shoot through about every part of my body as I enter the Caffeine Castle and walk to the counter, thankful there is no line.

There is an older man behind the register, about half-bald, but fit, as if he hits the gym and tries to hold on to any bit of his youth he can, if not his hair. I've never seen him before, but then I don't come in often. I order coffee for me and Jack, pay, and when I should step aside, I reach in my purse and slide the envelope on the counter. "Can you please give this to Mike when he gets in? Discreetly, please?"

"Sure. He's already been in today. We probably won't see him until Monday. Is that okay?"

My spine stiffens, everything inside me resisting the delay, but there is no solution but to wait, not if I plan to follow through with this mission in a safe way. "Yes. Yes, that's fine. Thank you for doing this." I eye his name tag, and the ice in my chest is back. It reads ADAM. "Your name is Adam?" There is accusation in my voice I cannot quite tamp down.

"It is," he says, grabbing a cup, an ink pen hovering just above the paper surface. "And yours is?"

"Mia," I state. "My name is Mia."

He scribbles that on the cup. "Okay, then. We'll call your name when your order is ready, and I'll get your envelope to Mike."

"Thanks," I say softly, but there is still the ice in my chest, which seems to have slid down my body and frozen my feet to the ground. What are the odds of this man's name being *Adam*? "How long have you been working here . . ." I pause for effect and add, *"Adam?"*

"About a year. Know Mike real well. He's been coming in awhile. Don't you worry. I'll see him Monday for sure."

"Thanks," I repeat, but my hope is now fear, and my fear is controlling me much as Adam does, with every beat of my once-happy heart.

Chapter Eighty-One

Adam.

That name is haunting me. I literally handed "Adam" my tell-all on "Adam."

I'm berating myself for what feels like a stupid move during the walk to the library, but there's really no time to process my own possible bad move. My cellphone rings, my earbuds announcing my father's call. "Answer," I order my Apple device, and the moment my father is on the line, he says, "I just saw the news. Did you know that young man who was in the bar fight? They said he worked at the library."

"I did," I say, but hearing his voice punches at my emotions and drives home how much I have to fight to keep him and his problems off Adam's radar. "It's a bit of a shock," I add.

"Were you at the happy hour? The news said a group from the library was out together when the attack took place?"

"That's what I hear, but I was at dinner with Jack."

"Oh, thank God," he gushes in relief. "I'm thankful you were there and that you're safe and well. Makes you really realize how short life can be. All the more reason to get this patent sold and secure my family's future."

"Please don't use Akia as a reason to sign a contract with Big Davis, Dad, and especially without meeting with the second attorney."

"I'm meeting him today. Jess got me the name, and I set-up an appointment, but, Mia, if this new attorney says the contract is golden, it's golden. It's a lot of money on the line and a hell of a lot of security for my family. That means you, baby girl."

"I care about you and your invention, not money." I round the corner to bring the library into view and halt at the news trucks and crews all around the building. "I have to go, Dad. The library is surrounded by press and chaos right now. Just please think hard before you sign. I love you."

"I love you, too. Be safe."

We disconnect, and I hurry forward, spying what appears to be a memorial for Akia in front of the library, flowers, and notes, and random items displayed for all to view. Because no matter what a jerk he was to me, he was a human being with family and friends who loved him. He didn't deserve to die. Nearing the entrance, I press through the crush of the crowd and activity, showing the police my credentials and eyeing the line to enter the library. Even our security guard is a police officer today. Once I'm inside, I spy Jack behind the help desk, a line of people waiting on him. I hurry forward, join him, and offer him his coffee.

"Thanks," he says. "I need this. It's chaos here."

"Have you checked on things upstairs?"

"Our team is holding down floor three. Here is the problem. Half the staff down here called in sick. Apparently most of them were at the happy hour with Akia when he died. They aren't taking it very well, as you can imagine."

I can imagine, I think, wondering how many of those people were close to Akia, even his version of my two Js.

"Well, let's handle things so they don't have to," I say, and with that in mind, my phone goes into the pocket in my dress. "I'm ready," I add, opening the cabinet beneath the counter and shoving my purse inside, ready to get to work.

With speed in mind, Jack and I break the line in two, offering aid where we can, in every way we can, but there are a lot of people just curious enough to want to ask questions. Lookie-loos in the library, which is really not cool at all.

Worse, there's an event in the auditorium that doesn't cancel, and I'm forced to manage. It feels weird to do my job that I was scheduled to train Akia to do this very morning—creepy, even, and I fight off guilt. I allowed Adam to know too much about my conflict with Akia.

Once I've ensured the group renting the auditorium is settled in, Neil corners me in the hallway. "Thank you for taking care of the auditorium. The police want to talk to you."

"To me?"

"To everyone. They're looking for suspects in Akia's murder last night."

That's all he says, just that, before he turns and walks away.

I draw in a shaky breath and press my hand to my belly. I'm going to be a suspect. He took my job. I'm the person everyone is going to point at. I'm starting to spiral when one of the employees calls my name, a call really for me to get back to work. I hurry down the hallway to attend the employee and a patron, which morphs into another employee and patron.

At some point in the midafternoon, I exchange texts with Jess, but I barely remember the content for the craziness around me. It's around three when Jack and I slip into the zoo break room and manage to down a couple of bites of cold pizza that someone, maybe Neil, ordered hours before.

"They think Kara has an ulcer," Jack informs me after slugging down a drink of sugary Coke. "Her husband called to check on you hours ago, and he told me. I just never got a breather to tell you."

"Oh wow. Well, that explains a lot about her chronic problems. How is she?"

"In pain, but they are working on getting her on the right meds."

I've just taken another bite of my slice when a uniformed police officer steps into the room, the sight of him in the doorway jolting me, as if Neil didn't warn me this was coming. He did. I just seem to have lost the warning in a sandwich of chaos and questions, or, I imagine, more of that mental self-preservation. I didn't even warn Jack this was coming.

"Can I ask you two a few questions?" the officer asks.

My spine stiffens, my body tense, the line along my jaw tight enough to pop, and yet somehow I manage a friendly enough, "Of course, Officer," moving to the seat next to Jack to allow the officer to sit with us at the little table we've been sharing. "We have pizza," I offer, "but it's pretty cold."

"I'm good, but thank you." He's a young man with dark hair and wrinkle-free skin. I can only hope that indicates he doesn't have enough experience to coax guilt and a confession from me over pepperoni pizza.

"I'm Officer Kelley," he informs us, claiming his seat and pulling out a little white notebook like the ones you see officers use on television. "This will be fast," he adds. "Where were you both last night?"

Jack is quick to spare me, answering for us both, explaining our trip to the hospital and then the taco joint that neither of us can name, even under pressure. Officer Kelley scribbles notes on his pad, then takes down our addresses and as much detail as Jack offers him. "We'll confirm all of this easily enough," he assures us before he flips to a page, shuts the pizza box, and sets a list of names on top of it for our review. "These employees were at the bar with Akia. Do any of them have a reason to want him dead?"

"Want him dead?" I ask. "One of his friends and coworkers? I thought it was a bar fight?"

"We work on floor three," Jack replies before Officer Kelley can answer me. "We don't know Akia or his group well at all. We're just covering for them because most of them are out today." He glances at the list. "Those are all his coworkers from this floor."

"Exactly what I was going to say," I interject, but my mind is racing. I should tell Officer Kelley about the job situation, but Jack grabs my hand under the table and squeezes, as if warning me to keep my mouth shut.

"We do believe it was a random bar fight," Officer Kelley says, answering my question. "But it's standard practice to cover all bases." He reaches in his pocket and hands each of us one of his cards. "If you think of anything or hear anything we need to know, please call me." He nods and stands, exiting the room.

I twist around to face Jack. "I should have—"

"No," he says, his tone soft but absolute. "That information serves no purpose. You kept your pay. You were not at the bar. The end, Mia."

"But others will tell him."

"The only others who will talk were at the bar and are far more worried about themselves right now than you."

"Yes, but—"

"No, Mia. Again, I say, *the end*." He stands. "Let's get back to work."

Chapter Eighty-Two

The library closes at six that evening, and Jack and I wrap up the paperwork on floor three. "You want to come over?" I ask. "Jess is coming by, but there will be pizza, much better than what we had at lunch."

"I told my sister we'd go to dinner since I'm skipping the wedding tomorrow. And the party, by the way. I'm not sure I told you that or not."

"I'd still like you to come, Jack."

"I'll cover here and let you leave early. We have piles of paperwork for both floors to catch up on. I might just order dinner here tomorrow night and do it all. I wish I could do that tonight, but apparently Akia dying has freaked out my sister. She wants to see me."

I'm reminded of what my father said this morning and speak my own version now. "Life is short. Take care of those you love."

"Yes, it is," he says. "And that's why I'm driving you home."

It's fifteen minutes later when he pulls into the driveway of the bookstore and then folds me into a big hug. "You didn't kill Akia," he says when he pulls back and meets my stare. "Don't go trying to convince people otherwise, especially the police."

If he only knew the truth, I think. If he only knew about Adam. I don't know if I've ever wanted to tell him as much as I do now, but I also don't know that there was ever a worse time to do so, either. Instead, I bite my tongue, nod, and slide out of my seat, shutting him inside his car and watching him drive away. Only then do I enter the building, and at this point the bookstore is closed for the evening, but it will be open bright and early tomorrow. I hurry up the side stairs, halting abruptly when I reach my loft level only to discover a small, jewelry-size box sitting in front of my door with a red ribbon. My stomach twists in knots. Adam is no longer silent.

I pick up the box and open my door. Once I'm inside, I sit down on a stool at the kitchen island and stare at the box, unsure what to expect. Does he know I dropped off that envelope to Mike? Is this some kind of punishment or warning? Oh God, is this something that tells me Mike is dead? With my heart beating like a drum, I rip off the ribbon and tear off the lid. I blink at the sparkling diamond necklace resting on black velvet but refuse to admire it, mentally rejecting the gift, all his gifts. Underneath I discover the cards I placed in the ceiling tiles. "Oh my God," I whisper.

My cellphone rings, and I know without even looking that this is Adam calling, even without the alert from my earbuds. I hit the answer button, the earbuds allowing his voice to sound closer and more intimate as he says, "Hello, Mia."

"Hello, Adam," I reply.

"Do you like the gifts I gave you?"

"The necklace is beautiful," I say tightly, but I have not missed the plural reference in the question. I'm just not sure what to make of it yet.

"Wear it tomorrow night," he orders. "I'll be close. Watching you."

Did I tell him about tomorrow night? I don't think I ever told him. "How do you know about tomorrow night?" I ask cautiously.

"Why would you miss Jess's awards ceremony?" He doesn't give me time to answer, not that it's really a question. "What about the other gift?"

Does he mean the cards or killing Akia? It doesn't matter, I decide. My answer is the same. "I want you to stop giving me gifts. *Please.*"

"I told you. Talk to me. That's how you earn your independence, Mia."

"I was handling it," I say, not able to say Akia's name aloud. "My boss is out sick. You have to give me time to make things happen."

"You mean you were waiting on your security blanket to return. You do like your security blankets. That's becoming a problem for me, or, more importantly, you."

"She's not a security blanket. She's my boss."

"So is Neil."

The buzzer goes off on my door. "That's Jess. She's bringing dresses over for me to try on for tomorrow night's event."

He's silent a moment before he says, "You refused to talk to me, Mia. Don't do that again. And as for the cards, what I give you serves a purpose. Read them. Think about the messages. Learn from them. Keep them close, not far away." He pauses again, and the buzzer fills the silence. For some reason that I cannot explain, I can almost imagine his smile of satisfaction as he adds, "I look forward to seeing what dress you pick." He disconnects and the line goes dead.

He's silent now, but he is not gone.

Chapter Eighty-Three

Jess enters the loft with her arms piled high with garment bags. "I brought you so many great dresses. You have to try them on before we eat. I know you. You'll hate everything when your belly is full." She's already walking up my stairs toward my bedroom.

She's not wrong, especially considering I haven't been for a jog in a week, but the last thing I feel like right now, on the day I've learned of Akia's murder, is trying on dresses. Even more so when I know this game of dress-up pleases Adam. "I'm starving," I call after her. "And we need to talk about my father. I think you should leave the dresses and let me surprise you with the choices."

She pokes her head over the side of the loft. "Are you serious? You know I love to play dress-up with you."

The one thing she has in common with Adam, I think, but she was at my door this morning, comforting me while he stalks me. This is for her, not him, I remind myself. "Fine," I say. "Fine. Dresses first."

She grins and disappears over the rail again. I hurry up the stairs, and soon I'm inspecting gowns that she's laid out on the bed, instantly drawn to a long fuchsia-pink gown. "That one."

"Oh my God," Jess says, shoving a lock of blonde hair behind her ear. "Yes. The belted ruffled silk organza gown. That's a Maison Common, my newest brand obsession." She runs her hand over the skirt. "Look at the ruffles in the skirt to match the bodice."

She has me at Maison Common. I've never heard of the brand, and it's not a brand Adam has bought for me. Sold times a hundred, in fact. While, yes, I'll be forced to wear the necklace he just gave me, which is presently stuffed in a drawer for my eyes only, at least tonight, I don't have to wear anything else that remotely reminds me of him.

A few minutes later, I stand at the mirror and stare at myself in the gorgeous gown, in love with this as my choice. "I don't have to try on the rest," I announce. "This is the one."

"Yes," she agrees, stepping beside me. "Yes, it is. You look marvelous. I love it on you. It's almost as if I bought it with you in mind, which I did not, by the way, but now I feel like I need to give it to you. It's just so you."

"No," I say. "I will not wear it if you plan to gift it to me, because I might not know the brand, but I know it's expensive if you love it."

"One day I'll rank as high as Adam, and you'll let me buy you things. Just wear the gown and love it for the night then." Fortunately, as usual, she doesn't push hard and moves on. "Do any of the heels Adam gave you work for this dress, or do we need to try on shoes?"

I rotate, eager to continue the purge of all things Adam in any way possible, and my eyes land on a pair of strappy crystal Cinderella heels she's set out for me to inspect. "Those," I say. "I want those." I unzip the dress and step out of it. "And now we eat pizza."

"And now we eat pizza," she agrees, ordering for us.

It's not too much later, and we're sitting at my kitchen island eating pizza from one of our favorite joints, delicious pizza that makes up for the horrid pizza earlier today, when she says, "No more glasses. We never talked about that, you know. Still the Adam effect?"

I'm stuffed or she'd have just ruined my appetite. "I suppose so," I agree, dusting off my hands. "I went to the eye doc right before all this mess happened with Akia."

"Hmm. Well, that's a bad subject we'll avoid tonight, but you look good. Beautiful, Mia. I'm so happy you're starting to let yourself shine a bit. You deserve to feel good about yourself."

"I didn't feel bad about myself before," I argue, "and I'm not sure I prefer this new me to the old, anyway, so don't get used to this."

She holds up her hands. "No pressure." She reaches for another slice of pizza and takes a bite. "But since Jack isn't coming tomorrow night, you want to invite Adam?"

"I think a you-and-me night would be nice," I say quickly. "Unless you have a date?"

"I don't," she says. "I'm on a dud streak. What does a girl have to do to get a man who can kiss properly and knows when to touch and when not to touch? I'm all in for a you-and-me night."

And for a moment it's just like old times.

Me and Jess, hanging out, laughing, us against the world.

But it's not us against the world. It's me against Adam. And if I don't win the battle, she could end up just like Akia. *Dead.*

Chapter Eighty-Four

Saturday morning I wake to nothing but my alarm. No calls. No door buzzer. No text messages. It's uncomfortable, the eye of calm taunting me with the promise of very bad things to follow. I check my phone just to be safe, but there are no messages. There is nothing.

Once I'm awake I actually relish the feeling of nothingness, avoiding the drawer with the necklace and the note cards in it in favor of simply enjoying my coffee and reading a chapter from the book that I haven't touched in a week. I enjoy this escape so much that it's a struggle for me to force myself to slide my letter opener/bookmark behind a page to mark my spot.

An hour later I'm at work, well before Jack. I've agreed to open and take the early shift to allow my earlier departure at five since I'll be attending Jess's awards ceremony. Jack joins me midmorning with the intent of staying for the late-Saturday closing hour of seven.

When I depart for the day, it's with another offer thrown in Jack's direction. "You sure you don't want to go with me? It doesn't take you long to get ready, and we can be a little late."

"Not a chance," he says. "When we close, I'm going to go up to the records room, crank up the music, order dinner, and catch up on all our paperwork and inventory. Me and this place, with no one but a security guard as my unseen and unheard companion, is a sweet spot I haven't felt in a long time."

We are two pieces of the same puzzle, this man and me, and he doesn't have to explain the joy in his words. I understand them with every piece of who I am. Our friendship was kismet, no doubt about it.

I leave the library, actually feeling a little jealous that he will remain here, secluded from the world, as he loses himself in his love of the library and all the books that line the shelves.

I am no longer the me I know, I think, and not for the first time.

This is my first thought as I stand at the mirror, staring at my reflection in the gorgeous fuchsia dress and sparkling shoes, having a bit of an out-of-body experience. Of course the dress and shoes are stunning, but the girl, the *woman*, wearing them has my hair, my eyes, and my body—it's just all arranged differently these days. It's who I am beneath all those changes, and tonight's glam and glitter, that I question. I do believe some part of me always felt that if I looked more like Jess, I'd be more like her. That felt so far from possible I didn't even try. But now, looking at myself in the mirror, I am the closest I will ever be to my version of her, and while I do feel different about me, I'm still not sure it's in a good way.

My phone buzzes with a text message, and I grab it from my nightstand to find a message from Jess: Me and the limo are about three minutes out.

That's my cue that my time is up. I walk into the bathroom, where the velvet box sits, and open the lid, and as I had when I opened it, I barely glance at the necklace as I lift it and attach it around my neck. It falls just above my cleavage, a platinum round diamond pendant that glistens in the light with the clarity of the stones. It's stunning, and yet every place it touches me, my skin crawls with the idea that Adam will be looking for it and watching me tonight.

I glance down at the cards he'd insisted I keep close. He wanted me to read them again, but I refuse to be transported back to the moment Kevin was rendered extinct. I close the lid down hard, sealing them inside the box, and then set it aside.

Jess left me a collection of evening bags to choose from, and I walk to the bed and pick up what Jess informed me is a classic Jimmy Choo black velvet Bon Bon bag. I have no idea what is classic or not classic. I chose it because my letter opener, bookmark, and potential weapon, per Kara, fits inside. A smart accessory for someone being stalked by a stranger who has proven his willingness to kill not once, but twice.

Chapter Eighty-Five

The limo is white. Jess's dress is black lace with a flesh-color, skintight full-bodied slip underneath it. Chanel, of course.

"It had to be Chanel," she purrs. "You know how I adore Chanel. And you, my dear, look gorgeous." Her eyes catch on my necklace. "Oh my. That's new, isn't it?"

"Yes," I say, and when I'd be forced to say the devil's name, Adam, I'm saved by my phone buzzing with a text, though I'm not sure it's really a save if Adam is the person contacting me.

Steeling myself for the worst, I withdraw my phone from my velvet purse and read the message from my father: Can you come for brunch tomorrow, baby girl?

Welcoming the chance to talk to him about Big Davis, I quickly reply with: I wouldn't miss it for the world.

"My father," I say. "He wants me to come to brunch tomorrow. Maybe I can talk some sense into him then."

"A little late for that now," she murmurs. "But maybe you can prepare him for the worst."

My brows knit together. "What does that mean?"

She twists around to face me. "Wait. You don't know?"

"Know what?"

"Oh, Mia, I'm sorry." She grabs my hand and squeezes. "I assumed he told you, and you just didn't want to talk about it today, after Akia and all. He signed the contract. Every attorney involved swears there is verbiage in the contract to protect your father."

"But?" I ask, sensing that's where she's going.

"I heard through a press contact Big Davis always puts an image clause in tiny print buried in a weird place in every contract. If your father hurts his image, the deal will be edited, and done so in Big Davis's favor. So after I found out about this, I asked Nick to look for it. Mia, it's there. Your father signed it with that clause in the contract, and I swear I blame myself. Not one of the attorneys I recommended did their damn jobs."

"I don't understand why he did this," I say, dread for my father's future humiliation on national television filling me. "He knows what Big Davis did to him in the past."

The car pulls up to our destination, and Jess says, "It's like you've said in the past. Humans radiate toward habit and what they know. Your father obviously sees the familiar just like you do. A security blanket. All we can do now is prep him for his television presentation and pray he conquers it." The doors to either side of the limo open, and it's a good thing they do.

My defense mechanism over my father rears its ugly head. My father does not need a security blanket. He was just trying to get the most money for his family. My angry words are blotted out by the activity that consumes us the minute we're out of the car. There is a literal red carpet to walk, with cameras flashing here and there. Jess catches my hand and leads me along with her, forcing me to pose with her, smile with her.

In what feels like a million years later, we are led into a pre-event room, with twinkling diamond chandeliers above us, ice sculptures, and expensive art adorning the walls. We're both handed champagne and instructed by a man in a tuxedo to enjoy the random tables of delicious food. Jess is instantly pulled away, and I walk to the cake table, and it's with white cake in my mouth that I almost choke on a memory. I toss my plate in the trash as Adam's words come back to me: *"You mean you were waiting on your security blanket to return. You do like your security blankets. That's becoming a problem for me, or, more importantly, you."*

How does he know everything, even what my friends say to me? *How?*

I wonder if he's approached Jess and Jack, acting like a stranger, prodding them to talk, or if he simply hacked their electronics. I hug myself, aware that he is here, somewhere in this crowd, even if it's simply by way of the cameras he's using to spy on me—and, really, everyone here.

"Time to sit," Jess says, appearing by my side. "The ceremony is going to start."

Jess and I slide into seats near the front of the many rows of chairs, sitting side by side. "This is it," she whispers, grabbing my hand again.

She's very touchy-feely tonight, and I wonder if that's Jess's version of nerves. I wouldn't know. In all the years I've known her, I've never actually experienced any insecurity in her unrelated to daddy triggers.

Jess's award is one of the biggest of the night, which ensures we'll sit through many others before her name is called. We're almost to the end of a long ceremony, at least per the schedule I'd found in my seat, when there are inappropriately timed murmurs in the room. I glance about, noticing a number of people eyeing their cellphones. Curious, I grab mine and allow my Apple alerts to flash across my screen. One such alert has me sucking in a breath as I read: Big Davis killed in a car accident.

My hand goes to my neck with the certainty that Adam has struck again, that Adam knew before I knew that my father signed with Big Davis. I show the headline to Jess, who shocks me by shrugging. "At least your father's fake security blanket is no more."

That's when her name is called. She hugs me, and I hug her back, but as she walks to the podium, an icy-cold sensation slides through me. *Security blanket.* She said it. Adam said it. Adam knows everything about me. Jess knows everything about me. It's an insane thought, but my mind goes back to pasta-and-wine night with my two Js, when Jess had lectured me and Jack: *"I'm going to say it again, as I've said it ten thousand times," she'd stated. "You are both"—she'd waved her fork between me and Jack—"what you choose to be. If you feel invisible, you are invisible. And you both feed this in each other. You use each other as security blankets."*

If I'm right about any of this, Jack is the next target. I feel it in my gut.

And what if next means now, right now?

I text Jack: Where are you?

Still at work. How is the ceremony?

Jess is at the podium speaking, and I reason that Jack has security at the library. He's safe. And Jess is not Adam. She's *not* Adam. And yet, for reasons I cannot explain, I need out of here now. I'm near the end of the row and quickly ease my way out of the seating arrangement. I don't look at Jess. I just walk and walk as fast as I can. I know only one thing. I need to get to Jack. I need to see him alive and well. I need Jack to talk sense into me.

I need him to tell me any idea that Jess is Adam is impossible. I've seen Adam. I've seen him, and yet when I exit the building, and I'm only a few blocks from the library, I find myself saying high heels be damned. I'm running in that direction. I'm running toward Jack.

Chapter Eighty-Six

It's nine when I arrive to the library in a huff of heavy breathing, a rage of wild thoughts, and a general feeling of falling apart. The time forces me to enter through the back-parking-lot door and key in my security code for entry. I do so and hurry up the stairwell that will lead me directly to the back room where Jack and I often escape to work, where he'll be working tonight.

My feet pinch in the fancy shoes as I climb the stairs, clinging to the steel railing, relieved when I exit to a hallway and follow it to the records room.

"Jack," I say, stepping into the doorway to find him missing, but his cup is on the desk, files sitting about here and there.

Exhausted but relieved to be here, to know he must be here as well, I just need a minute. I round the desk and drop into the seat, my purse plopped on the desk next to the coffee mug. My phone rings and not for the first time. I open my bag and reach for it, eyeing the screen. Jess has called me ten times and texted me just as many. The messages are not kind: Why would you leave? How could you do this to me? This is such a bitchy thing to do. I swear I thought you were my sister. Instead you're no better than a piranha who is using me and wearing my dress and shoes.

I do a double take at the nasty words that seem as if someone else is typing them, not her, not Jess, not my best friend I consider a sister. Why would she be this angry without talking to me? Unless . . . unless she knows I came here, that I came to Jack when I was supposed to be with her. Did she talk to Jack? Did she assume my destination when I left? Is she jealous? Even then, the accusation that Jess is involved in all of this feels over the top. *Unless,* I think again, unless Jess is somehow Adam. No. No, I've seen Adam on video. I adjust the thought to a more logical view. Unless Jess *hired* Adam.

The sound of a door opening and closing has me reaching for the letter opener and setting it on the desk, just in front of my purse.

"Jack?!" I call out.

Crickets and more crickets, while blood rushes in my ears.

"Jack?!"

Jess appears in the doorway, holding her trophy, of all things, considering it looks heavy and rather large with a big gold world at the end of a tower. Her hair is in disarray, as is never the case with Jess, her dress torn at the bottom as if she caught her heel in it, her expression pure anger. I don't recognize this as the person I know and love. I pop to my feet. "Jess?" I ask tentatively, though I don't have to inquire as to how she got into the building. Jess has brought me dinner here when I worked late several times. She has my code.

"What is this?" she demands, storming toward me.

A moment later we're standing at this side of the desk, facing each other. "Why aren't you at your event, Jess?"

"Why aren't *you* at my event?" she counters. "Why did you leave and come here of all places?"

"I thought I figured something out," I say. "It was silly, but I wanted to know Jack was safe."

"You left for *Jack*?! Are you serious? Tonight was my night. Tonight was *our* night." Her words are a hiss and punch all at once, and I swear she grips that award a little tighter, like it's a weapon she intends to hurl at me.

She is not okay, and in that moment my adrenaline soars, and everything comes together for me. I was right. God, I was right. It's as if some part of me knew even before tonight. "Are you Adam, Jess?"

She laughs this bitter laugh, throwing back her head in this jerky fashion before her eyes meet mine. "I have never touched all that money my family left me for anyone but you, Mia. Just you. Do you know that?"

The impossible has happened. I'm afraid of Jess. Not only is she not okay—now I'm worried I won't be, either, if I don't get out of here and do so now. I want to reach for the letter opener, but it's slightly behind me. I'm terrified if I make the wrong move, I won't get my hands on it, and I'll trigger her in a way I do not presently want to trigger her. "How?" I ask, trying to keep her talking, trying to buy time to figure out what to do. "How did you spend it on me?"

"I wanted you to love yourself. I wanted you to let go of that damn victim act that you and Jack just freaking perpetuate in each other."

"Because he's my security blanket?" I snap, allowing anger to win, when my anger is not the way to calm her down.

"Yes. Yes, *he is*."

"Where is he now?" I demand, afraid for him. Afraid he ends up dead just like Kevin, afraid he already is.

"Thankfully he doesn't seem to be here," she snaps, her tone dripping with disdain. "If I saw him right now, I might kill him myself."

Ice slides down my spine with the absolute hate for Jack etched in her face, in her voice. I believe her. I believe she'd kill him. I'm afraid of my best friend, the person I considered a sister until right now. Now I don't know her at all. Will she kill me, too?

Talk to her, I tell myself, trying to calm myself first, then her. If I can understand her again, maybe I can bring her back to her right mind. "How did you spend your money on me, Jess?" I press.

"Adam," she says. "He and his team of experts. They were paid and paid well to teach you to get rid of your problems or do it for you. And what do you do? You walk out on one of the most important moments of my life. You betray me and desert me."

Shock rolls through me, a boulder traveling mountains of disbelief. "You had them *killed*?" I demand. "Kevin? Akia? Jess, did—"

"Yes. Yes I did. And don't forget Big Davis. Damn right I had that pervert killed. You and your father can thank me later. The second bidder on his invention is more than willing to step up, and in a big way, but Big Davis was intimidating him. No more, though. *Now he's dead.*"

Panic overwhelms me, a wild river dragging me into the bloody bowels of hell, and I have only one coherent thought. I need help. "Jack!" I scream. "Jack! Help!"

It's the wrong thing to do. She lets loose a wicked scream that doesn't even sound like her and tries to hit me with the statue. I manage to catch it before it blasts through my skull, but suddenly she's holding the letter opener, her face distorted, *evil.*

"Jess," I plead before she plunges the sharp end into my belly.

I gasp with the pain, and for just a moment my world blacks out and spins. But she isn't done with me. I see it in her eyes. The statue has fallen to the ground, and in some part of my mind, I'd heard the heavy thud of that moment. Somehow I'm still standing, but Jess is bending down, reaching for it, and I know she will crash it into my skull. Somehow, someway, I manage to pull the blade from my belly, numb from the pain.

By the time I do, Jess is already holding the statue high, ready to blast it against my head. Instinct, survival instinct, kicks in, and I plunge the letter opener into Jess's belly. The statue hits the ground hard enough to rattle the floor. She doubles over, holds on to the blade, and whispers, "Bitch." She yanks it from her belly as if she doesn't feel it and tosses it on the desk. "Such a bitch," she adds, but she stumbles backward, trips on her dress, and goes down.

I grab the letter opener, no, the knife that it has become, and I start running.

Chapter Eighty-Seven

My eyes open abruptly, staring at an unfamiliar white ceiling, the scent of medicine teasing my nostrils, a chill to the room around me.

I jerk to a sitting position, my gaze ripping around what appears to be a dimly lit hospital bed. A movement in the corner draws my attention as a large man unfolds himself from a sitting position. "You're awake."

I blink up at the familiar face. "Mike?"

"Yes," he confirms, catching my hand, an IV dripping in the crevice of that same arm, a numb sensation in my belly, I don't quite understand. My mind is a jumbled, blurry mess. "I got your letter, Mia. I'd have preferred you gave me time to help before you went off and got stabbed."

My hand instinctively goes to my belly. "How did I get here?"

"One of the off-duty police officers working a shift at the library found you and got you here to the hospital. I'd already talked to him about looking out for you and Jack. He called me right away. I'll explain everything I know so far soon. Right now, you just need to know you're safe." He hits the call button. "And we need to let the medical team know you're awake."

In my mind I object to the interruption to the answers I crave and need, but already a nurse is rushing into the room, and Mike is backing away from my bed, disappearing out of view. The nurse, a woman

I guess to be midfifties, with brightly colored reddish-brown hair, asks me random questions. "What's your name?"

"Mia Anderson."

"Like Mr. Anderson?" she teases. "You know, from—"

"*The Matrix*," I say. "Yes. I've heard that more than a few times." I shift, and a stabbing pain rips through my belly.

"Easy," she murmurs. "You had a pretty deep stab wound, but the good news is it missed all the important stuff. You're going to be just fine. How bad is the pain?"

"Bad, but just when I move."

"That's what *I hear* a lot. And you know what I say?"

"Don't move?"

"Exactly. Now we've had you well checked out. You're going to be just fine, so I'm going to let you finish your chat with Mike." She slides the call remote into my hand. "If you need me, just hit the button. And, Mia? I'm Mia, too. Bet you won't forget my name." She winks and then backs away from the bed.

Mike remains out of sight until the door to the room opens and closes. That's when he rolls a stool to my side. "You up to talking now?"

I try to sit up and grimace. He captures my arm. "Not a good idea."

"I guess not, but yes on talking. I need to know what happened. I need to know—so many things. Like how are you here? They told me you wouldn't get my letter until Monday."

"They being the Adam you left the letter with?"

"Yes. Yes, him. I was afraid he was working with the other Adam."

"Adam is just a barista who happened to be on duty when our team called in a big order that afternoon. He delivered it and your letter. I was surprised you left something for me, so I opened it right away. Needless to say, you got my attention. I was working on finding the other Adam and getting you help, but you had to get yourself stabbed before I got the job done."

"I see," I whisper, memories flooding my mind. My lips curl, biting back the question I have to ask, my lashes lowering as I whisper, "Jess?"

"She's dead, Mia."

My lashes lift again, tears burning in my eyes. "I killed her?"

"You hit a major artery. She bled out before we ever found you in the back parking lot behind the library. Neil has cameras in each records room. It's all on film. We know it was self-defense."

"I don't care what you know," I say, my voice lifting. "I care that she's dead. I care that I killed her." I huff out a breath, my voice lowering, rasping painfully from my throat. "I loved her. I didn't want—"

"I know you loved her, and I know you didn't want her dead. Believe me, I've done enough research in the past twenty-four hours to know more than you think I know."

"I don't even know what that means."

"Start with what you do know."

"Jess said she hired Adam and a team of men to basically fix my broken life." I swallow the bile in my throat. "I think she paid them a lot of money."

"She did," he confirms. "Based on Jess's journals now in our possession, and the contracts and communication we found on her electronics, Adam and his team of men were part of a black ops mission. Once we saw their contract, which wasn't new to us, we pinpointed who they were, and the investigation came together. The FBI is actually aware of this group, and while they've proven slippery, we've compiled a great deal of data on them. Pulling that prior knowledge allowed me to demystify a lot of information related to your case."

Perhaps the whole black ops mission should be where I home my thoughts, but the very nature of Jess was to go big or go home. Adam was an actor is what plays out rather brutally for me, and with a sharp twist of shame in my belly. I bared my soul to that man. I dressed up and let my hair down for him. I *exposed myself* to him in all kinds of emotional ways, and even now my cheeks heat with the idea of his men listening in to our conversation, perhaps laughing while they did. I wonder if Jess listened and judged me incapable of functioning on my own.

Even beyond the murders, how could she not see the betrayal of trust all this created between us? I answer my own question. She didn't. Jess really believed she was my guardian angel—she always did. No one has to tell me—she planned to fix my life and ensure I never found out.

Now I wonder if she's actually made me a target for killers. "Am I in danger? Will I be considered a liability?"

"I've talked to the task force. This group, DC9 is their name, operates with strict rules, no credit, and no favors. They only do what they are paid to do and nothing more."

"What if she prepaid for their services?"

"Again, we have her communications with DC9. She only gave them one name at a time. She paid them a lump sum up front. Then her estate paid them a bump fee every time she added a name. The estate had no idea what they were paying for. The bottom line: they're gone. You're safe."

"I'll be safe when they're in custody. Please tell me that's happening."

His expression is grim. "They're slippery, Mia—we don't even know why they call themselves DC9—but they've moved on. And I promise you: this is now personal to me. I'm going to push for answers."

"She had Akia and Big Davis killed. And Kevin." My throat is dry and raw as I add, "She killed my ex-boyfriend, Kevin."

"I know. You told me in your letter, remember?"

"Did she have anyone else killed?"

"She intended to have the two attorneys working on your father's case killed. That didn't happen."

I laugh, a cackling, crazy sound I barely recognize as my own. I told Jess how that man, my father's attorney, hired her look-alike. I know how Jess feels about certain types of men, how she places them in the same perverted category as her father. Add to that the way he let Big

Davis, who had a reputation for being handsy himself, get over on my father, and it was a kiss of death. In her state of mind, she saw red. She saw blood.

I almost got them killed.

My mind darts to Jack's coffee cup on the desk in the library last night. It was there, but he was not. "Jack?" I ask urgently. "Is he alive?"

"He's outside with your parents. They're all fine. Under the circumstances, I just asked to talk to you before they did."

I press my fingers to the bridge of my nose, trying to fight the burn of tears that threaten a waterfall. "I can't believe she did this. I can't believe she could kill people or have them killed." I drop my hand. "She tried to kill *me*."

"Did you know Jess had been in therapy off and on her entire life?"

"*No.* I had no idea. I mean, her father molested her. She needed to be in therapy, but she rejected the idea when I brought it up."

"Yes, well, based on our research, she was in therapy until a few years back and just stopped. We suspect that's when she spiraled. But as difficult as this might be to hear, we think she hired DC9 once before." His expression tightened. "To have her parents killed."

I wait for that to feel wrong, but it doesn't. "How did someone as young as she was back then, college age, hire DC9?"

"She had a sizable trust fund, a resourceful mind, and powerful people around her, some of whom also did not like her father. We're looking into who might have helped her. Bottom line, Mia: she was not okay. She was never okay. And you were never going to be okay with her intimately involved in your life. You're lucky to be alive."

"Because of you."

"Because of *you*. You fought back. And you won. I'll be around, but you have some people who really want to see you right now. Do you want to see them?"

I nod. "Yes. Yes, please."

He stands and walks toward the door, and panic rushes over me at the idea of him leaving. "You will be around, right?" I call out after him. It's silly, but right now he's like the rock that's holding me up in a sea of confusion.

He gives me a smile over his shoulder. "I'm not going anywhere, Mia."

And unlike Adam, when Mike says my name, it's comforting, not unsettling.

He exits to the hallway, and the next thing I know my parents enter in their own version of a hurricane. Of course my father is in as much disbelief over Jess as I am, while Mother claims, "There was always something off about that girl." I don't argue. Jess was a tormented person, and I blame myself for where we are now. I lived with her for years. I knew her as no one else knew her. There were signs, symptoms of a troubled person I didn't want to see. Her anger flared over certain men, and certain behaviors, in a volatile, unpredictable way that was not normal. She found out one of her college professors was sleeping with a student. She deemed him a disturbed man, stole his glasses, and burned them. He was out of line. I actually called her a hero. I didn't look hard enough to see the truth. Maybe if I had, she'd still be alive, and so would Kevin, Akia, and Big Davis.

My parents linger in my room with me a good, long while, but they eventually decide Jack deserves some alone time with me before visiting hours end. They leave, and Jack enters with rocket speed and seems to say to hell with my stomach, drawing me into a painful hug. It hurts, but I don't care, not one little bit. He's alive. He's here. He's safe.

"I'm so sorry," he murmurs, pulling back to look at me, sitting on the bed. "I know you came to the library looking for my help and me."

"I'm glad you were gone. She might have killed you."

"I have to be honest. I started dating this woman off a dating app, and it was confusing, Mia. I didn't want to tell you. I didn't know how to keep our friendship alive and have this relationship with her. That's why I suggested we date—well, that and my fear Jess was pushing me out of your life, at the same time I was as well. I was confused as hell. And look what happened: I left to meet her and you—you're here like this. And Jess"—his lips thin—"Jess is dead."

All of a sudden his phone calls and weird behavior make so much sense. "You should have told me about the woman. What's her name?"

"Sara."

"And you like her?"

He nods. "I think I do."

"Well, as long as she doesn't kill people for you and tell you it's for your own good, then that's a good thing. I'd love to meet her. When you're ready."

We sit there together and chat about everything that has happened. Despite Mike assuring me Adam is long gone, I ask Jack to look at a photo of Adam on my phone, wherever it is now, but he doesn't have to. Mike already showed him one. Jack didn't recognize him at all. Of course not. Jess knew Jack would be protective of me. Jack was dangerous to her agenda, which I still don't fully understand. I shiver with the idea he most certainly must have been on her hit list, but I don't want to know if he actually was. I just don't want to know.

Eventually the nurse warns us I need to rest. "Mia" gives us five minutes. Jack hugs me again, and as he's about to leave, I have a thought. "Hey," I say. "How did you know I was wearing Chanel that day?"

"My sister is a Chanel whore. I'll see you soon. Rest."

He exits to the hallway and I shut my eyes. I'm tired, so very tired. More tired than I've ever been in my life. But I make a mental note to make Jack's sister the new face of Chanel. Then I can love it the way he loves her, not in the way Jess thought she loved me.

Chapter Eighty-Eight

The next day I'm released from the hospital, and at my parents' prodding, I agree to stay at their place. At this point, I'm simply not ready to go back to my loft or the library. So much so that I officially take a month of leave from work to get my head on straight and decide what comes next for me.

I mean, how do I ever return to the place where Jess died?

The place where I ended her life?

Over the next few days, Mike and numerous other FBI agents from the task force visit with me and ask me questions. Part of my own mental health is helping them, doing all I can do to give them anything I can to stop what happened to me from happening to someone else.

The task force controls what the media knows. Jess's attack and mine were reported as part of a random attack, someone who followed us into the library from the parking lot door. It's all part of their need to control not what the media knows but what DC9 knows.

It's Mike, though, who I save my questions for, and he proves more than willing to offer honest answers, even if they are not the ones I'd prefer. On one occasion, while sharing coffee on my parents' patio, I actually bring a list of open-ended topics and hit him with them all at once. "There was a cleaning guy at the bookstore under my loft. Was Ben involved with DC9?"

"Ben has disappeared. We can't find him. So, yes, we do believe he had involvement, but based on his work history, his background check, and a number of other factors, he was a real person who was probably paid to aid DC9."

"But he disappeared?"

"Yes."

"Is he dead?"

"Or paid well enough to start a new life."

"In other words, he might be dead," I say.

"Yes, Mia. He might be dead."

"Thank you for being honest."

"Of course," he says. "What else?"

"There was a man at the library who was even in a presentation I gave. He had dark hair and always sat on floor two. There should be a camera feed from the library to show him."

"We've looked at the camera feed, and yes, we're aware of this man. We can't identify him. The library believed him to be a financial performance auditor hired by an investor, but that proved to be false. He also showed up right when DC9 was on scene and disappeared when they disappeared."

"How did you know when DC9 was on scene?"

"The journal I told you about, the one Jess kept, was a treasure chest of information."

A part of me wants to read the journal, while another part wants to do what I have too often done in my life: hide from what I might find. "What did it say about the man?"

"He was there to monitor you and those around you, but he was also there to ensure you knew you were not invisible anymore. He and Adam combined were supposed to help you feel pretty and worthy of male attention."

My cheeks heat. "God. This is so embarrassing." I don't give him time to reply. I don't want to know what he will say. "Can I read it? Perhaps I can help you understand some things."

"I don't think you really want to see this side of your friend, and we're already talking to you about the missing pieces as we discover them." He tries to move on and prods, "What else?"

"She was *my friend*, Mike, a sister in my heart. I need to know more about what happened to her, which also happened to me. I feel guilt, real guilt, over the people who died. She hired DC9 because of me."

His lips press together, and he gives a quick nod. "I'll see if I can get you a copy of the journal, but it may be a while."

"I don't know if I can wait that long for answers."

He studies me a moment and says, "Her spiral started several years back, as we suspected and as her therapist confirmed. That's when she went off her meds. She told her therapist they were dulling the way she looked at life."

"Did she write about me?"

"Yes, she loved you to an extreme, Mia. She was obsessed with you. She wanted to make your life better. She even believed she could tell you Adam was her gift to you and that you would thank her when all of this was over."

My hand goes to my throat. "Thank her? She thought I would thank her for killing people?"

"You did nothing to create that belief in her. She thought the world would thank her for getting rid of her father, too. He was a monster, a molester of children, who would hurt someone else if she didn't deal with him."

"And her mother?"

"An enabler who was almost no better than him."

"Was he a monster?"

"We have nothing to support or disprove that accusation. You didn't drive her to do this, Mia. You are a victim. It wouldn't hurt for you to talk to someone yourself."

I shake my head. "Yeah. Yeah, I think I might do that."

"What else can I say right now to help you deal with this?"

"How did I not see her spiraling?"

"The therapist said she was very good at acting normal."

"But this was me. I lived with her for years."

"But you didn't live with her in the past few years. Cut yourself some slack. What else can I answer to help you deal with this?"

"This sounds silly, but it's bugging me. I had an Uber driver named Jack. Any idea if he was DC9?"

"Yes. Jess mentions him in her journal. She was trying to surround you with symbolism and help you decide what repeating themes had to end in your life."

"Jack," I whisper. "Was he going to be next?"

He gives a small, sharp nod. "Yes, Mia. Yes he was."

My eyes shut, and I pant out a harsh breath. "I need some time alone."

"Of course," he says, surprising me by patting my hand. "You got this. You will get to the other side of this hell and be stronger for it. I believe in you."

His confidence is remarkably comforting, perhaps because Jess was my cheerleader, and now she's gone.

—

As for Jack himself, he comes by to visit me often, and he even brings Sara with him one day. I like her. She is pretty and sweet, and when she screams at a spider in my father's workroom right along with me, I decide she's no killer. Therefore I like her even more. And it seems Jack isn't invisible to Sara at all.

It's two weeks later, and I'm feeling better, at least from a physical perspective, up and on my feet, but at present actually sitting in the lounge area of my father's workspace. I'm reading a book, trying to find my happy place again, when he joins me with two cups of steaming coffee in hand, one of which I happily accept. It was only a week ago now that he signed the backup offer on his patent, and it's a life-changing offer. Five million up front and 40 percent royalties on his product sales.

"We've decided to stay here," he says. "The house next door is up for sale. We're going to buy it and turn it into my workspace. Then remodel the main house."

"Well that's fun," I say, thankful that neither he nor anyone else has any idea what really happened to Big Davis. I don't want his dream to become about guilt and shame. No matter what has transpired, outside his understanding or knowledge, he has absolutely earned this success. "I can't wait to see it all."

"Also," he adds, "there's a house two blocks away. If you love it, your mom and I would like to buy it for you. We'll pay for you to remodel it and make it perfect."

"Y'all don't have to do that, Dad."

"We have the money," he says. "I've worked for this dream. Your mother held on to the dream with me for a lifetime, and so did you. Treating you to this is part of that dream. And I know you don't want to go back to the loft. I can tell. I mean, you're here, hanging out, with your mother."

I laugh, but the laughter fades quickly, honesty at the forefront of my reply. "No," I say. "No I don't." I hug him. "Thank you. Thank you, Dad."

"This came for you by certified mail," my mother announces, entering the room and offering me a large envelope. My brows furrow at the name of an unfamiliar law firm in the corner address area. I open it quickly, my hands trembling, and I don't know why. I swallow hard and read the letter addressed to me.

> Dear Ms. Anderson:
> Many years ago, Jessica Pierce made arrangements to ensure you would be safe, comfortable, and protected should anything ever happen to her. You are the sole

> benefactor of her will. The sum is quite large. Why don't you call me and come by my office to chat?

I'm dumbfounded, not sure what to feel or think.

Jess left me her money.

Do I even want it?

I slide the letter back inside the envelope. "It's about Jess's final affairs," I say. "I need to handle some things."

Neither of them says anything—no, not even my mother. Even she understands all things Jess are sensitive subjects. There wasn't even a funeral. Apparently her estate was given directive to cremate her and do so as silently, and as outside the public eye, as possible. Details I only know because of Mike's candor.

I don't tell my parents about the money. I'm not sure I'm going to accept it.

On the morning I'm to visit Jess's estate manager, I meet Kara for coffee. She is on the mend and still in disbelief of all that happened. "I can't get my head around the idea that the gift I gave you was used as a weapon."

"Well, that gift allowed me to fight back," I console her, but I'm also eager to change the subject, which is sticky, considering the details the FBI has allowed to be public knowledge, or, in this case, disinformation, for a good cause—catching up with DC9. "Tell me about this ulcer of yours," I urge. "Will it flare back up?"

This works, and we chat a bit before her candor kicks in. "Are you coming back to the library?"

"Well, I have to pay the bills," I reply, laughing a bit awkwardly at the difficult question. "I'm just not sure I can go back to the place where Jess was killed."

"I expected as much. Which is why I have another offer to present. There's a job working in library administration waiting on you if you want, and it comes with a raise. Your email can be thanked for that offer. Not me. You impressed the right people with your thoughtful words. This offer was already in the works when tragedy struck. But you need to know that it's in the administrative office. It won't be working at the main library around the books you love. I'm not sure how you feel about that."

No books to love. I don't know how I feel about that at all, but the offer is a compliment. "Thank you and everyone involved in the offer. I just—I need to think."

"Fair enough," she says. "And I think you earned that right."

After a few minutes, we hug goodbye, and I walk to the office where I'll soon discuss Jess's will. Jonathan Jackson, the man in charge, is in his sixties, rather distinguished, and reminds me of a more polished version of my father. This, to me, explains why Jess was drawn to him to manage her estate. She was drawn to my father. He was the father she never had but wanted.

He sits behind a massive mahogany desk and documents, which I read with shock and revelation. Per the words on the page, I'm to inherit $15 million. I literally gasp, my gaze lifting to his. "Fifteen million? This can't be right."

"She invested well and never touched her parents' money until recently, when she withdrew a million dollars."

A chill runs down my spine. Now I know how much she paid to DC9. One million dollars to turn my life into hell while ending the life of three men. "I don't want it," I say, offering him the paper back.

"It's yours. If you want to donate it or give it away, that's up to you, but it's yours." He holds up an envelope. "A letter from Jess."

I shake my head. "No. Keep it. Maybe one day I'll read it. I can't now."

"Understood. Just get me a bank account, and I'll transfer the funds to your name. It's your money, Mia. I'll have to start charging you to hold it in one week."

Anger bristles, and I don't know if it's at him or Jess or maybe myself. "Did you know? Did you know she needed help?"

He pales. "I did not. I barely spoke with her, but she left you her fortune. You were all she had."

I can feel the blood run from my face. His statement guts me right where I sit, a $1,000 leather chair hugging my body. I *was* all she had, and the hardest part about all this has been knowing she did bad things for me. She killed for me. And she was so lost and tormented inside that she didn't even know why that was wrong.

Guilt is my enemy right now.

I don't know how I will ever forgive Jess, let alone myself. I wonder if there is anything but time and therapy that will allow that to happen. I pray there is, though, because time moves far too slow, and there is an ache in my chest right now I'm not sure will ever go away. The only thing I know for certain is that this man can't help me.

I stand up and leave the room.

Ironically the coffee shop where I left Mike that envelope is right across the street from Jonathan's office. Of all the places that remind me of the recent tragedies that I've been avoiding, I find I'm drawn there, perhaps because it's where Mike and I reconnected. It's where I launched my battle against a dangerous enemy and started to win a war. I hurry across the walkway and laugh as Mike reaches the door at the same time. "Perfect timing," he says, opening the door for me and dressed in a suit that screams FBI agent, his dark hair trimmed to the scalp, never more than an inch high.

A few minutes later, we sit at a table together, and I'm struck by his blue eyes, the shade of a perfect summer afternoon, not too dark and not too light. Friendly eyes, intelligent eyes. He's gone above and beyond for me during the hell of the past few weeks. "I need to tell you something," I say. "A confession of sorts."

"I'm an FBI agent. I love a good confession."

Oddly, the comment and the man do not create unease in me. I just spit out the words, say what I have to say. "Jess left me her money."

"I actually already knew that long before you did. Law enforcement looks at every piece of a puzzle that points to motive for murder."

"Murder?" Now my heart is racing. "I didn't know about the money," I add quickly. "I just found out, and I don't want it. The estate holder insists I have to take it now and do with it whatever I want, donate it or whatever."

"Easy, Mia," he says. "You know we know you didn't kill Jess for her money. We have the video of the event, remember?"

"Right. Right. Sorry. It's just a touchy subject. The money stuff feels weird, too."

"Let me ask you this. Why *not* take the money? It's a lot of money. Life-changing money."

"It feels like blood money. She used it to fund murders."

"That money is gone. This money is yours now. Do something for you with it. You earned it. More than most will ever know."

"I don't even know what I want to do now at all. I love books. I loved the library, but I don't want to go back to the place where—where Jess died."

"So fund a literacy charity and spend your life helping others learn to read. Do something good with the money."

I perk up, my spine straightening, a fizzle of excitement inside me I did not expect to feel now or ever again. "That's actually a great idea. And my dad bought me a house. I don't want to go back to my loft. I can pay him back for that. Thank you. You really have helped me today."

He considers me a moment, then reaches in his backpack and slides a notebook in front of me. My heart races in my chest. "That's—"

"Jess's journal. I wasn't going to give it to you, but I think it might help you understand how out of your control what happened was."

Swallowing hard, I drag it closer. "I don't know if I'm ready to read this, but I think maybe I could book that therapy appointment and take it with me."

"Good idea. Excellent idea, actually."

A few minutes later, we're standing outside, waiting on my Uber, when Mike asks, "Have you been back to your loft?"

"No. I haven't. I just don't feel safe there, but I have to go pack up."

"I'll take you. I'll help. And I'll tell you how to protect yourself."

"Don't say a gun or a security system. The letter opener got used against me like the gun could. The DC9 isn't fazed by technology."

"No," he says, "but Sasha would put the fear of God in them."

My brows knit together. "Sasha?"

"My German Shepherd. I make a lot of enemies in my job, but my girl keeps me safe."

"German Shepherds are very intimidating."

"She's a sweetie. Why don't you come over Friday night and meet her? We can order in dinner. She'll help you decide if you want a dog like her. And the answer will be yes, I promise you."

I blink at the surprise invite, but my answer is easier than I would expect after all I've been through. "I'd like that."

"I'll pick you up. Seven?"

"Yes. Seven."

My car pulls up, and he opens the door for me, winking as he shuts it. The driver pulls away from the curb, and hope fills me. The kind of hope I never thought I'd feel again. Maybe even more hope than I ever had before. I also decide that maybe Jess was right, at least on one point. Being invisible is a state of mind.

ACKNOWLEDGMENTS

This book would not have happened if not for all the support around me. Thank you to Emily, who—for ten years—has taken on every book and deadline in superhero mode. Thank you to Diego, my husband, for all the times you say, "Let's talk about it," and we do, and then I know what comes next. Thank you, too, to Louise Fury for bringing me and my editor together. Thank you to my editor, Megha Parekh, and her team, for the enthusiastic response to a story I hope speaks to the vulnerability we all feel at times.

ABOUT THE AUTHOR

Photo © 2013 Teresa Lee

L. R. Jones is a pseudonym for *New York Times* and *USA Today* bestselling author Lisa Renee Jones, whose dark, edgy fiction includes the highly acclaimed novels *The Poet*, *A Perfect Lie*, and the Lilah Love series. Prior to publishing, Lisa owned a multistate staffing agency recognized by the *Austin Business Journal*. Lisa was listed as #7 in *Entrepreneur* magazine's list of growing women-owned businesses. She lives in Colorado with her husband, a cat who always has something to say, and a golden retriever who's afraid of her own bark. For more information, visit www.lisareneejones.com.